Acclaim for H. G. Carrillo's

loosing my espanish

"A linguistic wizard, Carrillo creates . . . a syncopated, jazzy rhythm . . . its sentences twist and turn, first embracing then rejecting pure, uncontaminated English and Spanish. . . . It is written with a level of style that shines . . . endearing."

—*Los Angeles Times*

"*Loosing My Espanish* is a novel that exists in a realm where beauty and memory and longing are one. Mr. Carrillo's talents are formidable, his lyricism pitch-perfect, and his compassion limitless."

—Junot Díaz, author of *Drown*

"*Loosing My Espanish* begs comparisons to James Joyce's *Ulysses* or Gabriel García Márquez's *Cien años de soledad*. . . . [It] takes linguistic and imaginative risks seldom seen in contemporary letters. A gem of a book." —*El Paso Times*

"Did you know that language can be read and heard and seen and touched? That you can smell it, taste it? Try *Loosing My Espanish*."

—Eduardo Galeano,
author of the Memory of Fire trilogy

"Heartrending and be

a truly original and compas sm and passion . . . effectivel ant experience and creates ry can, indeed, become one."

n Blade

"H. G. Carrillo's remarkable prose captures memory, loss, and desire like a net made of language. In its trappings we find all sorts of gifts, from history to puns to love songs. *Loosing My Espanish* is enchantingly brilliant. What we are witnessing is the evolution of a great American writer."

—Ernesto Quiñonez, author of *Chango's Fire*

"[A] stunning fiction debut." —*New York Post*

"Joyous. . . . Carrillo blends vibrant language, vivid imagery and complex personalities into a bilingual stream-of-consciousness narrative that weaves its way through time, space, and the Cuban diaspora. . . . You will be enchanted."

—*Cuerpo Magazine*

"In *Loosing My Espanish*, paradoxically, the great winner is Spanish, not only for the way in which the text is subverted by that language, but also for the splendid way in which it has given blood, spirit, and conviction to a moving novel that breathes Cuba in a major key."

—Mayra Montero, author of *Deep Purple*

"Stunning . . . Carrillo delivers a narrator who erupts and disrupts the pavements of the Cuban-American experience by showing us that the most accurate, if not truthful, fact comes from the memory of the impassioned heart. The rhythmic beauty of Carrillo's commanding storytelling leaves you with the urgency of trying to catch your breath."

—Helena María Viramontes,
author of *Under the Feet of Jesus*

H. G. CARRILLO

loosing my espanish

H. G. Carrillo's work has appeared in *The Kenyon Review* and *Glimmer Train*, among other journals and magazines. A Ph.D. candidate and instructor in the Department of English at Cornell University, he divides his time between Ithaca, New York, and San Juan, Puerto Rico.

loosing my espanish

H. G. CARRILLO

ANCHOR BOOKS
A Division of Random House, Inc.
New York

FIRST ANCHOR BOOKS EDITION, OCTOBER 2005

Grateful acknowledgment is made to the following for permission to reprint previously published material:

Agencia Literaria Carmen Balcells, S.A.: Excerpts from *Informe Contra Mi Mismo*, by Eliseo Alberto de Diego. Copyright © 1997 by Eliseo Alberto de Diego. Published by Aguilar S.A. Ediciones, Madrid. All rights reserved. Reprinted by permission of Agencia Literaria Carmen Balcells, S.A.

University of Arizona Press: Excerpts from *The Keepsake Storm* by Gina Franco. Copyright © 2004 The Arizona Board of Regents. Reprinted by permission of the University of Arizona Press.

The Library of Congress has cataloged the Pantheon edition as follows:
Carrillo, H.G. (Herman G.), [date].
Loosing my Espanish / H. G. Carrillo.
p. cm.
1. Cuban Americans—Fiction. 2. Community life—Fiction.
3. Chicago (Ill.)—Fiction. I. Title.
PS3603.A77455L66 2004
813'.6—dc22
2004044545

Anchor ISBN-10: 1-4000-7814-8
Anchor ISBN-13: 978-1-4000-7814-1

Book design by Pamela G. Parker

www.anchorbooks.com

Printed in the United States of America
10 9 8 7 6 5 4 3 2 1

En recuerdo de

David Robert Herzfeldt, A.I.A.
1961–1989
My Beloved Heartfelt Light

The Ghost will bring rum to the table.
Seats are reserved for those who will be absent.

Eliseo Alberto de Diego, *Informe contra mí mismo*

You want real? Draw your thumbs along
the backbones of fossilized fish
and press your fingers into the brush
of vertebrae, the singular eyes, fronds
of fins. See? Self-portrait. Osteichthyes fanned
in accuracy, bone-hollows that are you
exactly, you perpetually, you
who thought yourself detached from sand,
salt, and cannibal rage. Now sit outside
this tank. Want in? Want to be sleek? Too bad.
But imagine being made that way. Whose reel,
You think, wouldn't you relent before fish-
mouths, the O a cavernous word out of the belly
where God is mean and fresh?

Gina Franco, "Fishing," I

loosing my espanish

WELL YOU KNOW sometimes you no know you no going to like something until you right in the middle of no liking, Amá will say whether things are good or bad. She'll say it at the start of something, or in the middle, or long after it's finished, which makes it difficult to tell when you've gotten to the moral of the story. Will things get better? Are they about to get worse? You never know if her eye is fixed on a distant horizon or clouded in some memory right in front of her.

She said it when Joaquín-Ernesto—the Santiago Boy—went through the ice that winter after we moved up from Miami. And again as he began his ascent into sainthood here in what little there is of Cuba in our tiny community in Chicago.

None of us in Troop 227 had seen it happen. It was after Christmas, bright and cold. On the bus ride out Father Rodríguez and our scout leader, Mr. Sáenz, said that the older boys were to keep an eye out for us younger ones, but the moment the doors opened to the wide expanse of Starved Rock, we ran and shouted and shoved at each other like rams; like wild banshees, Father Rodríguez said. All that morning we followed raccoon tracks as they appeared and vanished under dustings of snow. There had been lunch at the lodge and the discovery of an abandoned hummingbird's nest.

We had been sent to trace the flight patterns of nonmigratory birds when Mr. Sáenz began yelling for us to divide up in twos and look for him. ¡Vamos! ¡Vamos now, goddamnit! Father Rodríguez was yelling.

And later, when we all got back to the city, Mr. Sáenz was crying he never, never, never, never, never lost a boy in all his years.

The wind stood the few long hairs across his bald head on end.

Other than the murmuring that continued long after the Santiagos were led home, the only sound was the icy clatter of leafless trees. Forever after that—because the body had not been found that day—it was easier to focus on the bald spaces on Mr. Sáenz's head. Somewhere in his eyes he had brought back a jagged hole in the ice just big enough for a boy to slip through, and by the time night closed around those twenty or so blocks where we all lived, we all knew that any one of us could fall into it.

And she said it again, Amá, just last week when she set fire to her kitchen, an act that took with it almost all of what little of Cuba we had here.

Nearly everything saved, wished for, prayed for in that tiny little casa blanca just off of Ashland Avenue that she had said was always and forever in the back of her mind seemed to willingly take to the flames, become unrecognizable, until nearly everything Amá had ever wanted was either altered or gone.

This morning, after spending hours at the insurance office, Amá and I went to her house. And even though we had spent the past two hours itemizing objects and appliances and books and glassware that had been lost or damaged, neither of us expected to walk into the kitchen of Román, Julio and my childhood, where we all had eaten the meals and told the stories and sang the songs and mucked the boots and did the homework, gone. Clear through the upstairs, all had given way to a crow caught in a hot gust of air above us.

The wooden back porch has been burned away and the sky comes in so now we might as well have been sitting in the garden. Amá took her place as always at the head of the table and gestured for me to sit next to her. The table's aluminum frame is still intact, though the linoleum top has melted into itself a little so that the blue and yellow and gray colors now all converge kaleidoscopically. Ay, Amá said smoothing her hand over the surface; it was the first thing she bought when we—just Amá and me then—were still living, just surviving in a small apartment off Logan Boulevard.

She apologized there was no coffee, and then laughed saying that it was something she had as a girl dreamed of: being the lady of the house who always had coffee and silver to serve when family or company came to visit. We laughed until we just sat looking through the hole that had been eaten through the wall to the garden.

The delphiniums are so lush, plentiful and purple for this time of year you can't see more than a foot into the yard. The rose thickets have come up so high over the back fence, and the smell of garbage and urine we had all grown used to over the years has been overwhelmed by the fragrance. They encroach so far—as if to make a canopy—there would be no way of telling there was anything else there, if from where we sat you couldn't see the peaks of three or four elephant ears, gigantic, seven or eight feet tall, in the air.

She told me, like always, all she did was set the rice on to boil. And then, like usual—Dios mío—she began to pray. She included the names of all of the saints she could think of; the week's numbers for the loteria; and the soul of Abuelita; and the pope who she swears must have at least a little Cuban blood; and the dearly departed Madre Teresa; and the world's starving children; and for her only sister left, tía María-María, and her husband, tío Néstor, and their daughters—cousins I only remember meeting once when we were all small children—Julia y Wilma in Santa Fe; and for the sisters that Amá has always said that she has had the good fortune to adopt and be adopted by since leaving Santiago for La Habana, and then La Habana for La Habana Pequeña, and then leaving Miami for Chicago; said she has always considered herself lucky to have had two of the most magnificent mujeres to walk the face of the earth—las doñas Liliana y Cristina—as friends without whom life in this country would simply be unbearable; and for the three boys they all raised together—Román—El Blanco—who she said they would all see on the television one day, y Julio—El Negro, Román's gemelo, doña Liliana's sons though they have different last names—who she said she wasn't sure what it was he did but however she was quite sure whatever it was would one day change the course of the whole world; and then of course for me; she always prayed for me, her own whom she could not be more proud of; and, she said lowering her eyes, she even prayed for Juan Ocho, who did nothing for her—she reminded me even though she said she was certain that I already knew—that Juan Ocho and his trumpet playing did nothing at all—nothing for her and certainly nothing to her—except give her a boy with the same castellano hair that any woman—no matter how good—might have fallen into, which is why, she said, when she prays she never includes herself; it just wouldn't be right.

Gone now are the pictures of the sea-green dress—the one made with the exact color fabric as doña Liliana's eyes—that Amá and another girl had to sew her into; no zippers, so that her attendants at a coming-out party would say that it felt like they were holding an angel, they say, like a cloud, like nothing in their arms. Singed, after years under gilt and leather covers. Their edges and centers melted into the plastic sheets leaving behind a gloved hand and the famous swan ice sculpture that stood nine feet high and the fountain that sprayed pink champagne.

Gone too is the picture of Juan Ocho and his wavy castellano hair and his shirt opened to his trim waist and his ojos malos the color of asparagus water that no woman could resist no matter how good.

Left is the lady's hand door knocker: her fingertips gently resting on her tambourine, placidly, calmly, as if nothing happened, merely caught in una siesta between fiestas. Also, the aquamarine brooch in the shape of a dragonfly doña Liliana is said to have thrown away because the clasp was loose that Amá or another of the girls working in the grand house in El Vedado is said to have pulled out of a wastepaper basket. And the gold-rimmed plates doña Cristina managed to get on the plane with her—a setting for seventeen and a quarter—though mostly broken. The credenza and buffet in the dining room stand steadfast though warped into blackface caricature. Though gone too are the photos of tío Néstor y tía María-María at the Santiago bar where Néstor and Juan Ocho's band played: Los Americanos—merengue, rumba, samba, jazz, boleros of heartbreak, loneliness and betrayal—everyone used to wait all week just to hear them play; Amá says they were so good they almost had a record contract, says they were set to tour South America before Castro.

Upstairs a charred box still holds the silver cuff link doña Cristina says Amá stole from Juan Ocho with the hope doña Liliana could find someone who could put a spell on him that would bind his feet and keep him from straying.

Fisted into a cinder was the packet of letters addressed to Amá, but meant for all of us, from my prima Carolina, still in Cuba. Like plaintive songs caught in an ever-constricting throat, they once read of long-ago and far-away: Mireya, you know I haven't had a new dress in an age; Mireya, you have no idea what it costs to get any lipstick, let alone a good one and you know the closer I get to thirty chances slip by me; Ungüento, Mireya, send ungüento in a hurry, with a quickness; Send the one like the one like we see in the ad that comes over fuzzy from America on the tiny little television a girl down the hall from us has . . . send the one that cools the burn and eases the pain like they say, for I work now, we all do . . . in the fields all day with a machete, like a man or an ox . . . no, querida tía, like a burro . . .

The gutters lay skeletal around where the back of the house has been eaten away, though every math test Julio, Román or I had ever taken, every paper we had written was preserved by a fallen mirror.

The baby shoes doña Cristina had bronzed when Román must have been all of thirteen were steadfast, though the door we had stopped open with them—the door to what had been the room Román, Julio and I had shared—looks as if it had been snarled and slathered by a toothless black mouth.

We both sat there, Amá and I, wishing for cafecito in perfectly crafted, painted china cups with matching saucers.

Amá looked around at what had been what for so long she told everyone was the reason we had left Cuba and said, Well you know mijo, sometimes you no know you no going to like something until you right in the middle of no liking. And although we were staring at smears that trace the carpet along the hall to the sewing room that Amá y las doñas had fixed so nice, I knew that she was talking about both that moment then as well as when we first came and lost the Santiago Boy; and the moment we set foot in La Habana Pequeña, as well as the first sentence that I heard Amá say in English. Sometimes you no know you no going to like something until you right in the middle of no liking.

And maybe today I'll know something, maybe I'll be able to say something like: But you see, señores, this is how myth is made—from just these shards—this, this is historia . . .

ESCUCHEN SEÑORES—HOMBRES jóvenes; all of you who have sat in these seats over the past several years; mensajeros del futuro; mis iluminadores, mis casas, mis escuelas, mis corazones, mis playas; mi sentido común; mis yucas locos—I forget all the names that I have had for you—Shiny Distant Shores. Even yesterday's too long ago, a fever-dream broken into floes of hunger and want and then more want, it is so far away now.

Óiganme. You have no idea, given how ill-disposed I am to looking at myself in mirrors, how surprised I am to find myself—in the rear- and side-views of my car, in the glass awards cases that line the halls on the first floor—like now, still talking to you. Sometimes to years of you long gone. And surprised to find that what's being said about me these days—that I have begun to occasionally mutter to myself—may be true.

But it is strange how something that I have always done—rehearsed my lectures, made lists, figured out what comes next—is now an act of self-consciousness, that now what's in the past has made me appear to be something other than what I am.

I've only thirty-four more of these opportunities, and I'm finding time comes flying back on me whether I want it to or not. All of a sudden, I find myself mouthing years of attendance rolls, record books of grades, notes for lectures that now will probably never be given. My muttering. Muttering, they say, as though I have not always been trying to make these corrections; as though I haven't been always thinking them as loudly as I could these things that they say that I now mutter; things I believe they believe I say as if I have no idea what's coming out of my mouth anymore.

Ay but in all fairness, I've done very little to be understood.

So thirty-four more times—if we take out the days we're off for Easter—there are, mis hijos. Only thirty-four more opportunities to prepare these lectures and stand in front of you in classrooms that have become all too familiar, so much like home, mis chicos queridos. And I finally have some answers to some of the questions that you have asked me, now.

Traveling past the nurse's office to the principal's office, Father Rodríguez's and Father McMillan's offices, I wave, tousle the heads of a couple of passersby, congratulate a victor on the field for his recent win, answer quick questions about assignments due, agree to meet about an essay, a letter of recommendation. He's very affable; Likable . . . all of them like him . . . they all seem to learn from him, everyone says so; a mí me gusto mucho; Been so good to all of mis hijos, I've overheard mothers say when they were certain that I was within earshot. More than once has someone's father come to me after a soccer game to say that he'd never thought that he'd see the day that his son could take charge; take the ball down the field that way; once it was described as if in an afternoon a son had shed all of his boyhood, run it off down the field and appeared a new and different person. Wonderful pedagogical skills, highly organized, very demanding although his students all seem to love him, Father Rodríguez has copied each year from the first of my annual assessments as if nothing could or would ever change; or as if the only possible change that could occur is that eventually I would sit in his place copying the same words into the annual assessment of someone who had once been my student.

Each morning as I pass the portico into these hallways on these last days, these final days, I wonder how I haven't noticed the din that pours out from the cafetería: a howling—like caged animals—the murmuring grunts, the flung cereal boxes; the clatter of cutlery. Or the smell that is not all that different from the locker rooms as I pass under the cupola by the large stained-glass window that looks out over the bell tower, the green, the parking lot and the play fields.

There have been many times over the years that I have been tempted to simply sit in the window niche on the second-floor landing under the cupola, and rather than going on, just watch the dust particles ride the sunlight, watch students cross below me scurrying, already as busy as the men that they will grow up to be, taking on the roles that will one day make them feel important, satisfied, safe, trusted.

It could be that it is this building. That despite its disrepair—the cracks and leaks, the peeling everywhere, the broken lockers for which there is no money; there will be no money coming in; nada, nada; nada—the something grand, the something particularly ambitious that made the immigrants who came to this area nearly two hundred years ago to look back to a medieval France, and an ancient England, a Renaissance Italy with hope enough that they pooled pennies earned at factory jobs and the domestic chores of others a little at a time in collection baskets still lives here. Years ago, when Julio and Román arrived from Cuba by way of Miami with las doñas Cristina y Liliana, Amá thought it important to see to it that the boys were acclimated to their new home: she took them to the lake, made sure they had new uniforms, showed them how to take the bus in the rain instead of the route that she laid out for us. The first opportunity that I had to show them something on my own I took them to the cupola—the same way anyone who has gotten to be a boy here and shown someone else—stood them on the opposite side from me and showed them all I had to do was whisper the words comemierdas and putos for them to hear. The three of us spent more than a half hour their first day on the cracked mosaic of the Sacred Heart calling each other moco, estúpido, chica, until Román or Julio let go with a belch that resounded the dome and peeled us off running in fits of secret laughter; as if we had gotten away with something that no one else either knew about or could recapture again.

Sometimes it may just be enough to watch, boyhood, I often want to tell my colleagues as we've whined about test scores, curriculum, textbook choices and the like into the fretted muck that we like to call faculty meetings. And although I have never bothered to do it yet, lately I've come dangerously close to asking them, if like so many things that thrive on their own, do the boys really need us the way we think they do, the way our egos tell us they do, forcing them to do the things that we demand of them as if we know any better? It has been a long time that I have wanted to take each of them, one at a time, by the hand to this window and simply say, Mira. And then watch them, my colleagues, see everything that they had hoped for, everything that they had dreamed was already realized right before them. Even boys have their seasons, I'd say: in the winter, they leave their houses bundled for the cold, and halfway, something switches them on high and they're sweaty and shoving at each other, coats open, gloves lost. I've a cardboard box filled with scarves under my desk that no one will claim; as soon as the weather starts to get warm, they fill up with a harmless venom, boys do, that sets them on a fidget that either makes them want to tell you an elaborate lie, smash something or build something out of nothing. And I want to tell them, the boys, to hold on to it, this moment, it goes away as if it were never there at all, but I never do. Never say it to either my colleagues or the boys.

Instead, for years I've left the echo of the cupola with all its dust and smell of oil soap, rounded the gritty terrazzo steps and headed toward the end of the hall on the third floor, the furthest from the stairs, where all the new teachers, younger teachers have been assigned since I've known of this place.

I suppose all I had to look forward to was moving to a lower floor in the succeeding years; closer and closer to the vestibule a little at a time had I not been shown a quicker way out.

And—not unlike the first time that I came to this school, and Amá handed me my lunch, straightened my tie, used her saliva and finger to rub away at the corners of my mouth while she told me that this was one of the moments in her life of which she was most proud in spite of herself because she always wanted me to know that my successes as well as my failures would always be my own—I cross myself, kiss my knuckle, inhale deeply, push down the battle in the pit of my stomach y . . .

Escuchen señores. Óiganme todos, as you have all heard at this morning's assembly, this school will no longer exist as it has during the past hundred and three years and I will no longer be a fixture here. We are the last school in the diocese to go coeducational because of the lack of funding, they say, and you now know that I am not listed among the teachers who will be returning next year to meet the challenge.

Challenge, Father Rodríguez has told me. That was the word he used, challenge.

Ay, what challenge, señores?

But I suppose that many of you already knew this. You've heard the rumors. And I suppose that this kind of education—boys being taught to be men separately from girls being taught to be women—has been arcane for a while, a thing of the past, and it's time for some of us to move on. Some of you will graduate, others will move on to your senior year though none of you will be able to nudge your little brothers and say, Take Delossantos' class.

I've heard you say it. I've heard so many of you say it.

I know an entire generation of you have been telling each other, He's an easy A, a pushover.

And I suppose it's true. But someone should be easy on you; someone should clear a path for you. After all it is an awfully indifferent world, a dangerous world, a strange world that we send you out into with little more training than an infant would have to take the helm of an inflatable life raft.

And of course, there are those of you who I have let leave—years of you have passed through here—with me biting my tongue.

Well, no more.

You are my last. Not that I had had any plans of abandoning my position, no. But still, you are my last.

I've heard the chisme—like old ladies, you are—in the cafetería, on the playground, in the hallways for weeks now all I've heard is that so-and-so's mother told someone's uncle's cousin that Delossantos was getting sacked; he must have murdered someone, or embezzled from school funds.

And it is true, that it was no coincidence that I accompanied my mother to the insurance office during this morning's special assembly. I suppose the good Father Rodríguez wanted me to save face in some way or another. Though my absence had nothing to do with the freshly inscribed message above the third urinal in the third-floor boys' room, which as a result of poor grammar leaves me somewhat befuddled. In the event that the author is in this room, stand corrected that were I to have a predilection for canines I could joder perros; or might have jodido perros; or were it the beginning of a poetic assertion, the rather flowery Mr. Delossantos, que jode perros, may have made a rather lyric opening to an ode or ballad on the theme that could have easily wound its way down the line of sinks and back behind the last stall where you all hang out of the window to sneak cigarettes even though you think the faculty doesn't know about it. As it stands—Mr. Delossantos era joden los perros—it is not only untrue, but may be an indication that I have failed those of you who have come to me seeking help with your Spanish grammar.

Señores—los hombres apacibles jóvenes que van a heredar la tierra un día as the world's bankers and accountants and businessmen and garbagemen and husbands and lovers and doctors and lawyers—every morning for the past twenty-two years, I've cleaned my glasses, knotted my tie and after toast and coffee and a cigarette, stood in front of rooms full of you tracing the generosity of a Spanish queen through to the Declaration of Independence; the launch of the Americas; and the trajectory of the greedy fists of the English, Spanish and Portuguese slave traders as they were hurled over centuries into the faces of the unsuspecting of Hiroshima and Nagasaki, who knew nothing about baseball and apple pie, or American History.

As freshmen most of you had me for World History; American Government when you were sophomores; some of you have been in my homeroom. I have helped coach the soccer team, and I have tutored many of you through Spanish and English exams. I have waited for this moment. This class—Histories of Latin America: From Colonialism Through the 1960s—is an elective; so all this semester, I have assumed either you want to be here or could fit nothing else in during fourth period and need the credit to graduate.

And so far this semester, we have established the dollar amount fixed into Cristóbal Colón's hand and computed its value in today's market, the cost of the ships included. We've speculated on what acts of love, what promises of romance, were exchanged between the queen of Spain and the Italian.

Even though after examining the Delacroix portrait of the dashing Colombo and his son at La Rábida, as well as pictures of the Randolph Rogers alto-relief bronze doors at the Rotunda in the District of Columbia—an entire district he gets—and pictures of the paintings of Colombo at the museum in the Vila Baleira of Porto Santo, none of us has any idea if the Genoese Discoverer was really "tall of stature" or possessed "an aquiline nose" or "blue eyes" or had a light complexion, or had white hair by the time he was thirty though blonde as a child, because none of the images we have of him were created during his lifetime as is written in history books. And what do we know about Isabella and the rather homely Ferdinand? We speculated on the beautiful Spanish woman in *The Assumption of the Virgin* and wonder if she is the patroness of northern European artists of her time like Miguel Zittoz y Juan de Flandes, who were renowned for their infinite attention to detail, yet really know nothing of her beauty.

However, once we've conceded a romance we've also committed ourselves to a mustard field near El Cerro de Cabeza de Toro.

¿Por qué no?

A mustard field in full bloom, where under the watchful eye of La Virgen de Trujillo, the Genoese Discoverer chases his beautiful, regal mistress, his patroness. There are those who would say that she was girlish in her coquetry, hardly what one would expect of the sovereign of Iberia. There are those who would say that her hair was raven-colored.

Does it matter if there were mustard fields in bloom in Trujillo that spring before the Genoese set out? No, I'm not even sure if mustard grows in Trujillo.

Pretend, imagínenselo.

Imaginen.

When Román, Julio and I were boys, by flashlight we'd read to each other in hushed whispers tales of marauding pirates and invincible sea monsters, and ghost ships that flew through the night. And for each unearthly soul that flung itself out from the sea to take revenge, to right an injustice, to yowl its indignation, Julio would stop us to ask if it was true; if it really happened. Did the captain dance the mizzenmast, sword in hand, as flames engulfed the deck; could a galleon really hold the wealth of an entire small kingdom? It would seem silly now, I would be hesitant to ask either of them now if they remembered the dark, remembered the slightest sway of wave that we could set down the densest, darkest of tributaries into the roughest of waters out to an open blank. In fog, we read, ships called out every two minutes with the clanging of a brass bell to hush the roar of that eerie silver-gray light of possible oncoming danger: a head-on collision that would slice the more vulnerable of the two between stem and stern, send hundreds scattering like grains of rice against a polished black floor.

¿Verdad? Julio would stop us and ask. A desperately incredulous ¿Verdad? for each maiden and maidenhead, and ¿Verdad? for every moment that caught him wide-eyed and openmouthed, thinking, Who knows this, who saw this, who lived to tell?

And if tomorrow I were to show up downtown at the actuarial firm where he works with its long floors of men in shirts and ties sitting in cubicles and was able to tell Román apart from anyone else so as to ask about Julio's doubt and his own anxiousness to Go on, Go on, Vamos—It's about the story, he'd bark back across the dark of the little bedroom we shared in Amá's house as boys—I wonder, señores, if he'd say the same thing now in response to where your textbook reads that that year—the year the Genoese sailed—the mustard came up purple; and add, fields and fields of purple causing a luster in the queen's eyes that allowed the Genoese to know what she was thinking before she ever said it.

It's a romance we speculate, history, a fiction.

. . . FOR YEARS I'VE had you all pile into rowboats in the strip of a lagoon that runs between Lincoln Park and the Drive. Sit close señores, I've said, close, close and close your eyes; allow yourselves to feel the inescapable movement of the current. Some years I've asked you to imagine how the topography surrounding the Río Magdelana varies as it opens out into the sea; others, I've said imagine that by 1830 you have been declared El Libertador of your country, you know each tree along this path, the parrots flying overhead, the blood running into the sand toward the freedom that remains out of reach; what you dread most, señores, is merely this feeling of constant constant movement like something eluding you, slipping from directly underneath you.

This year for the first exam, each of you received an envelope sealed with red wax, however the crest was indistinguishable. The message inside whispered: Presidente Allende, the Alliance for Progress is on your heels, the wealthy want your testicles sautéed with a crème bordelaise served on gold plates accompanied by a chilled champagne. What will happen to you and us? Who am I, and why must I whisper? Why do you whisper back?

Señor Fuentes' mother made the tortillas when we recreated the photograph taken of Villa y Zapata early December 1914 in Mexico City. By the way, albeit true the tortillas were delicious, and we all made pigs of ourselves, señor, your mother's efforts will not guarantee an A for you in this course; you still need to make the effort to get here on time, and complete all the assignments in an acceptable way; not in that way that you like to do, with the dog-eared corners and the half-written sentences.

Óiganme, señores, I understand that our unseasonably warm weather combined with the nearness of your graduation and the mystery around my leaving makes it difficult for you to suspend your disbelief long enough to entertain the facts of history. Rivers and terrains no longer on maps or places that were renamed and reclaimed in bloodshed so long ago are nearly impossible to distinguish from the tales of storks and tooth fairies that have brought you this far.

Incredulity—I know, like the rats scurrying the corners of the ship on which we joined Pedro de Menéndez de Avilés and the Timucuans that afternoon in 1556 and sailed up the Saint Johns to claim Florida for Spain—rears up ugly and hungry on its hind legs sometimes even when it's your own life you're hearing about.

I understand incredulity, mis amigos.

I look at your light blue shirts and navy pants and matching ties, and find it hard to believe I once sat where you sit. It seems like a tale of long-ago and far-away that before attending school here—like most of you—I too attended the Jesuit grade school just across the courtyard.

How is it that I came to a time when Padre Martínez from Amá's church gives a liberation mass every year in my classroom on the anniversary of El Salvador's La Matanza from a time that I sat where you are now, thinking some of the very same things that you do, with very little thought of how easy it was to get here unless, instead of a measure of time, history is space, like a series of rooms that we can just as easily step into as out of?

Well, no more.

I didn't fuck any perros—such an easy verb to conjugate—nor did I murder anyone, and I will leave here right after you graduate nearly as poor as when I first came in. It was just a letter. A letter written long ago, to a long-gone person that was tucked in a history book.

No dogs.

No smoking guns.

Ay, miren aquí, as you all know this pink country here is Spain y aquí, this blue one es Santiago. Though no map that the Jesuits see fit to bring you gives you accurate proportions here. South Africa. The Cape Blanco. This one here is ironically called the Cape of Good Hope and then on to Santiago; and then from La Habana, here in blue to . . .

Ostrovski—thin and wan, though strongly suspicious—you've echoed the voice of the ever-strengthening muscle of doubt that has been with me since my first year of teaching when I thought I knew something, where to next? No we are not talking about something that happened over three hundred years ago in a country that none of us can even go to; and you're right—you've been right all semester, you've all been right over these years—we probably should be more concerned with diseases for which there are no antibodies or drive-by shootings or skinheads.

I don't blame you. I don't blame any of you. It is the combination grip of this early heat and unrelenting uncertainty of your fates. Some of you—those who graduated not long ago—are just starting families, and realize that I have never told you anything that really means anything.

Once you leave the air-conditioned comfort of the school's walls—and might I note, there was no air-conditioning when I was a student here—there is a hot out there that's so strong and so willing to close in on everything you think you know. Lately, I even find myself watching the chalk dust ride the streams of bent light that is refracted through the high windows of the classroom—not because I'm distracted by it, but because for the first time in a long time, I can; little matters now—but within an hour of our lesson I can feel your fear rise up in steam as you run away to some foggy world that's neither here nor out there. I can smell it. It's raw and new. It gnaws the heart.

Though without it, óiganme mis compadres, without your fear with what would you arm yourselves against those things you fear most: Terrorist Invasion; Global Warming; Joblessness; Homelessness? Who makes change? Who moves things forward?

Each and every one of us wakes each morning and quickly gathers up tiny bits of our pasts to know who we are. And it is by telling them over and over to ourselves that we live. First it's the song on the clock radio, then a picture across the room, the need to pee.

Miren my hands. This color on the map, this bit of orange here. Illinois. Chicago stares me in the face every morning when I shave, señores. My face, this color, a subtle legacy of the British Royal African Company, is, as they say in the vernacular, el color of my Espanish.

I LOVE IT, doña Liliana said as only she can, by rolling the L in love long and fat and delicious out of her mouth. No, I no love it, she corrected herself, I love love it; I am so in loving with it, she said running across my kitchen to turn up the radio.

And she mamboed back to the table, her broad hips swaying, her neck thrown back as if the graying bun knotted at the base of her scalp was still the pale blonde—Rubia de Harlow, Marilyn Monroe Rubia, they say they called it—that she maintained even after the first few years of Castro when she had to do it herself; she danced as if the dishrag she held were a pair of satin evening gloves that she clasped behind her imaginary partner's neck.

Guantanamera.

Anytime it played, in any version, she and doña Cristina knew all the lyrics, knew when the singer would change the look, the face, the attitude of la guajira; the girl up from the country flew into rages, was sweet as dulce con leche at the singer's whim and las doñas Liliana y Cristina seemed always to know all the words.

La guajira, when she was a temptress, they said they sang her eyes green green and her walk haughty, hips rolling over legs so long you'd need a trail of bread crumbs to find your way back. When she was a bruja, her skin was smoky; her eyes—haunted from sun in the cane fields—cast spells over them that tightened and convulsed them into a dance that left them sweaty and aching.

Guantanamera, guajira Guatanamera, they sang when her skin was a cafe con leche y her thighs were soft as the belly of una paloma, la guajira's neck was theirs for biting and her innocence was at the ends of their fingertips.

Guantanamera, guajira Guantanamera, they sang, and although the girl in the song changed, the country girl from Guantánamo, she was a new lyric each time they sang the song.

But Amá never joined in.

Of course you know it was always a man doing the singing, doña Liliana said.

To which doña Cristina answered with a click of her tongue. She then took a look at the dishes doña Liliana had just rinsed and stacked on the drain board, and ran hot soapy water, rolled up her sleeves and began to wash them all again as she had done so many times when we all lived together years before in Amá's little casa blanca.

And then, as we have seen so often over a sink of soapy water and doña Liliana's poor efforts at dishwashing, doña Cristina's face broke into what none of us have ever known if what we were witnessing was a battle to combat tears or a fit of hysterical laughter—something I've only seen actresses do in old movies—as she gracefully leaned and fell into one of the chairs as she sighed, La pobrecita, la preciosa . . . a safe haven, a palace she made for us . . . just close enough to the sea so we wouldn't feel so homesick . . . that little house.

And even though doña Liliana knew she was talking about Lake Michigan, she never bothered to correct her. She merely answered by clicking her tongue, which I took to mean the same as the tongue click she issued before our collective silence anytime over the years we let doña Cristina recount the stories of our lives together as if we ourselves had not been there to have lived them.

Tell us about when we were babies, Julio, Román and I would beg. And doña Cristina would remember which of us started up with the croup before spreading it between the three of us; who had to be quarantined from the others sick with fever from the measles. It has always been as if doña Cristina has held memory for us all. Even though she hadn't been there, she recalls with great detail, as if the pains had been her own, how the gemelos came: first Julio—as though he'd break doña Liliana's pelvis in two—then Román, turned backward, curled up in a ball at the far end of doña Liliana's womb, born black with a purple arm on one side up to his shoulder half an hour after his brother—and then eleven months later, she says, I flew, as if shot from a cannon out of Amá the following April into the midwife's hands.

Our first steps, our first words have been gathered and arranged as if she had picked them up as easily as photographs the day that she came into all of our lives; and so convinced we were of her powers to hold on to exact moments, precise details, that as boys we'd hand her leaves, ends of ice cream cones, baseball score sheets as if she could hold on to the thrill that ran through us hearing a home run cracked in a tie game with extra innings, the perfect combination of sun and breeze, the smell that clung in our clothes when it was suddenly autumn here in Chicago.

Doña Cristina, any one of us can ask, tell me about when, and she'll know the day, know the weather, tell you if you took a bus, a train or a car to get to wherever it was that you ended up.

Guantanamera, guajira Guantanamera, doña Cristina sang along sadly with the radio and took time out from the pastelito she was picking at with her nails to look over her shoulder, I assume to see if Amá was in the room as she began to tell the story of months when she and doña Liliana were waiting with Julio and Román in Florida for the call, for money, for Amá to tell them that they had someplace in the world to be; someplace that we all could call home, she said. You can ask doña Cristina anything about the time they were detained in Miami, and she'll unravel yards and yards of concertina wire, dogs with vicious teeth and feet and yards and cubic miles of forms with thousands and thousands of blank spaces to be completed; English, and being made to feel stupid and like a hero and unwanted and saved all at the same time. It was as if we dangled from a little piece of twine over the Florida Straits, she'll start when asked, and then she would add sharks underneath them, and raging, gun-wielding revolutionaries and politicians—both Cuban and American, depending upon who asked—in the sea and the air around them. That little casa blanca was there for us, for all of us your mamá did it, doña Cristina said grabbing my hand.

Tell her you had the time of your life, and you will have come from an evening with twice as many kisses than were given you, from the races having won the trifecta, when you overhear the story retold; you will have been thought the best dancer at a party, and the most handsome in the room, but whatever it was, that feeling you had when you had it is something that you'll never forget. That, she'll hold for you exactly the way that it was.

Once—against doña Cristina's protest of several rapid tongue clicks—doña Liliana said she thought I was old enough to know; she looked over her shoulder before saying, they said, they say that Juan Ocho sung Amá with his trumpet playing from the wall where she was standing. Julio and I had found the only picture that I had seen of him in a little silver frame tucked between tablecloths in the sideboard and asked, and doña Liliana whispered that—la luna negra, guajira—he sang her up to the makeshift platform for the band that had been set up in somebody's—she could not remember whose—patio.

But it was doña Cristina who corrected, he sang Amá, his luna negra, rising over the cane fields, like sugar on the mouth of the sky that betrayed that it sometimes kissed the earth; two hundred years of the sky kissing the earth yields la luna negra de Guantánamo, guajira Guantanamera with a golden halo.

Doña Liliana had tried to continue telling the story when doña Cristina chimed in to say that Amá was wearing that gold Dior Liliana threw out probably after only wearing it once or twice, as if to make sure that we hadn't gotten lost in what she calls doña Liliana's spinning of the truth.

¡Ay ya mujer! Doña Liliana scolded with a single cut of her eyes before turning back to me to say, She lookeded muy elegante.

She lookeded overdressed—as did you in those days—is what she lookeded, doña Cristina said while examining her own fingernails with disgust.

How do you know, you weren't even there, doña Liliana snapped at her.

To which doña Cristina responded, I have had years of seeing the pictures.

And they commenced in a clutter of tongue clicks back and forth at each other before doña Cristina cautioned, If you're going to tell the boy the story tell it so it makes sense. You put her in that gold cocktail dress that you wore to some party or another and had shortened only to find out that the style had changed to long dresses; y you piled a switch atop her head and made her up for I don't know what with that pink frosted lipstick that you thought was so chic, and stuffed her into those high heels that were too small for you—size fives when you know very well you were an infant the last time you wore a five—all for a party the domestics were having at somebody's house who was in Miami at the time. Ay benditos, doña Cristina insisted, Lilianita, if you're going to tell the boy the story tell it right; which only caused doña Liliana to click her tongue several times rather vigorously before remembering a second lyric she heard from somebody who she couldn't remember that Juan Ocho sang stars into Amá's deep-set eyes, the smell of the sea near Santiago in her breath. Guantanamera, guajira Guantanamera, she said, they said he sang.

When I asked only a few years ago, Why Juan Ocho? it was doña Liliana who said she heard it was because it was his lucky number; he had one of those hand-painted ties with an eight ball on it; he told people that he was born on the eighth day in the eighth month; but other people said, she said, it was because he could neither roll seven nor eleven; really he was Ocho por defecto, doña Cristina confirmed, and she seemed to remember—she conceded even though she hadn't been there—something about his having a pair of cuff links made of dice: tres y cinco.

Tres y cinco, tres y cinco, doña Cristina muttered under her breath, and then she began clicking her tongue against her teeth like a playing card against spokes on a wheel. What I heard is that his name was Arseñio Ramos and his people come from Holguín; farmers is all. Goats, I think, she said she seemed to remember.

Guantanamera, guajira Guantanamera, they say he sang, Juan Ocho, and although in none of the things that Amá and I picked through after the fire was there the man in the little silver frame holding the trumpet. Wavy castellano hair, tie askew and shirt open wide though cut off before you could see if there was an eight ball painted on the bell of his tie.

Doña Cristina said she wasn't sure—even though we both knew—and that maybe I needed to ask my Amá. She had made an effort to pull on the half glasses—which I once overheard doña Liliana tell Amá she knew doña Cristina didn't need, only wore on that string so that people would pay attention to her when she was about to say something—up off her bosom.

Of the wavy castellano hair, doña Liliana whispered so that doña Cristina couldn't hear, thousands of women could have fallen into that. And even though she didn't seem to have heard what doña Liliana said, doña Cristina who had never laid eyes on him began to add rather absently that he had a way of drawing on a Montecristo that made your heart stop, and he wore those big pants and pointy shoes pachucos wore back then; and I seem to remember that he wore lacquer on his nails. Not a color, clear. But still nail lacquer; not even the wealthiest from high society wore it, no, it was a sign of the type that wouldn't think twice of calling on you without an apology two days after he left you stranded without a ride at a party, or thought nothing of kissing the hostess' hand in the most elaborate of fashions and then later relieving himself in a corner of her patio. O he was a wonderful dancer—all hips and glide—the type that would make you so dizzy you had no idea when he transferred you over to one of his friends so that when you saw him across the room you thought you still were the woman he was dancing with.

Pero, yo no know, doña Liliana said, I have no idea what his real name is. Maybe you should ask Mireya.

By the time I asked Amá, Julio had lost interest and was playing ball with Román and some of the other boys in the street in front of Amá's house. By then the notion of a father for them was something like knowing the composition of green or yellow light; when they asked their own mother, doña Liliana would smile gently, lovingly and tell them that they were hers; Amá once began to answer that doña Liliana went to the mountains, but she could not finish the story because, as if by surprise, she realized that was all she knew, and sent them to their mother; not even doña

Cristina, pressing her fingers into her temples, could give him eye color, a way of sitting, a mouth; did he adjust his crotch openly, chew with his mouth open, use foul language in front of ladies and go into their purses—all of which we were told were things a gentleman never did—or did he brush his teeth after meals, keep his neck and nails scrubbed, smell of soap, mint and barber's lotion? We had no idea. They, Julio y Román, seemed to be content with the light that doña Cristina seemed to remember coming through the trees, the thinness of the air, difficulty breathing in the rough terrain, and the chill it took on after dark, but not much more. And of Juan Ocho that day I first asked, all Amá said was he was a man who sometimes called himself Juan Ocho, and other times introduced himself as Juan Ocho Dellaspalmas, and when he was looking to get his way he referred to himself as Juanito. But all she knew was that in her past or in another life she must have done something so terribly evil for which she must pay by having to raise a child so ungrateful and cruel that he would go into places that he knew that he was not allowed and begin to ask questions about things that were never discussed with him.

And that was that until she told me she prayed for him the day of the fire.

Guantanamera, guajira Guantanamera, the radio sang, though we were no longer in Cuba. Julio watched the World Cup in my living room; on the couch beside him Román was asleep holding his potbelly with both hands. Guantanamera, guajira Guantanamera, part of long-ago and far-away and Amá's little casa blanca and the life we all had there too were memory.

Later, in my dining room doña Liliana squatted over the boxes of clothing that Julio, Román and I had salvaged from where Amá's storage closet once stood underneath her stairs, and she had left the swinging door to the kitchen open for doña Cristina's commentary which was not unlike what you would hear at a fashion show with each dress reminding her of doña Liliana's memory of a coming-out party; of two weeks' vacation spent near Santiago; of a month spent in Valencia—everything was either strapless or off the shoulder that season—and then Seville, Majorca and then Italia. Ay, sí, Italia, as if she too had been there, as if we had all been there as doña Liliana put dresses on over her clothes, twirling and changing and walking the length of the dining room table as if for a much larger audience.

It only made sense that Amá come and live with me while she decided what was next. No one ever asked. I had both an extra bedroom and a study, a double storage locker in the basement, was closest to the area she knew best, near her shop and church. Julio's apartment was too far up on the Red Line and Amá—although she has threatened many times—has never learned to drive. Doña Cristina's apartment was small and comfortable yet with its limited furnishings somehow seemed monastic. Doña Liliana had devoted her spare bedroom to her winter wardrobe, the dining room to cosmetics, shoes line the hallway between her bedroom and the back door, the counter space in the bathroom had four curling irons that were spiderwebbed to a multiple adapter so that they could all be in use at once. It hardly seemed a question; no one thought of asking Julio, none of us would. My place seemed the most likely, maybe simply because it was now the only place where all of us could still fit, still have dinner together like we always had, and it felt less like the unpeeling of an onion that had begun as Julio, Román and I began graduating from high school and starting our own lives.

Pobrecita, doña Cristina said under her breath, and then she continued clicking her tongue as she filled the sink again with hot water and soap and began to rewash the dishes that she had just rewashed.

Outside it had begun to rain again. A quick thunderous

shower in fits of starts and stops. A sulfurous smell seeped in through the windows that tasted like I was being fed mouthful after mouthful of tarnished spoon each time I exhaled.

None of us ever know if it is the coming or if it is the going, the rain, that will remind doña Liliana of a time when she was a girl and her father—who was a very rich man—had had a party and many very famous people from Hollywood attended; or when her father—who was a very politically connected man—had had the entire ballroom of La Habana Hilton shut down for her sixteenth birthday; or when her father—a considerate and influential man—had sent her to Paris just to pick out dresses for an engagement party that she never had to a fiancé who never proposed.

I worry, doña Cristina said as she finally began to dry and put away her collection on the dish rack.

I reminded her that doña Liliana gets like this when it rains.

Y doña Cristina said, No not Liliana, I never worry after Liliana; no one need ever worry after Liliana. No, it's Mireya. Mijo, I'm worried for your mamá. And not just the fire. I think she may need some help; she may need a doctor, doña Cristina started when she was interrupted by doña Liliana as she came in with a little charred box of half hearts.

Doña Liliana had stepped into the sea foam dress without a zipper; the one that there used to be pictures of that were taken the night Amá and another maid who didn't last long enough for any of them to remember her name had sewed doña Liliana into so that in the arms of her attendants she was a breeze, a wave, and then nothing more than a lingering. Even sewn together, now the dress could never close around her. The bodice fell forward when she dropped her hand from her chest and revealed the gold Disney World appliqué T-shirt. Where the ballet-length hem ended, jeans that were faded into a precise crease ran to the tops of freshly washed tennis shoes.

Doña Liliana's hands, cheeks and neck were streaked with soot. She drew another black line across her forehead as she brushed back hairs, and happy with guile saved from girlhood, thrust the box forward, smiling, Mira.

The half hearts in their cotton bed, untouched by the fire, glittered between burnt bits. Mira, she said, they'd only give you half; Antonio, Roberto, Reynaldo, Chucho, Rubén. Your name was supposed to go on the other half. Pero, I think most of them had their own names put on both halves. Sí, mira, I have two from Chucho; hijo de puta, Jesús, drank so much he had no memory and no conscience; entonces he gived me the half he had intended for una china he didn't know I knew he kept down near calle san Lázaro. Y entonces he asked for it back, telling me his sister was sick in the hospital. Sister! ¡Dios! You would of a think the son-de-the-bitch would have known better—or at least have been raised better—to think he could try that one on a girl who had grown up in El Vedado, she said, tongue clicking.

No, no, the next time he came to my father's house—my father's castle—I have Mireya turn him away right at the door. Y Óscar, tu mamá lookeded at him like he was an already forgotten, she did. Down the nose like she said, La señorita is a no longer accepting the visit from you, señor Chucho, you must go now before I have the man set out the dogs on you, tu mamá dijo. Y we no even have no dogs, doña Liliana laughed tossing her head in a way that let me see the crown of gray roots close to her head that she would no longer go into the shop and have Amá take care of.

Too vain, doña Cristina once said of doña Liliana's gray hairs, too proud to let your . . . even your mamá that she . . . well . . . we . . . chico, we's all getting old.

Y Guantanamera, guajira Guantanamera, they said

they sang—las doñas Liliana y Cristina—as they cleaned the kitchen and dining room, wiped down the tables and counters, and remembered a man named Cristóbal and his brother Rodolfo who had tried to pass themselves off as twins although there was clearly a decade between the two. Razor-thin moustaches, matching guayaberas—each always with a gardenia in the buttonhole—the older one could hold the younger in a handstand above his head with just one arm, and they would end their routine on doña Liliana's father's richly adorned patio with perfectly coordinated backflips.

Román had left and I was prying the beer from Julio's hand, covering him with a blanket and turning off the television when las doñas remembered Rodolfo y Cristóbal's aftershave that permeated the air even outside and was stronger than the boutonnieres they had worn, stronger than the combination of flamboyant, verónica, orchid or magnolia that surrounded doña Liliana's father's overflowing patio, yet not strong enough to mask the celery and onion smell of their breaths or the fungusy smells that came out of parts of their bodies that neither Amá nor doña Liliana wanted to begin to think about.

Ask Mireya, doña Liliana said as they were leaving in doña Cristina's rusted Corolla, ask tu mamá, she served many an iced glass of champagnes y lots of those little cocktail sandwiches that were so popular back then.

And it would have seemed like any Saturday night—Amá's cooking, las doñas Cristina y Liliana remembering and cleaning up; Román y Julio and me eating ourselves stupid—except that there was no longer the white house that my Amá had dreamed, prayed for and imagined herself—when we all lived in Cuba, when Amá and I first came to the United States—the lady of.

When doña Cristina's call came half an hour later to let

us know that she and doña Liliana had gotten to their respective homes safely, I took the call. Buenas noches, I called into the phone as if it could have been any evening the six of us had been together, when she started to tell me she was serious about Amá needing help.

Since the fire, casseroles have come the fifty or so blocks by bus and El, have been walked—pulled behind in little wire shopping carts—over from the ruin of Amá's house to my apartment, dropped off while dutiful sons and daughters waited downstairs in cars and mothers, aunts, chismosas from Amá's beauty shop, ladies from the church had cafecitos and cake. A long line of them all week. And then late the Sunday morning after Julio y Román and las doñas Liliana y Cristina had been to my house for dinner, Natalia Valdez McIntosh's—Naty, Antonia Márquez's girl as everyone calls her even though she's nearly forty—who makes the appointments and gives a hand with the shampooing and sweeping up at the shop, or, to be precise, it was Naty's mamá's casserole, pero everyone from the neighborhood knows señora Márquez hasn't left her house—solamente the grocería e iglesia—since her daughter's unfortunate marriage.

As Naty came through the door, she forced a dish I had seen wrapped in aluminum foil at hundreds of church potlucks towards me then enveloped Amá in an elaborate, jingling embrace. She carried a bunch of roses that I recognized as coming from over the back fence of Amá's garden. Their blossoms were slack from the heat and their own weight and their stems broken instead of cut. Naty's fingers had left droplets of blood in the wad of paper towel clutched around them. And Naty was made up for color TV. The lids of her eyes were extended out and up toward her forehead with a strong black line and shadowed in gradating shades of blue until they matched the contact lenses she uses to conceal her deep brown eyes. She was wearing false eyelashes that fluttered along with the rapid waving of her hand as she stood over one of the floor vents while it blew air-conditioning up her skirt and sighed, Ay, hace calor, ¿no?

She took a long time to light on the couch next to Amá. Her brittle blonde hair was swept high on her head; her bright pink nails extended and curved to such a length that it made the dexterity with which she handled the spoon I gave her to stir her coffee remarkable. Her bracelets, earrings and key chain—a cluster of charms, trinkets and keepsakes surrounding the single key to the front door to her mamá's house where she has lived since, after only three months fifteen years ago, she left the redheaded güero nearly everyone in the neighborhood said looked like un topo—never stopped jingling even after she and Amá were settled on the couch.

Amá hasn't gone to the beauty shop for over a week. Though Naty assured us that since the fire, all the standing appointments—the weekly pedicures, hand and neck massages, the hair appointments—had been placed on hold until La Señora is herself and ready to return. And though this was a social visit, she was careful to preface, she still was a little curious as to when Amá planned to reopen.

She said she and the other girls from the shop wanted Amá to know that she was more than just the neighborhood beautician. Señora you provide a service, she said, even Padre Rodríguez was concerned and offered a special prayer for you and the loss of your house and so many of your belongings. She told Amá she should have been there; Naty had never heard so much tongue clicking in all of her life as he recounted the loss and the devastation that had happened to one of our own.

Which, Natalia said as she added cream and four sugar cubes to a cup so small that she needed to rattle her spoon against its sides for what seemed an eternity until the syrup she had concocted met her approval with a loud smack of her lips before adding, probably set the ruby-tongued chismosas into overtime. There probably wasn't a phone line available for miles for a whole hour after mass, she then added as she lifted the saucer daintily to her lips.

Y Ave María, Señora you only need to see señora Figueroa's roots! There's no way that she is ever going to convince anyone she was una rubia natural as a child ever again. Y those Paredes girls, the indianidad has jumped back all over their heads, there's no way of telling what it will take to wrestle those wild Mayans back into submission.

Amá sat quietly, nodding as the girl continued. She smiled at each elaborate description. Gently stirred her coffee around in the cup—cream, one lump of sugar—without drinking any. She closed and unfolded her napkin two or three times in her lap, and neatly closed her legs in what I knew her to believe to be a ladylike position as she smoothed her skirt around them.

Naty took time out to cut the tiniest sliver of cake without crumbling, licked her fingers with a noisy jingle; then, with gestures and voices, began recounting the week's cliffhangers from her favorite telenovelas. Amá was pressing cake crumbs against her plate with the back of her fork, and Naty was alternately imitating the lascivious Doctor Zuniga and the libidinous Nurse Sanchez as I tiptoed out of the room.

I shut the door of my study against Naty's jingling. The room was cool and dark. Outside, kids had opened a hydrant. Its spray filled the street, their mouths were wide, toothy silenced squeals of delight from where I was sitting. They ran with abandon, without care, without thinking how baths, dinner dishes, laundry would be curtailed until the fire department came around to stop the spray flooding the street and restore the water pressure. And although every winter we have complained that one day we may all die in the snow, outside, in swimsuits and underwear, the littlest ones either naked or in diapers, some even in clothes cared only about escaping from the heat.

¿Quién sabe? ¿Sabe, verdad? I wrote on the page in front of me.

¿Sabe, verdad? and then the year 1460 and sat back and tried to anticipate the questions students don't think to ask.

Imagina, Óscar, Mr. Delossantos, the blank stares you'll receive when I ask, señores, for whom is it 1460? Certainly not the Taínos who arrived on the island from the Antilles before el conquistador?

Future managers, supervisors, superintendents, lowly schoolteachers of the future, I had planned to ask, what time will you need to be at the office, on the showroom floor, in your classroom? What time do you tell your sales staff, the receptionist, the guy who sleeps at the computer service desk, your students to show up?

For those who will punch a time clock in the future, whose time is it that you'll begin to make the doughnuts, mop the floors, bag the groceries, slide under somebody's SUV to begin installing a new exhaust system? Clock-watchers of the future, how is it that you will know that you have just enough time to get papers off your desk, check race forms on the Internet, flirt with el jefe's prima in the short skirts who has been given a posh job answering phones at twice your rate even though a college degree was necessary for your position?

How will you know that you have just enough time to take an extra coffee break, grab a smoke; how will you know when there's time enough to take the sports page in the men's room with you? When does 1460 become 1460 in what is now Santiago, La Habana, Holguín, those of you whose futures will not involve dirt under your nails or chalk dust on your clothes or carpal tunnel syndrome?

Future bankers, lawyers, dot-com moguls, future futures seers, those of you who are destined to fail no matter how hard you try, how is it you'll know that it's overtime you'll need, time and a half you're calculating; will you know how to calculate vacation time?

How is it that you'll know you have free time; that there is more flexibility to the hours of your day than there was when you were a drudge pushing papers in a cubicle? And although you'll dream through the window of your towering office of swaying palm trees and waterfalls with deafening spills, how will you explain to yourself that the concrete parking structure you're looking at is exactly what you're supposed to see?

Who makes time, I had planned to ask.

Imaginen, I suppose is the next thing that you're going to say, Juan Ocho guessed.

He leaned against the doorway of my study, the air in which was mostly being eaten up by his verbena hair oil, the smell of rum and the clouds of smoke from a cigar held in his grin. He wore a rumpled cream-colored linen suit, a blue silk shirt unbuttoned to his waist; his panama obscured his eyes. He carried a plate covered with aluminum foil.

¿Ay, hace calor, no? he said as he took off his hat and began to fan himself. When he smoothed his castellano hair into a wave, a crumble of ash fell off his Montecristo and ran into the Oriental carpet and set the koi swimming around our feet in the rug's blue water.

As he made his way across the room, the water splashed against his trousers, the chairs and the couch. He threw his hat on the couch, set the plate on the desk and removed the aluminum that slipped silvery from his hand, fell with a heavy plop into the water and swam beneath the desk; I could see its shadow move along the bookcases, around the floor lamp and under the couch.

Juan Ocho ran the unlit end of the Montecristo around

the flan before sticking the majority of it in his mouth. He rolled his eyes and rocked on his heels, his trousers tented with a large erection.

Guantanamera, guajira Guantanamera, he hummed reaching underneath his belt. Guantanamera, guajira Guantanamera, he sang, con guayaba, guajira. He removed his hand from his trousers, brought his fingers to his nose and inhaled, blowing on his fingers and then inhaling again as if testing the cork from a bottle of wine. Yo soy un hombre sincero; De donde crece la palma, he sang before his eyes shot open and he said, Sí, sí, verdad, Mireya. Nobody could figure out how she did it, flan con guayaba. Con guayaba. Can you imagine? Well I suppose you can, you've been eating it your entire life, ¿no? Entonces, you must know what she does with the seeds. They're so small, ¿no? Tiny like the lunarcitos on her hip.

I told him that I wouldn't know.

And he said, O sí, yes, of course you wouldn't. Well they aren't that different from the ones on her throat, except more embedded. You would miss them if you didn't have a light touch, if you know what I mean.

He ran the wet end of his cigar around the flan again. Ay how does she do it? A sieve? Cheesecloth?

Dije, yo no sé, I told him.

You must have watched, he insisted. How could you not help but watch? It was the talk of El Vedado. All the maids were sent to discover her secret. He said they were instructed to become her friend; ladies of the house who had had tea or dinner with Liliana's comemierda of a father would beg their maids, And while you're at it, learn how she bastes a stitch so cleanly, and keeps a house so nice. You should learn, they told their maids. You must have seen her do it at least once, ¿no?

I never have, I said flatly.

Well, he said sucking his teeth with disappointment.

And he placed his hand into his trousers and brought his fingers to his nose again. Guayaba, mijo, he said; very few things in the world make you want to eat them and lick them more than when they open themselves up to you as guayaba, he said as he produced one from his pocket and defied gravity by balancing it on the very edge of the desk. He held the cigar—which never grew shorter, was only smolder and coal-red tip between his teeth—as he produced another guayaba from his pocket and set it next to the first. Guayaba kept coming from his pocket until there were over a dozen of them on the edge of the desk. He opened one with the letter opener, and the juice ran down his arm, his trouser leg, and colored the water at his feet a light pink.

He balanced the letter opener on its point in the center of the lecture I was preparing for the next day and said, If you're polite you get it on a nice chilled plate with a little lime. If you're unfortunate, you have to grab it off of the first tree that you pass; shove your thumbs in it and suck for all you're worth. Pero if you're lucky, the sun will split it open for you nice and pink—mira mijo, like this one here, he said thrusting the fruit toward me—and all its juice will come running at you just because you're pretty. At least that's been my experience, he said with a phlegmy chuckle.

I told him that I didn't think that we should be having this conversation.

¿Por qué no? he asked. It seems to me we should have had this conversation the moment that the first few hairs sprung up around tu verga.

The drag of the water around our ankles and the koi—that responded by schooling about each peel of guayaba as he dropped them, bloodying the water—slowed me down as I attempted to make my way out of the room; and by the time that I reached the door, Juan Ocho had already casually draped himself in front of the opening.

Forget all that silken gloved hand shit Liliana, he sang,

Guantanamera, guajira Guantanamera. Instead of some bored, spoiled, pale debutante, mijo, imagina una guajira brown, lean, long-limbed crossing La Sierra Maestra in her bare feet with a plate full of flan con guayaba in her hands. Ay bendito, could your abuelita make daughters.

You never met her, I said, you never met any of them.

Did I have to, mijo? he said, You call yourself el maestro de historia, you make the math. I known hundreds of them coming over La Sierra Maestra at the time: inocentes, brown as la caña, and twice as pure. No mestizaje, all of them hecho con sangre africana. Negras, negras, negras, negras. Negra negra, like cafecito solo. No leche until mine comes around. Like they come up out of the ground that way. Grown in the fields, raised in the sun, guajiras, he sang as he danced around in the pool that was now teaming with koi.

I was lying on the couch in my office. At some point I had taken off my pants and shoes. It was barely morning, not quite light, still dark.

In the hallway on the way to the bathroom I could smell Amá's kitchen burning, and I could hear her praying, Dios mío. Dios mío. Dios mío. Dios mío. Dios mío.

When I turned the light on, I found her standing in a red-and-white flower print dress that must have come from one of the boxes in the dining room. Her hair was perfectly brushed and she was wearing black patent leather shoes and holding a matching handbag.

Amá, I called when she didn't respond to the light, Amá?

She smiled politely. Perdóneme señor, pero you know when the bus comes?

Amá, I said, it's me, Óscar; soy Óscar.

I'm headed for La Habana, she told me in a very girlish voice. My mamá saw a baby that I have to catch. A baby dropped in La Corriente del Golfo. Woolly-headed girl, what have you done now? she asked me, while she stared with her eyes wide at her throw for me of the corie that lay on the scarf that held the story of her life in front of her. Woolly-headed girl, mi preciosa, mi niña, with the whole of your life ahead of you, you've done it now, she said.

She stepped and asked, ¿Señor?

Amá it's me, I said as I reached to touch her arm, but she ran down the hallway towards the living room.

No, I need a bus, she said as I chased her, a bus, la guagua; woolly-headed girl, mi preciosa, mi niña, she said to me, that crying, that crying you hear is your baby.

Daylight was beginning to light the windows as she dropped her purse and ran through the swinging door between the kitchen and dining room.

Amá! I called.

You hear it too? Escúchame, she whispered as she paced the length of the kitchen table, Escucha. You hear it too; I know you do, señor. Porfa, ayúdeme, ayúdeme. We need to get to La Habana, we need to get to La Corriente del Golfo and swim to the bottom. You'll recognize him in sea-weed. He's mine that one you hear, mine, the one with asparagus-water-colored eyes and castellano hair, the one my mamá saw in the corie. Por favor, señor, she wailed.

Soy yo, soy yo, es Óscar, I called. And all of sudden, she knew me.

She looked at her dress. At the room, at me, and back at her dress. She smoothed the skirt as she caught her breath. This is doña Liliana's, she said as if asking. She wore it for tea with some diplomático americano, and once for a charity luncheon. It has a blue sash, she remembered.

I started the coffee while she changed into her bathrobe.

When she came back she was brushing her hair and pinning it up as if it could have been any morning back in her little white house just off Ashland Avenue. She asked if I had gotten the paper off of the porch, and had I made sure the coffee was good and strong.

We said nothing for a while. I buttered toast neither of us ate.

As I left the room to dress for work, she said something about not opening her shop again for another week; none of them are going to die without getting their hair done, pero I do worry about Naty.

She came into the hallway to kiss me good-bye when she asked, Mijo he was here wasn't he?

¿Quién, mamá? I asked.

Juan Ocho, she snapped.

I don't know who you mean mamá, I told her, to which she responded, Of course you don't, all the same he was here. I heard the two of you talking, I saw him leave out of the ceiling.

She looked at me to see if it could be true and covered her mouth.

Her face began to crumble with fear. Oscarcito, por favor, she said, as if I could explain how she had wet herself without knowing it.

And for the first time in sixteen years—possibly because I was frightened, or because I had no explanation as to how guajira changed at the will of men's eyes that would satisfy Ostrovski or Palacios that didn't begin, Once upon a time near Santiago, near the bay of Guantánamo—I called Father Rodríguez and told him I was sick.

. . . AY SANTOS! ¿RECUERDO? ¿Bromeas? Don't be so silly as these two here, of course I do, Amá told Doctor Canales as the very pretty woman listened intently and a nurse took my mother's temperature, examined her heart, then her lungs, and took her blood pressure.

Maybe it was Julio who first noticed that something was going on. But I paid no attention to it then. Weeks ago, months ago, it was still cold out, we had met for dinner, and he told me about being at Amá's house earlier in the week, taken a dress doña Liliana wanted let out, or was returning something, a dish, a thimble, a pair of scissors, a bolt of fabric, a nine-year-old Hindu—I don't remember now that I need to—that his mother wanted him to return, and he found Amá in her boots and housedress standing in the three inches of snow in the garden, staring at something—and I do remember this clearly—yet he was not able to determine what.

Óscar's abuela—mi madre—her cuervo, Amá told the doctor switching again to Spanish, Pirata.

Pirata, mi abuela's cuervo o cuervos, one out of the thousands of thunderous murders of black, iridescent crows or entire murders down and over from the Zapata peninsula that, for her and her alone, had somehow found their or its way to Santiago.

Pirata—though Amá has always said up until now that only Abuelita had been able to see them or it—still Pirata, for either the one or for them all as they streaked the sky with a screeching smear of gawwaaak-gawow, as they headed toward their communal nests in the trees right above where Amá had been discovered shirking work, lazing about like a good-for-nothing. His shiny black eye, their shiny black eyes—the good one—could peer through banana leaves, see through the night, through the dark, into corners, around bends and deep into rivers of conscious and heart-of-hearts.

Pirata, Amá told Doctor Canales, because of his or their one blind eye and the tale that followed him or them from the galleon with a bare-breasted mulata figurehead—the likeness of which, they say, favored a woman famous for murdering husbands and eating children—that started in Grenada and rounded nearly every port in the Caribbean; Barbados, Jamaica, Saint Domingüe, and back around the Canary Islands like a knife through blue water, it cut open the sides of trade ships, of marauding ships, of ships in illegal waters, in uncharted territories and places that were full up with, spilled over with silver and brazilwood and coffee and gold and hides and tobacco and mahogany and copper; split them open and sucked their contents into its own hull; y they called him or them Pirata for the ribbons of blue curses in the most ancient of Catalan he or they would unfurl at anyone who came close to harming his abuelita, anyone who had an unkind thought or who was thinking of throwing el ojo malo in her direction unloosed a streak of damnation from that bird that made the sailors—who sucked their teeth in a nasty way at the rock of the hips and breast of pardas y morenas—even they looked away, at their boots or the mud, the birds' curses were so accurate, cunning, lethal and filthy; Pirata for the gold earring he or they plucked from the ear of a visiting española—bloodstains all over the bodice of her white silk gown—as she passed by with her black postillón in one of the many quitrines they would promenade up and down the major boulevards in; and Pirata for all of the gold watches that would go missing from the houses that servants would be blamed for, and the left shoes and thimbles and scythes and lace spindles and pocket watches the loss of which brought on beatings; at night people kept a good hold on babies, and the souls of the old and the ill were always guarded over—many a fine gallina's throat was slit to honor Changó—and wine was poured into the ground in front of the houses of young untouched girls, even the unattractive ones; he came, Pirata, they say they said, with el mareo that killed so many all the way back in 1833; they say they said you'd find them dead in the boiling rooms, standing dead right at the kettles; they'd walk dead around the cane fields with their distended bellies and hollows for eyes until the vibrating that came back on them from the blade against the stalk would finally send them back and flatten them out; and as their bodies split and ran into the soil like overripe mango under the sun, it was Pirata, they say they said they saw that wide wingspan—a blue-white, the color of the lips of a dead coffee heiress—that flew through the boiling rooms and into the huts while they slept and circled the fields during the day and paced the moon until morning, until the very few that were left—some of them close to dead, others nearly dead, some just standing, it was—when the men and the boys who could headed towards the brush surrounding the fields that led towards the forest with torches in their hands; some say they said it was the heat from the fire what broke the fevers—the brush and the forest all gone before they could finally get them put out—others say it was all them tarántulas—thousands of them what come out when their nests start burning—that sucked the poison out, no sé; pero although no one found any of the missing hat pins or silver crab forks, and possibly things went missing at the same rate as before, Pirata was neither seen and didn't nobody blame him for anything—except the few who could only blame a man dying in the prime of his youth on the bird or the birds—until the day of course when he stole mi madre's, Óscar's abuelita's, afterbirth.

An omnivore, a thief, indifferent and impatient with human frailty. It was Pirata, Amá said.

And the teacup and saucer? Doctor Canales asked. What were you feeling when you couldn't figure out the teacup?

The sudden sound of the doctor's English in the room seemed to startle my mother. She looked around like a child caught rifling in a drawer where she had been told repeatedly that she didn't belong: first at the nurse, then doña Cristina, Doctor Canales, then me before training her eyes on something out the window.

The doctor's offices at the edge of the Drive overlook Lake Michigan heading east at such an angle that no shoreline appears; just a stretch of water that seems to flatten and fall off where you can't see any more. I tried to figure out if it was the old electrical generator, the sails on a passing boat or just the water that drew Amá's attention.

At that dinner with Julio, we never got back to whatever it was that he thought that Amá was looking at, what she might have seen across the garden. We talked about his car—whether or not he should get a new one or wait until next year—and what the upcoming spring season had in store for the Cubs. Looking at the platter of cleaned ribs and smeared barbeque sauce between us and his tie tucked into his shirt to avoid dragging the tip through his plate that mirrored mine across the table, I recall thinking that I was uncertain as to why he called—it is not something that we do often—when he asked if I remembered a girl that he had dated years ago. The name—whatever it was—seemed familiar enough, yet it took a physical description complete with the holidays and parties that she attended for me to have even the vaguest picture in my head of the very small, dark dominicana who put on airs when in a roomful of cubanos that he was talking about. It seems that Julio had run into her, didn't recognize her, in fact, they hadn't recognized each other. You remember her, 'mano, he said, she was so pretty back then, spicy, sexy; and apparently she had said that she remembered him strong, muscular; invincible with an implacable sense of humor. What happened? he said she asked. What happened, he asked me, how did it happen that one day we were all kids and suddenly the next we're adults asking what the hell happened? Such a pretty girl, that spooky, gets into your blood kind of pretty, so terribly pretty she was, man.

The nurse finished her tabulations, collected her things off the counter and waited for a glance from Doctor Canales before leaving the room.

Ay bendito, Amá finally sighed before giving in to English, you no can expect me to remember everything all at once all the times! He, my son, he make too much from everything. I remember, por ejemplo, when he was born that he had the colic for precisely sixty-three days, and that on the left side of his bottoms he have a birthmark like a caracol.

And she, Amá said pointing at doña Cristina, she should talk; she's forever sick with something or one other. ¡Por favor! You know what, let me tell you some things, when she was about nineteen or twenty and we was in Cuba, she no have a date or a new dress to go to a coming-out party or some kind of big celebration they was holding near La Plaza Armas for something or another—a big thing it was with blue-and-white striped tents and all—and for nearly two weeks she cries, needs to be put to bed; they call for the doctor then too. And another time, she have to return an engagement ring, because she have three at once, but it was the one that she like the most—the ring not the fiancé—pero the moment he come to the door she faints . . .

Mireya, no, that was Liliana, doña Cristina quietly interrupted, that was Liliana. It was Liliana; she's the one who always thinks she's sick.

Amá looked back out of the window.

The boat had passed.

That dominicana was beautiful, beautiful, beautiful, dark and lovely, 'mano, Julio had said, she had a voice on her too, could sing, always sang in the morning, a Billie Holiday song, completely blue and hollowed out by the caballo she rode—rode hard, he'll tell you—that he said he remembered all of the words too.

It seems that he had called because he wanted to remember something that had been lost to him and needed someone else there to help put it back together for him, but never remembered, never got back to whatever Amá might have been staring at that afternoon he had gone to her house with whatever it was doña Liliana wanted him to bring over, never got back to what Amá might have said once she realized he was standing next to her.

¿La taza, señora, la taza para té? Doctor Canales asked again ¿Qué pasó? she said calmly.

Well I don't know what you're talking about, Amá snapped. For very kinky hair, no matter how much they complain about the way that it burns, vain as they are they want to feel like they have hair like a guërita even before it has a chance to take; taxes for the shop are due in April, August and November even though they call them quarterly; Roosevelt, Taft, Wilson, Harding, Coolidge, Hoover, Roosevelt—again, but a different one—Truman, Eisenhower, Kennedy, Johnson, Nixon, Ford, Carter, Reagan, Bush, Clinton, Bush, and if you need to know anyone before that maybe you're right; on that day everyone says they saw it I really did: while standing with nearly the rest of La Habana, I felt the first of what would become two hundred and fifty-eight days of nausea, bloating, back pain and swollen ankles only to culminate in what would be thirty-two and one half hours labor pains beginning just as the two famous doves landed on the shoulder of el presidente; Óscar, after all that time pushing against me the wrong way, he suddenly turn around on his own and come in such a big rush they say that he come out like a cannonball, and was so small and angry and red then that I thought that I had done something wrong, thought that I had not taken good care of myself; I knew I was there to catch the baby mi madre had predicted, I just had no idea that it would come without warning; he had been there inside me for nearly three months before I had any idea he was roaming around in there; the last time my ladies' visitor came was seven years ago on the twenty-sixth of March, and if she begins to show up again I will definitely show her where the door is; today's date is April 8, I know because a week ago—the Sunday before the fire, I made a ham with 7UP the way that it said in a Ladies' Home Journal that doña Liliana had thrown away in La Habana back in 1965, with cloves, canned pineapple rings and maraschino cherries—I remember thinking that at one time nothing seemed more exotic, more americano—I don't even like it, but the boys—Óscar, Julio and Román—have gotten used to it at Easter, they expect it; I couldn't even read the magazine, but I remember the ad very clearly; me and all the other girls who worked in El Vedado at the time, what did we know, we all thought it was called ZUP; el presidente's reforms sent us out in the field then for our patriotic duty: we couldn't work for people in El Vedado anymore, so by then with a machete in your hands, in the cane fields that most of us had fled, so dreaming of America or even just

Miami meant that you could have tea with Rita Hayworth once a week and dance at the Palladium while Dizzy Gillespie played; we had no idea; the November when Óscar was eight, and we were already in Miami, he had mumps and because I couldn't take him with me to the Refugee Relocation Office, and I left him with a neighbor who tied him to the bed so that I would have grandchildren; I nearly killed that woman, her husband and brother-in-law had to pull me off of her; on Mondays, señora Mena comes in for a wash, comb and set even though she hardly has any hair anymore—we make what looks like a cloud to float above her head; Tuesdays and Saturdays, doña Cristina comes in and lends a hand; Wednesdays, Naty and I are busy all day long with . . .

You want more? Amá suddenly stopped in English and looked around the room at me, at Doctor Canales, at doña Cristina.

She pulled the examination gown up on her shoulders in a slightly indignant manner. And when Doctor Canales asked again about the teacup—and the morning just a few days earlier as I was getting ready for work and had watched as Amá, coffeepot in one hand, flipped the teacup over and over; first with the saucer on top, and then with the bottom of the cup facing upward; she then placed the inverted saucer on top of the cup when she began to pour—Amá flicked her carefully lacquered red nails up into the air as if it was nothing.

He worries, she worries, Amá said, again with a flick of her nails in doña Cristina's and my direction, all these years I've been the one who has taken care of them, made sure they have had what they needed, and they worry. I tell you Doctor, you seem like the reasonable woman. Who wouldn't have the hard time putting the life together again after burning it down, ¿no?

Doctor Canales nodded, but before she had an opportunity to ask another question, Amá told her the number of eggs in a dozen, the orisha you need to protect against el ojo malo, the square root of nine—which she says she remembers from helping me with my homework—the number of days in the past February and the next February, a recipe—with precise measurements—for fabada.

When asked, Amá was able to supply an elaborate list of our family tree, including primos that I only knew from letters and stories: una prima, whom I have only known through the legend of her black black hair and the red red heart she kept for a man she saw just once coming out of a barbershop, for whom she is eternally peeling an oleander flower leafing its petals in the breeze she hoped he might have left behind; rum-soaked cigar smoke might fill a room and craze all sense; the Robles sisters—her oldest sister, María Sofía—will put curses on anyone soulless enough to steal money from the felt hat at the feet of the blind man standing at the corner of calle Monte.

Amá made my tía María-María appear as loud and colorful—with bracelets and necklaces—and as brashly made up as she and doña Cristina had always made her appear; María-María because there were two in as many years in front of her named María something or another.

It was Pirata that told my abuela that Amá was coming, my mother told Doctor Canales in Spanish.

The night she, my mother, Óscar's abuela, returned her husband, my father, Óscar's abuelo, to the sea, they say they said, they saw Pirata cross the moon as she headed back up the beach, and climbed the rocks, and the entire time he was singing a bolero that was popular at the time. Mireya, she said he sang, mi cielo, mi iluminador, mi casa, mi escuela, mi corazón, mi playa, mi guayaba, mi sentido común, yuca mío—I forget all the names I had for you, Shiny Distant Shore; Too long ago, a fever-dream broken into floes of hunger and want and then more want, it is so far away now;

Although at times like this, when it is quiet and dark and warm and there is just enough wet to hang melancholy in the air that I am brave enough to look; Y mira—scratchy phonographs that sent the song flying through the air from parlor windows, from open shopwindows; if you listened to the novelas in the evenings, you could hear it between scenes, garbage collectors and fruit vendors sang it in the streets; it was whistled in the fields; orchestras played it at cotillions; and it was rumored that a very famous courtesan, popular with both American businessmen and Cuban government officials, paid Lacouno a great deal of money to arrange it as a dirge—she even paid him a commission and made him sign a statement promising that if she predeceased him he would conduct the orchestra at her funeral—only to die the great-grandmother of eleven and the widow of a prominent Miami realtor; a millionairess, who with her husband silent in the grave for nearly forty years, was able to reinvent herself as the daughter of a sugar planter; the only part of which was true was that she did indeed come from Camagüey; it seems that somewhere along the way that along with her country accent, her inability to read in either Spanish or English, and two sons—one in La Habana, another who was raised by his father in Barcelona—she also chose to forget that she had a black mamá once her own American children came out pale with eyes color de tiempo.

Mireya, Mireya, they said they say, Pirata sang at the foot of her bed every morning that she carried me, and every night before she went to sleep. And why shouldn't she trust him? Since the day that he stole Madre's afterbirth, the bird had been her constant companion. When she was little and had had worms, she said, Pirata went into el baño with her or out into the field where she had to squat and ate them; he cured her by leaving his droppings in her hair and in her dinner, on her shoulders. When all the other children—with their bloated stomachs and their screeching after seeing worms come out of their bottoms—Madre said she was fine, with a good appetite and a happy disposition, ready for work or school, while the others complained and lived in fear of nightmares. They called her bruja, and where some were told to stay clear of her, others became dependent on her.

Known for her accuracy, Amá has always said that mi abuela seemed to navigate the future rather than divine it. When Amá was old enough she would set up a folding table in the marketplace and turn the corie. They would gather around her greedy as nursing infants asking, asking, always asking. Would a daughter who had left to work in a Miami hotel send money back? Would the baby Dulce Núñez was carrying so low be the boy Carlos had been praying for? Could they expect rain so late in the season, it's been so dry?

Amá says they said that Abuelita would wait for Pirata to fly down from the flamboyant where he would perch, whisper in her ear. She always knew.

Amá told Doctor Canales she could always remember being proud of her mother and proud, maybe too proud, of the good dresses she was allowed to wear to market that were handed down from the house where Abuela was a maid, and then to each of her older sisters—María-Teresa, María-Gabriela y María-María—before coming to her. Made of lush fabrics, their full skirts would shift and recoil around her legs, Amá said, they were a joy to spin in. People would see her in one of these dresses and tell mi abuela, Qué bonita the littlest one, what balance, what grace, what a long neck, like a black swan. While mi abuela saw to the future Amá would find a patch of grass nearby. Colors sped around her; the grass was cool between her bare toes; dizzying herself, her tongue tasted snow; at the bottom of the ocean, in the heart of a cove with a school of remora, she would spill up in the foam and glisten in the sand. Arms at her sides, head thrown skyward, round and round again in the opposite direction until her hair grew in raveny waves down her back and her dress became the same ivory tulle as the one mi abuela had made for the daughter of the women in the house where she worked; until her lashes were elegant and her skin was like milk and her lips held her heart out toward one of many suitors on a night in a garden bathed in music and light from paper lanterns blowing in the breeze on a veranda of a house where mi abuela was la doña de la casa and had so many maids that there was one just to hold a plate of chocolates and another who did the washing and another who tuned the novelas in on the radio in the afternoon while mi abuela rested on a chaise longue brought all the way from Paris with nothing else to do but keep her hands soft.

Amá could not remember if she was six or seven when mi abuela's hand reached in and pulled her out. Mi abuela told her it was time, she was old enough to see what wanting got you. She dragged Amá back onto the dirt and over to the card table. The corie, the table and the earth still swirling in front of her, she closed her eyes. Amá could hear a baby crying in the weaving, distant darkness. That's yours, mi abuela said. Amá was just barely able to make out the thin hard jaw of the woman handing it to her; her bony hands were inky against the infant's yellow body. The gleam in the woman's fierce teeth opened a light onto the surface of the table where Abuelita had thrown the corie that was clear as warm oil; the baby's arms, an eye the color of asparagus water, and Amá ran to catch it by forming a basket with the skirt of one of the best dresses that she had, with anything that was made available to her. She could not see it, could not feel her legs moving, but she could see herself running underneath the sound of the infant's cries. Past the clink of ankle shackles, past women sweating in field after field of azúcar, past women tending white children, until she could run no longer and fell panting on her knees still holding her skirt, poised and now surrounded by acre upon acre of wild pineapples.

Mireya, Mireya, Pirata sang as he sat on Madre's shoulder, she said.

She said it was my abuela's voice that caught her ear as she prayed on the day of the fire. Clear and alive in the eye of a storm coming over the Straits of Florida calling her back, it sung her U.S. life, and made fun of her English, made fun of the secondhand mink that she would have only needed for show had she stayed put—never for the weather—and only if she had been a white woman in La Habana. She said Abuela asked her what did the daughter of a maid, a girl born on a farm, know about running a beauty shop? Where had she been going for the past forty years: to sweep up other women's hair, and tend to their smelly feet? She said, clear as if she were standing there Abuelita said, The wild pineapples, Mireya, the wild pineapples are coming up in the garden, niña, go fold, mija, outta of the mirror; don't think you're better than anybody else, remember, negrita. Negrita. Negrita, there's laundry still on the line; there's ironing to be done; cover your hair, negrita, nobody wants to see that wool; what is in La Habana, mija, who will tend to the bananas, there's wild pineapples coming up in the groves.

She had set the rice on to boil as usual. And as usual she sat down to pray—Dios mío—including all of the saints and the souls of Abuelo y Abuelita—and though she usually keeps her eyes closed, it was a flash of light that caused them to open. There was something in the glass in front of the photo—one doña Cristina had taken on a wisteria-covered patio wall in El Nuevo Vedado—something on the image of doña Liliana. At closer inspection she discovered it was Pirata's dead eye, the eye of a ciclón, the kind she said she would watch forever since she saw one coming over the Straits of Florida the day she took a bus from Santiago for

La Habana. Dark, cool and liquid. Ay bendito, she forgot she had been talking to God. And it wasn't until she heard that damned Figueroa woman that she knew the house was burning.

Amá began reciting multiplication tables, first in English then translating when Doctor Canales replied by saying that she wanted to run some tests.

Amá looked out of the window with the same incredulity of a woman who was watching herself fall: a keen awareness neatly coupled with disbelief in the unstoppable.

All this over a teacup? she said weakly.

That and the fire, the doctor replied without looking up from her pad; these incidences may be completely unrelated to each other and they may be an indication that something else is going on, señora. She smiled graciously at Amá who had turned away from the window, and asked, Could you come in a week to get started?

Amá looked at me and then doña Cristina before saying if that was what we wanted then she guessed that it would be OK to waste the money.

A marvelous woman in all ways, Julio had told me sometime after he had allowed me to pay the check and we were waiting for his car to come, to be brought around by the valet. Julio had scarcely gotten the word brown out of his mouth when the young man answered, Alfa Romeo, and without taking Julio's ticket went off for the car.

I just think, Julio continued, what my life would have been like had I made that choice, gone with that woman, been her man or whatever it is that people say nowadays; would I be looking at her now thinking, What is this heavy, slack, beaten down once beautiful woman doing in my house, and how do I know her?

When the valet came back with the car, Julio just said, Cállate and get in. He peeled off to the end of the street, turned the corner on edge with a shrieking sound and soared until we had circumnativaged the entire block and were back in front of the restaurant.

We got out of the car. Alfa Romeo, Julio said longingly, lovingly as he handed back the keys and this time his ticket to the valet as he told the boy, No, no, he had forgotten, it was an eight-year-old brown Saab that we were looking for. Julio ignored the look of horror on the valet's face, and when we were in his car, headed towards my house, Julio thanked me for having dinner with him, for indulging him; he confessed he wouldn't have taken the car ordinarily, but he just couldn't pass up the opportunity to steal candy with someone who he knew, knew just what it was to steal candy the way he stole it.

I had left the room so that Amá could change. When she emerged with doña Cristina and Doctor Canales in the waiting area, Amá's arm was hooked into Doctor Canales'.

You know Señora Doctor, Amá told her, that color—Féria Burnt Cinnamon number twenty-eight, ¿no?—is good for you; it brings out your eyes nicely, and goes with your skin almost just right for not having it done professional; what you need is a good conditioner; not the one you're using; what, from the farmacia? You need one that gives you manageability and shine; one that washes clean, not with those dull residues that you got there. If you give me a call before my next appointment, I remember to bring you some. ¿Claro? Claro, Amá answered for the doctor.

And Doctor Canales smiled; she was smoothing the back of her hair with the palm of her hand as we were leaving.

Y ENTONCES, of course, you would all know this because you have all read pages two thirty-three through two seventy-eight for today's lecture. It was the British who brought this color to what the Italian lothario called the Jewel of the Caribbean. Isla Belle, Belle Caribe. Preciosa. The most beautiful place that he had ever seen in his entire life, I believe he wrote, the Genoese explorer.

La Flaca—the Skinny, a woman's slipper of an island—the Spanish sailors called it. As you remember from a couple of weeks ago: at an approximate latitude of twenty-one degrees north of the equator, and a longitude of eighty degrees west of Greenwich; four thousand nineteen feet above sea level at its highest point, it shimmers fifty miles off the coast of Miami. Y it was just there, simply a found-bauble in the Spanish crown for over two hundred years; no silver mines to exploit; no golden veins running though it like Mexico, o Péru if you prefer. However, miren. Remember señores, this is just una historia up until this point. You should not have been surprised if as you read last night there was a wolf or a wicked stepmother or a garden made completely of azúcar to be found.

Miren my hands. As you read earlier in the semester—pages five through eleven in the preface—it was in 1501 in the common era that our Catholic monarchs—Catholics, you know, just like you and me—approved the establishment of this color in Hispaniola, but it was not until the early seventeen hundreds that anyone knew what to do with it en La Flaca.

Azúcar, mis hijos, cane field after cane field. As we see on page two forty-seven, the color to mine La Flaca's gold was negro. The Caracas agent who wrote the information in the center of the page worked for the Royal African Company to inform them that there was to be no one of a yellow cast en La Flaca. No, they wanted the deepest black—Congo and Angola Black—without cuts in their faces nor filed teeth. The men to be well grown, neither too tall nor too short; the women were to be of a good stature, not too short nor too small, and without any long breasts hanging down as it says on page two thirty-seven.

Some died along the way; the Asiento Trade was not necessarily the easiest way to get to the Americas. Some traveled from the Cape Coast as far as Caracas before coming back around, before arriving at ports in La Habana y Santiago with their sweat and their yams and their magic of forever and their blackness. Over seven thousand by 1737. Blackness as commodity. Blackness coveted in the field and in the house, blackness that could be inherited, passed down for centuries. But I get ahead of myself.

Por ejemplo, mi abuela—born in the last century—was reputed to have been blacker than most midnights. Her dowry collected from the cane fields, from kitchens, to nurseries and back to the cane field.

Talk goes, mi abuelita—a tiny woman but very strong—could lift a bowl an inch off a table without touching it; could instantly cure a cold by steeping a root into a tea; could convince a turtle to abandon its shell; and people outside of Santiago say that at an age well past when anyone thought that she would find a man, she pulled one from the ink of the night's surf by his woolly hair. As black as she was, he was light. Still negro by all accounts of his features and hair, pero they say, years in the sea had washed the color out of him, and they say, they said he had no eyes and rarely spoke. Some say that he was found naked. Others claim he was in tatters, and that my abuela had gone to the shore with a linen shirt and underclothes she made herself. There are those who maintain that they were awakened that night by such a sharp light from the moon that it seemed to roar like the roar from a hive, and upon going out to the convenience or stepping outside to catch a breeze, they saw the two of them—mis abuelos—walking arm in arm. He was wearing a blue guayabera and cream-colored linen trousers, though was bare-chested and barefoot; others said they had thought an albino eel had wrapped itself around his waist, his member dangled so close to his knees. There were those who could have sworn that he was a first cousin whose family had been hiding out in La Sierra Maestra to avoid working on the fincas for nearly a century living with los indios; and there were those who from the time Abuelita was a little girl were frightened of the predictions she made regarding crop yields, the folds of livestock and litters of puppies, called her bruja and swore she conjured the eyeless man with seawater, mercury and blue thread.

Miren señores, all they agreed on was that it was mi abuela leading a man up from the sea. They all recognized the edges of her untamable hair that was legendary for the nearly six inches it gave her in height before cascading to her waist. And no one doubted that the eyeless man had an uncanny knack for carving leather. No one remembers him asking for the tools he used, no one remembers how he got started. Pero there were hundreds—some say thousands—of belts, and saddles, seat covers and tables transformed into spilling-overs of pineapples and coconuts, plantains and bananas; horses, cattle, sheep and goats; roosters and parrots; snakes, scorpions and tarántulas; waterfalls and mountains. There is—or was—a picture of him, standing next to a round tabletop that had been turned on its side and was as high as he was tall, on which palmas reales rose in full flower with fronds that cascaded over the tabletop's rounded edges. All without eyes, without knowing, so many were to have said to have said.

In the three years they were together, he gave her four daughters. And then one day, he wandered back into the sea; and then one day, he left with a traveling circus and was taken to the United States where he was put on display alongside Johnny the Half Boy for the shock and amazement of others; and then one day, he eloped with a contorsionista mejicana; and then one day, he was taken to Los Arados by the Cobas Hernández clan and sacrificed as part of a ritual healing ceremony. And then one day, eighteen days to the midnight after the last of their daughters—mi madre—was born, mi abuelita dragged him by the collar of a shirt she had ironed just that morning back to the sea.

No sé.

Of course there is no way to verify most of this. My Amá never saw her madre do any of these things; she and her sisters were far too young to remember their mother having anything to do with any man. But they all knew all of the stories.

Just lathering this face with these hands to shave every morning I am telling myself this story, mis amigos. And then I have someplace to start. It may not seem important now, but one day you may find that the life that you lay out in front of you isn't the life laid out in front of you.

Y no, señores, I have not attempted to misrepresent history as we know it, as Señor Ostrovski and you, Menéndez—from whom I am missing the last two homework assignments—will no doubt assert when we have our question-and-answer period. Though it is true that for all the years I have been here I have made an attempt to direct your eyes—and the eyes of your older brothers, your tíos y your primos—toward some of the more interesting highlights than the texts the archdiocese approves of represent.

No matter.

Though I suppose that it would be wildly irresponsible to do otherwise.

. . . CLOSE THE DOOR y abran las ventanas.

Sí, abran las ventanas.

Sí, sí, sí, of course, all of them.

This building was never meant for air-conditioning, we didn't even have it when I was a student here and none of you will fall over like tulips. ¿Es verdad, no? No deposed royalty here. No princes or barons. No earls. Not one of you is in line for a duchy or has been secretly betrothed to a prima who is the sovereign of a small country, ¿sí?

Abran las ventanas.

Sí, sí, sí, both, from the bottom and the top. Menéndez, grab the window pull; those of you closest, raise the shades all the way, all the way up. Vamos. No grumbling. Vamos. Vamos. Stop being such sucky babies. It's only just past eleven; at most, it's in the mid-eighties now; the real heat of the day won't be around until at least one.

Abran las ventanas.

Hombres, we come from tough stock, all of us. We've been peasants, we've been farmers. We come from long lines of men who have stood on the ends of a plow, and have driven cattle, oxen, burros through our own sweat into the shit of the earth, into the shit of others and have come out on the other end. The fact we're even here is an act of colonial alchemy: hombres de mierda; or at least, men from mierda.

Push the tables back. All the chairs against the wall.

That's right, all the tables and chairs against the walls. And choose a seat on the floor; someplace you don't normally park yourselves. Away from the cabrón you eat lunch with, the vato you exchange critical glances with when I ask you to do something other than that what you're used to. Sit on the floor; sit on a desk; stand on a chair.

The heat, the heat, the heat.

Sí, señores, yo sé, yo sé, I know it's hot. All these days—over three weeks now, ¿no?—it's been hot. These days, a heat index at a hundred and one or two degrees at least. Ay qué weather.

And late in the day, nearly every afternoon while you have been in Chemistry or Phys Ed, wherever it is that nobody demands that you abran las ventanas—of course they never would—the sky has knotted itself angry like a fist black and bloodied overhead until cracking open in spiteful hisses of lightning without thunder for only an hour of what they say is more rain than the city has ever seen.

Vayan a las ventanas later today between one and two when whatever classroom you are in suddenly gets dark.

If you have not been listening, on the English-speaking networks and both Spanish stations, the weathercasters have accurately predicted and traced a swirl of warm air from the center of Lake Michigan that moves across the Gold Coast to its hover over the fifty or so blocks above the neighborhood here where we all settled.

Nobody knows why the rain doesn't move inland or to another area of the city.

Some say it's the lake effect; los otros dicen el diablo.

Yo sé.

I know it's hot.

I know it's a mean heat.

I know you're warm.

If necessary, pretend.

Pretend, my Amá says on a day like today, that you are an ice cube, or maybe just a sliver of ice in a limonada, melting away. Pretend you are a breeze, a gust of cool air, the chill running up the back of a strapless dress.

Pretend.

Oh, why not Ostrovski? ¿Palacios? ¿Por qué no, señores? If I've taught you nothing in the time that we've spent together, let's hope that I've taught you that history is space—much more so than time—like rooms that can be stepped in and out of.

You've done it when you've walked out of school these past afternoons and the gutters and the eaves are overflowing with dirty water; the streets are wet and littered with tree boughs and leaves, and the garbage you took out the night before is spilled across a lawn a block from your homes.

Some of you have gone home to flooded basements and downed awnings. Found the race cars and the coloring books and baseball mitts you had long forgotten, but thought would be somewhere safe if you wanted to pick them up again, floating out of your back doors and down the alleys. Y you, Della Peña, who lives around the corner from my mother's house? Wasn't that your first bike: the one rusting on the curb near Ashland with the tiger print banana seat? I seem to remember your father running behind you yelling, ¡Vaya, chico, vaya! That's it! That's my boy! ¡Ése es mi chico, ése es mi hijo!

Laugh if you want to.

It's so easy.

But all you're doing—all of you—is telling yourselves the story in which you tell yourselves that you do not care, it doesn't matter. Or as Palacios and Rodríguez are likely to say, one of which they could care less, I'm sure to the disgust and horror of that poor new little señorita Jonas, whom you call Miss Twinkie behind her back, the hostess with the mostess, and the horror of every other English teacher that didn't hesitate and slash his or her own throat before issuing you a passing grade.

And just as easily as any pretty blonde with a slim waist and an ample bosom can be reduced to a snack cake—never has to be a woman like any of your mothers—you absent yourselves as you leave here each day. Stepping over huge puddles of rainwater that swelter and steam in this heat, you tell yourselves the world around you isn't changing before your very eyes; that this—this unseasonably warm weather—couldn't have anything to do with what chemical companies do, or what the manufacturers that you may go work for do. No it's not changing, you say, slipping through all the concepts of reality that you've ever been given without even knowing it.

Why does it rain so; why is it so hot? After all it's only April. It must be, you say. And then you fill in the blank, make something up that allows you to spend unfettered hours in an arcade, or in front of the television, or doing whatever it is you do besides reading the pages I assign.

Señores, you say you don't pretend. If so, then why do you say that it doesn't matter when things don't go your way, or you can't explain them to yourself or each other? Laugh if you want, but how does Della Peña hold on to an entire childhood, let alone that moment with his father so many summers ago that it seems like it happened to someone else now that his bike has been picked up, carted off by those guys who salvage scrap metal?

If you are not so adept at pretending, why hang those pictures—in your lockers, and your closets, and your bedrooms—that you cut out of those magazines that you've secreted away from your parents under mattresses, in the garage, down in the basement? Y what about those magazines? I suppose you're right, one day one of those ladies—scantly dressed as she is—will alight from her perch, wings spread, breasts heaving. And after she has made you feel like the man that you feel that you are, she will produce a plate of frituras just like your mamá makes, iron a crease down the sleeves of your shirt that resembles a razor's edge, tell you—coo in your ear—that you complete her before she returns to her place between an ad for a product guaranteed to give you control all night and one that will lift your belly, support your back and give you the physique of an Adonis. Entonces, if that's possible, the rain could be your own ardor come back on you, or a mistake returning and returning.

So hace fácilmente. One day will replicate into the next until—stuck in the ordinary of washing your car, building a sundial out of snow for a future daughter, reaching into your wallet for your credit card, or some touchstone that feels so much like an act of faith—you'll find that unseasonably warm temperatures or the predictability of torrents of rain are unsatisfactorily explained by God, science or the devil, and you'll begin to tell yourself a story of a land neither long ago nor far away that you'll cling to as if it suddenly were your soul hovering outside your body.

In atonement you say the oppressive heat was brought on by the neighbor you've cuckolded, whose hedge trimmers you've jammed, whose dog you once cursed and kicked one night when you had one or two too many and the moon danced the sky on the back of a marlin. It'll be a serpent's kiss; an eagle's curse; the cure of a murdered woman who entered the heart of a thrice-decorated general who up until that moment had always been thought venerable and chaste; or the bitterness of that innocent left pining for a hand that was never imagined, never thought of, never projected onto some improbable, impossible, poor unsuspecting vato.

Or rain that comes as a great wringing of the shirts of the millions and millions of the underpaid and underappreciated. Fruit pickers and waitresses, sí. Pero, what about the girls who never get asked to the movies? Any of you have a parent, a relative, a tío who works in a factory? What story of what vacation in what distant future in what amount of time floats and bobs in a mist above no surface for him?

¿No?

Ostrovski? Díaz? Paredes? Palacios?

No, I didn't think so.

It's nothing, we say, when the sky has cracked open each day for weeks—every day—and spills over us for an hour or so; nothing, again, when the heat indexes rise so far above normal that the meteorologists on television and those who write for the newspapers are stuck with their mouths poised for flies, their fingers hang over the keyboards in their office waiting for some explanation; es nada, pinche nada, when you find the baseball field and the soccer green sodden and muddy; neither the hand of God nor the devil's spit, and nothing, again, when there's talk of shifts of barometric pressure, cold fronts, tropical tempests, a hole in the ozone layer and everything else we can't see. Because, when we say it's nothing, nothing is the kind of story that allows us to live.

Sí. Se hace just that fácilmente.

Of course they all need context, the stories, all need to fit in with the other stories that are told around it. Por ejemplo, we all pretended that winter that we lost Joaquín-Ernesto—the Santiago Boy, pero it was 1969 then—before any of you were born, pero many of your parents were there—and many of us were just coming here to where it snows for the first time. Díaz, I remember the way your father stammered all the way up until he was in the ninth grade, and Paredes I remember the first slow dance your parents had here on our very own gym floor. For many of us then the language was new, and hope—that thing with feathers—made us want for nearly anything to be possible.

We began using only his birth name at his memorial service and after that no one could remember what we had called him before. Joaquín-Ernesto they said. Joaquín-Ernesto had been a good boy; had always kept a watchful eye for his sister; had never let her cross the street by herself. Always kind to his mother; a perfect gentleman. Joaquín-Ernesto was always at the driveway, so many remembered him carrying his papi's lunch box; every evening—it didn't matter the weather, he was always there. Paredes, ask your father, he will remember him.

During the service, Troop 227—the same 227 that so many of you quit before you could know what it was like to wake up under a sky crammed full of stars—stood honor guard. A woman who had only seen his picture in the Spanish newspaper had come from the edge of the city, had called a cousin and told her all about the boy who was exactly her own son's age. Hundreds of veladoras had been lit; thousands of rosarios passed between thumb and forefinger in the name of Joaquín-Ernesto.

People who didn't know him, wouldn't have been able to tell him apart from any of the others the same age or height in the 227, stopped what they were doing in the middle of their day in a collective moment of silence; change from the empty tomatillo cans above sinks was given for flowers. Ay, y señores, their fragrance—white roses, orchids, lilies shipped from warmer places—took the air above the sea of brown people, crested the lace edges of the occasional black mantilla and swelled up thick and hot and steamed the windows of the church and glazed the doors shut against the cold.

Over there, across the parking lot, in the basement of our church, a woman whose name I can no longer remember told Amá tostones had been his favorite. Well, her tostones, she conceded as she peeled the foil from the platter and let her face roll with tears. As I recall she had very orange hair with at least an inch of black root. She said she had never seen a boy who could take food as spicy as that Joaquín-Ernesto; everything salsa, just like a little man.

His family sat at the front of the hall. People took turns filling their plates and coming up to talk and touch his mother and his little sister. They nodded at his father, who sat barely moving, looking far far away in his too-tight suit. His hands—hairy and enormous—rested on his knees.

Y aquí señores, it is here that I want you to pay close attention. Because it was one of the most amazing acts of storytelling, or remaking of history, that I had ever witnessed to that point. Palacios, ask your father, he was there; as I recall he was the one who used a permanent marker to draw a beard on his face—the rest of us had used soot from the chimney, but no, he wanted to be real—he was with us running around the tables in our little uniforms. Y, as I recall, he too had been captured with us by the revoluciones they were rounding up and holding under one of the tables with a jump rope as we awaited our trials and executions in La Sierra Maestra, in La Habana.

Pero, we had escaped and guerrilla-crawled from table to table under the paper tablecloths, headed back to La Habana when away from the Santiagos' table, over paper plates of potluck, we heard people's whispered stories to each other of esperanza y recuerdos. A man who never looked up from his shoes told Mr. Sáenz a story about a woman who never cut her hair and never seemed to grow a day older. Women gathered up the paper plates and cups, saving the forks in their aprons to wash and use later. All the while—wiping up and pushing in chairs—one of the women told the others: Was the blood oranges what cured my Víctor when he get out of the army, she said; he was all scrawnied y tan pale; and I taked him back home when you could still go home and he eat the blood orange all day long; I make it in a juice for him and put it into his soup and he's so strong now, and married with a good job and he give grandbabies—dos—both boys, she said.

A patio in Holguín was remembered as being slick with evening dew and lit with strings of colored lights that revealed a dark corner where a man with a gray handlebar mustache quietly recalled—for the benefit of the group of men surrounding him—fingering the most beautiful mulata he'd ever seen in his life. The mention of Holguín made someone think of three sisters, all named María something or another—María-Teresa, María-Elisabeta, you know the type, he said—girls so naïve they thought they could get jobs in the city as hostesses or shop clerks even though they had had little school and knew nothing but farm life.

Of course, they all knew people who had died since they had come north; some had even been children. There was a woman who lived just off of North who lost a baby every year for the first five years of her marriage; and lost her husband to a hit-and-run in the sixth, and then her mind in what would have been the seventh. But old age, illness of any kind, any horror, a drunken blanquito driving recklessly, a knife fight, a mugger, a frying pan thrown across the room in the heat of an argument were all so much more comprehensible. This, though—so foreign, so distinctly northern—made them want to surround themselves with palm trees taller than you could imagine, and an almond that yielded bushels every morning on the front porch of a house that overlooked a valley where a horse fifty hands tall and pale as the sand ambled in front of the sea.

Y ay señores, at the heart of each of these stories was the sun. You'd have thought it was right there in the room with us. It burned so strong and real and directly overhead that for a while nobody thought about the cars that they would eventually have to dig out, or the furnaces that might not kick on in the middle of the night, or the terror of frozen pipes, or the empty box upstairs in the church that the Santiagos could neither fill nor bury nor get warm.

So then señores, you pretend something else.

That night Amá and I walked home from the bus stop through hard teeth of snow. The wind disregarded our new boots, hats, scarves and gloves. It cut and burned my scout uniform and the red union suit we bought on Chicago Avenue that morning. Our small apartment was dark and quiet. We could hear water drip in the bowl that Amá used to mix the flan we took to the service. The streetlight shone on the foldout couch Amá would fix into a bed for us every night. We sat for a long time huddled on top of the radiator. Outside the snow whorled itself into a giant down the center of the street, making the June just months before seem imagined.

If we had ever sat in the shade of a banyón in the park near the housing project where we had lived the July before in Miami, it would have had to have been in a book I was reading for school. Suddenly there had never been bacalao swimming in a barrel just down the street; no one took thread out of a store into the light to compare it to a swatch of fabric; no one turned the future over with the corie in front of the botánica. Daylight had not come through the tree at the precise second Amá's finger had fallen on an accordion fold of a map she had smoothed out in front of us, never lit the exact area as she said, There, there, there, she pointed, in Chicago we will have our own place, we won't have to share with relatives or anyone, you will go to a good school where they will make you speak good English all of the time so that you can grow up to be a diplomat. She had never said that she might learn to drive, might even buy a car. She had never said, Mira mijo, there they have snow in this wonderful place were we are heading; it glitters and cools the earth like magic, as she ran the flat of her hand against the map from end to end.

In the morning, I could feel my mother turn in her sleep. The wind outside had died, leaving icy granules of snow to angle in the air in a thin steady veil. I was hungry and my head ached so badly it sang out in regular intervals like a clapper in a bell. We were both still wearing our coats.

There. Sí. Se hace just that fácilmente.

Without knowing it, just knowing that story—and you have all heard a version of that story; some of you have fathers who were actually there with me; others of you have heard it told by other people; each time any of you pass the brass plate commemorating his attendance at this school in the lobby, it's a story that somehow has attached itself to you, become inextricably part of you—you've just a little of Cuba, my Cuba, the Cuba that the very few of us cubanos around here can tell you about that's always part of your history whether you're Cuban—Martínez, Chávez, Ostrovski, Babcock—or not.

Imagínenselo.

You're an icicle in a thaw, or the puddle in the snowdrift underneath it, and the runoff as it makes its way across the pavement and burrows under another bank of snow. Imagínenselo. Ostrovski, Babcock, Palacios, Suárez, perch on top of a desk, each at one corner of the room e imagínenselo.

Sí, sí, sí, Ostrovski, on top of the desk.

Ándele, we haven't all the time in the world, and it's not as if I'm asking you to crochet me a pair of booties or perform the second act of Swan Lake. I'm asking that you sit on top of a desk.

Vamos. E imagínenselo, the four of you, imagínenselo you have a wingspan strong enough to glide across La Sierra Maestra to Santiago and then to Matanzas where the water is so blue; muy claro, hombres, y there's no reflection, and from directly above, schools of fishes seem to pass through you; imagínenselo from high above while you—Chávez; every year there's been one of you: early to mature; full of life, ready to find fault, poke fun, take flight in the smallest things; Quiñones y Martínez—lie here.

Sí, here on the floor, shoulder to shoulder with your heads pointing west. Castañeda y Cartagena lie on your sides—one of you on either side of Chávez and Martínez—heads facing west, toes east just like Quiñones y company.

No laughing, this is not that funny.

Move in close señores. Close, close. Muñoz, Paredas, Peña, come join us; the three of you lay down like Chávez and his group; Johnson, you and Calderón vamos y assume the same position as Castañeda y Cartagena. Alvárez, Santos, Kelly, you know what to do; y Parker and Juárez, on your sides like the others.

Why? Well it is an inherited history of why, isn't it, even when you're told you have the whole story . . .

. . . MARTÍNEZ, IF IT is 1835, just months before you and Chávez were deeply concerned with the celebration that honored the ascension of Quiñones as the sovereign of your area of the world, of the world as you knew it up until this moment now. For weeks and weeks there has been nothing but singing and dancing in your village. As hunters, you've been part of a band of men who have been responsible for seeing that there was antelope, or some such animal was part of the celebration. Antelope, only the savoriest of savories for Quiñones—ascended from the fiercest—Quiñones—ascended from the most kind—Quiñones—ascendant from the most honorable, you cheered.

No laughing.

Just because señor Quiñones has been known to hustle some of you out of a few dollars in the pools you vatos have held that you think faculty has no idea about the last couple of football seasons doesn't mean that he can't be descended from honorable people.

Young girls, sí virgins—¿por qué no?—danced for him, laid flowers at his feet; they made him whatever he wanted to eat, and took his fantasies for their own. He was given his choice of a wife or many wives. No matter he's just a young man; crowned just a few days before his seventeenth birthday. Chávez, at one time you and Martínez placed all your faith—your futures—into Quiñones' divine ability to lead your village.

However faith on that order, mis chicos, it is the kind of thing that will make you believe that you can hold it in your hand. And it comes with you whether you want it to or not. Your hands are bound; your legs are manacled, so you carry it on your chests or in your mouths.

It's the secret that you keep under your armpits, between your toes as you pass over waves and swells in the sea that you tell yourselves is not the sea; not the sea now that makes you sick up all over yourselves during the first month or so out, but the sea that you watched from the Cape of Good Hope; that you've watched your whole lives from either side of the shore; no longer the shoreline where you watched the fishing boats come in or the traders bombard.

Yo sé, yo sé, it's hot, pero just as easily as you can see the ripple of heat waves, the heat can be gone, gone.

Pretend.

Pretend you're no longer lying in your own urine and excrement or that of the man next to you.

After all, how different is it from sitting all these years in these rows of desks next to the same group of men? The one next to you forgets his underarm deodorant, the one in front of you farts—no Chávez, this is not an opportunity for a command performance; ay, like little girls you all giggle—but when it happens you absent yourselves from it; you may complain, pero your first impulse is to flee to some place free of the odor of the man next to you; you tilt your nose, you think of something else, someone else, some place else, and in seconds you're gone.

It's something like what happens at the beginning of a lecture, or when you're sitting in church, or when I begin to ask about the reading that you were assigned the night before.

So I can't imagine that it would be too terribly difficult

for you to watch as Quiñones' spirit tells the story of the beloved familia you all are about to be born into, children of Las Casas.

Sí, los hijos de las Casas from the bluest of eyed to the kinkiest of haired; closer, close close, señores.

When we were boys—Julio, Román and I—Amá and las doñas threw cautions over their shoulders before we headed toward the beach or when we went to play in the street: Stay out of the sun as much as you can, don't get too dark, don't stay out too long.

Children of Las Casas, move close, mis compadres.

There is no heat, no hunger, no stench.

You've forgotten Quiñones has been dead twenty days since the boat has begun to move underneath you, has been rotting since; but how does that matter anyway, none of you have seen the light of day in twice as many days.

Later—when you confer with others who will lay claim to similar journeys, when you're old and you tell the children who gather around you in the starless dark where you cannot be heard by anyone at the hacienda—you'll remember a gasp coming from his mouth that you will describe as coming from Satan's ass as he turned to take Quiñones away. You'll be dead nearly a century and it will be your great-great-great-grandchildren who will be able to tell you—will be able to pronounce in your new language—that he died on an escuna, a goleta. Seven sails high, swift and sleek to the helm.

Closer, mis compadres, closer, as Quiñones, back from the dead, takes the form of the dead. Not too unlike the picture on page two twenty-nine: pinched nose, somewhat beady eyes, receding hairline; a horseshoe, I think they call it. Completely bald on the top with just a ring around half his head, like the gym teacher, Father López; nice, ¿no? The venerable, the lauded, el célebre Fray Bartolomé de las Casas delivers you.

Closer, mis compadres, closer. There's no heat here, with just his appearance, you are cooled with the waters of Redemption, as was Lazarus. Las Casas, a finely featured man with little or no traces of Moorish Invasion in his skin tone, nor was there any of the darkness of color that would come that would be part of how much of this country imagines the landscape of Latin America. Celibate by all appearances, or as celibate as any man can appear celibate in the face of a pregnancy or many pregnancies at once for that matter. For, señores, as easily as any man can bring into question his hand—or whatever—in any pregnancy, it is equally as difficult for a woman to hide or deny some sort of direct involvement with some man. In fact, I know of only one historical case of virgin birth that has any sort of widespread acceptance and even that has always been open to conjecture. No, señores, when we ask where are you from we're asking what kind of Spanish did your mamá teach you, what kind of frijoles went into the arroz, did she use pork fat, manteca, chicken skin, goose grease, did she hang the sheets out in the midday sun, was a razor-sharp crease ironed down the sleeve of your shirt, were there cakes with each cumpleaños with blue icing and racing cars, and that your eyes were brown—your eyes were green, hazel, black—and hers were not, in fact each time that she has looked at you as you've grown has presented her with a moment in her history that grows progressively further and further away from her, what is your country, what was her country, where was the earth where you first planted.

Mi moreno, mi grano de café, mi negrito, mi tiny tiny negrito, doña Liliana would call out when Román had been out in the sun for the afternoon. Julio and I would be playfully chastised for allowing ourselves to go from brown to black to navy blue, it was never the same with Román. And even though he was still lighter than Julio or I, it was as if she had a surprise visitation from the good father; a legacy like a way of standing or tilting a head, a tick, a simple gesture—like rubbing the side of his nose when he thinks, Román does as if he had always seen it, learned it while on a fishing trip or just sitting there watching it done over and over again—something from the past, brown rising from black, African black las Casas ushered in boatload by boatload.

The tongue of fire above his head illuminates the ship's hull; the robes of his friar's habit unfold over all of you as he opens his hands and extends his arms out over all of you.

Mira, I don't know about you, señores, pero I'm struck by how his hands are depicted—dexterous, deft, skillful—in your textbook. Not a day of hard labor, or fields to plow when he tells you all just as eloquently as if he were reading it from the page adjacent his picture:

Now Christ wanted his gospel to be preached with enticements, gentleness, and pagans to be led to the truth not by armed forces but by holy examples, Christian conduct, and the word of God, so that no opportunity would be accessible for blaspheming the sacred name or hating the true religion because of the conduct of its ministers. Behold, this is nothing other than making the coming and passion of Christ—he refers to the founding of Iberia, if you can imagine such a thing—useless, as long as the truth of the gospel is hated before it is either understood or heard, or as long as innumerable human beings are slaughtered in a war waged on the pretext of dispersing religion . . .

Ay what's all the giggling? OK, I paraphrased.

Pero, had you all done the reading this would not come as a surprise to you. Oh, I see. Señor Chávez—in rare form—has decided to add a bit of realism to the moment. Señor, what would we have done all of these years without your prodigious and noxious flatulence to turn us green since kindergarten, ¿no?

Pero, the venerated santo Fray Bartolomé de las Casas cannot be immured even by señor Chávez's most powerful of issues. Las Casas' decree is the word of God and God once again is moved by its endeared, entrusted, endowed monarch, who is quick to be guided by Las Casas' vision of a people—for those of you who claim the island of Puerto Rico as your home, the islands in the Caribbean off the coast of Colombia, the Dominican Republic—dark-eyed like Meléndez and Alvárez, with the same strength and tenacity of will as a Suárez or Cartagena show at the penalty kick: strong backs, strong arms; the ability to work long hours in the sun; skin used to sun, made for sun, made from the sun. It wasn't that he was an evil man, Las Casas, a wicked man, no, he was a man of God who merely saw a similarity in climate that made you better suited for work in the fields, for work, for toil or slavery than the bodies of the indigenous.

Close, close, señores, even closer.

No señores, not even Chávez could distract this stalwart champion of las Américas. Following Isabel's Genoese lothario on a mission of compassion blessed by and ordained by the church, he earns his encomienda by less salacious means. He is el salvador de los indios, their protector, el conquistador of the fair, the just, the good. It's God who tells him los indios need prayer. God's voice—mean and fresh—he hears on Pentecost Sunday in 1511 while listening to a sermon delivered by the equally venerable yet not as celebrated Father Antonio de Montesinos on the voice crying in the wilderness.

Closer señores, por entonces, Las Casas, through the dead Quiñones, past the haze of Chávez's farts, will tell you that it was from that moment that he knew the truth behind the pronouncement: In the beginning was the Word, and the Word was with God, and the Word was God.

Las Casas will gather you all up in his gigantic arms as if you were his children and kiss you each on the forehead as he promises: He was with God in the beginning. Through him all things were made; without him nothing was made that has been made. In him was life, and that life was the light of men. The light shines in the darkness, but the darkness has not understood it.

And you'll feel safe as if nothing can harm you, as if nothing will ever be as dark as this moment in the ship's hull will never happen again.

Closer señores, porque Las Casas and his golden heart is about to tell you of a life devoted from that moment on—from the moment that he heard de Montesinos' words—when he became at one with los indios.

So close he is able to push Quiñones' dead body—dressed just like the example of a Taíno warrior on the following page—out of his chest and cradle him like a newborn in his arms. Ay señores, Las Casas has big arms. Arms strong and large and wide enough to embrace all los indios de las Américas, he tells you. When he tells you of all los niños indios in 1513 that he scooped into his arms even though he was fighting for Ferdinand, Isabel, for Ponce de León and for the friends of the handsome Genoese; when he tells you of las indias with their children in tow, you hear the cries of Las Casas, El Último; Las Casas, El Honorable; Las Casas de Dios. Even from under Las Casas' priestly sandal, the voices of Caribes y Taínos sing out in the clearest of Spanish, in Spanish only spoken in the court of Ferdinand y La Reina todo poderosa.

Closer señores. There's no heat, there are no waves.

Las Casas—had you been born indio—saves you for he knew that God was in the world, and though the world was made through Him, the world did not recognize Him; He came to that which was his own, but His own did not receive Him; yet to all who received Him, to those who believed in His name, He gave the right to become children of God—children born not of natural descent, nor of human decision or a husband's will, but born of God.

Las Casas would give up his lands, give up his indio serfs, women and song, mijos, and walk with God against the tyrannies of the encomienda and the repartimiento as institutions that exemplified the mistreatment of los indios for the rest of his life.

They asked him, Then who are you? Are you Elijah?

He said, I am not.

Are you the prophet?

He answered, No.

Finally they said, Who are you? Give us an answer to take back to those who sent us. What do you say about yourself?

He replied in the words of Isaiah the prophet, I am the voice of one calling in the desert: Make straight the way for the Lord.

And he did, our Las Casas.

Closer señores. Head to foot of the man below you; shoulder to shoulder with the man next to you, mis hijos. It's a tight compression in the chest of the father from whom you are about to be born. Because it is with the same stroke of the pen, through the same voice of God speaking through Las Casas—your new father—that exalts the Taíno warrior on page two twenty-nine who gives you new birth on the shores of Matanzas where they say the water is so blue, on the docks of Santiago where they say las playas are so white and the sun is richer than anywhere else on the island.

Imagínenselo, mijos.

Imaginen you did the reading you were assigned last night.

Imaginen while you read you tore the hundred or so pages from the book that separate you in the hull of this escuna, this proud goleta, and you would be witness to the milagro, this act motivated by the hand of God, in an act of kindness that will for centuries ahead of you turn your blood, black blood, into sugar.

QUIET AS IT'S kept, señores, as much as we want to complain, this is a familiar heat. Ay, mis casas, mi azúcar, it is a heat in the blood. We brung it with us, Father Rodríguez said this morning. I have no idea exactly what he was talking about, but knew what he meant as I watched him pulling at his collar the way he does—you've all seen him at morning mass—when he has uncomfortable things to tell you.

Mijos, since before I was your age, I've watched him pulling at that collar at weddings, funerals and Boy Scout jamborees; in faculty meetings, he will pull at his collar and attempt to fill a nearly full glass of water before he responds to the simplest of questions. Father Rodríguez, someone will ask, do you think we should salt and plow the driveway to the rectory, or will plowing be sufficient? And he'll tug.

Julio, of course, remembers a time that Father Rodríguez taught a class here called Christian Growth—he and Román were allowed to take it; Amá at the time said she had never heard of something so inappropriate in her life; and although I had a changing body there was no need for me to know anything about it until it was time for me to know something about it, and I recall doña Liliana asked when Amá thought that that might be; and although Amá conceded that there was a lot to learn, she also added that she really hoped that I would never learn it, but if need be it would be sometime after I had moved from her house—but really the sum total of learning that went on in that class was a lot of meatus jokes made throughout the year, which only encouraged more collar pulling out of Father Rodríguez until the class was never offered again.

For those of you who have served mass with him in the mornings, you know every now and then he tugs at that collar at the very moment he sets the chalice down. You know after he has finished wiping the front of it, and he's closed his eyes to pray; and when he opens them, he'll go at that collar.

Palacios, you would know, you started serving mass here when you were what, fourth or fifth grade, ¿no? I was in fourth or fifth grade too when I started serving mass with him. Altar boy is what they called it in those days. They didn't start calling you servers until I was away at college and members of our sister school there across the way needed to get into the act. A strange thing that, pero, no matter.

Ostrovski—were he here and not in some dark and undusted ossuary of the library where his sinuses will not bother him, away from the ragweed or hay fever or whatever that is that makes him wheeze and turn so pink; someplace where they keep all the books on birds, I'm guessing—he would tell you, as I can tell you from years of serving mass with the dear padre, that there is a moment—the same moment that you begin to taste the residual alcohol left in the blood of Christ—that Father Rodríguez will tug at his collar. I suppose not in disbelief that the actual transubstantiation has taken, or does take place but possibly with some doubt of his ability to act as its agent.

And of course if you think about it, mis hombrecitos, why shouldn't he?

After all he's only a man, like any one of us, subject to the same gastrointestinal eruptions that señor Chávez is so famous for; the same holes in his socks; were not all his shirts black, you could match any of his sweat rings to ours. And maybe the subjects of transubstantiation and the weather cause him the same anxiety as our own anxieties about things in which the hand that moves is unseen; it makes those of us who have put our trust in the Father Rodríguezes of the world uncomfortable in some sort of way that maybe it's best not to discuss it here.

But, no matter.

I think it important though that you know for those of you who yourselves are questioning the veracity of this trip that when he asked me this morning where I was taking you on this field trip, and when I said it was a field trip therefore I was taking you here to a field, he tugged at his collar.

Father Rodríguez is at a crossroads with me, and doubt is an insistent taskmaster.

He administered my First Communion, corrected the first essays that I wrote, counseled me through my confirmation and has heard many of my confessed sins. He even wrote recommendations for my admission into college. Pero, now that he is a part of the committee that has decided that this place would be better off without me—I am told during the ill-fated assembly he announced that regrettably señor Delossantos will not be rejoining us this year—and when I walk in, he looks over his coffee at me in the teachers' lounge—which incidentally it is not nearly as interesting or as glamorous as you might imagine it might be—and questions the possible merits of a field trip to a field right outside our own windows.

Regrettably.

Pero miren, none of you are ever out on this or any of the fields here on the campus without some activity to guide you. Soccer, baseball, football, marching band. Some of you only cross them to get from the school to the bus. But, now sitting here, you have a clear view of Ashland Avenue; you can see anyone coming or going from that store on the corner that for years has sold nearly everything. Of course, when I was a student there was no bulletproof glass. And there's the bus shelter, and the Wendy's, and the traffic headed in and out of the tire shop.

Mira, there's Father McMillan who's been here for ages, long before Spanish masses. He's on his way to the rectory, where he will spend the rest of the afternoon holed up in his office; who's to say if it's God's work or if he's lounging on the leather chaise that señora Castañeda keeps polished and soft? No matter, really.

As he walks by, we will all—in our heads—write the story that best suits us. Has he had a secret love for señora Castañeda that he dares not articulate; does she secretly wish to kill him in his sleep for the lust that she feels him directing towards her and does she do penance for these sinful imaginings by tending to the leather of his chaise with the type of care she only reserves for her grandchildren now? When the secretary comes to work and sees Father McMillan's chaise polished so carefully, does she tell her sister-in-law over Saturday laundry that she believes its gleam comes from the rhythm of Father McMillan's trouser seat? Viejo McMillan, she might say, after all of these years listening to our music coming from the cars on Ashland Avenue, he has finally fallen into it and while laying back on that couch trying to put together his Sunday sermon, he can't help but shake those withered white nalgas of his while he imagines himself under una palma.

OK, I agree señor Palacios—there is no need to hide your opinions under your breaths—a certain amount of this is bullshit. There is no reason for any of you to hide what you're thinking.

Let's have a moratorium of honesty, señores. Let's weave no more obscure dramas that we write each other into. After all, what do you think it was like to come back here after taking just a day off to tend to my mother, to find that in the fourth-floor boys' room I've been turned into the loco by one of you—one to whom I gave a seventy-three percent on his last essay—who is looking for escape? Dios mío, por favor, deliver me from this fucking loco history fuck, I believe the latest inscription reads.

Pobrecitos.

Why remain las víctimas de la historia when it's yours to write, yours to control. It's simply a situation as to whether or not you are watching or being watched.

We've come here to observe, señores, sit and watch. Already, Father McMillan has offered himself as a subject. Though at the same time, we too are the subjects for someone else's observations.

Watched, or being watched, señores? You tell me.

Which are you the moment that you walk out of your front door with your hair crazed and your shoes shined as you head to the end of the block, as you head into the bowling alley, put two dollars onto the counter at a convenience store, fifty cents into the newspaper box? Even though you think you're in control—writing the story of your entire day—another one, in which you've stolen something in the back of the store, in which you're worthless, one in which a no-good, a rapist, a cad, about to cause some havoc somewhere is written as suddenly across the street, across the aisle on the bus, at the corner of the block; you—just your walking down the street—are a promise of something, the commencement of something, the betrayal of another, a sacrifice for someone else, of something else. Until they all converge on top of each other with neither rule nor certainty.

Por ejemplo, Safe as houses, English people say. An idiom I've never been quite able to figure out. None of them who said it had ever seen a car flying in the eye of a hurricane. And of course it, Safe as houses, remains much more allusive today for me than ever. Pero, they say it.

No matter.

Y miren, there's señora Figueroa on her way to a southbound bus, and by the scarf on her head on such a hot day, I believe that she is on her way to Pilsen to have the black put back into the crown of her head by some Mexican hairdresser that only knows her as a client; are we to assume that this mejicana in Pilsen does a better job, or does señora Figueroa think that my Amá—whose shop is just around the block from señora Figueroa's house—is such a chismosa that Amá is the one that told everyone in the neighborhood that señora Figueroa lies about her age?

But don't let yourselves think that you are safe just as spectators here, mis parotids. As much as you're watching, you're being watched. So why not take the school tie off, take your shirts off and wave them over your heads; run around, howling and screeching, acting in a way that people will later describe, as if you had no sense at all; as if you're all out here unsupervised; that Delossantos, years from now they'll say they said, he lost control of his class; lost control of his mind; was a child molester if you're wondering why he never married; entiendes; cuarenta y uno; always too close to his mother; he gave his class drugs; I've always known.

Pero, you'll be the only ones that know that it was heat—heat Father Rodríguez says we brung with us—that we were after.

The day my Amá's house burned, someone brought a glass of iced tea, cautioning her to just take small sips and someone else reminded her to take deep breaths between them. Señora Figueroa gasped when she saw her husband bringing one of their best living room wing chairs—gold tassels, plastic slipcovers and all—out into the street for Amá to sit in. Shttt, he said waving his hand in front of his wife's face, leaving her mouth open without anything coming out but a wheezing, doña Cristina—a family friend whom I trust—said. However, the Monday after the fire Father Rodríguez called to find out how my mother was doing. How long did I expect that she would be in the hospital, he asked, how severe were her burns?

Burns, I asked.

At mass on Sunday señora Figueroa accounted for her shortness of breath on the day of the fire—the wind taken out of her so completely that she believed herself to be taken out of her own body, I believe he said were her exact words—when, through the picture window of her well-appointed living room, she saw my Amá fleeing out of the side door of her house and running through the garden, upsetting the crèche of La Virgen del Cobre—up and down the street like a madwoman—with the top of her head and the back of her dress in flames.

Miren, people as they move from the bus stops and El platforms, quickly into the shade, from around buildings to areas of shade where you can't even see a tree move or into the air-conditioning of any taquería or video arcade and say ¡Ay, hace calor! As if saying it in Spanish to someone who knows exactly what you're talking about somehow makes your mouth drier, your clothes stickier and the headache you get from the sun more vivid.

Quiñones, you pride yourself on your strength. Two years captain or cocaptain of the wresting team; fullback; shortstop. We need a demonstration of your athletic prowess. Go across the street into that weedy lot—the one that used to be a panadería where you could get the most wonderful tortas for cumpleaños, and from where the smell of freshly baked bread that came up out of it when we—Julio, Román and I—got off the bus in the mornings—sí, right there where the weeds and garbage collect from the entire rest of the strip, was intoxicating before it was blown up by one of the gangs or whatever it is that goes on around here nowadays. Go and act as if your tie were a machete.

¿Como? The idea of being watched bothers you under

another context? No matter, I'm sure I'll get other volunteers who are looking for an additional twenty points on their next quiz; the possibility of a passing grade for many of you who would ordinarily . . . sí, I thought that that would remind many of you of the reading that you didn't do last night.

Imports had gone from $1,292,000 in 1770 to $25,217,000 in 1840; exports from $759,000 to $21,481,000; but I suppose that none of this made sense to any of you, particularly for those of you who didn't bother to read it. You could think of it as the year that Junípero Serra established the San Carlos Mission in Monterey. Sí, sí, sí, I realize of course that this is in no way associated with any music or video or computer game program, but if you were to think of what you ate last Fourth of July—barbeque, ice cream; did you sneak a beer behind one of your tíos' backs?—and remember instead of celebrating the opportunity to stuff your faces, you were to be commemorating this country's revolution, which doesn't occur until six years after Cuba begins to establish itself as a financially viable Spanish colony.

What purpose does knowing this serve, Ostrovski?

What purpose?

Ay pobrecito, hombres history is only the memory of others in which you insinuate yourself.

Por ejemplo, psychologists say that it takes the memory of two unrelated things to come up with the third thing that you are trying to remember. The one you want. The taste of candied apple and the smell of tar or vomit may bring back a summer's day at an amusement park. The sound of rain and a run of gooseflesh up the back of your neck can sicken you with the same queasiness as when the penalty kick that you thought that you'd miss or the penalty kick that you missed—the sound of the boot against the leather, the tang of mud in your nostrils that is nearly a taste, blood that filled your mouth, teeth fiercely brutalizing your lips—as you positioned for the block. Regardless of what the two disparate things are, which two you put together, somehow you wind up in the middle.

If I say Monterrey, 1770, and come up with the recipe for Chávez's mother's mole—his mother's family comes from Monterrey, you know—why it makes you want more the more you eat; which color raisins to use; at what temperature to melt the chocolate.

It is what allows each port dotting the coasts of the island to spill over into the rest of the world. Chocolate, handmade linen, flour, rice, wine, soap from Spain, lumber, cotton goods, metal; and in return the island gave up coffee, tobacco, copper, hides, mahogany as the result of azúcar. And of course slaves. The 1774 census lists 171,621 inhabitants, fifty-six percent white. By 1846 a total population of 900,000 lists fifty-three percent of who were either slaves or free people of color, if you can image such a thing, mijos.

And I suppose that it is an easy thing to write from this end of time. It's the same phenomenon you'll see when this bus celebrating Jennifer Lopez's prodigious posterior passes.

Multiply the labor there across Ashland Avenue times the number of students in this year's graduating class, and then again times the number of times that you open the refrigerator in your homes just to peer into it, and then again by the times in your life that you think that you'll drive-thru for french fries, and then again by a million billion, and you'll have the approximate number close to a billionth of the number of strokes, beads of sweat, bleeding fingers and broken backs that lined the sugar bowls of the best of houses in La Habana, in the palatial estates of Santiago, and it all got there without an acknowledged voice.

It's as if under that four-year-old advertisement for a program that is no longer on Telemundo—or Univisión or whatever it is these days—across the street there, beyond the limits of La Habana, Matanzas and Cárdenas, soil rich in fireable red and black clay running twenty feet in depth that grabs on to cane shoots and resists erosion during the rains of hurricane season, we were to start a story that begins: Once upon a time. Were these happy people; were they oppressed; were they overworked; were they beaten; should we—those of us here in let's say La Habana circa 1950—feel guilty or repentant about the American cars we drive, or the Parisian perfume we wear?

No matter.

Whatever it is it is relative to what we write down, ¿no?

Por ejemplo: With most of my mother's house gone now, it's—I suppose most of you know without my saying—common knowledge on Amá's street that el viejo Fernández wears bikini briefs under the coveralls he wears to the factory every morning despite his hanging belly; and he covers the bald patch at the back of his head with something that comes out of a spray can: señora Figueroa just happened to have seen from her back porch when she was airing the rugs the week before last.

It is also known that after twenty-five years of marriage and nine children the Garcías will go at each other in a loud ravening fuck in their upstairs bedroom every Sunday morning at seven o'clock.

Y Luz Maldonado—with all that money her husband's pawnshop on Ashland Avenue brings in you'd think they'd move out of that third-floor apartment—still, the glowing tip of the cigarette she sneaks on the back porch right after her husband has passed out on the couch can be seen through the leaves of the cottonwood that fills that yard.

Does el Viejo Fernández see Elvis when he looks in the mirror; is an aphrodisiac part of the huevos con chorizo, galletas y cafecito señora García serves on Sunday mornings, or is it señor García who cooks; and for those of you who know Maldonado with his gruff manner, is it gin, or rum, or vodka, or tequila on his breath, and is it the back of his hand that his wife fears as she cowers on the back porch?

And who is this collective we that we're talking about when we say we, mis hijos?

Just days before the fire at my Amá's, Ay hace calor could be heard translated on the streets, in the stores, hanging out of windows, collapsed on their porches, nobody can remember since coming to the States, since moving north a time it raining so much; it being so hot; having to be so careful about leaving food out; nearly fainting walking from the bedroom to the bathroom. So hot, it was recalled that there were days for someone in Guadalajara—tan humid y as they call it sultry—that if you hung sheets to dry in the morning, by lunchtime you'd find them so alive with green moss they'd crawl down the street after you. Which was—no matter what it was—nothing according to señor Ramírez, who lived down the block from us, scratching his balls vigorously through his filthy overalls and pointing a wet end of a cigar at whoever would listen. He was saying there was a summer when he was a boy in Jayuya when the air was so hot and wet that the Spanish moss would become carnivorous and would lunge down and devour hundreds of little tree frogs at a time. Señora Figueroa said that she didn't believe a word he said; and he argued every word of it as the truth, for the whole of that summer his mother and sisters refused to leave the house without scarves.

Is it the same heat for each as what the other has brung as Father Rodríguez offhandedly said this morning while blowing into a steaming Styrofoam cup, clumps of that non-dairy creamer floating on the top; I have no idea how he . . .

Well, no matter. Is what's important how much, how many, and how does that translate into dollars today?

Claro, there is no reason why any of this should matter, Pérez, you're right. Pero mis hijos why should it matter whether or not we attempt to fill in the gaps between pages two thirty-three and two forty-five? Or read those pages anyway, as many of you clearly have not? Y miren, you could tell from here, from this distance what negotiations, what barters, what transfers of funds, what brutalities were exchanged for babies, bodies, lives, land. And if you can't, a simple story that ends with, Slavery was wrong, the colonists were bad and we all moved happily on to the twentieth century, el fin, should do.

If where they are working near the alley there in the soil rich in fireable red and black clay running twenty feet in depth is an end row, and it's the eve of the end of the Spanish-American War, they say they said, mi abuela—the eleventh of a brood of girls—slips down the legs of a woman who was just entering her thirtieth year.

Water broke, baby, afterbirth and all with just a swift stroke of the machete; no different from ten babies before; no different from hundreds and thousands of babies from the days and years before. Same sun, same rows of cane, until mi abuela, who howled so when she hit the earth, they say they said, that for the few moments that her mother looked down at her in surprise, that you could not hear the sound of chopping. Without permission to go get water, without permission to have her baby a month early; as a woman fortunate enough—la mujer de la fortuna, they called her before, mi abuela—to have all ten of her other daughters working, living on the same plantación, abuela's mother gathered her up in her shirt and tied the infant to her breast and continued chopping. Pero, unlike the other girls who had slept quietly against their mother's breast during the day—happy to be safe in the moist folds of the powerful woman (for she was known for her strength and her ability to pull down as much cane in a day as any man within the province)—no, mi abuelita, they say they said, was not lulled by the sound of chopping, the jiggling of her mother's breasts; her mother's whispers of Querida nenita, nenita dulce, dulce dulce, querida nenita, dulce querida, dulce dulce, were unable to quell the baby's screech. A hollow screech, a deafening call, a yowl that was said to be so piercing that one man's left ear ran a line of blood from the day the baby was born until he died many years later.

Not pain, not hunger, pero malevolencia, they say they said, it was because it came from her own mother's insides turned out; the stoic manner with which she raised her babies, got on with her work, met the next day as if there was some difference from the one that had preceded it and the one that would follow it; so loud no one noticed the cuervo that would follow mi abuelita the rest of her life and steal the afterbirth—did it eat it? no one knew—before the women who usually assisted with babies coming into the world could get to it, could give it up in offering to keep the baby safe, keep the baby far from the devil, return the baby's alma to los siete santos africanos when the time came. Y and as if a spell was broken during the weeks and months that followed the appearance of my screaming abuelita—once the Americans took over, and change filled the air as neatly explained in tonight's reading assignment—anyone who had been near the baby or were within la zona of her wailing began to complain of blisters that ran with pus but wouldn't heal, and food once vomited up even the dogs wouldn't go near it, and joints that separated so far from the sinew of a shoulder, from a back that they appeared to be only a long tobaccoey strand of spit.

It's easy señores, ¿no?

If you think not, do tonight's homework. No moaning, pero one thousand words.

Dije, no moaning. You'll want to call yourselves men one day—strong men, able men, men without fears or reservations able to command other men to do your bidding or at least report to you in some office somewhere downtown; responsible for thousands—yet you whine like children when you're asked to think what it must be like to take on the work of just one woman.

One thousand words in which you take all eleven or twelve years of what you know about Father Rodríguez, and write what you believe his response would be to the question: Padre Venerable, Padre Sabedor, Sabedor Padre, why is it so hot, has God forsaken us, or is this what we have brought upon ourselves?

Bring them to class tomorrow; we'll compare the answers.

Ahora, Pérez bring them in off the fireable red and black clay, slop them, run them through el río y tell them of tonight's assignment.

Anyone who sees Ostrovski should tell him, por favor, he's to see me.

IT OR THEY, Amá said, was Pirata.

Says wings ran shadows over the front of the house, the roof, and blocked out the moon. She called out to me, in her nightdress and slippers, before getting caught up in his tailwind of debris, dust and molting feathers—el viejecito—and, ay mijo, the lake, the lights at the planetarium, down Michigan Avenue, you've never seen them that way.

And she took a breath as if she was beginning to describe what came next.

But nothing came. And the more there are of these moments when nothing comes, the more of them Julio seems to remember. Over the week he's called to replay moments in the past year when Amá has seemed to go and come in the middle of conversation, moments—he says he knows that I've seen them—in which she seemed to hang in an air pocket over a set of ellipses before lighting. He reminded me of the pride señora Figueroa took in telling us that recently, after seeing the wire grocery cart Amá drags behind her from the store sit full in the sun for over an hour, she had to come over and knock on Amá's door.

And suddenly knowing what all of this may mean is as sickening to me as seeing a pot roast set out on the drain board to thaw and forgotten until it had begun to attract flies.

I watched as Amá's face fell into what looked like bewilderment. Whatever it was she seemed to be trying to find lay like pick-up sticks in front of her: the way pictures of events, parties, birthdays, vacations you've heard so much about, and the story of something that happened someplace you weren't, never seem to come together, yet it is all so familiar.

Instead, she shook her head as if to send it away from both of us. She turned away sharply and began to chip a tiny hole a stir at a time with a spoon against the bottom of her cafecito.

Sí, Pirata, she hummed merrily to herself. Pirata, she wove his name into a tune without any other words that she was making up as she went along; sung or hummed for me as much as for herself. Pirata in the trees, Pirata over the mountains, Pirata across the Straits of Florida, with each clink of the spoon against the porcelain cup. Pirata—she sang as if she had been caught dressed as a princess, or a ballerina, or in her mother's makeup and high heels—he flew in circles, dive-bombed ladies' Sunday hats for paste cherries.

In the teachers' lounge this morning, señorita Jonas complained that she might as well not be there; no one pays attention to her anymore. They're out the window, in the clouds; they climb the walls and the room smells like trapped, ripe, sweaty boy. She says she believes that she'll go mad if there's not a break in the heat before the semester ends.

She was in the middle of saying that next year she's hoping to be on maternity leave, but would be willing to assist in any protest that we might wage against the administration to cancel school in the event that it's this hot next year.

This is no joke! she exclaimed. These old buildings, with their jury-rigged air-conditioning, she started.

I tried to interrupt her by saying it never gets this hot at this time of year, but she didn't seem to hear me.

The rooms never get cool, the boys are everywhere and there'll be girls; Óscar can you imagine what this place will be like if it was this hot and there were girls too? And then she stopped all of a sudden. Her eyes filled with tears as she brought her hand over her mouth; Ay Oscarcito, lo siento, lo siento.

And I found myself stroking the back of her hand, rubbing her shoulders—Estás OK, es OK, nenita—as if it had nothing to do with me.

It's so unfair, she gasped, you're a good teacher; they have no right; it makes no sense.

I changed the subject. Told her a joke about twin sisters and a photographer. And she laughed until she forgot about what we were talking about; until the boys in the composition class that she was facing the next hour resembled cucarachas scattering in a suddenly thrown light; and the heat, the administration and whatever else that was bothering her seemed to wash off of her; until she exclaimed that she needed to get away from me before she wet her pants from laughing. It wasn't that I was ungrateful. She's kind, maybe too kind. Maybe I did it because she wants so much to believe in the things that she believes in; maybe I did it because I want to believe it, want what she believes in too.

But by then I was no longer paying attention.

Even though just minutes afterward I stood—as you'll all recall, señores—here, in this room, telling you about La Habana that rose up out of the mist from the nineteenth into the new year's morning of the twentieth—y ay bendito, what a glorious morning that must have been—I couldn't go with you were I to be able to take you all into my confidence and be honest with you now.

I couldn't allow myself to be taken down the shimmering Corriente del Golfo past El Malecón and make the bend around near El Parque de los Mártires and allow myself to fall into the Bay of Havana, where for over the fifty years that followed ships came daily, freely from the Bay of Biscayne bringing americanos dressed in their best for traveling. It was a time, señores, just before the time when the best warm-weather clothing was purchased for the journey. Before sailor suits were fitted for four- and five-year-olds, and debutantes in Manhattan had Italian sandal makers come to their Park Avenue apartments to trace their feet a month prior to sailing; between the dawn that launched the last millennium, before a market existed for winter houses—when there was only the occasional yanqui—in Mantazas, I had hoped to be carried up in the harbor's spray with you as the first light of the twentieth century flexed a slow brave muscle over the Bay of Havana, but I kept returning to a hole in the glass the size of a fist that that morning Amá claims to have flown through on the backs of a flurry of crows that she claims whispers.

THE HERE-AND-NOW, here and now?

Well of course, señor Ostrovski, you're right.

All of the señores Ostrovski over the past years have been right about this. Why ask about the past when the future is always the most important question? The one of you with the carrot-colored hair and freckles—I can't remember your name now; you sat there in the third row the year I bought my first brand-new car: an '82 Tercel; black with brown interior—Comemierda, you bought this shit so that it looks like leather, Román said when he helped me install the radio—you're right, señor, it ain't like we's gonna walk backward in time.

Y otra vez, that same year—I don't even think the two of you were friends; the name Cedillo comes to mind; pero, as if it were yesterday, that sullen glower out the window for the entire period, the eye rolling that went on anytime a date in the past was mentioned—it's hard not to know that the two of you were thinking the same thing.

Ignacio Villaciergo, I think he was called—from four or five years ago; played football; broke his leg in his senior year; dark good looks; his entire class looked up to him. He too couldn't imagine how he was connected to the Spanish-American War or to the French Revolution; in fact, there were a number of historical figures that he at one time or another said could kiss his shiny brown ass. As I recall, Khrushchev was a candidate, as were Lincoln, Napoleon and, of course, Hitler. He was one of the ones who I had in a class nearly every year before he graduated. There was some point in the semester, some moment of breaking clarity for him, that would cause him to screw himself round in his chair and ask his worshippers if they believed a word of what was going on. Ay sí, nalgas the size of casabas, he has. Ask him about it. I see him occasionally as I pass that row of arcades on Ashland Avenue. I think he has a daughter, two, and another one on the way: he was with his wife at Amá's church a few Sundays ago; Ay, both of them, only twenty-two, twenty-three, and she seems to be quite far along; and for every baby it seems that he takes on a sympathetic twenty or so pounds. Ask him, and he'll tug at his daughter's arm, pull her closer to him, as he tells you the number of yards he ran his junior and senior years; and about the scholarships: Northwestern, William and Mary, Michigan. Grief, glistening like a raven's wing, will cover his eyes as he tells you, 'Mano, I was the shit . . . I could fuck the shit up, couldn't nobody touch my shit, see what I'm saying?

He'll pick his baby up and tell her, Just like Delossantos, never looking forward. And he'll plant a wet kiss between her eyes.

And.

No matter.

Señores, all of you, turn to page two forty-seven.

Use a ruler; if you don't have one—well, of course in my days as a student here you wouldn't have dreamed of coming to class without one; preparedness for nearly any situation was the mark of a good man, an honorable fellow, they used to say; trust no one who is not ready to do the job that he says that he's setting out to do and that includes showing up with the right tools to do it, Mr. Sáenz used to tell us, but that was also in the days when he had more hair than he does now; and I'm sure most of you know he's the type of man who can pour things without spilling them—any straightedge, the side of another book, a pencil that hasn't been broken off or chewed to shreds will do.

I'll graciously assume you've done the reading for today. If not, no matter.

Primero: Crease two forty-seven by folding it over onto the inside gutter of the book.

Miren.

Segundo: Carefully insert your straightedge into the fold; for those of you who are using another book, you will need to unfold the page and place the outside edge of the cover of the second book against the fold that you have made in the first.

Sí, sí, sí.

I should have had you do this long ago, years ago.

Pero, don't start yet.

We are only going to go three quarters down the page. Right after all that drivel about sugar production—as if it mattered how much, where it was shipped to—and before the nonsense that they give you about the reasons the United States entered the Spanish-American War.

We can count on Quiñones and Cartagena to keep those dates for us. They are very good at that sort of thing. Even if they are gone.

Mira, with the straightedge placed thusly—just below the date April 11, 1898; it seems that you'll have to bisect the portrait of William McKinley in half to do so—and pull.

You'll know you've done this properly if you're holding his head in your hand and have tidily left his collar and tie along with the puffery of a coat in the book. Any more, say if he were still wearing his collar and tie, it will be difficult to attach him to the end of a pen or a pencil eraser.

Try it.

Just like a Javanese puppet, ¿no?

You'll find that somewhat pious gaze toward the light of heaven that makes him look nearly cherubic in the book transformed into a sneer; he'll look as if he is about to spit on whatever it is that you're writing.

Or fold what you have left into what we used to call footballs. Those triangular works of origami that for years I've seen sailing across the classrooms when the past gets particularly dull; sí, sí, sí, we had those too. There was, at one time, what seemed like a staggering amount of lunch money put up for a semester's worth of field goals. Don't worry about the information you're thwacking across imaginary green, Olympic fields, the Super Bowl, there have always been those like Quiñones and Cartagena, and I suspect they—people like me, I suppose—will always be there to remind you, bring you back to the Here and Now here and now by inserting a date by which the past can be recaptured.

Oh you're wondering how I know about those little triangles of paper? Footballs, ¿no? Sí, sí, sí, I was a boy once too.

When I was here we even had golfing matches—a legacy it seems that we didn't pass on—in one of the science rooms in the basement; one of the ones that is still lined with those old tables with a hole and the spindle where you can hook a Bunsen burner.

Image.

Imaginen each table was a green, the hole the hole and the spindle for the Bunsen burner the flag, and the entire room can suddenly become a series of different courses with caddies and clubhouses along the East Coast.

Spitballs propelled by Bic pens with the caps bent to resemble putters and drivers were the start of an unsanctioned PGA tour that began my freshman year and culminated with a pros tour of which Román was a part during my junior, their—Román y Julio's—senior year. Y Father Benítez—none of you would know him; dead long before I finished college and old the entire time we were students here—stood there reading, as he always did all year long, for each and every one of his classes he read the textbook from beginning to end, for years. Never looking up, Father Benítez, never engaging in conversation. Just reading, as if the boys in front of him were not there at all.

Close to spring, as Father Benítez was finishing a book Román remembers being called Physics. And only twice in the semester did he look up. The first time was during the semifinals in which four other classes were involved—Father Benítez's chemistry and his three other physics classes—and Román says it was a bank shot from the tee closest to the door, off the window across the room, against the front of Father Benítez's desk and into the hole that set the room into spontaneous cheering and Father Benítez to nearly fall off of his chair as he was shocked into looking up. Román says there was something smug in the old priest's expression; like all the cheering was about the joy of physics, Julio says.

The second time the finals were well under way, even closer to the end of the semester. Not unlike a day like today, it was warm and half the room, those who bothered showing up, because Benítez never took attendance, were restless and bored in the heat. It was all up for grabs, Román says, someone drew a caricature of Benítez on the board sitting in his cassock on a high stool reading with a mushroom cloud behind his head; a poker game was taking place at one of the tables; and all of the finalists from every other of Father Benítez's classes in the golf tournament were present even if it meant skipping other classes.

Someone had begun a hushed commentary that detailed each of the shots in the match, though success couldn't be recognized with the customary round of polite applause; the nod, Julio says, and the wink were their signs of affirmation. And it seemed as if the PGA final Tour of

Champions—which very few of us students didn't know about, didn't have some portion of allowance or lunch money riding on—would have gone on successfully until a winner had been determined, until someone—Julio can't remember who—began lighting matches and throwing them.

Now it is important to note, señores, that of the three of us—Julio, Román and me—Román is the most likely to remember a phosphorescent mist beckoning us through a cracked window when the rest of us only felt the run of a swift, acrid chill as we passed an abandoned house; the further we walk from each woman we pass on the street, the more beautiful she becomes, the more inviting, her personality sweeter, her stories smarter, her abilities to cook, to love—I mean really love, he'll say if he has had a little too much to drink—to care for him, the stuff made of legend. Nearly all his windmills are dragons.

So what I can tell you for certain is there was a fire drill that day, I did smell smoke, the fire department came, just as everyone—all of us students—gathered around Román as he told of the one match that had fallen into the twelfth hole on the green, that from where he was standing appeared to be out, and of the helix of smoke that curled—like a cobra, I believe he said—up, and of the jack-fool who cupped his hands and blew into the hole, knowing full well that oxygen and years of collected spitballs mix well.

Holy shit! were the words Román says Father Benítez used—although there are those who said the old man yelled ¡Puta Madre! and ¡Madre de Dios! Holy shit! became the consensus anytime I heard the story afterward—Holy shit! Román says the priest said, cassock and rosary flying as he pulled the fire extinguisher off of the wall and clearly having never read the instructions, covered the hole the flame was coming out of with the nozzle at the end of the hose.

For a while all you had to do was say, Holy shit, and others laughed around you. Now when he wants to make us laugh Román will tell the whole story to Julio and me, complete with accurate impersonation of Father Benítez later telling his colleagues about the chemical reaction and the principles of physics that caused the fire. There was something clearly explicable, Román starts when he goes to tell Father Benítez's side of the story. Something of the here and now that makes the then and there—the inexplicable when the two stories are placed side by side—reside comfortably together.

And then again—when taxes come due, or the heat or gas bill, a repair on a car, prevents us, me or Julio or Román, from buying a new stereo or a boat or something like that, something that would make us feel like we still had cojones like barrels—we say Holy shit about a lot of things these days. I suppose I don't know whom it is I'm reminding, you or me, when I start stories out with, I too was once a boy.

Señores, you have no idea how easy, if we were to say 1968, as easily as I can place a hand on the back of my neck, close my eyes, I can switch places with many of you as you were when you first started here. Sit across the courtyard on one of the lower floors of the grade school. Trade cheese sandwiches for tuna. Shove in line to make sure that you got chocolate instead of white milk.

That January afterward, if you were the right height to have been in Troop 227 when Joaquín-Ernesto disappeared through the ice, you could feel yourself being counted as you walked down the street. While I was waiting for Amá to get off of work, I watched Marta, the owner of the beauty shop—Amá's beauty shop now—where, back then, Amá was working as an apprentice, stop and walk to the window and wipe the fog away; first with her palm then more violently with her smock. She did it so many times that the woman in the chair asked if her permanent would be done while she was still young enough to get her husband to notice. Marta said that she had seen three niños go into the alley across the street but only two had come out. The woman in the chair started upright, and then indicated, waving her red nails frantically, for Marta to hurry and go wipe; go wipe the window again.

All the women in the shop stopped and peered through the sweaty circle in the middle of the shopwindow until the last of the boys emerged tugging at his zipper. The women signed their relief; one of them crossed herself and kissed her knuckle several times.

Tucked in the mirror behind the three operators' chairs was Joaquín-Ernesto's carta conmemorativa, which included his fifth-grade picture—his hair parted wetly on one side—and prayers to both the saints for whom he was named as well as one to San Iago in memory of the far tip of Cuba from where he and his family had come. Marta had carefully placed it between her pictures of the pope and one of herself in a pink-and-white candy-striped bikini that she swore by summer she would fit into again.

We were told to never, never, ever go anyplace alone. The mothers on our floor of the apartment building all planned last-minute trips to the store so that three or four of us would have to put on coats and boots and hats and gloves, and go together. In the carnicería Joaquín-Ernesto's carta conmemorativa was arranged with the crucifix and the dusty dried palms from the previous Lent above the meat lockers. In the farmacia, the same picture that appeared in the Spanish newspapers had been blown up and taped over a lighted display at the front of the store. Before, a pretty woman had blown smoke rings upward with a bright smile of perfect teeth. After his disappearance, the light from the display shined through the part in Joaquín-Ernesto's hair and made halos of his eyes, while the caption continued to read above him: ¡Kool Milds, Me Gusta!

The snow that had fallen the week before Joaquín-Ernesto's disappearance through the ice locked us in as it froze firmly and was shoveled and piled and heaved aside to make room for more snow. Daily, new gray mounds were shoved from the streets to the middle of the playground at our school and nightly a blanket of an inch more would cover it.

Insistently, steadily, concentrically the days moved from haze to murk to black until there was no room for us to run at recess. Instead, we were shown films on protecting ourselves from strangers and the evils of drugs. There were filmstrips called the Chronicles of Jesus, and we were shown His birth, death and resurrection—one frame at a time—and back again. Twice while outside the temperature spiraled in windchills far below normal. The floor of our gym became dangerous as the steam radiators at the ceiling slicked the walls with condensation that ran onto the lacquered surface below making it unfit; unfit, as Father Rodríguez put it, for sport, for play; like glass, he put it with more anger than I had ever heard him use before, it would be like giving you pieces of unbroken glass to play with. We were warned about the jeopardy of simple exposure: You could die just from standing outside; you could freeze for being foolish enough to go anywhere without a hat and gloves and a scarf and long underwear. Each morning Father Rodríguez would have us kneel by our desks. Pray boys, he said, pray that you'll grow strong and honorable; Pray you'll have a body that is finely tuned for sports and a mind clear for long division; Pray you'll gain the patience and wisdom to know true fuerza y true grace like our dear, dear Joaquín-Ernesto.

The past, señores—you're right; listen to Ostrovski—never really matters that much until there's a moment in time when you have to gather yourself up, find yourself, and move on.

None of you have any idea how many times I've come to this page, or to pages like this in the books I've taught out of, and looked out at rooms full of you and realize that I have disappeared. There are no dates, no events by which I can mark my existence. I suddenly have no right to be in front of a room; the literature denies my existence; I am disappeared by the very text that I quote: pues, señores, yo soy the apparition that speaks for ghosts. Somewhere between the grand sweeping mention of Latin American slavery and the Spanish-American War, voiceless, nameless—sin azúcar, sin boca—I'm left the blithe espíritu negro de los campos y cabaret until el 8 de enero de 1959 when Castro rides into Cuba to declare all of la Isla mulato.

It's all very confusing now that I'll no longer be teaching here anymore. You'll think me naïve, pero these were not things I ever considered. I never thought that any of you would question what any of the dates that I rattled off meant in terms of your futures, or that you would develop a valid hostility—one that goes past that schoolboy malaise; I know it, I was raised to think of duty as a virtue and lethargy as a vice; the good man is one who keeps both mind and body healthy; Trustworthy, Loyal, Helpful, Friendly, Courteous, Kind, Thrifty, Brave, Clean and Reverent, but therein lies the lie—that prohibits you from blindly taking up with ghosts when you've worked nearly all of your lives to not believe in them.

Fresh-faced, straight out of college—I didn't know any better, I was the best at what I do; many thought I should go on to graduate school; and it was an honor to be asked to teach here—Father Rodríguez and Mr. Sáenz had all the ladies from the church cooking the whole week before. A mass was said and pews of people turned around and looked at me, Amá, Román y Julio y las doñas Liliana y Cristina as Father Rodríguez announced his wish that everyone would welcome back señor Delossantos—I was suddenly señor Delossantos—one of our own who has returned to give back to his community. As the congregation applauded Amá beamed and feigned embarrassment the way she does anytime she is ashamed of being proud.

Claro, even now, were you to ask me the socioeconomic advantages behind the famous execution of 1536 as well as the more lascivious ones, I could tell you; although the sixth finger appears in many of the portraits that were made before and after her death, it may or mayn't have been true; and the number of warts and moles attributed her seems quite ludicrous given the egocentricities of her monarch to whom it must have occurred that were he to produce the much-sought-after heir he would eventually need to sleep with her and therefore make them highly unlikely. There are seventeen letters written by him to her held by the Vatican—God knows why—in which he professes an undying love, unwavering passion. Although, señores, the lines between love and passion are oft too frequently confused. Both so violent, so jarring—great upheavals of the soul, however unclearly defined, always bleed the cruelest punishments—that her last plea could have easily been, But sire I thought you loved me. To which he could just as easily have responded, That, madam, of which you speak is governed by the sovereign prick of state, which, make note, towards you points a downward neigh. Or he could claim the letters to be of his own invention and therefore, as king, his own to destroy. Why not? It is from the same sort of information—the years that she lived in France during which she is said to have developed a taste for things French—that we assume that as her head was separated from her body she was fashionably dressed for the continent.

With 1517 in the common era, I have scattered this very classroom with oceanfuls, five centuries of tears shed for and in the name of La Llorona as she watched from her wedding bed as her husband removes the guayabera—ivory-colored: white yet yellowed with just a hint of Old World aristocracy—bespattered straight through to his long undergarments with the blood of her countrymen. It's blood and tears easily drawn into this classroom; it's a virtual deluge that splatters the banks of the Río Grande and the Tejas border, and spills into the Gulf of Mexico. In Brownsville on a sunny July fifteenth in 1859 they ran out of the face of a man who was being pistol-whipped in front of his friends and family by an Anglo marshal, and then again out of the marshal's shoulder as a result of a bullet wound inflicted when he wouldn't be stopped; and they wash back toward the border only to be taken up again as el corrido tells us in June 1901 in San Antonio and run from the chest of yet another sheriff thinking all mejicanos look alike, and they part the ground on the road to a christening on a hot day in July 1923.

These are just a few of the things that I have needed to know—know well—to do what I do.

So if I were to tell you, There in that hole I had you rip out, write 1844—a date I've never seen in any of the books that I have used over the last twenty-two years—I could set Gabriel de la Concepción Valdés running in the window made by the rough edge. Plácido, he called himself when he wrote; Plácido—a name for sonetos, plegarias, declarations of suffering and independence, desire and contempt—runs through streets named for so many politicians, diplomats, lands claimed by the names that they are named after: por ejemplo, I could send him running down calle O'Reilly—named for Field Marshal Alejandro O'Reilly, the man most responsible for Spain's reorganization of the Cuban military after the Seven Years' War that ended in 1763, one of the few places on the island where you could get an English-cut suit, broadcloth shirts and monogrammed cuff links—even though with his brown skin—the illegitimate and orphaned son of a Spanish dancer and a pardo hairdresser; the winner of the 1834 contest held in La Habana in honor of Francisco Martínez de la Rosa where he beat out eleven white competitors which makes him in demand to write lyrics and odes of baptisms and birthdays—pues, he isn't allowed to shop in the best of shops; instead he's chased, hunted and finally executed.

Children of Las Casas.

También, I suppose that it would be his ghost that I'd need to float across the Florida Straits up the south stairwell and into this classroom next to me, and have him say, Here, aquí, this señor Delossantos, qué neither jode perros nor is a loco, I am his past by which he stands in the here and now.

And I could be fairly convincing, ¿no?

OK, maybe not all of the time, but most. Maybe. I no longer know myself.

Pero, señores, what I do know of the here and now is its hold on the then and there. And there's so much that you need to know, need to have hold of that I still find myself unable to say. Standing here talking all this time about exports and trade agreements the same way that I've done for so many years, in a way that I can do in my sleep, I find myself wishing that at least one of you could hear what I think. What I've thought so loudly that sometimes I have had to catch myself during my lectures of the past two weeks or so to make sure that what I thought and what I've said are not the same thing, only to seconds later find myself wishing that they were.

One day, in a very intimate space, at a very intimate point in time, when you think that you couldn't possibly get any closer to another person, the question who—if you could be anyone in history—would you most like to be may be set in your ear. And maybe, just that once, if you're lucky enough to be close enough to where your nose breathes in at the base of a neck that smells like overripened casaba, you'll realize that you would be the person you were the moment before you were asked.

Sí, es verdad.

Anyone who has ever really loved anyone or any place has done it just this way.

IT WAS PIRATA, Amá said as I was sweeping broken glass off of the kitchen floor this morning. And again as I patched the window with cardboard and tape, and took measurements for glass to be cut at the hardware. She pointed to the hole in the glass—the same size as one of Román's balled fists—and said, Quieres la tierra y la luna.

La tierra y la luna, she was saying when I asked if she remembered talking to Román last night; remembered me coming into the kitchen and helping her patch Román's hand. Did she remember helping me get him to the couch and did she remember asking me to sit by him until I was sure that he was asleep, sure he didn't toss with nightmares?

Anyone who has been to the small apartment Román has lived in for the past ten or fifteen years just outside the city in Maywood knows he has never thrown anything out. Receipts are bundled together with paper clips without regard for order or date. Years and years of groceries, notices for years-old license renewals from when he was still allowed to drive a car, laundry chits, are stacked in dusty piles along the counter that separates the living room/dinette from the kitchen.

Is good he don't get the newspaper, doña Cristina has

said nearly every time when she, Amá, doña Liliana, Julio and I have gone over to clean when the drunks got to be too bad and someone from the garage where Román works called to tell us they hadn't seen him in a few days, which are the only times that I have not heard doña Liliana respond to nearly everything doña Cristina said with a click of her tongue.

They mop; they sweep; they wipe the trophies for baseball, for basketball, the one for lacrosse, the medals for swimming, all the ones for soccer free of dust and the film from cigarette smoke; they polish the big silver cup—MVP his senior year after the regional championship—awarded to him on the green just outside the classroom windows on a day not too unlike today. Pero it was June I think, right before the end of the year, and Amá and doña Liliana wore hats fancy with wide brims and silk flowers, even doña Cristina wore a sundress though she covered her shoulders with a sweater much too hot for the day, and the band played in full uniform, sweat ran down the faces of the men that stood around looking at their shoes and off into space, then and now if you asked, stood around them, in between tales of the goals lost and blocked at the penalty kick, goals that sent them up onto the shoulders of their teammates, goals that made heroes of entire towns back home, they would have said that they said the kid is going places.

Julio and I lift the chairs, the couch, move the bed out of the way of the vacuum. Doña Cristina always says that she has no idea how anyone can live with so much dust as if it were the first time that we stepped over empty vodka bottles, pulled half-finished fifths from cupboards and drawers.

On the second and fourth Fridays of each month—pay-days—I leave the back door unlocked though in all of these years I've never told Amá or las doñas.

A back door unlocked, in this city? Amá would say, why

wait for the assassin; grab the boning knife and go ahead and slit your own throat from ear to ear. And I can only assume that she locked it back sometime after I had gone to sleep.

I hadn't heard Román's footsteps on the wooden back porch or his fist against the glass. Without completely leaving sleep, it was my toe hitting the bump where the floorboards meet at the threshold between the dining room and kitchen. A stream of moonlight ran the length of the kitchen floor from the opened door.

¿Dónde usted ha estado, señor? Amá asked. There was a tartness to her voice—something that I didn't know, had never heard before—mock reproach whispered into the dark, issued as if she knew Román would respond, Nowhere else in the world; everywhere in the world; waiting.

Solamente un hombre, Amá snapped, estúpido engreido.

I know, Román said, yo sé.

Like there ain't been babies to raise and mortgages to pay and all the time . . . well it ain't like I wanted you back or nothing, I just wanted your responsibility of which you have none.

Sí eso es, eso es, Román said swaying on his feet as if he would fall forward or back, his tongue thick in his mouth, Eso, eso eso es.

There's been a lot to do all these years, Amá scolded, babies to raise, work to be done, and you were . . . you weren't . . . you.

I watched as Román moved through the shadows towards Amá; he hung his head so that his chin rested on his chest and his lips were poised between her eyebrows before he whispered, Hold me.

Amá raised her arms around him and closed her eyes to the kisses that he placed along her hairline.

Eso, eso, eso es, he whispered.

I turned the light on, and Amá stepped back, unaware of me, but surprised to see Román there.

Doña Cristina is the only one who has ever lain claim to have seen the red sandals since we met La puertorriqueña. Why would he keep such a thing? she asked one evening after we had spent most of the day at his apartment cleaning.

How am I supposed to know? I asked. Román has never confided in me; I've always been little Oscarcito to him.

You could ask, Amá pleaded, he's your 'mano, he'll talk to you if you ask.

But she knows that we don't ask. As much as she and las doñas Liliana y Cristina wanted the three of us to act like brothers even though I was of no blood relation—other than Las Casas—to either of the two of them, Román y Julio, we've taken it all on—the rivalry, the envy and I guess some of the hero worship too—to the point that we have mimicked Amá and las doñas and never ask. We never do, Julio and I, because if we did, the kind of dreams that boys learn to covet in secret at the appearance of the first few scraggly hairs in our armpits or the cracking of our voices—like the real existence of a man who can leap buildings in a single bound or sports figures that will somehow become our best friends—might never come true.

Though there had been a lot of tongue clicking the spring Román met La puertorriqueña in red sandals that he brought to Amá's house, we didn't ask. It was clear while Amá and las doñas cooked and set the table that as Román, Julio and I waited watching the White Sox in the living room we would not say anything, not ask any questions. The way Román's hand, with its never completely clean broken nails because he was already working at the garage by then, lingered over her belly—stretched out on her belly; smoothed and resmoothed the fabric of the flowered sundress that ordinarily las doñas would later have said didn't go at all with the shoes she was wearing—no one would ask why she didn't offer to help in the kitchen, or what her father did.

We all would remember the sandals the same way that we'd remember the pictures taken in Amá's garden after we had all been down to City Hall; and the harvest of peony and pink cabbage roses Amá cut that morning that La puertorriqueña—Ana Sofía, that's it, that was her name, Ana Sofía—carried stretched themselves wide open in the heat of the judge's chambers and dripped a trail of petals down the hallway, down the street and the steps of the subway; and the way doña Cristina—who has never been one to be engaged in casual conversation with the neighbors or shopkeepers—would whisper the word parto, as if señora Figueroa doesn't intimate it to anyone who will listen when she tells them that that girl looked like a gitana with all those wild black hairs, red lips and so many jewelries; slap his face in public and scratch his chest, like she was a cat; y no modesty at all, bosom all showing, legs all showing, she'd let him push her up against his car for hours right in front of my house, y that the girl couldn't be a day over thirteen—even though she was nineteen, my age at the time—and that she appeared to be having twins if not triplets, even though the baby, a girl, came more than a month early.

Small, red, we only saw her through glass. The end of July, the first week of August, I don't remember.

Eso, eso, eso, es, Román murmured as Amá picked the bits of glass from his hand with a tweezers, cleaned and dressed his wounds with more gauze than seemed needed. She made him drink a cup of tea. She untied his shoes, and turned her back to us as I helped him out of his pants and onto the couch.

If doña Cristina had actually seen the red sandals in the back of a closet, under Román's bed, rolled up and hidden with his undershirts, none of us would have touched them. Just hearing about them, knowing it could be, brought about a scarlet ember of embarrassment that got passed from bare hand to bare hand much in the same way the discovery of a four-leafed clover pressed in between the pages of a borrowed book of poems could thrust any one of us into the middle of someone else's wish, open a box containing a summer's afternoons spent.

Just as easily, the hottest of sweaty summer nights can bring about snow from a long-ago afternoon that Amá was sewing the gloves that we bought that morning on Chicago Avenue into the sleeves of my coat when I first heard her use English more than to say Yes or No or Thank you very much. It was right before Passion Week and the three-month anniversary of the loss of Joaquín-Ernesto. I had been chosen from the 227 to read at church in his honor at yet another service. I watched Amá as she knuckled hard quick stitches into the sleeves. She tucked her lips into her mouth as she worked and she wouldn't look at me even after she had cut the thread with her teeth. She never said anything about us not having enough money for me to keep losing gloves. She didn't need to; I was standing next to her when I heard her tell our landlady she was sure things would get better and that she would ask Marta for more hours.

I was begging her not to make me read at the service. While she wiped our breakfast dishes I told her that I was sick, couldn't do it. I followed her into the main room and back into the kitchen and then back again while she got water and starch to iron her dress on our foldout bed. All the while begging her not to make me read; I would make her ashamed of me; I'd pee my pants.

When she was finished with her dress she went to the kitchen and pulled the flan out that she had made the night before. She motioned me to leave the kitchen and I sat on the radiator watching her back as she attempted modesty stepping into her dress and then wrapped the flan in aluminum foil. She put her coat on and stood at the front door holding it when she said, You know mijo, sometime you no know you no going to like something until you right in the middle of no liking it, then is OK to no like it. She smiled and held out my coat and the flan pan. Her hands were raw from shampooing, rinsing and conditioning other women's hair. She slipped them into a pair of my sweat socks and hid them in her coat pockets.

At the buffet table in the basement of the church, the woman who told us at the last service of Joaquín-Ernesto's love for her tostones grabbed Amá's hand and said, The boy reads well, nobody, nobody had the dry eye. Her eyes moved over me like a searchlight as she told Amá that I was very smart. Tan smart, she repeated still looking to see where it had come from, he might even grow up to be a doctor or a lawyer. Amá looked up from unwrapping the flan and said, Or maybe a diplomat. The woman ignored her completely, took up a plastic spoon, ran it around the edge of the flan platter and placed it in her mouth. Her eyes seemed to glaze over involuntarily and close as if she had been taken somewhere so far away that clearly, for a second, she had no idea where she was. ¿No is no bueno? Amá asked timidly. The woman's eyes shot open as if she had been slapped. She said it was good, good enough, might be better had the guayaba paste been made fresh and not come out of a can.

Other people did not seem to mind that Amá's flan had canned guayaba. As the line wound round the buffet table, down the hall, out of the social hall and up toward the steps that led to the church, you could hear them saying, Her there, la negrita with the boy who did the reading; the one that came over just a few years ago and just came up from Miami, ella aquélla. Each only took a little as if to make sure everyone got some. They stood in front of Amá allowing it to melt on their tongues before looking at her in astonishment.

How creamy, how delicious, how much like home, they said. She makes it, flan light as nothing, light like dreaming, como el paraíso.

It was all gone when Joaquín-Ernesto's father came to the table. The woman with the tostones tried to hand him a piping hot plate of them with her salsa verde. He paid no attention. He looked at Amá and then fixed his eyes on me. When he realized he was staring, his eyes went quickly to the top of my head.

Is gone, Amá said with her head down, pushing the platter forward for him to see.

The suit he wore was shiny from wear at the elbows and knees, and the cuffs of his shirtsleeves were frayed and too short: his hairy wrists, the backs of his hands, ended in broad fingertips that were raw and bitten and a little bloody. Without seeming to hear what she had said, he ran one of his hands around the well of the plate several times and walked away with three of his fingers in his mouth.

Once he was far enough from the table to be outside of earshot, the woman with the tostones said, Ay pobrecito, and then asked Amá if she knew why Joaquín-Ernesto's mother and little sister weren't there. Amá shook her head pretending not to want to know, focusing on wiping the platter clean and putting it in the grocery bag she had folded neatly under the table. The woman with the tostones continued anyway and asked Amá if she could see the woman across the hall: Mira the one with the blue rinse; well she lives next door to them and she tells me that his wife took the girl and just one bag and—if you can imagine in all this snow—walked, walked, nenita, from here to the Greyhound station on Harrison Avenue.

Someone else who overheard the woman with the tostones talking looked over her shoulder to make sure that she too wouldn't be overheard by anyone else before she added that she heard that before Joaquín-Ernesto's mother left with his sister someone had seen her up on Ashland Avenue at the pawnshop with her wedding ring and the rope of pearls that she had been given by her sainted abuela for her trousseau.

The four of us were silent as we watched Joaquín-Ernesto's father walk up from the basement to the landing that led outside. He threw all his weight on both spring-latch doors and went outside into all of that snow without a hat or a coat or gloves.

Sit with him, mijo, Amá instructed before heading for bed, make sure he's good and asleep before you leave him; talk to him, mijo, until you hear him snoring, before he's taken off by nightmares.

And I began to wonder how many times since that afternoon in early September that they sat through a second showing of The Changeling back when there still were movie theaters downtown and you could pay once and sit through showings of a film all day long how many times since did he look at her empty seat, hear her whisper that she was going for popcorn, think, if he had only checked earlier; how many times had he looked at his watch, craned his neck into the darkened back of the theater; over and over again, did he watch that crazed man, that over the years would begin to look like a crazed boy to him, holding a pair of red sandals in front of a downtown movie theater that is no longer there off of State Street.

Ana Sofía—that's it—that's what señora Figueroa says when she tells the neighbors he sat on the front lawn—Ay pobrecito, drunk beyond standing up, drunker than I seen anybody gets, she says when she recounts the story, adds a new story, layers story on top of story—crying, he was crying, Ana Sofía, holding her red sandals in his hand, rocking, rocking until Julio and I were called to help him into Amá's house.

But none of us know, know for sure.

Amá brushed her teeth, and I could hear her weight against the floorboards head toward the back of my apartment. She would brush her hair out and pin it before saying a decade or two of the rosary before the light that came from under the door of her room went out.

Thinking Román asleep, I moved to head towards bed when he turned quickly to stop me. Mira Oscarcito, he said, tengo un secreto. He beckoned me closer, close, until my ear was nearly resting against his lips when he said, Las mujeres . . . a mí me parece fascinanate . . . Es un misterio . . . mean, mean, mean . . . with all that delicious chaos between her thighs. He then whispered, Eso, and his mouth opened as if a grape had fallen out of it before he turned and began to snore.

I found Amá staring at the hole in the glass in the morning.

She insisted it was Pirata.

. . . SUGAR PRINCESSES. . . .

Sí, Ostrovski, dije, sugar princesses. Dígame señor, which part of it do you not understand, or refuse to believe? Is it sugar? Or is it princesses? We'll wait.

Sí, pensé así.

First a few dozen, then a hundred or so. Sugar princesses from Oriente, from Santiago, from places like the area between Vega and Manzanillo where their fathers had inherited refineries from grandfathers and their great-grandfathers; from the cattle ranches y fincas bought from sugar, spun from sugar, powered with sugar where they needed to concern themselves with choosing fragrances that lingered in the air long after they had taken their leave and avoided the possibility of heart palpitations brought on by the heat.

Although when Castro and his compañeros came down from La Sierra Maestra . . . and what date would that be, Castañeda? Señor Chávez? Paredas?

Sí señor Ostrovski, I see your hand. It's just that I wish that someone else beside you had done the reading. It would be nice to know if after all these years all of the Ostrovskis that have passed through here had done any of the reading. If only to tell them that maybe they had been right. Right and wrong at the same time. I'm ashamed now of the years of A's that I have given out because you have known the exact date. The exact date American allies landed on the shores in Normandy was worth five points; you could get an additional ten if you could give the date when the words A heavy burden has been laid on me by my brother's will in transferring to me the imperial throne of All Russia were uttered; ten more if you could identify the circumstances and the speaker. With whom was President Lyndon Baines Johnson speaking on May 27, 1964, and about what particular conflict did he have doubt seems less important now than whether or not during this conversation he rubbed the cuticle of his thumb raw with his index finger out of nervousness.

Claro, señor Ostrovski is right, the date in question is 1959. I'll give you ten points bonus, though I doubt that the school will recognize a grade above an A plus, least of all from me. Pero, estoy rodeada de reliquias de una vida que ya no existe.

No matter.

Pero before that, before Castro, sugar princesses, sí, sugar princesses were already burying English and Georgian tea services, place settings for twenty including escargot forks, ladies' soup spoons, asparagus tongs that their families had been bringing over from España since as early as 1551 were buried in well-tended gardens that were equally as old and cultivated.

Irony, no, them putting into the ground exactly what they came for in the first place and didn't find?

Doña Liliana remembers debutante after debutante that came out the years before her and the ones just after that were suddenly learning things that they never dreamed they would be learning, like how to remove canvases from their stretchers, roll them into tight tubes and ship them off to distant relatives in places like Mexico, Spain and Miami.

Pero señores, flight from Cuba was not a new thing, it is nearly as old as the Spanish language's debut on the island; it had been going on since the morning of July 10, 1555, when the honorable corregidor of La Habana, Juan de Lobera, woke to find a French corsair—one Jacques de Sores—rummaging through his things in the Castillo Real de la Fuerza of which there was an illustration, pero I believe that we tore those pages out last week. Talk goes, if you can trust historians, de Sores—purported to have been dashingly handsome and fiendishly relentless in his pursuit of booty . . . sí, señores, let's all say it, get it out of our systems . . . booty, booty, booty . . . making him not too unlike any of señor Pedro García's three older brothers who barely got out of there, they were so distracted—de Sores' pride seems to have run a singularly directed course. To a pirate by trade, the gold, the silver, the jewels of las Américas headed back to Spain, retrieved from sunken galleons and housed in El Castillo were irresistible. So on the morning of July 10, 1555, he and his men sailed into the narrow harbor of La Habana, raging hard-ons sticking out in front of them, and took what it was that they wanted. They say they said they said, it was all over in just half an hour, and they say de Sores and his men took great pleasure in humiliating their captives, and accounts range from numerous atrocities—ay, just some boyish pranks some say, they say they said, they were just playing with them—against the poor, some say they rode priests like they were horses through wagon ruts fetid and muddied with garbage, human and animal excrement that are now the streets of downtown La Habana. It only took thirty minutes, they say, to loot El Castillo, terrorize the settlement and set de Lobera towards the instantiation of a tradition of fleeing Cuba that is so intrinsic to the culture that doña Liliana—who would say, she or any girl from El Vedado at the time—might have liked to lay claim to some French ancestry.

Sugar princesses, however, from the beginning of the 1950s began to appear on the covers of magazines, invitations to their parties were the most sought after; rubia like a starlet, like an heiress, no matter how you had to get it, no matter how many hours were spent in your hairdresser's chair, no matter how burned your scalp became, rubia. And suddenly thin, like Ana Lucía, doña Liliana says, thin was in, like Audrey Hepburn before there was Audrey Hepburn, La Flaca they called her.

Though nearly thirty years later, Ana Lucía would remember it was the year—1951, the year Eddy Chibás put a bullet through his belly on national radio—that they all said they said it was the year of La Flaca. But they meant her there, with night's moon in her gaze; someone else; her there in the photograph on the piano in her house in Miami: cool and distant, but also within reach of their carefully manicured fingers.

Somehow, they had forgotten the skinny girl in pigtails with a history of questionable blood. They called. They stopped at her father's house in El Vedado, leaving their damp cards on the credenza in the hall. They pressed their damp hands into her gloves across dinner tables, and into the backs of dresses that newspapers reported came all the way from Paris. She was seen at the opera, on the beach, getting out of a government car with the son of one of Batista's highest-ranking officials in front of La Hilton Habana. She had been at a friend's house. The boys fixed drinks out on the patio, while she and the other girls went to the powder room. She remembered it being warm. She was dabbing Guerlain—they all wore it then—at her wrists and temples. The radio had been turned up; they were waiting for their favorite radio novela: they would find out that day if the heroine, Rafaela, would tell her husband that she was having an affair with their doctor who was also his best friend. There was a commercial for Hiel de Vaca from Crusellas and Kolonia with a K, before she heard Eddy Chibás' voice return. She heard the boys laughing and imitating Chibás' nasal high-pitched voice: Integrity Against Greed . . . Integrity Against Greed, they mocked. Her head had sung with a hangover the next morning. She was to go shopping with a girlfriend. Her father's driver had let them out in front of a Dior gown in a window on calle Paseo. A soldier stood close by with a gun on his hip. Another was at the corner at attention with a rifle across his chest. The night before they had gone to dinner and then a nightclub where una negra sweated out song after song under a spotlight.

It would be nearly a year before she and most everyone else she knew in Cuba would know of Chibás' last call to the country or the thirty-five-caliber bullet he put into his belly, years before they would know more than that Hiel de Vaca from Crusellas and Kolonia with a K was delicate to the skin. And to this day, nobody knows whatever happened to La Flaca.

Doña Cristina claims the chisme around El Vedado—if you believe the talk had around cafecitos and the tiniest little watercress sandwiches you've ever seen, talk at the vanities of fashionable powder rooms and in the dressing rooms on calle Paseo—La Flaca was first sighted in Santiago with a black drummer who wore skinny ties and a blue sharkskin suit who was popular with heiresses and haunted by smack. But as time passed, sugar princesses were flocking to the port of Habana with Louis Vuitton steamer trunks full of party dresses, mink wraps and tiny little shoes made by an italiano who each spring and early fall would be admitted into the most select salons and sitting rooms to trace the feet of those who were escorted to the christenings of yachts and first male heirs. Their photos were taken at

Martí—planes ready in the background—on board private boats harboring in Santiago, and they were retouched to accentuate the aquiline familial noses or the prominent foreheads and swan-like necks before they appeared in the newspapers. Their signature wave meant—at least to them at the time—that they were off to be educated in places like Switzerland and Paris, they were summering with relatives in Majorca, relatives in Miami.

And for just as many that fled into or over La Corriente del Golfo, ten more surfaced in the most fashionable places to be seen in Miami. Some would claim relation, and would have had lunch with her just the other day; others would have met the very rich and very young lover that she was with. Of course, there would be those who by the poolside, under the shade of a dripping mimosa, in the thick liquid of a Miami afternoon would confide in a friend the pain of her historia. Though whether they ended up married to a wealthy dominicano, and summered on the Côte d'Azur, or at the Estée Lauder counter at Marshall Field's, like doña Liliana, questions about La Flaca—what is she wearing, with whom is she seen; where did she summer; I'm sure she must have married one of those Hollywood people, or a Texan, doña Liliana tells doña Cristina when the question is brought up—seem as fresh as the headlines on the fashion and gossip pages that asked, where was La Flaca now in those couple of years before Castro came down from La Sierra Maestra.

You couldn't have told them that just twelve years ago, they could have passed her on the street in downtown Miami or at La Galleria and not have recognized her.

Aureliano, her son, had passed his boards and was interested in some blanca who spoke perfect Catalán up in Chicago; Couldn't ever see coming back home to stay now mamá, he said. His sister Pilar would have to see what was going on with Miguel in November—he has been stuck at the office late every night since the beginning of the year—

if not then for sure in December, she would come alone with Carolina for at least a week. We'll shop and cook and lay out on the beach together, mamá, it'll be fun, just us girls, you'll see.

Two months before her fifty-first birthday, Ana Lucía García Carrera née Pérez found herself somewhere between cheating at canasta with the wives of other cubano businessmen at the yacht club and listening to her husband, Alberto, snore. But it was her babies, Aureliano y Pilar—out free in the world; far from her, far from here—that buzzed lively like a scorpion born in the center of her brain; alive as memory, they fluttered like breezes of flamboyants, whirling ripe pollen clouds in the distance. Around the canasta table the most common lament was los niños. They never called; they didn't write; they had no idea if their madres lived or died. Pero por Ana it only filled her with the satisfaction that her job was done. Alberto was very drunk. Harmless. From where she stood, lighted in a river coming from the television, a slackened sock hung off the end of his foot. She allowed the wind to take the front door behind her with a slam that reverberated through the hallways. Her keys clanked loudly against the marble table in the vestibule.

The heels of her shoes clipped along the polished tiles towards the den. She stood in the expansive arch that led into the room. His belly rose and fell in slow, rolling, languid presses and spills. One leg was braced against the carpet next to a spilled drink; the other was stretched over the back of the couch. His knees were so far apart she could make out the heavy outline of his balls on the inside of his leg. She could not see his face, but she could smell him: his hairiness; his socks; cubano rum smuggled through Mexico.

The sound on the television had been muted. The woman on the screen was young and pretty. She could have easily been the grown-up version of any of the americanitas Pilar brought around the house, or Aureliano's rubia with her clear blue eyes and facile, cultivated, lisping Spanish. Ana watched as the girl fought against the wind on an abandoned street. She faded and reappeared in between connections and failures of the signal. Her hair flew and her microphone wavered. All of Dade and Palm Beach Counties were shaded in an outline of the state of Florida that suddenly illuminated the upper right-hand corner above her head. Warnings of a severe weather watch detailing funnel clouds, a fifty-foot wall of water headed from the south, hail and dangerously high winds rolled across the hand that clutched where the girl's raincoat covered her breasts. Behind her, a newspaper box had been dragged from its moorings at the curb into the middle of the street.

Ana imagined the sound of its scrape as it inched its way down the street. She reached into the darkened part of the room to where she knew a vase was that she and her decorator had shopped for for weeks with chips of cream, eggshell, egg cream and ecru paint samples filling their handbags. It teetered on its carefully dusted spot on the bookshelves with just a touch of her fingertips. With the whole flat of her hand, she could hear it tip over and roll before shattering to pieces against the tiles. A streak of lightning filled the bay through the French doors at the opposite end of the room. Past the gazebo and the slope in the yard she could see the straits overflowing the bay.

It took forcing all of her weight against the French doors to get them open. The ends of diaphanously sheer curtains were sucked out and threatened to be pulled off their rods and taken in to the night. Hailstones clattered into the room, onto the floor, against the glass front of the curio cabinet and into the open cave of the piano, causing the strings to cry. A sudden second flash revealed the hull of Alberto's sunfish banging against its dock. The thunder that followed rocked her towards the wall. She clung to the molding. It brought a shower of hail that ran the length of windows on the south side of the house. Another bolt of lightning cracked the center of the bay. She could hear the sound of the terra-cotta tiles sliding off the roof and falling into the circular expanse of the driveway at the front. Gutters began to sing out in mournful pitches at each end of the house. Alberto never moved. . . .

How do I know this? Ay ya hombre, how does anyone know anything? It was told to me.

It came to me over years of retellings, the kind of tellings of stories that maybe just now you're beginning to know something about.

At home, I have an office full, a house full of pictures, diaries, and letters, newspaper clippings. Pero, there are many, many questions that you have to ask yourselves, over and over. Like when on the page where the authors write that Guevara wrote—no need Ostrovski, I can find it, I know it—he writes of the pleasure it was to look out at his troops in the Sierra; very near to two hundred well-disciplined men armed with good weapons. He writes of the freedom to carry on conversations at night while resting in their hammocks; and permitted visits to the nearby villages where they established close ties with the peasants; and of the hearty welcome given by comrades.

I hear doña Liliana's indignant question, And where was I in all of this? as loudly and clearly as if she was standing next to me.

Miren. Vamos, señores, grab your books and your things. Vamos, vamos, there's little time before the bell rings and this random doubt begs for yet another field trip.

Where are we going? To the third-floor boys' room. Quiet in the halls, por favor, it's not that I mind what is said about me here anymore, not that it matters, but I am concerned that we don't disrupt others who may be working on much more critically important matters with much less concentration.

Come on, vamos, no need to complain, many of you were headed up here anyway. We'll all have a cigarette, I've only half a pack left, but I'm willing to share what I have with whoever wants one. Think of it as something that you'll be able to tell your friends, your parents—Had a smoke with Delossantos in the third-floor boys' room—and Father Rodríguez and the school board will take that and the fact that Brother Sessions will make it a point to casually mention how his typing class was disturbed by the noise and distraction of señor Delossantos' second-period class—all twenty-six of us since even though I saw them earlier this morning, señores Babcock and Suárez had decided not to grace us with their presence—thudding like a great herd of elephants, he'll say, if I know Sessions at all, as we pass through the hallway before the second-class period bell, and somehow I know that it will make everyone feel better, sleep better, more comfortably with the decision that they have made.

Pero, none of them will know what it is that you know until you tell them, it was Delossantos on another one of his crazy field trips. We are heading to see the latest artifact, or art-o-fiction, between the third and fourth urinals. I say art-o-fiction because there is no grounding fact, no firsthand knowledge to offer, is there señor Chávez? You'll collect flies, cállese la boca, señor. No need to be red-faced or deny it, I've spent four years with that tight, nearly indecipherable scrawl not to recognize it when I see it.

I'm not angry. And where I appreciate the accuracy of your translation earlier when I said, Estoy rodeada de reliquias de una vida que ya no existe, perhaps it's more accurate for me to say that I live in a world full of relics of a life that never existed. And because I don't want the same for you, I want you all to be there as art-o-fiction becomes artifact, as historia is transformed into history. We'll all have a cigarette together. Think of señor Chávez's inscription, Delossantos is a puto, as if you were an anthropologist regarding an ancient cuneiform, and watch it transform before your very eyes—even though I've never quite thought of myself that way—into truth. He said, you'll say.

Vámonos.

A RUSTLE SMALLER than a cat, larger than a mouse shot round the garden through the inkberry, the winterberry and the sweetshrub gave us all a start, sent Julio down the alley to see what it was, and caused Amá to tell him there was no need, she said it was Pirata.

Ay señora you are so lucky, Naty Valdez McIntosh said, either ignoring or unaware of the look las doñas passed, my muerto is either on vacation or not speaking to me anymore, or just not talking to me. And she proceeded to tell us about her date the night before: You know señora, she said looking in Amá's direction, the one that I told you about with the chocolate-colored Porsche. It seems after dinner there had been dancing, and a stroll along the lake; and there are times, she said, that a girl starts out an evening meaning to say no, wanting to say no, yet finds that sometime during the early morning hours, no isn't exactly what she's doing.

Doña Liliana raised the black golf umbrella she was holding over her head just enough for her carefully painted mouth to be revealed, when she asked, And you went to church this morning?

Naty attempted to feign shame behind her hand, pero the jingling of her bracelets betrayed her, and soon Amá, doña Cristina and even Naty's mother, señora Márquez—

who never went anywhere for fear of the shadow of shame her daughter cast, but insisted that she wouldn't miss one of Amá's birthdays for the world—began to giggle.

The rains that still come around noon, flummox and scatter us, had passed, set the sidewalks steaming. We were sitting in the side garden at the wrought iron table that I still riddle with pricks of embarrassment when I remember when the two cojoined swans whose heads and wings support the top were unloaded to open-mouthed sighs from the neighbors who gathered in the streets to watch; even señora Figueroa couldn't help crossing the street, and she sucked her teeth as she touched the details of the feathers. They've gone green with age since. And if Julio or I don't get over to cut the grass, in late summer they appear to grow out of, emerge from the lawn.

I have sixty-five años tomorrow, Amá had insisted the night before, even though doña Cristina had suggested that something just as nice could be thrown at my house, at her house, and doña Liliana—who never offers to pay for anything—suggested a restaurant; a nice little place, nena, where if you show them your ID on your birthday they bring you a cake with candles for free. I know what I want, Amá said as she left them in my living room to collect coffee cups and click their tongues.

After so many years of doing, we do without thinking. We expect Amá and doña Cristina to make the congri, yuca y malangas; this year there were empanadas con pollo y bisteca, pues, Amá insisted, she wanted everything to be like it always has, pero, nobody's going to go over there and sit. Sit? Sit where from three o'clock in the morning? she asked, but when we drove up, Román—red-faced and beer in hand—was standing over the barbeque pit, and the familiar smell of roast suckling pig that has meant holidays and cumpleaños since the first New Year's we spent in Amá's tiny little little casa blanca. Doña Cristina wiped down the table and chairs while Julio and I carried food from the car; Román handed us beers, limonadas to Amá y las doñas, and even had lime slices to shove into the cans of Diet Coke that he brought especially for Naty; he was the disc jockey of an unending stream of merengues y boleros that came out of the largest barrio blaster I'd ever seen; from her bejeweled gold bag, doña Liliana, with exaggerated ritual and the practiced dexterity of an aerialist making certain with her umbrella in one hand that not a single ray of sunlight touched her face, produced a thermos of coffee and two bakery boxes of pastelitos y dulce con leche, that we knew later—when we were all too full to move, languid and stupid as cows when they were offered round the table—Amá would merely scrunch her nose with a smile and say, No, gracias, too sweet.

The sun had moved lower in the sky when two men's voices sang, Fuera, en pos de mi amada que está tan lejos para hacer nuestro nido, allá en el cielo, through the garden in such close-knit harmony with a guitar that for a moment we all headed limp and damp with humidity into our own private spaces.

Julio's snoring, Naty's assessment of her bracelets, Román's openmouthed stare at nothing; even doña Cristina's nervous glances at what needed to be done, what needed to be cleaned up, put in order, set into place before we all went back to our respective homes and prepared for the week ahead cut between the voices. So that when they floated into a brash trumpet wail under Celia Cruz's calling, La negra tiene tumbao y no camina de lao, doña Liliana realizing that she hadn't slipped her limonada under the table for Román to pour a bit more—Solamente un poquito más, she said—from the paper bag that he kept in his back pocket, straightened the umbrella over her head and switched the focus to Naty.

Naty tell us more about your yanqui and his chocolate-covered Porsche, she asked.

Chocolate-colored, the girl giggled, not chocolate-covered.

No matter, doña Liliana said and smiled her sweetest smile; the smile she said should have been in magazines, the smile doña Cristina has always said no good can come from.

Señora Márquez went scarlet.

Liliana, Amá said as she moved doña Liliana's limonada toward the center of the table.

Porfa Naty, doña Liliana cajoled, we'd all like to hear about it.

Amá touched Naty's shoulder.

Unaware, Naty cheerfully said, No hay problema, no señora, is OK. And began, Well like I said, and she started by telling us what she had been wearing.

Black is always best, doña Liliana sneered from under her umbrella, smiling.

O I could not agree more, señora, Naty said, and she told us how nice he smelled—well-mannered and all—a dark blue suit, no rumples, nice tie, a shine on his shoes; he opened the door for her.

Was this the front door, doña Liliana asked, recovering her drink with the tips of her fingers, or the one to the chocolate Porsche?

Both I think, Naty said, and then looking off to the side she appeared to be taking a mental tally of each door that she went through that night, before confirming, Sí.

So he opened all your doors, doña Liliana said only allowing her mouth and nose to show, How nice for you.

O sí señora it was very nice; the nicest, Naty told us. You have never been on a date like that. The wine. The food. Ay and the dancing. It's a small club, ¿no?, and very dark.

Dark? doña Liliana now allowed her eyes to become visible for a moment before telling Naty that it was good that she was seen in her best light.

What do you mean by that? What does she mean by that? Naty asked around the table.

I mean nothing—she means nothing, doña Cristina echoed flatly—Really, nothing, doña Liliana repeated. Un poquito más, porfa, mijo, she pushed her limonada toward Román. I tell every woman who comes to my counter at El Marshall Field's with your crow's-feet and the beginnings of all kinds of sags that I may have nothing here for you, pero you can always choose how you are lit. Or is it lighted? she turned and asked Julio.

Liliana . . . be nice, doña Cristina said and covered her mouth when she had no idea for whom to be embarrassed.

Cristina, quizá en otra vida, cuando ambas seamos gatas, doña Liliana snapped, ¿Qué? A woman cannot give another woman—a girlfriend—a beauty tip and not be thought of as una perra?

Naty gathered herself up and said, Now that you mention it, and I didn't want to mention it, but the sun has gone down enough to expose yourself safely without having to be afraid of turning to dust.

Doña Liliana gave us the benefit of her full face and part of her turban as she hissed, How nice of you to want to not to, before covering up again.

Por favor, Liliana, what are you jealous? Amá admonished.

Which is when doña Liliana reminded all of us that she once danced the merengue at the Tropicana in a dress so thin, so red, so tight—tan sexy, she said they said, they said—you'd have thought you'd died and gone to heaven . . .

Gracias señora, I love it when you talk about olden times, Naty tried to interrupt, but doña Liliana continued only louder.

. . . and under the lights of the nightclub she'd arch her back and throw the waist-length hair that they would later argue was either the color of maíz o miel verano. Béseme, chica; Béseme; Besitos, besitos, she said they said they all begged, they all wolf-whistled, they all sucked their teeth, and fanned themselves with napkins as she passed their tables. They disagreed—there were arguments aplenty—as to what it was she wore that reminded them of jasmine; of vanilla; of orange peel; of bergamot.

And she may have gone on to tell us about the opportunity she turned down to go on safari, the night a diamond ring the size of a small latticino Julio and I fought over until one of us lost it was thrown in a suitor's face, or when she was envied because her feet were like a little girl's—like a china doll's—tiny, smooth, with little moons in each nail, unmarred by years of hours behind the cosmetics counter at Marshall Field's when Román knocked her limonada into his own lap as he shoved his hammy hand across the table toward Naty with the loud, beaming invitation, Báilame, chica.

Neither his wet sagging shorts nor the difference between the rum in him or that that remained in the bottle in his back pocket seemed to set Román off balance. Equal parts garbo y macho, he danced Naty who never stopped jingling or talking—Ay you are such a wonderful dancer, you; y your back and shoulders, muy fuerte—to the back garden and around the side, through the hedge of day lilies that have already overgrown the créche of La Virgen del Cobre despite the earliness of the season. Román's big hand in the small of her back caused her to throw her head back making her look regal, beautiful.

Chiflada. Puta, doña Liliana said under her breath, crumpling doña Márquez's face before she ran from the table.

Doña Cristina followed.

Cállate, Liliana, Amá said so quietly I looked up to make sure that I hadn't thought it.

¿Qué? Liliana asked.

And then I heard Amá say something that I had never heard her say before. She said, Dije cállate, Liliana, this is my house and I would like for you to be quiet. And with that, Amá took the umbrella from doña Liliana's hand and closed it.

Naty and her mother made sure that Román got home safely. Climbing to the second floor of my apartment, carrying the leftovers and the cooler, Julio and I were met by a wall of heat from the day that had risen up off of the ground and stilled itself there.

¡Dios! What happened to your air-conditioning? doña Liliana asked producing an ivory and black lace fan from her purse.

The overhead lights and the lamps came on with a flick of the switch; the refrigerator was still running; the answering machine was blinking with doña Cristina's message letting us know that she got home OK. But try as we might—Julio and I, with a flashlight and my toolbox in the sweaty confined space behind the furnace—we were unable to get the compressor to kick over.

When we returned upstairs, Amá had turned all of the lights off and opened all of the windows and the back door, doña Liliana had fallen asleep sitting up in a chair. Over the noises of traffic and a distant argument being had in Ukrainian, I could hear the shower running and Amá singing, Fuera, en pos de mi amada que está tan lejos para hacer nuestro nido, allá en el cielo . . .

I know that song, doña Liliana proclaimed cheerfully as she woke gathering herself, adjusting her turban.

Vamos, mamá, I'll take you home now, Julio said offering her his hand, bowing slightly at the waist. And she took it, alighting as though he had said they were headed for a barge on the Nile or Katmandu, somewhere there was a flurry of white waistcoats and stiffly pressed handkerchiefs, silver platters lined with paper doilies cut to look like the most intricately spun lace.

The chair where doña Liliana had been was saturated with her perfume. I sat waiting to hear Julio's car drive off, listening to the Ukrainian argument move from inside the building next door into the street, when the buzzer rang. Julio asked if I'd come down and meet him at the door, I left the car running, 'mano, he called into the intercom, and you know what Her Majesty is like when she's tanked.

When I got downstairs my portly pink and hairless neighbor, dressed only in an athletic T-shirt and white briefs, had put his car between himself and a very thin, beaky, though heavily made-up woman who was pounding her fist on the hood of his car as the woman shouted in English, You are a crazy, you are a crazy.

Doña Liliana had gotten out of Julio's car to watch at a safe distance and fan herself in what she has always said was the prettiest of ways which was to pop it open and set it aflutter, and although she has a great affection for lace fans—has a great many of them—even without one, particularly when she's drinking, she has never seen the need to abandon the gesture completely.

You forgot this, Julio said, handing me the white paper bag that earlier doña Cristina says that Amá left on the counter at the pharmacy and then left in her car after her last appointment with Doctor Canales. Vitaminas mostly, doña Cristina had told me, things that will bring blood and light to parts of her brain that are going dark. She didn't seem too bad today, Julio offered, maybe. Maybe, I repeated as the woman in the street began throwing her shoes at the man in his underwear. Doña Liliana called out, Olé, as each of the heavy platform sandals hit the pavement.

My mother has become small suddenly. How big she seemed when she still slapped the lies before they were completely formed from my mouth; how wise, I thought, when she ironed labels in T-shirts and undershorts for summer camp; and how kind, when I was the only one in my cabin to discover a different treat rolled into pairs of socks that she had labeled with the days of the week. She looked tiny to me, swallowed up by my white terry cloth bathrobe when I came upstairs to find her dancing in the hallway in the light that came through the windows on either side of the building.

It was a wordless song that I didn't recognize yet it seemed familiar, something that I had heard all of my life but have never known what it was. She looked like a little girl as she stopped and I watched as she began drying the back of her neck with a towel, when she suddenly discovered the moon and the stars reflected at her feet. She knelt as if to grab at them and we were both surprised to find that they broke apart in her hand, poured through her fingers and reappeared at her feet.

I pushed past her and rushed into the bathroom, turned off the shower, and released the plug from the tub.

Blinking and shocked by the sudden light, Amá demanded to know the meaning of this. ¡Espere, señor! ¡Contésteme! She fought me as I pulled all of the towels and the sheets from the linen closet and threw them onto the bathroom floor and lined them down the hallway.

¡Espere! ¡Contésteme! ¡Contésteme! she was yelling at the end of the hall as I mopped on my hands and knees. ¡Señor! ¡Señor! I demand to know what you are doing!

Amá, I said, it's me. It's Óscar.

She shot me the kind of look people give when you've said something in a language that is foreign to them that sounds so much like something they know. She said nothing; she looked around her as if searching for an escape. Amá, I asked, what day is it?

El domingo . . . el domingo . . . es mi cumpleaños, she said timidly, and then with a certain haughty indignation she held out the hem of my bathrobe and asked why else would she be allowed to wear her good dress.

And there on my hands and knees, yelling before I realized that I was yelling, I cried, What year Amá? I need for you to know what year.

When the floors were dried, I made my mother a cup of tea.

He was here last night, she said.

Weary, I answered, Who Amá, who? ¿Pirata? ¿Juan Ocho? Amá, I'm tired, I have to work in the morning, let's get some rest.

No, she said, tu silencio.

¿Mi silencio? I asked.

Sí, tu silencio, she answered as she turned my teacup on its side and allowed what little that was left to separate from the leaves that clung to the side.

¿Y quién es mi silencio, Amá? I exhaled, not looking at her. Not knowing all my life, señores, that same way that you all already know that a child, no matter how old he gets, knows what his parents need him to be—intrinsically, instinctively—but not knowing what to call it until just then.

O that's the one, she said, that you pray silently to yourself—Dios, por favor, ayúdame—when you find yourself alone at a restaurant or in a darkened movie theater—Quítame este dolor, por favor—when you find yourself having to make a decision to take a vacation by yourself—Llena mi soledá con tu amor—each night when you arrange the extra pillows lengthwise against you. She wiped my cup clean with her index finger before washing it in the sink.

I was still sitting at the table when she turned the light out on me—Por favor, Dios, ayúdame, por favor—she said she had never heard it before, tu silencio.

Es Pirata y mañana, hoy tenemos ternera, she said before heading to her room for the night. Buena noches, she called back into the dark.

. . . BELIEVE IT OR NOT, at one time you could ask Father McMillan—the one you call Old Boy behind his back—any question that you could think of that involved time or space. He could add, multiply, subtract, and divide up to six decimal places in his head. They say they said, that during his prime, years before even I was a student here, your scalp would crawl with uneasiness if you caught him through the window in his morning ritual as he stood at the board—long and angular underneath his black cassock—writing the day's problems with his left hand as he wrote out the night's assignment with his right.

The exams he gave were taunt knots of two planes traveling at the same rate—one from Moscow the other from Berlin; two buses—one leaving Istanbul at 0415 hours, another departing Bangladesh twenty minutes later—a rocket fired from the school courtyard gains velocity of . . . as it soars in trajectory to an apex of . . . spirals out at a radius he was able to catch in seamless projections of calculable reason. So it only seemed logical after Joaquín-Ernesto went through the ice that winter that we all turned to Father McMillan to explain the milagros that followed.

Easter came that March on the coldest day on record. Slush—made soft and runny by rock salt and passing cars—

pooled at the corners of main streets and lapped up the sides of solidly entrenched snowbanks on the sidewalks. More than one brand-new pastel dress and matching coat was ruined by drivers so insensitive to what day it was that it was decided they had to have been heathens or Satanists or puertorriqueños. Shoes that had been polished to gleam proudly were riddled white with striations of salt.

We stood in the fragrance of incense and candle wax. Few of the lilies were real, most were silk or plastic; the cold weather had destroyed them the instant they were taken from hot storage. We gave thanks for the benevolence that had been bestowed upon us, and the everlasting light that had been shed over us. Father McMillan asked us to remember those who were no longer among us, and as the list of those who were sick, dying, dead or lost was read, those of us who allowed sideways glances saw that Joaquín-Ernesto's father was sweating with his head tilted back and his eyes closed like the sun was real and hot and bright and directly overhead.

He was not at the social hour after mass, though the crimson tongues of las chismosas whispered as they laid out their plates of food: Didn't he look haggard; poor, poor, pobrecito; did you see his face, so unshaven; his hair such a mess; his hands, so dirty; he smelled. Someone saw—as he was leaving the church—that he took his tie off over his head and let the wind take it; he unbuttoned his shirt and walked out into all of that snow; and wind; Ay no in that wind, Dios mío, she sighed.

It was shortly after that what people would claim as los milagros of that winter began to happen.

Father McMillan was first called when a young woman who had been racked with an arthritic pain that people said was cruel and far too ancient for her years, slipped and fell right in front of the beauty shop when it was still Marta's. She was helped to her feet and her groceries were collected, to find that her hip moved freely; like warm oil, she told Amá. Though by the time the woman's doctor told her that he had heard of isolated cases just like hers, the rumor had spread that the image of La Virgen de la Caridad del Cobre could be seen in the frost of the beauty shop window. Later las tías of the restored woman came in to beg Marta to turn the heat off in the shop. The two of them stood arm in arm, wrapped in matching black crocheted shawls. They just stood there looking at Marta like crows on a wire and only separated when one or the other went to relight the oración de Santa Bárbara that they had placed in the snowdrift where their niece had been cured. Marta could put up with them for half an hour or so before announcing that she refused to allow them to hold their vigil outside of the shop and insisted that they come in off the street. But the women continued their vigil, suggesting that Marta might could use a little prayer herself.

Rubbing the cold off her shoulders, she told Amá las vírgenes viejas had always given her the creeps; even when she was a little girl. Amá said it was best to just ignore them. Though finally, afraid that the two women would die in front of the shop, Amá sent me to get Father McMillan.

And even after he had spent an hour with the two viejas over tea at the manicure station, hearing of their widowhood and their devotion, Father McMillan's comfort and assessment of the shopwindow, once they were all gone, Marta, Amá and I stood in the street peering curiously neither admitting nor denying what we did or didn't see.

The next morning's snow turned to sleet and then into hail that nipped and raked at any parts of our faces that we dared leave exposed. At school, we stared out the windows in resignation at where the playground should have been. Our landlady said she was washing dishes as the sleet began spitting a pattern, a message, against her window.

She wasn't sure at first what it was telling her as she

watched the woman in the building across the alley making breakfast for her husband and children, when all of a sudden she knew—just as if someone had come and whispered it in her ear—she knew where her husband had been going every morning for the past year. Without thinking, she pulled the red silk quilt off their bed and went out. By the time she got a cab, the hail had turned into an icy rain that soaked the color from the blanket causing it to run in bright orange lines down her legs. The rain turned to hail again so hard that the driver had to stop and pull to the side. They sat there for more than fifteen minutes while the driver smoked and the heavy blanket melted into her. Her arms; her hands; in the rearview mirror she could see a woman—wild hair, wild eyes—who had streaked her own face orange from forehead to cheeks with the clawing of her fingers. The cab was battered like a tiny tin box, until the sky cracked in a bolt of lightning and an icy flap of rain. Our landlady said she had just moved to wipe the fog from the window when she saw that they had stopped right in front of the puta's house and her husband ran out the door holding a newspaper over his head toward his truck.

And for days, she said she told Father McMillan in the confessional, the image of him leaving that woman's house turned and turned at the center of her belly. Why then—after all these years, at the age of forty-two—did that morning she realize for the first time that she was pregnant? He had to answer.

Everything went glossy and slick with ice as over the next three days two boy babies were born at the exact same moment; each was named Joaquín-Ernesto and respectively called Jugey and Ernie. A woman from Camagüey who was thought to be well over one hundred finished her ironing and lay down for an uncharacteristic nap in the middle of the day from which she never woke up. At church the following Sunday, we were asked to pray for the babies and the woman from Camagüey whose hand-knotted lace ran the length of the altar, and of course, for Joaquín-Ernesto's family.

After mass, a man believed he was introducing Amá to his wife for the first time as la negrita who made flan con guayaba like home, though she, the wife, and Amá already knew each other from Marta's shop. The woman pushed past her husband and said Mira as she removed the scarf from around her neck and began to tell of the goiter—her embarrassment, her shame for so many years—that she turned while waking to find on the pillow beside her. Just the night before she was coming home later than usual and she had seen Joaquín-Ernesto's father dancing in his underpants in his backyard. Her husband added that Joaquín-Ernesto's father never goes to his garage anymore; his brothers are running the business completely by themselves. His wife interrupted to add that he was dancing there—there in the middle of the yard—with both his arms outstretched in the rain and the snow. She said the sight caused a chill to run through her so deep that she wasn't sure if she had really seen what she had seen, all she could do was get home and get under the covers. Y mira, she said displaying her neck proudly. And they all ran to Father McMillan, looking for proof, searching for an answer. Could it be? But wasn't it possible? Didn't God sometimes? they asked and asked.

Our milagro—Amá's and mine—began the following Monday when a delivery truck skidded down our street, nearly missing us on the corner. It slid its way to a halt at the far end of the block, dropping two cases of mangoes: Paraíso, from a much warmer place, Amá sighed letting her scarf drop to her shoulders. The crates broke open and the fruit thudded and rolled and spread in a rose and orange and yellow and green carpet on top of the gray slush in front of us. Without thinking, Amá bent quickly and handed three to me; she put one in each of her coat pockets and slid two into the sleeves of her coat before the driver could get out. We glided on the ice around the block to the back of our building and ran as fast as we could up the stairs. Amá and I fell onto the couch laughing breathlessly. She pressed one of the mangoes to her nose and then held it to mine. With another I imitated her and rubbed it against my cheek and neck. She dug her thumbs into the skin of one of them and put her lips against it and then handed it to me. Flamboyants, Amá sighed, acres and acres of them with the bright red and orange flowers grow along the edges of Santiago. She was in the middle of telling me that you could be in the middle of the grime of the city and all you had to do was start running toward their fragrance when all of the lights in our apartment went out and the refrigerator stopped humming.

An object set into motion by human force, given the gravitation pull of the earth in rotation, can remain in motion, skate air currents, for how long, what was possible, and what was milagro and what was physics? I wanted to ask Father McMillan. Could, por ejemplo, Ana Lucía García Carrera née Pérez from the lovely Dade County home where she had resided for over thirty years on an evening when a hurricane made its way from La Habana across the Straits of Florida, let an object free and have it remain in space, propel it with such force that nearly twenty years later I would catch and covet it so many miles away?

The story goes, she walked through the rest of the downstairs, Ana, turning on every light switch she passed. She pulled the chains on the delicate porcelain lamps so sharply that they either fell to the floor or broke in half from their bases. One fist malleted against the other freed the latches on the doors in the living and dining rooms causing one of them to swing out against an espalier of wisteria, smashing the frame and panes of glass onto the south patio.

The copper-bottom pots that lined the kitchen ceiling clanged loudly against each other as she forced open the windows above the sink and in the breakfast room.

Ana banged with her fist against the door to the maid's room until the heavy charm bracelet burst from her wrist into hundreds of poorly recalled fragments. The room was empty. Graciela was no doubt still at her sister's in La Habana Pequeña; Ana imagined the two of them and the sister's three children huddled in the girl's one-bedroom apartment. Fearful and superstitious of spirits they had brought over with them from Cuba, Ana knew they would all now be sitting in the dark with their feet off the floor to avoid being struck by lightning. When Ana lifted the latch into the windows to the maid's bathroom the green dress the girl had hung to dry on the shower rod took to the air and went out to dance with the palm fronds that nearly touched the ground.

She took the back service staircase two steps at a time, leaving a shoe on the first and fifth steps. A small light illuminated her face and shoulders as she stood at the three-sided mirror on her half of their bedroom.

The pink silk dress slipped to her ankles. As she reached around to turn the hooks of her girdle, she suddenly caught the reflection in profile of that strange woman. Ana unpinned the woman in the mirror's hair and it fell in dark coils around her shoulders and down her back; a white ring glowed at the crown of her head; none of those expensive Miami hairdressers understood the shiny raven of her youth; complete otherness, that chin that flowed generously toward deep cleavage. She could feel her hips round out well past her pelvis, and the line of her belly as she tried to lift it, force it above the waistband of her underpants.

For weeks, for months, for years she could go without encountering this strange fat woman. Sometimes ridding herself of her was as easy as pushing back waking from a dream. Though other times, on the turn of a moment, comparing fabric and thread or trying on a dress in a department store at one of the shops in Miami, she would find that for a long time she had been caught in a memory that was slim-hipped, rapacious and indifferent, that bobbed upward so the grace of her pronounced clavicle could be seen through its dress, and she would find that she had sunk her thumbs into the mango she was testing in the grocery. Or a song on the car radio would bore its way so deeply into her ear it would leave Aureliano stranded at a friend's or Pilar waiting while the other girls went home from their ballet lessons just at the moment Ana found herself—fully dressed—wading up to her hips, arms outstretched away from the Bay of Biscayne.

Of his mother Ana Lucía García Carrera née Pérez, Aureliano Francisco García Carrera often said she set things flying; she could pass through you in a hall, hollow tiny burrows and throw up castles in the sand next to you; forever throwing open windows; you never knew, he said.

Father Rodríguez was holding Aureliano's eighth-grade picture in between his thumb and forefinger as if it were a featherless dead bird. When I came into his office I could see Father McMillan, but seated across the wide polished mahogany, he was fused in the sunlight from the window behind him.

Who is this? Father Rodríguez asked as he paced the length of the room, Who is this boy that you've written to, this, this, this boy that you say in this letter that he is the wind, the shore, the sea?

Not to the boy precisely Father, I said, but to the boy that was once the man . . .

The man who once was the boy, he interrupted.

The boy who was a man, who . . . I said, but I didn't have an answer.

Never having put words to something and not knowing

what it is are two very different things, caballeros. So many of you have had this experience and have yet to realize that it has come and gone. ¿Chávez? ¿Babcock? ¿Señores Torres, Cartagena? You've been called into Father Rodríguez's office, sat in that same chair and found that questions like why have you been late or absent without an excuse for more days than school policy allows, or why were you drinking vodka from a thermos with your friends when you were caught one night underneath the bleachers on the back green, don't bring about answers more than they open a bead of sweat in an armpit that, despite your shirt and undershirt, will rush to splash against the cinch of your belt. It's difficult connecting why you dodged class that afternoon with the jagged thrill that tore through your legs as you were chasing through El cars all afternoon, slipping past passengers and train security; why you spray-painted the word fuck into the asphalt of the parking lot means less than the anger that was discharged out of you, seared like a torch out of the top of your head, your ears, your mouth, though it's not the same thing as saying something, calling it something. In fact, it—that thing that makes your tongue go fat—is the same thing as having nothing to say at all, because once articulated, it can be repeated over and over until like the wrapper on the condom that you keep in your wallets the promise, the hope and excitement it holds is slowly creased away.

. . . Escúchame Perfecto, mi cielo, mi iluminador, mi playa, mi sentido común, yuca mío, I forget all the names I've had for you, Shiny Distant Shore, Father Rodríguez read. To a boy you wrote, he accused, a boy.

He paced the room denting a waffle tread in the carpet, creaking the floorboards underneath him. Señor Delossantos, need I remind you we are in the business of boys? he said holding the picture in front of me. Who, who, who is this,

this boy? he asked. He had me look at the letter, verify it was my handwriting before snatching it back.

Aureliano Francisco García Carrera, I heard myself saying, though by the time Father Rodríguez repeated it, it had become something else, something foreign, language that had neither cadence nor currency for me. He crumpled and pressed the letter into his temple as he tried to remember a boy by that name who attended school here. And before years of boys, streams of boys, naked, showering after soccer practice, seeing me privately after school in the small office that I share, accepting rides home from me when it had gotten too late, before boys placed under my care could be imagined unsafe and compromised in front of me, I told him, No, never, never.

Well we can all thank God for small favors, he was nearly yelling when Father McMillan stopped him by clearing his throat.

The two priests stared at each other. And although I could not see all of Father McMillan's face, there caught up in the light of the milky blue of his one cataract-coated eye was the answer to how long—calculating both time and distance—after Ana Lucía García Carrera née Pérez opened the window to her only son's bedroom during a hurricane in which they say they said she was seen standing completely clothed, up to her waist in the Bay of Biscayne, and they say they said she was whipped by lightning and wind as she fought to keep her arms stretched; subtract the number of years, and the ratio of resistance created by the wind that kited Aureliano's eighth-grade picture multiplied by the distance between Florida and Chicago, factoring in many, many long winters, its misplacement in a book or a photo album before it's coupled with a letter written on a September afternoon so long ago that all that's left of it is an ache before it ends up in the hands of a parent who demanded Father

Rodríguez to tell her what the hell is going on, what was the school going to do about this?

If you had only told us what you were, Father Rodríguez started.

And I interrupted, What am I? What am I? I asked.

Yet before he could answer, I told him, I am a history teacher and someone whom you've known most of his life.

Pero that's the funny thing about time and saying something, señores, because the exact moment I said it was the same moment that it began to be untrue.

So I sat there with Fathers Rodríguez and McMillan in front of me like a calculus final for which I neither had a final answer nor the ability to show my work.

AURELIANO.

Señores, what can I tell you? If time and propriety allowed, I could say that he was the kind of man who spent hours picking out a tie at the haberdashery counter, would spend a fortune on a pair of shoes that he'd wear daily without polishing or caring for until they fell apart on his feet. He'd spend hours at a tailor's having a suit altered—questioning measurements, the drape of the garment—yet not own a pair of undershorts or socks that didn't have holes in them.

It was there at the edge of Alberto García Carrera's property that Aureliano says his mother, Ana, says she had first seen her: the woman who she was and wasn't at the same time. Alberto García Carrera had placed her there with tea and brown toast the morning after she had been spirited over the Straits of Florida.

The linen, china and silver were the best, his housekeeper courteous. Her hands were shaking under the warm Miami sun. She was wearing the same strapless, sea blue dress she had been wearing the night before. Just hours ago, she had stood at her dressing table in El Vedado choosing the necklace and earrings that she hid in a pocket of her purse on the plane. She had been at a coming-out party at the Hilton Habana for a cousin she barely knew. Festoons of lilies and rushes poured out of towering crystal vases on each of the tables. The dance floor had bobbed with corps of white dinner jackets. She and a group of her friends had sequestered themselves in the ladies' room to decide where they would go afterward. Instead of the one who took all of his clothes off every time he got drunk, or the one who would show off with great displays of ennui and quote Rimbaud, it was her father's driver that met her outside of the ladies' room. He had bruised her arm getting her to the car. And it was at that moment that she felt her slip out of her, suddenly and as easily as getting sick, La Flaca was outside of her. An hour later, Alberto García Carrera's toothy grin met her on the airfield at Miami International. When she asked who he was and what she was doing there, he replied that she was safe.

For months, Ana watched her there as sheaves of blue linen stationery piled on the ground around her. Until they were to her knees, then her shoulders, until they rolled down the slop of the ravine, to the dock and into the bay. Her father's only reply to why she was where she was was to send his spirit to wake her bolt upright in bed with the clipping of his heels against the wooden floors or the smell of his aftershave. Alberto García Carrera would roll over in his sleep and rub her back, assuring in her ear that she was safe.

Ana would watch her evenings as she sat there with a transistor tuned to the radio novelas that came out of downtown Habana until the signal faded to static. There, so many nights she would be caught lifting a firefly to her lips by the time of the sound of Eddy Chibás' cry of Last Call and the thirty-five-caliber bullet as it rebounded and rebounded against the drum of his stomach, obliterating the lap of the waves against the dock and the fugitive radio signal. It was there, at the little table made to look as though it had come up from the earth, that she heard El presidente Carlos Prío

Socarrás had fled Habana. Ana had watched her walk barefoot back into the house and go to the cabinet where Alberto García Carrera kept his cache of rum cubano. After hours of listening to the same side of a Celia Cruz record and half a bottle, she ascended the stairs and allowed Pilar to be conceived.

The girl was scarcely out of diapers—just old enough to ask for her mamá's breast—when Ana noticed her hips spread over the sides of narrow wrought iron chairs. After Pilar had been fed, sung to and put to sleep, she dressed for dinner and found that she could not close the back of her dress. She suddenly realized Alberto García Carrera's hand no longer slithered through the sheets at night; he no longer caught her in the hallways of his enormous house and pressed up against her, or forced her hand in his lap the second the maid had left the room.

Page after page of her blue linen stationery flew off her writing pad, caught in the trees and sailed the air around her. They were no longer addressed to her father, but to an oleander en route to Santiago, a mango slice dipped in lime on a blue plate, her tía's singing. A mi yuca; a mi playa; a mi corazón; a mi sentido común, they were addressed. Each night she listened to her radio novelas, though now she no longer looked for fireflies to swallow; she was not interested if Doctor Ramírez would ever tell his wife that she only had six months to live. Instead, she waited for, welcomed the sound of the thirty-five-caliber bullet going into Eddy Chibás' belly. Now she always waited for it. She needed to hear it before she could sleep.

She told Aureliano that the last Ana had seen of her, her there—the woman outside of herself who she was but wasn't—Pilar had been offering her a Cheerio to kiss off the end of her finger when the news of the losses at Playa Girón came over the transistor. She had picnicked not far from there. She knew the area well, the slope that the announcer was describing. The shoreline that was so gentle for night swimming. The woman put her pen down, gathered the child in her arms and waded—waist deep—through the sheets of stationery back to the house. She cleaned the girl up, then showered and perfumed herself liberally. She took extra care in making her face up, and went downstairs to supervise the preparation of Alberto García Carrera's dinner. When he arrived home she took his briefcase and jacket. A drink was waiting for him by his favorite chair. She had taken off his shoes and rubbed his feet, while he ranted, Who the hell, just who the hell does this Fidel Castro think he is! A look of concern had come over his face; he had apologized immediately for raising his voice. He had stroked her hair and told her that she had nothing to worry about; she was safe.

After dinner he was far too drunk to negotiate the stairs by himself. She had given him her shoulder and used a soothing, cooing voice to guide him to their room. She had shut the door and unbuckled his pants. He had been as obedient as Pilar stepping out of them. She had taken down his shorts and pushed him backward onto the bed. She began by kissing the inside of his thighs until she had made her way up to his belly. As she straddled him, she had unpinned her hair and allowed it to fall over his face. She had slammed her pelvis hard against his. He had let out a groan, and she had raised herself off of him slightly and slammed herself into him again and again. He had then pushed her hair back away from his face. He had looked up at her and smiled as she made him, forced him to give her Aureliano.

Anoche, as I watched the weather report, Amá passed in front of the screen as she placed a glass of wine on top of the television to prevent evil from flying out of it and coming into the house. Repairs on the furnace can't be made until this coming weekend—since this sudden heat spell, a guy over the phone told me he's been up to his ass in customers, if you can imagine—which opens the apartment to the smells and sounds of the street. In the kitchen Amá rattled the pots, and ran water in the sink as she was getting dinner ready. Y señores, Aureliano Francisco García Carrera. Twelve years dead; thirteen this coming September. History by all logical standards, señores.

Though lists of what everyone says will one day fall away—on an evening when there is just enough warm, wet rufous light as the day slips out—cling in midair. The house may let out a groan that sounds so much like a barefoot hundred and eighty-eight pounds on the loose floorboard outside the bathroom; the deafening boom of a passing car radio can be as familiar and annoying as scraps of an old bolero whistled every morning between taps of a razor against the sink. Verbena rising out of a cake of soap is the same, can cause the world to spin backwards on its axis, as easily as the sweat-soured smell of the insoles of a pair of shoes in the back of a closet that you long thought that you had packed off for charity. Tubs of cottage cheese mellow and ripen green, initially threaten explosion, but eventually turn a benign gray as they devour themselves. However if things have been lavished with just that much neglect, a crystalline fur will have sloped the freezer over months of prepared meals that will go uneaten; their smell, stilled and faintly animal; they bruise the tip of the tongue and burn the insides of your thighs like razor stubble. And then it's gone, it just melts away.

Glee in the form of tiny squeals and a round of applause floated up from the street. Román was surrounded by a group of little girls in their swimsuits who had abandoned the wading pool and sprinkler someone had set on the front lawn to watch him balance a broom by the tip of its handle on the end of his chin. The girls shrieked as he duckwalked with it through the sprinklers. They called out and pointed at the wet spot on his pants. He tripped on the hose and pitched forward losing the broom and his balance, falling flat on his face to their delight.

Strange that. Seeing something that's there at all only because you want it to be.

The girls marvel as Román took an orange from his pocket, a softball and the ball the girls had been using for jacks—it's the bright pink I've also seen them use for a game I believe they've made up—and juggle them. Three, four, five circuits before falling backwards into the wading pool. They cheered and howled as though they were at the circus. Not a clown, but a dancing bear, an awakened life-size stuffed animal come to play. There could just as easily have been cotton candy, a sideshow.

Deplieguen las banderas. So simple, imagínenselo.

There are nights when he creeps up the back porch, Román, stumbling over the table and chairs, knocking over flowerpots and I am awakened by something as deeply imprinted as the marks left by the nosepiece of a pair of glasses; markers of spending time, time spent, there was a time long ago and far away.

Aureliano Francisco García Carrera. Aureliano. Llaño. Aure. Chico. Yaño. Reyo. Querido. Yuca mío, I forget all the names I have had for him. Shiny Distant Shore. Too far away, a fever-dream of loss, something else—I can't remember the words—and then more loss.

You seem to be someone with vision, he would say when he was trying to persuade someone of something, which he'd reinforce with a smile. And he had a way of curling the corners of his mouth that made you think that he was thinking the same thing that you were thinking at the very same time. Sometimes he wore too much cologne and got too loud when he drank. At a party he could make anyone think that he was charming and attractive despite the fierce sprouts of hair that came out of each of his ears. In the summer he would pit a dress shirt within five minutes of putting it on. His feet smelled, and he frequently left the half-and-half on top of the refrigerator for the entire day after getting his morning coffee. If he wanted a drink of water, he'd pull the first thing that came to him from the sink, even if it was a pan or a bowl and fill it. When driving, he rubbed the knuckle of his right thumb with his index finger; one of those drivers who looks at his passenger when he talks, he'd inadvertently cut other cars off without knowing it; there were always sudden swerves, screeching brakes, curses hurled in every direction. However once you get used to living life with your heart in your throat you get used to it.

He neither owned a comb nor a brush.

The little girls ran and peeked from behind the trunks of trees as Román rose like the Creature from the Black Lagoon from the wading pool, arms outstretched, hands grabbing the air in front of him. And the little girls pretended to scream for their lives—O no, they yelled; he's coming, they warned—yet none of them called out for a parent or an older brother or a tío having a beer on a nearby porch, none of them ran into the house. And their calls for help, for salvation, for aid, for escape were as light and unexpected as cottonwood flock. Cottonwood flock—if you can imagine so early in the year; so soon, too soon—cottonwood flock like snow, hot as it is, while the monster lumbered and the little girls bunched together like a cluster only to scatter as he got closer to them.

As I was backing away from the window, I stepped on a guayaba. The juice and the seeds and the flesh of the fruit sprayed across the floor and against the wall and soaked my sock. Two more rolled past her without her notice as Amá went to the window to call Román in for dinner.

I suppose I have always been skeptical when people have said, then things just happened or time just passed. But they have and they do.

I'm not sure where we were for dinner. In what country, at what time, as language shifted between English and Spanish and ran courses between centuries and us, across oceans and continents, hardly seemed answerable.

Amá said nothing of Román's wet clothes, or of the many times that he went to the kitchen to refill his coffee cup, or that he eventually forgot to leave the bottle of rum on the counter when he finally ended up setting it down on the kitchen table next to him. She cut the largest slice of flan for the fourth place that she set at the head of the table, and said nothing about the tablecloth or the finish underneath it when Román filled its water glass with rum to overflow. She even allowed him to pour a little for her.

The light shifted to just the flicker of la veladora for las siete potencias africanas at the empty place setting so that I was barely able to make out the faces around me. And although we talked about the weather, doña Cristina's need for a new engine, Román's new position at his office, around us a baby cried out, a baby stretched, calling out calling, calling, calling, running towards us, dodging past us, under the tablecloth between our legs. Had I been asked had I heard the baby, seen the shadow of the gigantic banyón as it crawled up from the baseboard, unfurled and crept up the blank wall behind us—already cragged and ancient—its leaves grown into a floating carpet in the air above the trunk, had they said, they say they say, as clear as the haruspex's cast, in the garden of the exile, the past can be a blanket, a comfort—listen to the lady's hand door knocker as she is tapping, tapping, tapping out a fiesta on her tambourine—I would have told them, No, never when I've called, Aureliano Francisco García Carrera. And there's been many a night.

Walled in by, stuck in this rigid circumambulance of historia, mis señores, the want to live through again a moment at the top of the Hancock Building when suddenly I was holding an envelope containing the individual letters—letters from a Scrabble game—of each of our names, or to watch him, Aureliano Francisco García Carrera, pull the bass nearly twice the size of one of my shoes out from the water near Prince Edward Island again and again stops me; doesn't come as easily for me as when la mujer—in a yellow dress so thin the black lace full slip she wore underneath it is the garment she wore—comes to dance herself out of her red sandals for Román, tell him she is his, bloody his earlobe with her teeth.

Where are you from? was the first thing that he ever said to me the day we met on a softball diamond in Humboldt Park. Where are you from? he said to me, Aureliano Francisco García Carrera. Strange question that. Though we ask it of each other, señores, we all ask it when we are in close proximity of each other's Spanish. After introductions are made—what do you do, how do you like it have been asked—Where are you from, we say, to ask, Tu familia, what river or rivers did they cross—¿mares?—what hardship did you inherit, what or who got left behind? It's a question you know you know can't be answered with something like Milwaukee and Damen. He wanted to know why mine sounded so much like his, like his father's, like his tío Arturo who took him to the cockfights on an Easter Sunday to his mother's horror and bought him a prostitute for his fifteenth birthday, that even though his father and all his other tíos knew about, slapped him on the back of the head and neck as he came back through the parlor of the house they had taken him to, it wasn't until twelve years later that the secret that nothing happened—they sat across the bed from each other, he and the prostitute, talking about where they would each go to college one day—was shouted out while we were caught, he and I, in a rainstorm under a viaduct near the Everglades.

Later, I found out that there was something about the quickness of my speech, the way that I said something on that day in Humboldt Park, he felt that he had to ask where are you from.

No me jodas, he said.

No mames, I said.

¿No mames? He laughed.

No mames, I said.

And he smiled.

Through the sweat and grit that came off of him—his team had lost that day in Humboldt Park—was the smell of spearmint chewing gum and verbena. I had no idea what it was before; it went into the water that he washed his sheets and underwear in; at the laundry around the corner, they rinsed the shirts he wore to the office in a solution that combined it with lavender; it was in the soap and shampoo that he used.

Sí, he owned a shaving mug and brush, strap and razor; said his barber taught him how after he bet the Tigers would edge out the Sox by the bottom of the seventh, and so by the time I met him he knew, had been doing it for a number of years, said he could show me too, but he never did, never got around to it.

And I never asked.

It seemed enough to know someone who did know.

Since Amá has come to live with me, there's no telling how many times she'll wake in the middle of the night to chase my tía María-María out into the ocean. Two little girls at play, mi abuela would call out to them, get in here you two, you'll end up so black, you'll need to smile so I can find you when I come to kiss you good night; you'll look like flies stuck in un dulce de leche in your yellow Sunday dresses. Or there are nights when her lace spools will clatter back memory of a shawl—forty meters long it was—Abuelita, Amá and my tías conjured to look like a peacock's tail in repose, something that rarely seems to happen during the day anymore. Instead the spools sometimes surprise her—What are they? Where did they come from? she asks—as she looks at them with the same sharp inhale of dismay and revulsion that I imagine someone would have at the sudden discovery of a litter of dead newborn kittens abandoned by the family pet, lifeless and flat among the motes of dust between the couch and the wall.

Though anoche, Román's snoring—known to the neighbors on either side of Amá's little casa blanca off of Ashland Avenue as la bomba since we were in high school—penetrated the walls. A drone that living this way now—with Amá's sleepless hauntings of the room where he, seer of invisible cities, madness broker, wanderer of places unseen, the youngest person in the state to pass the architecture boards at the time, señores, Aureliano Francisco García Carrera, kept his easel, so when I asked, cupolas, columns: Ionic and Doric, an Egyptian flotilla of abundances, likenesses from shadows, the past would be smudged in through a series of pencil scratches—La Playa Rosario, where the sand gives off wavery blisters of heat that stills the swells of green water in the distance, undulates in between that thin membrane between want and remembering.

Nights he's here, Román's snoring seems to press against something in Amá, push down that thing that sends her wandering into the night in search of the shovel, sand pail, trowel and sieve that she and María-María let be taken away by the tide or eaten by sea monsters, or as she has said many said, absconded by mi abuelo returning from the sea to reclaim his daughters; bit by bit you could feel him claw after you, she said they told her, a pail, a picnic basket, the sun umbrella that my abuelita had retrieved and patched from the garbage of one of the houses where she worked, until he had carried off all of the hijas dressed in their Sunday best. Best not to go in too far, she says they said; Best to stay close to the shore, she'll sometimes call out in all that I know of my abuela's voice.

But the rhythmic caw Román sends out when he is asleep on the couch, so reminiscent of waves against the shoreline, like two positive ends of a magnet, they seem to fix each other, Amá and he, in dreams that are both different and the same, and for the few hours that the house is quiet, and there always is the most beautiful mujer that you've ever seen in your life—black black hair tumbling down her shoulders, falling down to her waist as she unpins it, allows her dress to slide down to her feet as she tests the water with her toe—during a few stolen minutes, rapid-eye-movement minutes, señores, at La Playa Rosario.

Y entonces, I envy them this sleep, señores, you have no idea what it would be like to fall into those same kinds of feeble, unquestioning moments of then. In the mornings that follow them, Román wakes without shaking to the smell of Amá's frituras; Amá talks about reopening the shop, talks about calling to get estimates on the repairs that need to be made to her house, she packs us both a lunch; and Román agrees not to work too hard, to eat the extra orange she has packed for him, to check and see if he has enough change for the bus. No, never mind, she says, Óscar will take you, there's time, like nothing else there's time, she says.

I—like all the Ostrovskis, I suppose—am moored by dates.

Sleep rarely comes easily.

There is an exact time, on a specific day, caught in a certain longitude and latitude of place where he stopped breathing, Aureliano Francisco García Carrera. I have a copy of the notice I placed in the paper; the entire page, in fact; the day, the time, the week and all los otros he met on the way.

2:23 p.m. I remember looking at my watch—even then thinking it a strange gesture, a disrespectful act; quickly, I glanced around me at the sister that I met for the first time that day—so much like the pictures of Ana, his mother, that I had seen—her babies and her husband to make sure that they had not noticed me looking, checking the time as if I had somewhere to get to another appointment ahead, a plane that would take me away, away, away—as his body was lowered into the ground.

There was a time of day, no matter where he was or what he was doing, that he took a nap. Five minutes. He could have been in a meeting, his eyes could have been wide open, but he was long gone. Gone to nowhere, just a nap. If I said when, if any of his friends asked, there would be those who would remember him asking them to repeat what they had just said, seen his eyes glaze over as if in deep thought, watched him nod or pull his collar and tie away from his neck and wonder. And even now—telling—seems as if something private, something that was his, might be given away.

Aureliano.

Llaño.

Aure.

Chico.

Yaño.

Reyo.

Querido.

Aureliano Francisco García Carrera, I sometimes say at night when sleep doesn't come immediately. A chant, really.

I know, señores, it's hard to imagine. The same Delossantos who yelled, Confront your fears, señores! as we traversed rapids on retreat with Father Rodríguez on the Colorado—Open the mouth of your nightmares, reach in and grab what's yours! anytime any one of you has come to me with the words I can't—well there are nights that that same Delossantos sleeps with the lights on.

For years.

Verdad.

The light and sometimes the radio.

Talk radio: words like people in the room there with you, ¿no?

Por ejemplo, anoche a young woman—a girl about your age; could be someone you know—called a radio doctor to ask what she should do. Her boyfriend's family does not approve of her; will never approve of her, she says, but will not say why no matter how many times the doctor asks. But later, without her saying, she reveals that the boyfriend is educated and the woman barely finished ninth or tenth grade, and she is of a different race than he. They live several miles apart—it might as well be another country, you know, she tells the therapist, could be Africa or something—and he has a history of cheating on her when their geography and the undependable clutch on his car, an old Vega she said, keeps them apart for more than a week.

The therapist's voice is low, very low and mellifluous. They must add bass to it. They do that on the radio, you know. There seems to be a theory that the lower the voice is, the more secure, the more masculine, the more confidence it instills, suggestions made are salubrious. Soothing, as he suggests she go out and buy a home pregnancy test; concerned when he asks her age, and agrees with her that she does sound very mature for her age despite the fact that she never graduated from high school.

Night classes.

The G.E.D.

She tearfully agreed to them all, knows she is capable, ready for whatever lies ahead of her; she works in an office building somewhere in the Loop early each morning, six days a week. Day maintenance, she said, you know, toilets, wastepaper baskets; terrazzo that needs a coat of wax and a daily polish, particularly in the winter when nobody gives a damn, and they come in with their shoes and boots all messy, like they wouldn't notice if it ain't done, don't even bother to notice that it was done.

Sniffling, she added that there was no need for her to get all crazy about some little engreido, some guëro fool that ain't man enough to loose himself from his mamá's teta. There's a whole lot of vatos in her neighborhood that would want to get with her that would want to do the stand-up thing even if it was somebody else's business and all. That's for damn skippy, she told him. She knew she was slammin', she said, been told that her whole life, every morning when they are coming in, one or another of the business guys in the building where she works with their wedding rings and everything asks how she's doing, is she seeing anyone, wouldn't she like to see their cars, their condos; one even showed her a picture of a boat he wanted her to have dinner with him on, she said, she wasn't waiting for some white dude to validate her, that was madd loco.

Mi madre didn't raise no stupid perras, she said, and then quickly excused herself. She told the doctor not to get the wrong impression, he had to believe her; I'm really not all vulgar and all, just frustrated, she said. None of her sisters—she has two, both older—or her mother was ever dependent on any man, she told him. They raised their babies together; made sure they got by together; wanted for nothing together. And although she knew that she really, really loved him, that was hers, not his. He couldn't take that, wasn't responsible for that, that had as much to do with him as . . . well, she said, she couldn't think of what, but whatever it was, she knew it wasn't his to take because it was hers; I created it, she said, out of my own little imaginings, and it was hers to either protect or destroy.

Are you considering terminating this pregnancy if you are pregnant? the doctor asked.

No disrespect Doctor, the young woman asked, but are

you listening to me? Pregnant, I can handle. A baby or an abortion, I can handle. If he loves or not, I can handle. Them ain't my questions.

The doctor, after having attempted to talk and clear his throat at the same time, seemed to have been made self-conscious of what power his voice may or mayn't have at that point in the interview and simply asked, Your question is?

She wanted to know about her. This is more about me than anything else, she said. Doctor, what is it about me that always needs to look to the other side, you know, el otro lado, through somebody else's hedge and all? she said. It's like I'm stealing something from over there and coming back with it, yo, sneaking it over to my side to enjoy it. Yo, why it got to be about him, why it got to be about a baby, yo, why it got . . .

The doctor had regained the full range of his voice by the time that he interrupted. The girl's voice was never heard again. Maybe the therapist hung up before answering. Perhaps the girl gave up on the therapist.

Or I could have—lost in Aureliano, Francisco, García, Carrera—fallen asleep before I heard the girl's rebuttal, heard her rail curses at the doctor, tell him what she thought about his mamá, his sister, his greasy granny who got a hole in her panties, heard her sneer a threat to get his faggoty ass. No sé.

I understand, the doctor said.

Au

Re

Li

An

O

Amá is right, you know señores, each night before I can no longer hold on to consciousness—Dios, por favor, ayúdame; Quítame este dolor, por favor; Llena mi soledá con tu amor; Llena mi soledá con tu amor; Dios, por favor, ayúdame—I pray, but I have no idea how she knows.

It's a silent prayer, era es mi silencio, mi playa, mi escuela, mi sentido común. Since she's been in the room just across the hall where he, Aureliano Francisco García Carrera, played the merengues, tapped his pencils against the edge of his table, the bookshelves, against his forehead, I pray with my fingertips in front of my lips. Just whispers, no more, no more than puffs of air: as the girl on the radio said, it's mine.

Who knows where the girl went? What she thought, where she was headed after the doctor suggested that she talk to friends and family—people with whom she was closest—those that she felt had her best interest at heart, an ear for her concerns. She should seek counseling from a professional who could provide her with more than he could do then, there, over the phone, and he said she should never forget that she is an individual whose sense of self and well-being should transcend the selfishness of others.

But she was gone. Into the ether. Like the message for Hiel de Vaca and Eddy Chibás, pulled back into something that she wanted but didn't want.

The doctor hadn't heard, he didn't know, he didn't understand, or didn't want to know. Never once did he suggest that she grind glass into a nightly gin and tonic or sleep with a nest of scorpions. Or just lie there, lie there, lie there. Counting, counting sheep.

Had he kept her on the line just a little longer, she might have been able to tell him that if he didn't get it, still had no idea of what she was talking about, couldn't empathize with what she lived with every day, he could climb any El platform in the city, squat on his haunches with his face as close to the edge as possible as the train came in, whooshed past and burned his freshly shaven cheek. He'd find that although it would scare him nearly to the point of peeing himself, he'd also find himself wanting to do it again. He may not, but the want to do it will still be there.

It's like doña Liliana says, when her belly was flat, she wanted nothing more than to have a baby; when she found out that there were two crawling inside of her—Julio y Román—she spent a harried hour trying to shove herself into the smallest corset that she owned; she remembers standing in line at Martí, yelling at Román y Julio to stay close, not to stray, stay in sight, be quiet, yet all the time she stood there all she could think about was being in the comfort of an air-conditioned Miami condominium and stockings, silk stockings. And when she found herself in line again at Miami's Cuban refugee center, and later caged with so many others behind chain-link, like a German shepherd, she says, while paperwork was performed and Amá was contacted and she found herself yelling for Julio y Román to stay close, in sight, not to stray yet—like the girl who asked the radio doctor if he had heard what she said, was he listening—all she could think about was sitting in the garden of her father's house; a lovely house, a house any woman from El Vedado would have been proud to have come from, she says: sometimes when one of those wrinkly yanqui bitches comes to her counter wanting to know what will restore what vacations in the sun have robbed them of, she sees herself, Lilianita the carefree, la bonita, on the stone bench underneath the banyón in her father's garden watching las palomas that lived in the cupola above her bedroom window gather twigs.

If you ask doña Cristina, she'll say that it never happens. But cook chicken with onions, garlic, saffron and wine—lots of wine mixed with chicken stock that you've kept in the refrigerator for two or three days before you put the rice in—and she'll sing while she does the dishes, dance a little to the radio. Put just a little rum into her cafecito, and she'll weep with the heroine on her favorite radio novela as she continues to wait for the man she loves to say, mi amor.

For years now I thought that I slept on one side of the bed. This morning the light was still on. A newscaster cheerfully said, More heat. There was something sticky between my fingers.

At first I thought that I had cut myself, or had been cut, was bleeding from a wound that I couldn't find. I bolted from the bed pulling back all of the sheets to discover it was guayaba. Very ripe, nearly fermented. The seeds and flesh smeared the sheets, penetrated through to the mattress.

On my chest, neck, face and down my sides to my legs. It was on the wall above the bed and across the headboard. A trail of fingertip prints ran along the wall to the doorknob. The dresser drawer had been opened and the tie—a blue bow tie with white polka dots that he, Aureliano Francisco García Carrera, would wear with a maroon cashmere jacket, a white shirt, gray pants and a pair of black-and-white wing tips—had been taken out of the back of my sock drawer, tied and left hanging on the mirror next to the box where I put my wallet and change each night before I take off my pants.

Thumbprints were left where the tie had been pulled taut, and a line of guayaba ran down the wall in the hallway that faded just before it reached the bathroom.

I could see Amá over my shoulder in the mirror. Had I asked, she would have simply said that it was Pirata.

Who are you Amá, what journey are you on, and where have you taken my mother? I thought to ask, but couldn't. It reminded me too much of a time Román and I were walking across the east green, and boys from another school, black boys, boys who looked like us, heard our Spanish and asked, What the fuck are you? What the fuck are you? as they pulled at our uniform ties and scattered our books. Fuck you whatever you are, as the thermos containing the soup Amá had made the night before split open Román's lip. Fuck that, as we were kicked and head-butted, and the uniforms Amá said that they could barely afford were shredded and bled on. What the fuck? Father Rodríguez said under his breath as he paced into the shadows cast by Father McMillan's cataract-covered eye. Weren't you the boy who brought that dark dark dominicana with the big tetas in that blue dress to the prom; weren't you the best soccer player this school has had besides Julio; didn't I pin your fucking palms on you when you made Eagle Scout; wasn't it I who wrote your recommendations for college, and wasn't it I who hired you when you came to teach here; weren't you dating some chica that I saw climbing into your car one afternoon? I seem to remember your being engaged once: Father Rodríguez—José Victorio Rodríguez, S.J., since he was twenty-one, teacher, coach, mentor, Joe to his friends, señores, traced my history, laid it out in front of me in neat, well-organized piles in one quick, puerile, stolen, transgressive, What the fuck?

To which I still can only answer, No sé.

I remember Julio not showing that night. You get used to it.

Come here, come here, ven acá, was something he used to say, Aureliano Francisco García Carrera.

Weeks, maybe a month had gone by from the first time that I met him in Humboldt Park, when suddenly he was there yelling, Come here, come, here, ven acá, beckoning me over to one of the domino tables at a bar on Damen Avenue. It's still there. Caribbean food, mostly men, sawdust on the floor, poker in the back, domino tables line the windows as the bar turns the corner onto the side street. Casa del Sancti Spiritu, named for the hometown of the original owner whose name nobody can remember though if you're there late one night, right before closing and the real drinking begins, someone will drop the scratchy forty-five of El misterio de tus ojos in the jukebox and everyone still standing will raise one to Pepe, who resembled a raisin if you go by the portrait kept in memoriam surrounded by dusty silk flowers and a series of veladoras above the bar. The place smells like cervezas, sweat, manteca frying plátanos, cigars and urinal cakes. If you're looking for a puta or a cockfight, Rogelio, the bartender, he's the one with a toothpick in the corner of his mouth, is who you ask. I'll tell you now that he has teeth, pero he only puts them in at home. Too much fights here late a la noche, he'll tell you. He also knows the score to any soccer game played between Mexico and Cuba from 1959 on.

Even though I never go back, it's all the same, señores.

Sure I was drunk that first time. But never let that be an excuse, señores. For every drunken moment, millions of truths come flying. It's just the sorting them out as you look for your clothes the next morning that's confusing.

There are no more naked moments than the ones that you have sick on the toilet or in the shower, thinking about what just passed and who you are now. I was twenty-five, already a teacher here. Had never considered it. Never seemed an option. I was engaged to the woman Father Rodríguez doubtlessly remembers me bringing to mass, to school functions, she arranged flowers for the altar on high holy days, and sewed costumes for the younger kids during Passion Week. I hear, now she's married and living in Albuquerque. But I don't know that I've really thought of her, thought of her seriously as the woman that I almost married, since she returned the ring doña Liliana helped me choose.

He had eyes the color of blue wolf fur and a skin color that betrayed his mother's unforgiving blood, Aureliano Francisco García Carrera. But somehow I wouldn't discover these until months later, one night camping in the desert in Arizona, the same way I wouldn't know that he made an entire room smell like a casaba when he came in from a run, or the down that ran the center of his chest and spread out on his belly, in his navel, tasted like mango until later still.

For the longest time I was held by something that, like a fish in front of a shiny object, made me willing to brave the air to find out, just find out, what it would be like to know something that no one else you knew knew.

After we had toasted Pepe and staggered holding each other down the street to find a cab he said something that no one in my life before that had ever said.

He had gone back.

Gone back more than once.

Went back regularly.

Before college, through Mexico, he had found the fincas, the coffee plantation, the sugar-processing compound his father coveted, conspired to regain for Aureliano's mother and their children, with more fist-pounding, object-throwing tirades than Aureliano cared to recall from his childhood.

Through Barcelona while on an internship his last year of architecture school. First on a plane to Jamaica, and then only two hundred dollars got him a week in La Habana. He'd seen the Tropicana, walked El Morro, been in El Vedado. Knew where doña Liliana had danced the merengue in a dress so thin, so red, so tight, tan sexy they said they said, you would have thought you had died and gone to heaven.

Once through Canada to trek La Sierra Maestra.

Again through Canada, he landed in La Habana and spent three days crossing the island. But it was worth it he said, to wake and see the sun coming up over Santiago.

You'll like it there, he said.

And he was a singing man, Aureliano Francisco García Carrera—boleros, danzones, mambos, merengues of heartbreak and loneliness, pleasure and pain—first thing in the morning, in the shower, in the car, up from bed, before going to sleep, happy or sad, out of tune, from deep in his throat. It's just not something that you walk away from.

Come here, come here, ven acá, he said, once we got to his place. I don't remember who paid for the cab or paying for the cab. We staggered up the stairs—Come here, come here, ven acá, he said—as he beckoned me into the room where now Pirata finds Amá nightly. He brewed coffee that smelled like home, and then he drew the shoreline at La Playa Rosario, knew each curve it made, showed me how it seemed to be completely enclosed like an inland lake.

Come here, come here, ven acá, he said. And I followed him across the hall.

¿No me jodas? I whispered.

No, he said.

¿Verdad, chico? I asked.

Sí, he said.

He opened his mouth and lifted his legs over my shoulders.

Come here, come here, ven, ven acá, he whispered.

I could feel him smile, his teeth against my lips, his nose push against the bridge of my glasses, in the dark.

STRANGE HOW QUICKLY Román learned English after that day on the east green.

Like an American aristocrat, doña Liliana would exclaim, though because she couldn't name any—real ones like the ones back home, she once said—she is always ready with a list of movie stars just in case anyone asked.

As if he was born to it, doña Cristina told señora Figueroa and people who would listen times there was a line at the carnicería, and often making it a point while chatting with the ladies who used to come to make lace; afternoons at Amá's shop—for for years, even long before Marta left the shop to her, the custom has been to have either a standing appointment for the set and style of a bimonthly color or trim ladies keep no matter the weather until death; six-month touch-ups for permanent waves or straightenings are scheduled through December with each new year's calendar using the previous year's as a reference; though even emergencies to correct home-color applications or what Amá calls las penitencias de los unfaithfuls when regulars stray into dalliances at other shops and then return begging forgiveness and correction, they all, even new clients, expect a wait that can last up to two hours; nobody would think of factoring in the wait by approximating a time when a chair might be available; the rule is chisme for chisme, and where the woman who gives up her own story, tells her sorrowful woes of an errant husband or unloving children while Naty Valdez McIntosh cuts the crusts from the heels, files, applies nail lacquer, may be respected and trusted by the others, the woman who relays what she saw going on in the window across from her kitchen as she happened to be doing dishes later than usual one night or when she was awakened by the thud thud thud of a car stereo and needed a glass of water and an aspirin to calm her nerves just as a woman who routinely gets her roots touched up at the end of the month was getting out of a car that belongs to another woman's husband, or even better, seen a woman's husband leave another woman's house has certainly earned her value; better yet, however, and this has only happened once that I can recall, is the woman who had seen a woman leaving the house of a woman who had left her husband alone and taken her children with her to visit an ailing mother in Chihuahua, she is a woman who could have her complementary cafecito and fritura brought to the chair while her beauty is being restored; la chismosa with the ripest, sweetest, most succulent offering is the bravest and most daring because she also opens herself to exactly what she offers; which is why I believe that she always begins by saying, Charity for the sake of charity, doña Cristina, when she tells it—because somehow I believe that she believes that when she tells it she's setting things, all things, right.

Not a word of English he spoke, she tells it; none of us knew whether or not Román would ever learn, she says. And it was not like any of us besides Mireya y Óscar who could have known the difference anyway. She tells him shy and an unassuming kind of boy; she tells him very clever in Spanish, joking and happy. She talks him beautiful, in a mysterious sort of way, she says, as if she, Amá and doña Liliana never had to pry him apart from Julio or me in those first months that followed the dramatic arrival of la doña Liliana and her two wild boys—Julio, El blanco, y Román, El negro—in the December when we were eleven and twelve.

There was snow of course that they had never seen, and though Amá and I had been used to it for quite some time it was as if we were reliving something, the same things that made them curious and excited, perplexed them and eventually frustrated them by mid-February into a hothouse claustrophobia that blistered off in shouting matches over a baseball mitt that couldn't be used until spring, and the mate to a boot that somehow ended up unreachable on top of the garage. It all seemed deserved at the time and familiar to me, who was occasionally afflicted and often a perpetrator or one of a team of conspirators, and Amá who administered first aid in silence, calmed and returned las doñas to tea and proposals for dresses and curtains to be made.

Snow and finger splints, a split lip; ice, wind and freezing rain watched through the front and kitchen windows, our bedroom windows, were as easily connected to all of us as were the bruises, and the smell of liniment; for as many tents and forts and hideouts constructed under tables, in closets, using blankets between the single bed on one side of our room and the top bunk that we fought over, inside each of us were individual, separate armies of sloppy balled-up clumps of unreasonable hate that we hurled at each other across breakfast tables and in the darkness after we were warned there was to be no more talking, no more noise, not a peep from any one of us unless we wanted trouble for all of us.

They were a year older and bigger, taller, meaner, identical except for their color—Román, El negro y Julio, El blanco—and none of us boys could remember a time just a few years before that Amá and las doñas tried to remind us of when we all had played together so nicely in doña Liliana's father's well-appointed garden.

We were all put into the same grade because their lack of English seemed to be balanced by Román's ability to look at algebra problems and immediately know the answer without the use of paper and the fact that they were twins meant that the same was assumed of Julio. Father Rodríguez said he thought it a blessing that I should be given two older brothers, and seemed to ignore the fact that during that first year there always was a black eye between the three of us, or that both Román and I, on separate occasions, were placed in detention for attempting to drown Julio in the pool, or that twice Julio was placed in detention for attempting to drown me in the pool, or that Román had once vomited in the pool that winter Julio attempted to drown him, or that by our freshman year in high school, all three of us were suspended from pool privileges altogether; I don't want to see you little fuckers anywheres near this fucking pool, I believe is what Brother Núñez, who was the swimming coach at the time, said.

Though our desire to maim, bludgeon, disfigure lay readied, poised under the surface—had at the time I only gotten my hands on a poisonous spider; a silent, traceless arachnid, stealthful, efficient as the bomb that kills all the people but leaves the buildings standing—at home it was met with calm understanding.

It's what boys do, was said—as if any of them really knew anything about boys—when it was discovered that one of us was having a nightly pee in Julio's sock drawer. On weekends the three of us earned pocket change sweeping, taking out garbage, washing sinks and mopping floors at Amá's shop, and each week one of us would get his hands burned from having the broom wrenched from him, or ended up with a knot on his head for taking the most choice job, the easiest, which was restocking the supply room, breaking down boxes and setting them out for the vato who was the garbage man that week. All you had to do was call it first at the breakfast table on Saturday morning, but it meant that the guy who got the job also spent the rest of the day defending his territory, having to redo work that had mysteriously come undone while he was not looking. The best parts of his lunch—his pink Hostess Snow Balls or his potato chips—might go missing if he wasn't looking; an Orange Crush can easily, silently be tipped without notice if you are wearing a pair of Purcells. Hombrecitos was exchanged with a knowing glance over our heads, even when I needed to have three stitches put into my forehead and Román's arm was set into a cast.

No yelling, no punishments or lectures. Things that had brought about a slap across the mouth in the past mocked and defied gravity.

Everything turned inward where the thermostat was kept at seventy-five and pots of simmering fabada and baking bread caused the windows to sweat. An altar—that remained there until Amá set her kitchen on fire—was set in the entryway that in addition to a statuette of La Virgen del Cobre included the rosario doña Cristina carried to her First Communion and we later—the day we were allowed by the police and the insurance company to clean up after the fire—learned she had tucked the same rosario into her brassiere the night she lost her virginity to a man named Juan Rodolfo, who she said was so gigantic that like a bullfighter a porta gayola, she was submitting herself to the saints; there was also a photograph of my mother's mother, the last picture, Amá says, with all her daughters around her; and the plate to an etching that was made of doña Liliana's father's great house in El Vedado along with portraits of Jesucristo, Lazarus, Santa Bárbara and what seemed an unending supply of fresh veladoras, floras y cigarillos por los santos.

Ay, what did I know? I was just a kid, ¿no? Señores, you have to live through an energetic stillness, or a silent hysteria, like a virus, to know that one has passed through you. Passed by you. Surrounds you. Sí, like señor Chávez says, like the surround sound at the movies.

That year in that house of blended locuras of faith, boy-spit, fear and the need for as much Cuba as could be held on to in one hand while letting go of the same amount in the other, on the El platform, on the way back from her English class, while looking for work for the first time in her life, doña Liliana was confronted with a world that knew nothing of her or her father's magnificent house in El Vedado, or the flock of dressmakers, the italianito who traced her foot each spring for sandals, or the fragrance that a Parisian business partner of her father's had made for her; they knew nothing of the parties that she attended, gave or enhanced by her presence. Too light to be Mexican, blue-eyed and kept blonde as ever by Amá, after being pinched on a bus on her way back from her fourth trip in as many days from the INS offices downtown, doña Liliana found that she had come to a city where she could be pointed at after throwing a curse that caused the assailant to fall to the floor in convulsions; Pointed at by a child, she told Amá y doña Cristina as they attempted to calm her with tea and frituras. Pointed at her, doña Liliana told them, and then it said that the Puerto Rican woman did something and that man over there just fell out.

¿Puertorriqueña? ¡Puertorriqueña! doña Liliana cried as she relayed the story to the chismosas at the shop. But not only did it fall on deaf ears, it also seemed to seal her fate with them. And it wasn't until she looked up from her manicure—because even after all of these years, she has never trusted any of the manicurists that Amá has employed because none of them had the same gentle touch of the girl that used to come to her twice weekly back home—that she seemed to realize for the first time that she might as well have been trying to speak English.

Dark and light, looking back at her, was a line of faces under dryers, under coils of rollers, that knew that outside of the neighborhood, once they opened their mouths to speak, gave their last names to clerks, despite where they came from, it was decided that they were either Mexican or Puerto Rican. It wasn't news to them; most of them had spent most of their lives that way.

And who does she think she is anyway, señora Figueroa would say in front of doña Liliana until it became quite clear that the English classes that doña Liliana was taking were beginning to pay off. But it was long before that that doña Liliana began to say that it was so odd that these women—las chismosas in the shop—seemed complacent as cows that an entire city could take a question like where are you from and make it completely about them; use it like carnival barkers to guess where someone lived, how many children a woman had, what her husband if she had a husband did for a living, what might be found in her cupboards.

Is Spanish spoken exclusively in the home, I was to translate for the social worker assigned to make sure that doña Liliana and her sons were settled, fed and adjusted; No, doña Liliana answered, why would Spanish be spoken exclusively in the home when she, we, were neither Mexican or Puerto Rican?

I have no idea what I said—because in those days, señores, no one thought that it was important that social workers speak the same language as the clients that they were serving as much as they made sure that their clients knew how to make rice; una taza de arroz/dos tazas de agua was printed on the laminated card that the social worker handed doña Liliana telling her that she should pin it up above the stove—how I made it seem like I was translating exactly what was said. Because, even though I wasn't sure at the time why, I had a sense that neither woman was interested in what the other was saying.

I can no longer remember the social worker's name, but I remember her in drab brown clothes, small, and that she wore a fragrance that doña Liliana proclaimed so nauseous that she would throw every window in the house open if it weren't for the godforsaken cold. We met with her in the kitchen—Román y Julio, Amá, doña Cristina, doña Liliana and I—and doña Cristina thought it polite that we at least offer the woman a cafecito and some sort of pastelito, even though the woman never touched them. Just poor manners, Amá used to say, but doña Cristina corrected her, saying that Amá shouldn't think anything of it, it was merely the way Americans conducted themselves in other people's houses. Even when Amá reminded her that we were all Americans now, doña Cristina said she thought Amá a madwoman if she believed that it was a custom that we should all adopt.

The social worker asked about doña Liliana's educational background, and I determined that while she wanted to know about doña Liliana's time as a student at the convent school where she and doña Cristina met, she was probably not interested in doña Liliana's expulsion—for refusing to comply with the dress code and several afternoons that she left the grounds during recess, for which she claimed to be unaccountable—and how that expulsion was reversed when a sizable donation was made to the school by her father. I was certain that the social worker had no interest in the year that doña Liliana spent at university even after she was asked in her first week of a philosophy course not to return until she had come up with a sufficient reason for why she belonged there in the first place.

She went to a convent school, I told the social worker, and she attended Universidad de La Habana for one year. And I watched as Amá, doña Cristina, doña Liliana, Román y Julio sat in the kitchen tracking our conversations with the social worker back and forth across the table. They smiled when she smiled; they all mimicked her lack of concern and looked at me as if I had done something wrong; careless, as if I had mistranslated some nuance that betrayed doña Liliana's prayer each morning in front of the altar that compelled Santa Bárbara for strength and La Virgen for patience; because today is the day that my life begins, ¿no?

Doña Liliana once danced the merengue at the Tropicana in a dress so red, so thin, so tight—Tan sexy, they said they said—you would have thought you had died and gone to heaven. Béseme chica; Béseme; Besitos, besitos, they said they all begged, they all wolf-whistled, they all sucked their teeth, and fanned themselves with napkins as she passed their tables. They disagreed as to what it was she wore that reminded them of jasmine; of vanilla; of orange peel; of bergamot, was the story that doña Cristina never told.

What did you do before you came to the United States? the social worker asked doña Liliana though she was looking at me. Without waiting for my translation, doña Liliana answered, Era una revolucionaria. Dígale, mijo, she insisted, tell her I bore the babies of the Revolution.

Amá gasped.

¡Liliana, no! doña Cristina cried.

Mira, doña Liliana said gesturing like the women she'd seen caressing cars and washing machines on television toward Julio y Román. ¿Ellos no son muy hermosos, no?

And while doña Liliana fell over herself in laughter, Amá brought the social worker a fresh cafecito even though the woman hadn't touched the first; doña Cristina put another pastelito on the woman's plate next to the first, though both sat there until later; after she had left, Julio would lick them both so that neither Román nor I would ask for them.

Tell her, mijo, doña Liliana said, smiling, wiping her tears, tell her; what do I have to lose anyway?

Here, in a place where she had to be either Mexican or

Puerto Rican, she was abruptly disinherited from her own beauty and privilege, or the beauty that was her privilege that no longer brought about entrée or absolution. How would I know if I can still turn heads when I walk into a room, I once overheard her telling doña Cristina, when I have no idea who or what they see when they see me.

It seems like the long-ago-and-far-away sort of time, yo lo sé, señor Ostrovski, pero there was a time when all she needed to do was turn to the society page in El Diario de la Marina or the Havana Post with her morning coffee to find out who she was the night before. What she wore. On whose arm was she seen. Daughter of industrialist, each article starts in the spectral drift of microfiche. Sometimes they weren't even complete articles, señores, go to any library that has Cuban papers on file from the 1950s: Daughter of Prominent Cuban Industrialist, next to advertisements for Hiel de Vaca from Crusellas and Kolonia with a K was delicate to the skin, seen in a sequined Dior gown; at the ballet; on the steps of the opera house; at the opening of a pavilion; and of course, there were the great numbers of coming-out parties; charity dances; Señorita Liliana—daughter of one of our most prominent industrialists—qué bonita; lovely as could be imagined; reviving the scalloped neckline; clutching a spray of verónica and pink roses; accompanied the son of, the newly appointed, the up-and-coming, the next.

Until one evening, the Havana Post announced Batista had left the country.

None of you, señores, I realize, or for at least most of you, the fact that the president had left the country is somewhat unfathomable. For you, presidents—whether or not you happen to agree with their politics or not; whether you happen to know who they are or not for that matter, señor Chávez—are like fixtures and to have one suddenly leave the country would be the same as if you woke to find your street had turned into a river and you and your bed were floating headed toward the lake; shifts of who and what, when and where are so much less likely here; it's an easy, landlocked feeling—in the middle of the country—this, where everything is hemmed in just so.

But the cubanos who woke up to find themselves still surrounded by water had become somewhat accustomed to the idea that their president was a mutable shape-changer able to appear anywhere.

Ask doña Cristina, she'll tell you that they were all at a cocktail party—and this is only what she heard because she wasn't there herself to witness it—but she says they said it was an early-evening affair, right after dinner, before everyone was headed out to a dance so they were all in formal dress, meaning, because it was right before spring in La Habana, white gloves for the women, and the men would have been wearing white dinner jackets following the trend set by Hollywood at the time that April in 1952, when all anyone could talk about was Batista on the cover of Time magazine, standing in front of the Cuban flag. The caption read, Cuba's Batista: he got past democracy's sentries, the daughter of an American business partner of doña Liliana's father translated for all that bothered to pay attention. But hardly anyone bothered to pay attention, for there were cucumber sandwiches and someone had just come back from a trip that started in New York and ended in California with a stack of records and a recipe for daiquiris. And besides, for those who did last night's reading—and why do we bother kidding ourselves at this stage of the game, señores, with days like this, hot days, linked one after another, that seem to have plunged us into the middle of summer; unearned days that render daydreams of beaches, bring about the smell of sand, sea and suntan lotion, that take you outside of the confinement of classrooms and institutional disinfectant and chalk dust something like a northerly wind, a hurricane of change and destruction, everything leveled and readied for a cloudless sky, the sound of waves and the giggles that come from the scantly clad bodies that you imagine when you imagine, but of course, none of you imagine, but if you were to, how warm and moist, how slick with sweat are they; but the real question is where are they; are they part of some past beach or one in the future, entonces they surely are not here—the reading would have placed you somewhere between there and here.

Señores, for the few of you that joined the party last night and for those who would like to join us on the other side now, it's a thin membrane that you all use to get to the beach or to the arms you rest in right now or to another morning, another time, in another place.

Leave your towels, the cooler with its sandwiches and beer, the umbrella there on the sand. They'll be there when we come back. Vamos.

. . . CASTRO'S COMING DOWN from La Sierra Maestra wasn't the first time Batista fled the island, señores, no. The daughter of doña Liliana's father's business partner had always been known as a notorious flirt; the kind of girl you wouldn't leave with your aged abuelo if you had one for five minutes, doña Liliana says, for fear that the cuff links that had been in your family since the conquistadores brought the gold back to Spain would have been melted down into settings for diamond studs by the time that you got back. Though every one of doña Liliana's friends trusted her for translations; Time magazine to Hollywood Confidential, the latest fashion do's and don'ts needed words to make sense of the garish pictures that seemed to stare back with vacant drooling maws.

Helen or Ellen was her name they all seem to remember; Amá recalls that the best bedrooms in doña Liliana's father's house were opened, and the linen from Egypt that neither doña Liliana nor her father used was aired. Amá says the cook was given a list of things to shop for and prepare that would be pleasing to doña Liliana's father's American guests; they needed to be comfortable, the house needed to be filled with flowers, and sounds, smells and flavors that they would find familiar and pleasing, so they would want to come back, which is how Amá first came to taste caviar, and although she says that she enjoyed it, she also says waiting so long for certain things in life can etch away pleasure, make it nearly tasteless, the same way that debt can turn finding money on the sidewalk into just another day.

Amá says doña Liliana's father would say that he wanted the whole house to be just like it was when Liliana's mother was still alive. But because doña Liliana was a mere six days old when her mother—dressed in a peignoir of lavender-colored French lace that had been embroidered in gold thread—is reported to have shot upright from the shock of being awakened by the cries of the infant in the bassinet next to her before waving a hand in front of her face and uttering the word suficiente before she fell back into her pillows and died, not even the cook who was the daughter of doña Liliana's childhood nurse could quite remember what it was like when doña Liliana's mother demanded that there be freshly cut flowers on nearly every surface in the house, and disallowed slouching, and girls who smoked, limp aprons and messy hair.

Each year since doña Liliana's birth, her father would add a new thing and then a few new things about her mother. A mania of snakes, a fondness for orange rinds and yellow satin ribbon would come up as he took his daughter out for a drive when they were vacationing near Santiago, on a walk through the park or as he kissed her good night. Each new maid was instructed the way that doña Liliana's mother inspected underneath carpets and under the jardinières in the conservatory before a party; they all knew that she boiled a cup of water and steeped green tea, ginger and a bay leaf into the limonada before it was iced; and eventually they all knew the value of the triple-rope set of pearls with the diamond clasp she was wearing in the photograph on top of the piano that was to be dusted and returned to precisely the same spot—because you weren't really dusting unless you picked things up, were you—and they all knew, even if they only listened to the beginning and the end of the story, that they came into doña Liliana's mother's family by way of the sea; and they were to be Liliana's on the eve of her sixteenth birthday as her mother's mother had given them to her, mimicking the ritual of generations of women before. Until, after a while, anything that anyone knew about doña Liliana's mother came from doña Liliana's father's head.

She knew everything there was to know about social graces—the opera, the ballet, art museums—which was a very fine thing to have happen to a man who had spent his life on farms and fincas, in the military and then in offices, he told her in of all things a French restaurant in Rome the summer of her fifteenth birthday when he finally gave doña Liliana her mother's pearls.

He couldn't wait, she says he said, couldn't wait.

She says that he let her drink as much champagne as she wanted that night, and when she couldn't decide when the pastry cart was brought around, he ordered it stopped at the table and to the horror of the Romans who had no idea that he was dining with his daughter, caught glimpses of the two, as if in some fairy tale, frolicking with spoons, and allowed drips to fall where they may: on their chins, the tablecloth, the floor, doña Liliana says that she ruined the dress that they had bought just that morning with pastry cream, the two of them were laughing so much.

That night in a carriage ride, doña Liliana learned that her mother became horribly allergic to strawberries during her confinement; head to toe she was covered with hives the entire nine months, her father told her, because it was a luxury that she could not do without; it was what she craved, and she laughed at the ruddy color her skin took on, and she would have him watch as they spread out over her stretched belly. And he spared no expense having them flown in from anywhere he could get them. She wept when she heard Puccini and read the end of Anna Karenina, and on more than one occasion when they were first married he had walked in on her in her dressing room while she was seated at her vanity, listening to Puccini, a copy of Tolstoy's book at her feet, watching herself weep. She had no shame in my seeing it, he told her, she was a joyous woman who took all of life in her arms and tried to swallow it whole; no, very little about life made her uncomfortable or squeamish, your mother, she looked it all in the eye.

She would ride out on the fincas and set up camp with me and the other men, walk out into the factories in all that heat the same as she could spend an entire afternoon shopping on the Champs Elysées.

When they arrived back at the hotel, doña Liliana says that her father kissed her good night on her forehead before retiring to his room in their suite.

But Liliana couldn't sleep.

The entirety of Rome was spread out in front of her and there were so many stars that the possibility of a lifetime of wishes seemed hers for the making. She ran a finger over each of the pearls in each of the strands, and circled the diamond clasp over and over: her mother's throat was long and pale and when she wore her hair piled on top of her head, the most delicate V you have ever seen in your entire life formed at the top of her neck; a woman just as comfortable at the fights or a baseball game as she was at high tea with the wives of his business partners, he had told her, a most extraordinary woman she was.

Doña Liliana was unable to sleep the entire night; even though her body became tortured by little aches and twitches that flapped haphazardly like moths deep in her muscles, her mind ran ahead of the silver speedboat her mother was driving in the picture that her father kept at his bedside table at home; her mother's hair was tied back with a scarf, she was wearing white sunglasses and the perfectly drawn gash of red lipstick parted widely to reveal very well aligned rows of white white teeth as she turned to look at the camera; doña Liliana says were it not for the wild sprays that trail in her wake, she would have thought that her mother had been posing for a magazine cover.

All of Rome was lighting up in front of her as it officially became the next day, but doña Liliana says she still couldn't sleep, and she remembers remembering were she at home she might drink warm milk or lie on her back jiggling her foot until the muscles of her calf burned up its tight bundle of energy that caught another further up her leg which and so on until the house was set creaking with footsteps and echo, until her eyelids were so heavy that she couldn't lift them in response to the flashes of light she could sense around her.

Sleep would push her down as she tried to lift her head and follow the rustle of skirts as they passed back and forth in front of her bed, the click of a heel against the highly polished floors; tried to hear what was planned on menus, or learn how to plan an event, who to sit next to whom, how tables should be placed so that no one was too close to the music or too far away from the host; what to do with the investments and the savings left to her; whom she should marry. Warm nights in the middle of summer with the windows of her bedroom opened onto the garden, she could feel the mosquitero brush against her skin with every movement of the wet air, but try as she might she could do little to push herself from under the weight of sleep to search the room for the overwhelming smell of gardenia that carried her off and left her in the next morning.

But it was there in Rome the night of her fifteenth birthday. She had secured her mother's pearls underneath her mattress, dressed for bed, cleaned her teeth and prayed to La Virgen del Cobre that she would not grow heavy hips with pendulous breasts like the women they had seen in Sicily and that her hair would not get any darker when over her shoulders, curling like billows of smoke, she says, she began to smell the gardenias that grew in the garden back home. Gardenias and something like caramelizing sugar or burnt cinnamon.

She placed the gold crucifix she still wears around her neck into her mouth as she eased her door open and stepped into the sitting room.

It was everywhere, she says, the carpets and the divan, the flocking on the wallpaper like a wrist corsage and a ruined flan. Following it, she kept close to the wall, nearly falling out each of the windows as she pushed herself out into the air nose first.

The closer that she got to the source of the odor, the less she could shake the image of her mother on horseback crossing La Sierra Maestra. Forward in the saddle, bearing down hard the same way any man would, she rode hard, your mother, her father would say, like she and the horse were one pounding through the earth, ay it was something to see, I tell you. Hairs—that pale blonde hair doña Liliana had inherited, in the painting above her father's desk—that had come loose clinging to her mother's temples, her heart visibly in her throat pounding through her arms and hands in their clutch of withers and reins, through to her legs and into the horse's belly and its hooves as it pounds the ground; Imponente, her father would say, siempre imponente.

As she turned the handle to her father's room, her eyes began to water and there was a searing at the back of her throat. And he was naked on the bed, she'll tell you, it took some time to get used to the light—that weird, refractory, early-morning light, odd with both short and long shadows at the time night begins to break into pieces—and the room swerved in front of her through an outpouring of tears that no longer came from anything around her or inside of her, they just came as if they'd never stop, but she could see well enough to be certain he was naked. She had never imagined it before, or that his body might bear some relation to anything that they had seen riding the ceiling of the Sistine Chapel or the boys she and her girlfriends would hide to watch dive off of the pier.

Round and hairy, oddly pale in places, slack where once he clearly had been firm, muscular, offering his arm out of a car, onto many dance floors, crossing avenue and boulevard; she was so beautiful, he had always told her, more beautiful than any woman you could imagine, more beautiful the longer you spent with her. He was lying on his back with his mouth open. And she says that at the moment that she had discerned where it was that the overwhelming smell of home was coming from—gardenias and burnt sugar; mango y guayaba; salt drying on the back of her hand as she sunned herself after a swim—threatened to crush her, nearly causing her to swallow her own tongue, when the breeze in the room shifted, giving her her wind back and suddenly she was unable to tell which one of them, she or her father, had brought it with them.

Sleep came hard and fast. She was scarcely able to make her way back to her room; her legs were so raw and useless underneath her.

She woke in time for the last serving of lunch. Her father was finishing his cigar with newspapers from home, from Argentina, the United States, Guatemala and London neatly folded in quartered packets on the tablecloth in front of him by the time she reached the dining room. In a light pink silk shirt fitted for him on Savile Row, handmade Italian tie, pressed linen suit, trimmed and slicked back with hair oil he looked nothing like the dove in the last dream that she had had before she woke that had flown from her bedroom window back home to drop a mimosa seed into the center of the garden. And as the tree grew—sometimes the dove, sometimes one of the boys she had watched diving off the pier, hairy and naked, fluttered about the trunk and the branches, made love in holes that were not there before it started, let loose a spray of semen in its leaves that resembled a cloudburst before starting all over again, at the base up the trunk and through a canopy of intertwining branches that provided a trellis for a hungry wisteria vine to crawl up and over onto the roof; and right before she woke, the dove who was a naked man was flying in and out of the house as the roots of the mimosa moved into the parlor and along the great hall, turning over the piano with a loud thud, and purple and white petals of wisteria and mimosa filled the air as vine and tree together began to pull the house down.

Without looking from the Roman newspaper he was reading he told her about a farm for sale somewhere in the middle of America, in the middle of the United States, she says he said, six hundred and twenty-three acres for sale. Six hundred and twenty-three acres for sale, can you imagine, nena, flatland it says. Six hundred and twenty-three acres, no mountains, no sea, just nothing to look at, walk out of your front door every morning to nothing.

And no, she couldn't imagine it.

It wasn't until her food came that he looked up. He told her about the papal address the day before, and what the weather prediction was for the rest of the week and what it might be like when they arrived in San Sebastian, in the north of Spain, near France, Basque region where his abuelos were buried. It was the clattering of plates that caused him to pull the paper down from his face, and watch as it took two waiters to bring all of the dishes doña Liliana had ordered. The veal had sounded good, so had the fish, pasta, risotto; she had ordered three kinds of vegetable, a wilted endive with oil and lemon. ¿Qué es todo esto? he asked as the waiters dashed about wildly to get every plate onto the table steaming, amused as if he were watching clowns emerge from a Volkswagen.

Doña Liliana says that it was the first moment that she thought to be embarrassed, or that she had been aware of her own appetite for that matter. She had never awakened hungry before, and the waiter who took her order never flinched or questioned each plate she ordered. Sí signorina, he said, which sounded so familiar and inviting, it was the same as if he had told her that she was doing the right thing. Her thoughts danced, she says, she had no idea what she was doing, all she knew was that there was something ravenous inside of her that needed to be fed. Her eyes filled and she began to apologize, but her father waved it away as he folded the paper. Just like your mother, he said, needed the whole world laid out in front of her before she was able to make a decision; she had as many suitors as she had pairs of gloves, and dresses—ay Dios—a whole steamer trunk had to be packed for a weekend in the country; not that she wore everything, it was the choice; she wouldn't have been able to get dressed without it.

They once had been in Naples and their luggage had yet to arrive, he told her, and your mother went out and about in the same pair of shoes that she was wearing; the very same, he laughed, she needed choice, your mother, she did.

He began to eat with her, ignoring the additional empty plates that the waiters brought over, shooing them away as they offered to divide the dishes between them. He began to eat off of her plate, and with each mouthful, he sighed and complimented her on her choices. Never, he said, in his entire life had tomatoes tasted so sweet; garlic, lemon, spinach, olive oil, salt and pepper that he said caused him for the first time in his life to taste the color green. He paid no attention to the food that ran down his chin and onto his tie; he rubbed oils and sauce into his cheeks, the sides of his face, and continued, to the horror of the waiters and the few patrons left.

He told her that it was in London, days before they were to return to Cuba from their honeymoon, when her mother suggested that they abandon their plans and return to Lisbon. Choice you see, he said gesticulating upwards with his fork. Food flew out of his mouth with his excitement when he suggested that they go; to Lisbon, he said; there is a place, a cliff overlooking the sea, he said her mother said, where all of Europe ends, the very tip, where more than five hundred years ago it took courage to cross the ocean thinking paradise was just on the other side; let's go, he said she said, and pretend we're them, pretend we're Portuguese; let's find Brazil and spend nearly half a millennium envying Cubans. He laughed so hard he choked a little and garnered sour looks from thin waiters in their impeccably white long aprons.

I miss her so, nena, he told her, each and every day I thank God she left me with you and this ache in me that will never let go; it wasn't until I had her eyes that life began.

He stopped eating and looked at her. Vamos, mija, she says he said, vamos, let's go be Portuguese.

He ordered champagne when she agreed.

Which is why, she says, that five years later she looked on with curiosity at the creature whose visits from Boston were reason enough to have all of the muslin dust covers that doña Liliana's mother had made each time she brought a new piece into the house taken off of the furniture and put away like an idiot relative.

Helen or Ellen—doña Liliana always says she doesn't remember, and Amá agrees it was hardly a name worth remembering; messy; loud; got drunk a lot and slept in her clothes—sat translating the article about Batista in Time magazine that afternoon.

Afraid that she might snap the stem off of her glass, doña Liliana remembers having to set her drink down, she says, though no one ever commented, she was certain that she trembled violently in the presence of the woman. Who was this woman, this Ellen or Helen, and why was she in her father's house? doña Liliana found herself asking nearly every time she turned a corner or walked down a corridor and heard that hyena-like cackle of hers; y ay the way she spread herself out on a chair or, the later it got, on a table—and not in a pretty way, I might add—you would have thought that she was a stuffed pheasant on display.

She thought nothing of the fact the broad pink, black and white floral-patterned skirt of her dress clashed with the brocade silk of the chaise on which she reclined as she read, doña Liliana says that she was the type of creature this Ellen Helen that never would; completely oblivious, this Helen Ellen to the possibility that anything negative could be said about her, that there was anything unattractive about her, that the men who took her out in their cars also didn't tell everyone how easily her dresses unzipped or that she frequently was without panties.

Between playing with the crinolines under her dress and scratching her stockings with her fingernails, so that she was assured of the attention of every man in the room, Ellen Helen translated Batista's victory. When someone asked what did the writer in Time magazine mean by Batista no se conformó con el proceso democrático, Ellen Helen was no longer looking at the article when she told everyone in the room who stopped what they were doing to listen and answered, It meant nothing. Nothing really, she said, realizing that she had the attention of all of the men in the room. But when it was clear that she did not have the confidence of anyone in the room, she turned red and added, Nothing at all. Her eyes never met the page again, according to doña Liliana, anyone paying attention would have realized she was looking at the hem of her dress and pretending to read when she said, It only means that like this party, you wouldn't want to invite everyone, not everyone would appreciate it.

It was silly, seemed senseless, frivolous, doña Liliana says, but nobody seemed to want anything more from her. She says she said it said that Batista was essentially in the right by making choices for people who simply don't have the ability to make choices on their own—and if someone didn't choose for them, how would they get by; for godsakes someone with some sense has got to run the country—he had done all of Cuba a favor; a public service, she called it.

And even though the party seemed to start back up and continue around her—for weeks, breakfasts in the sunroom, shopping in the afternoons, evenings there were soirées to attend, openings and social engagements; the mothers of doña Liliana's friends asked about Helen Ellen, and when their fathers came to do business with Ellen Helen's father in doña Liliana's father's richly appointed study, in the afternoon or very late in the evening as doña Liliana says was the case, they made it a point to talk to this girl, give her gifts, asked her opinion of the opera, the ballet, politics, this young woman that doña Liliana and Amá both say didn't have two profound ideas to rub together, a woman who doña Liliana says really wasn't all that attractive with her close-set beady eyes and complexion that tended to get quite oily well before noon—yet she couldn't help wondering why the world cut such a great berth around her, around her shortcomings, her legs that nearly always appeared to be stubbly even through opaque hose.

Had she been her father's mistress, his lover, his fiancée, she says she could understand. But clearly that wasn't true. She asked, bribed and threatened maids for their indiscretion: Had that Helen Ellen been seen tiptoeing across the hallway in the middle of the night or early morning; had her father been caught in her room, or ordered breakfast brought into her room? Her father's secretary, the gardener, his gentleman's gentleman, and driver—all men—looked at her as if she had gone mad.

And perhaps for a while she had.

She wasn't sleeping or eating well.

Things that appealed to her in the past no longer held her interest, and she was often distracted and irritable.

And at night, she says, it must have been her mother, couldn't imagine what else it could have been that would come and guide her about the house and show her where things went.

It's not as if doña Liliana was hearing voices, she's careful to caution, but she knew something outside of her own body that pushed her about the house, showed her things she had never really looked at before until she was finally too tired to stand anymore and collapsed in her bed. A guardian of gardenias y azúcar quemada led her out into the garden, hid with her in the foliage that grew on the wall as one of the boys she had seen diving at the pier climbed over it and up the railing to one of the maid's rooms. It caused the night lizards to scatter across the dew-slicked stones and out onto the road, where they circled the house.

She says there were nights that she walked around the ground floor and saw shimmers of dust collect silvery on the floorboards in the moonlight and spiders throw castings from corner to corner. Grime crawled up the windows from the street. Moss reclaimed the porticos and pillars and the Spanish wrought iron railings where it found purchase enough to light on the shutters, spread and gnaw into the window frames. Mildew slithered in cracks in the door frames and walls made wider each night as the driver, clearly attempting something that was meant to resemble stealth, buoyed and bobbed the channel of rum inside him on his way to his small room. Moths found the corners where her father's secretary, thinking the entire house asleep, would edge himself into a shadow and, leaning against the wall, part his robe, reach into the slit in his paisley silk pajamas and make love to his hand with such ardent passion the boy with the lapis lazuli eyes he conjured would give off flashes of plasma-colored light as the secretary whispered his name.

The thorns—twice as many as she had ever seen them produce before—that studded the rosales on all sides of the house pierced the buds, devoured the petals, as they reached skyward toward the eaves. And from the very top of the house, holding on to the lightning rod, she could see the ocean and the bay. She says all of La Habana lay spread out asleep in front of her, and she could see the streets being cleaned and the shops unloaded. As she spun around, she could shut her eyes and wake everyone, set them into bustle. The mountains came into view, until she had cleared the way—farms and buildings gone, monuments struck—to the other side of the island while centuries went about their daily business: babies nursed, grew and seduced each other, plowed fields, painted portraits, opened a perfectly ripe higo with their incisors and plunged their tongues deep inside the hull until it had taken it bright red, seeds and all. And just as easily, by opening her eyes back into the dark, she could strike them all dead again, throw black headaches as if they were confetti, open sores where there had once been firm sallow flesh, she could disembody them and make their shouts the buzz of black flies as she wondered when would her life begin.

In the distance she could hear a nameless dog yelp, yelp, yelping, a very ugly, mean, nameless little dog, but could not locate the direction from which it was coming.

Do I believe it, señor Ostrovski?

No sé, as you would say, I wasn't there.

AFTER HOURS OF looking, I found Amá—close to hers yet too far from my house to imagine that she had walked, finding things is so hard for her these days; already beginning to get dark, the city had begun folding over on itself, readying for night, when there she was—in the fluorescent light of the Jesus bus stopped at the curb next to Wicker Park, watching others being saved.

Not in the kitchen, the spare bedroom, the yard, the basement. I had first called doña Liliana, then doña Cristina, then Román. I had driven around with my scalp crawling as I wondered out loud where on earth, what in the world, and imagined her lost someplace without a trace, frightened, thinking herself without family or friend, that she never caught the yellow baby her mother predicted, hadn't nursed me through months of colic, drilled me on math problems that she didn't understand, insisted I go to college and clean my teeth.

They had given her a doughnut and a cup of coffee and through the thump of congas and the jangle and snap of a tambourine she watched from a park bench as God—vibrant, spangly and purple—soared out of a very dark woman's mouth, rolled her eyes white and shivered through the shock of dyed orange hair that stood straight up on her head, through her fingertips and down her legs before dropping her to her knees on the grass.

Amen, sisters! Praise Jesus! called the crowd that scrambled around her thrashings, collecting shoes and earrings as she rolled onto the sand towards the monkey bars and swing sets.

Despite my cries, Amá followed the crowd as the dark woman headed toward the softball diamond. Other women along the way made sure that her skirt stayed down as the woman called out a bright yellow stream of Holy's between coughs, spits and clicks, macaw calls and gazelle brays, until she came to a stop under a poplar to sighs of Lord, Lord, Lord all around her.

Several tissues were produced to wipe the woman's tears and forehead as she was helped up from the ground. The woman was panting, a hand supported her head and someone at an arm on each side held her up. A small light brown man in a dirty white shirt and a tie pulled the Bible from underneath his armpit and held it over the woman's head announcing that Light had descended. Love had been bestowed. The congas and tambourine started up again, and as I was about to catch Amá by the arm she dropped the uneaten doughnut and cup of coffee, lifted her skirt to her thighs and began to dance a yambú.

There are those who would say that it was her mother's mother's mother's mother's yambú, or maybe just my abuela's, the yambú of a haughty negra who could turn cards with cigar smoke—legs low to the ground, her head thrown back; Amá says they said they said with the blood from a live rooster; with a length of nightshade measured against the joint of a finger; with the hairbrush of your beloved; with the name of your enemy; with five yards of gold thread; with the petals from a marigold; mi abuela could ask for the world to be shifted on its axis—but I had never seen it. I don't know if my mother had ever seen mi abuela dance the yambú, or that she had ever done it before. All I know is that it was something that she seemed to reach for easily, like a spoon or a comb, and it was there. At hand, suddenly there. In the same way that something that you have always known you knew, but had no idea that you knew; like following Aureliano Francisco García Carrera, taking his hand that first night he led me into the dark—Ven acá, come here, come here, he said—an easy grace, ancient and repeated; from the marrow, they say, when the baby knows things it hasn't been taught like words to a song no one in the house sings.

The onlookers clapped and shouted praises that begged her to search, find Him, look for Him. Let Him take you, sister, the woman covered in grass clippings shouted. They followed Amá's movement and rhythm as they repeatedly worked me—neatly as a sliver from a thumb—out of the circle they made around her. As if the strangers knew her better than I did, and like waves guided her along.

Amá, I called to her.

And even though she looked directly at me—our eyes met; Amá let's go home, we need to go home, I said—she had never learned English, there had never been a little casa blanca just off Ashland Avenue; her hands hadn't begun to gnarl from years of parting other people's hair or holding their heads under cool water. Her back was straight and her eyes clear. She was young, beautiful, the strange dark last daughter of the woman who smelled of bitterroot, whose hard glance even through a veil of blowflies could simultaneously confront you with your own fear as well as your deepest desire.

Slope-hipped and fluid, Amá was turning heads on the streets of La Habana, winning women's ire; making men want to risk the shame of questionable blood. She had not yet heard the high E Juan Ocho blew that women said nearly cut them in half, nor had she ever touched his hair.

Clouds covered the bottom of a crescent moon making it a golden horn rising in the sky; the crowd wove as Amá danced, as Amá leapt from her shoes, and the approaching night could have just as easily been day, here could shift to there.

She was within arm's reach, though I couldn't touch her. The sky could have opened up and split the ground into atoms. It was 1951 and I had never been born, as she looked at me, smiled and said, Sinatra's coming.

Helen Ellen had brought three friends with her from New York. All daughters of business partners of Ellen Helen's and doña Liliana's fathers—bankers, lawyers; men who merely referred to themselves as businessmen without ever referring to their business; men who blushed and conceded when their grown-up daughters called them Daddy—who made sure their girls came complete with clothes, shoes and handbags for every hour of the day.

Sinatra was coming, Amá will remind, when telling the story doña Liliana forgets when Helen Ellen and her father became regular guests in doña Liliana's father's house as if she were asking about an infestation of insects or about a bird that had come through a window.

Sí, doña Liliana will be jerked back in time and remember that looking like Ava Gardner had become the sole preoccupation of these women; doña Liliana says, Helen Ellen even traveled with the four or five chestnut wigs, and she had purchased a small dog that traveled in her purse. When asked the dog's name, Ellen Helen would grin and ask the asker if she or he would name their shoes or belt. The nameless Yorkie was nasty nasty nasty nasty doña Liliana says, never housebroken, always snipping at people, neither it nor Ellen Helen thought anything of its crawling out of her purse and eating off of the table; it always seemed either bored or hysterical and emitted long sighs and needed to lie down once it forgot what it had been barking about; it was jealous of a pincushion, one or two ottomans and the stray cats that got fed outside of the kitchen though too cowardly to do anything about it.

Spoiled and much too much like its mistress, it shat and slept and ate and shat again pretty much anywhere it wanted, and no one seemed to care one way or the other. Doña Liliana says that she only knew that it was male because it lifted its leg on trees and furniture legs as well as the andirons. And evenings when there wasn't some pressing event to attend to, Helen Ellen and her girlfriends took turns taking pictures of each other posing with it in what they called their One Touch of Venus dresses, they all attempted naming—FiFi, Killer, Spike, and at one time, after a persistent and unattractive caller who would eat anything for a kiss on the forehead, Claudio—none of them stuck, and they all eventually adopted Ellen Helen's sangfroid about it. It was it, and it needed to be brushed, it needed to be walked, it needed to be held even though it was known for ruining dinner jackets. Its favorite song was Desi Arnaz singing La Gonga en Nueva York, and visiting male guests—be a dear now, they were told—were sent back to the record player time and time again to play it for it one more time. It so loves it, doña Liliana says they'd say.

It needed to be fed, walked, shampooed and perfumed before any of the many events they had scheduled at the Hotel Nacional. Helen Ellen and friends had breakfast, lunch and dinner at the hotel; and then there were the strolls to be had through the lobby; doña Liliana says that she once overheard them enumerate the ways in which they could seem to be nonchalant, walking in front of the hotel, in one of the shops. Until finally one of them convinced her father that all of his business meetings needed to be held at the Hotel Nacional.

Ellen Helen and her entourage also moved into the hotel into a series of connecting suites, the sitting rooms of which were turned into dressing rooms. But even in all that space with which to giggle and spin in front of three-way mirrors, the girls' plotting took place on doña Liliana's father's patio: Why Mr. Sinatra, you smoke the same cigars as my father; although father was quickly changed to boyfriend, and then they dared replace boyfriend with lover which seemed corollary proof of a relationship between rum and libido, or at least of a relationship between rum and talking about the libidinous. Mr. Sinatra, they say they said, why thank you . . . it is the exact same perfume that your wife wears . . . that would be your new wife, I have no idea what your old wife would have worn, but I read in a magazine that this is the one Miss Gardner wears . . . or maybe it's just one of the ones that Miss Gardner wears, and what is it like to be married to one of the most beautiful women in the world, what did he think when he saw her first thing in the morning, did she look like that first thing in the morning, or did it take nearly every beauty technician in Hollywood to get her to look like that; it was agreed that if they received an affirmative to the last question the response that each would give was that they were not surprised.

Amá says that she saw the first lightning bolt of a storm that never came split a palm tree the day that the pictures depicting the departure of the honeymooning Sinatras appeared in the paper; it just hung there in the sky for a while, the storm, like blood caught in the tissue under the skin.

Helen Ellen and her friends required pitchers of mojitos, cold compresses and slivers of ice all afternoon to quell a combination of fatigue and hangover caused by the Sinatras' honeymoon. Funny, Amá says, we would watch them bored and stupid with nothing to do all day but get ready to go out all night and we'd look on them with disgust and say las americanas, yanquis, not knowing that one day we would all be one of them.

Which doña Liliana will never have any of. A Judas kiss

to compare us with them; Nunca, nunca, jamás, y never ever, she howls, Never ever did she do nothing but sit on her pretty little nalgitas all day long; never ever did she have nothing better to do but pluck her eyebrows all afternoon; never ever did she wait for something to happen to her, which when she says it, Amá and doña Cristina look at each other with both knowing and confusion.

It took a month or so, but Ellen Helen and her friends, one by one, left doña Liliana's father's house. A complete fumigation of the house was ordered by doña Liliana, which her father agreed to because shortly after Helen Ellen had left he needed to be in Miami immediately, though he made no mention of what it was he was going to be doing or who summoned him. While she had carpets beaten, windows washed and all of the rooms aired—and Amá says that it's true, doña Liliana made no pretense about anything and got down on her hands and knees and scrubbed with them—doña Liliana received a regular stream of telegrams and flowers; a weekly letter would tell of her father's health, business was always going well, he missed her terribly, would be home soon, did she want for anything?

Doña Liliana says that it was the moment that she thought that she had removed all traces of Ellen Helen and her friends that she looked back to find traces of the little dog they had left behind. Little turds, first on the patio and the stairs; once she left her lingerie drawer open while taking a shower only to find a surprise left for her when she returned. None of the household staff claimed to have seen it, the cook who fed the stray cats said that she would have noticed it. Like the knotted rags the servants had given it to chew, it dragged her to the edge between sleep and waking, and made her chase it through the dark halls.

She wrote to her father that she was fine, everything was fine, things were going well, and though she knew that it had become increasingly more difficult to conceal her sleeplessness; though, had she asked anyone in the house—Amá or any one of the other maids, the cook, her father's secretary, who said his weekly trips back to the island were for papers from her father's office or to deliver papers to his business associates downtown, the driver—Amá says that no one was aware or disturbed, no one had heard doña Liliana at night, let alone the dog.

And nearly a year passed this way.

Doña Liliana looking for the smell of gardenia y azúcar quemada—that meant home and peace—only to be distracted each night by the barking of that dog. She says that she was willing to give herself over for mad—she remembers thinking, So this is waking sleep, this not knowing if she had spent the night on the roof or merely dreamt it—and she began to settle into a life of distraction and insomnia when one morning, the cook noticed one of the stray cats dead on the flagstones of doña Liliana's father's well-appointed garden patio. Torn open and gutted like a fish at market, the stomach, heart, lungs, the intestines and spleen eaten away, and what hadn't been was covered with black flies.

Where the first was a shock, the second—which was discovered by the driver, who became nauseated by the animal's missing front legs, doña Liliana says, the tail had been gnawed up to its hindquarters—was a horror to everyone in the household except doña Liliana, who finally gave in to their demands and allowed them to bring a santera in the house. For two days the woman burned white sage in the garden, and after several implorations of las siete potencias africanas declared the house free of demons before collecting a donation that grew and grew at the point of collection as the old woman added the numbers of nietos that doña Liliana was feeding with her generosity and the places in heaven she was opening up for relatives who walked the earth restlessly and the warding off of enemies who the woman foretold intended doña Liliana great harm as well as the dead unknown to her—past inhabitants of the land, los indios, who sought its reclamation would stop at nothing, nada, señora, the woman cautioned, until it was returned to its rightful owners—until doña Liliana's purse was empty and she had slipped the gold bangles from her wrist.

Though the cook's screams the next morning alerting the house to the discovery of the third and fourth resulted in the youngest of the maids, the driver's daughter, being unable to stop crossing herself and pleading for protection for days afterward, doña Liliana says they said, long after she had fled the house without gathering her things or giving notice of her resignation.

And although the entire house held its breath, stood and watched each morning after that, afraid to approach the patio in the mornings, doña Liliana says that the strays no longer surprised her. For each that she shoveled up herself—because not even the men would touch them after the santera's visit—there had been a night—not every night but enough that there was always the queasy queasy rocking of a sleep-sick rolling in her—the dog woke her and sent her chasing. Her distraction had presented itself as something tangible, a weight at the end of a shovel handle, to strengthen herself against, bear up, or else be pulled down by.

Amá says she and the cook would watch doña Liliana collecting the carcasses at the end of her shovel and wondered out loud why she had refused the gardener's offer to take care of the strays during his twice-weekly visits; why she insisted if he wanted to be of any help at all that he bury them at the far end of the garden, beyond the pond and the fountain where the land pushed up in slight prominence that if you were standing on the top floor looking out of any of the windows—or from any of the windows of the surrounding houses—the tiny crosses that she had him fashion from scrap wood and whitewash could be seen.

Hurricane season came that year trapping doña Liliana's father in Miami she says he wrote. And though she never recalls him writing an exact date he planned his return, the letter excused his missing a return to her and their home and their life, a party where she could invite all of their friends to celebrate on the rains and his need to be in Buenos Aires the following week. Why he was going to Argentina and who or what had summoned him there he didn't write; business, he cabled her later from the airport in Miami.

After each of the torrential rains, doña Liliana went out to count the burial sites, retrieving and replacing crosses that had been washed away from memory, she says, because it didn't matter so much that they were exact markers but a tally that she kept so that when one had gone missing she would request a new one from the gardener. She wrote back to her father that all was well, she was fine, he should go in good conscience, take care of business, take exercise in the mornings and walks after dinner; the house was fine, his staff took care of her as if he were still there. She made no mention of the cats or that she had disallowed the gardener to weed the wild pineapple that after the rains came up across the lawns around the pond, and between the stones of the patio, turned bright green before it pushed red towards the sun.

When he wrote he had run into Helen Ellen and her father, and that Ellen Helen was delighted to come down and keep doña Liliana company for a while—You must be lonely, she says he wrote, without your old papá to be late for the lovely dinners that you plan so carefully, and to get cigar ash all over the house—she didn't write back about the little dog that Helen Ellen and her friends had left behind that had somehow survived the rains or that it continued to leave the remains of its kills—at least two or three a week by then—for her to find; nor did she write that since his departure the gardenias had grown several feet high and twice as wide, budded, yet refused to blossom—the pods fell, full, with a heavy thunk so often that in a stiff breeze, you would have thought it a shower of hail—nor did she write of her sleeplessness or her restlessness; no, she was as beautiful and bright and happy as ever, waiting for him to come home again; he should tell Ellen Helen that she would be waiting at the dock for her with open arms; because doña Liliana says she had no idea why other than she felt ready for it, or readied for it, and although she couldn't have told you at the time what it was that she was ready for, or for how long she had been preparing for whatever it was, all she knew is none of it frightened her any longer.

Helen Ellen arrived off the ferry with an enormous basket of Florida clementines and a copy of Time magazine with Batista on the cover. Without seeing the driver, she handed him the tickets for her trunks—Sí mijo, maleteros, dos, doña Liliana laughs when she tells it, pues I think that it is possible that she somehow knew that although she would leave the island several times before the Revolution that she would be bound to it forever—Ellen Helen threw her arms around her, kissed her hurriedly and repeatedly, and spoke of their sisterhood, and said with Batista back in office it was like they had been united forever, blood relatives almost, soon no one will be able to tell us apart.

A benevolent ambassador in her tight cream-colored suit, sunglasses, wide-brimmed hat and some arrogant and insistent fragrance, doña Liliana says she looked at her and smiled, took up the basket of oranges, which she later learned tasted of nothing, and said they needed to get back, she had ordered a cold supper, and there was just enough time to freshen up; friends were arriving later to welcome her.

. . . Though, of course, every time doña Liliana tells this story, I can't help but be reminded of the pictures of José Martí held by the Organization of American States that you have in your textbooks, señores, on page two fifteen, and the picture of Teddy Roosevelt disembarking into San Juan harbor in his white suit and hat on page two oh eight. I've brought supplies. Scissors, glue sticks, sequins, colored pencils, black markers and a few X-Acto knives that I would like to have back at the end of class without their having been used to make indelible the Magic Marker work of the rather prolific artist who seems to think that we need be reminded of the old familiar suggestion in a rather baroque style.

Babcock, Chávez, you'll do the honors?

Ay, señor Ostrovski, I do understand your desire not to desecrate any more school property, or school materials, you or anyone else who feels as strongly is free to come up and collect a library pass so that you need not watch what señor Ostrovski has described as an act of vandalism; I really do not wish to disturb those of you who are so constitutionally disposed. For those of you who do not venture into the library as diligently or as often as a student like señor Ostrovski—and for those of you who are not aware of the Scholars Cabinet outside the main office downstairs, señor Ostrovski has maintained a four point average over the past four years—you will find rows and rows of books neatly catalogued and completely organized within the confines of their bindings—save the occasional additions of underlining and, on the rarer occasion, chewed sticks of gum—that will help you complete the alternate assignment if you don't care for this one. You'll have the next two days to complete an essay on your notion of desecration in which you will first extricate the Latinate secrate from its prefix, and in the three double-spaced typed pages that follow how you are able to discern that which you consider sacred from that which you are told to consider sacred.

For those of you who have elected to stay—and I'm pleased to see that even you señor Ostrovski prefer this assignment—you first want to carefully fold page two oh eight so that the side the page number is on is tucked carefully in the gully in the center of the book; you'll find that you have eliminated the men at Roosevelt's right, dressed in black suits, disappear. Once secure, open the page again and cover the inside flap with a few strikes of a glue stick, and carefully smooth your seals so that Roosevelt eventually dries nice and flat so that we have the full benefit of Roosevelt's smiling face—a confident man—that we have to imagine as rosy because it is before Kodachrome.

Después, place a ruler in the gutter between pages two fifteen and two fourteen. This is where an X-Acto knife comes in handy, because the incision that you are going to make is clean and swift; even though we are going to eliminate these two pages, you will later need the quote attributed to the then president of the American Federation of Labor, Samuel Gompers—if you can imagine going through life with such a name—where he asks, Is it not strange that after entering upon a war with Spain to obtain the freedom of Cuba, now that victory has been achieved, the question of Cuban independence is so often scouted? And from these two pages, you'll want to carefully cut the picture of the battleship Maine floating in Havana harbor.

With these two pages missing, note how much bigger and jollier—like Santa Claus—Roosevelt looks than Martí. And Martí, small and dark, for the first time ever has the opportunity to look at Roosevelt with a furled suspicious gaze that never happened in life or anywhere on paper, and Roosevelt can smile gleefully back at him. Now they are neighbors. Good neighbors, I believe Roosevelt would have said.

Make your own choices now; you can either paste the picture of the Maine between them or you can paste it below or above them. And here's where the sequins and the colored pencils come in handy; though bear in mind, doña Liliana says she was wearing a light-colored dress and probably was carrying one of those longish purses, a thin one that fits so neatly under the arm like a folded newspaper, therefore allowing you to carry everything that you might need without destroying your silhouette . . . well, after all, it was in the middle of the afternoon in summer . . .

Señores, lost in the fire at my Amá's house is a letter from my prima Carolina whom I've never met where she writes, after asking for twenty one-dollar bills because she needed to buy an American laundry detergent—a good one, no wonder the Soviets smell the way that they do—Tía, you should see doña Liliana's father's house; none of the old glory of the olden days; there are bars on the windows and laundry drying in between them; there's got to be sixty to a hundred people living there; and it looks as if there is a tree, a flamboyant, has grown in through the floor of one of the front rooms and burst out through an outside wall; she writes that the last time she went by the house she was in a cab, but she thought that the tree had begun to bloom.

Helen Ellen had a passion for casinos—not that she allowed herself to part with any of her father's money that way, doña Liliana says, Ellen Helen thought them one of the best ways to be seen; according to doña Liliana, Helen Ellen thought the opera and the ballet a complete waste of time given that one and one's dress spent the majority of time in the dark, and then what was the point of getting all dressed up if you couldn't make other women simply emerald because as you know querida, she says Ellen Helen said, a full slip, high heels and a very nice pair of stockings was all any man required of you; a burlap sack would do.

Doña Liliana found that when Ellen Helen made grand pronouncements regarding proper etiquette and decorum at, por ejemplo, a cocktail party or some other such occasion that burlap sacks were often her point of reference. And to simply hear the impatience in her exasperated response—it's what potatoes come in, silly—to doña Liliana's question what was a burlap sack; and as much as doña Liliana never tired of seeing a look of stricken befuddlement flash across Helen Ellen's face, Ellen Helen never seemed to anticipate doña Liliana's response of surprise as she claimed to only ever having seen potatoes on a plate, preferably with sauce, and that she should make it a point of having the cook show her how the potatoes came when they were delivered, she says she said to Helen Ellen, nenita, you make it all sound so interesting.

Doña Liliana says she found that there was something perversely pleasurable about a certain kind of ignorance that she could use to display a greater ignorance in Ellen Helen that she couldn't resist. Which is why Ellen Ellen was translating the article on Batista that April in 1952 that she arrived, when everyone else in the room allowed the comparison of Batista's reinstatement to the exclusivity of a party to suffice as a plausible explanation as to why she thought the whole island should be ecstatic and return to drinking, doña Liliana says she turned the attention of the entire room back on Helen Ellen, closing her in in a wall of eyes, when she asked what the closing of the university and half of the police department in the streets have to do with party invitations.

The letters and telegrams that came from doña Liliana's father over the next year—the first from Buenos Aires, then Guatemala; Miami again; then the Philippines, Chihuahua and then Miami again—made no mention of when he would return home: he was fine, business was going well; there was nothing in the world for her to worry about, nothing in the world, she could go anywhere she wanted to; do anything that she wanted; there were private schools that she could attend, anywhere in the world, anywhere in the U.S.—wouldn't you like to live in the U.S. for a while, nenita?—Spain? Spain, he wrote, you loved Barcelona when we were there; why not go to Barcelona?

Doña Liliana walked along the expanse of pangola that ran along the shoreline near a summerhouse of a friend, well, not really a friend's house, she says, more the house of one of her father's business partners—two months' vacation that Ellen Helen said would do them a world of good; a change of scenery, pull them out of their rut—but the entire trip, doña Liliana says that she kept thinking, Why Barcelona and what rut? Barcelona? Barcelona? Barcelona? Until she couldn't think it past thinking anymore; it no longer really meant anything to her; she wasn't sure she had ever been there before. It's hard to imagine living in a world, she now says, in which you know nothing; it's tough to figure where you might fit and what you might be doing.

¿Verdad? ¿No, Martínez? Ostrovski?

Pick any day of the week and any article out of the newspaper. Not even an article if you are as averse to reading as so many of you have demonstrated. Pick an advertisement for something that will make your breath fresher or your armpits less smelly, señor Chávez, and tell me if you are able to predict the future. Will you be kissed? Will you get laid? Has the Parisian fashion designer who decides that we should all be wearing camouflage this year—the one wrapping it around our asses and our mattresses, covering walls and floors and car seats and baby strollers with it—divined war?

Ay, mis hijos, hindsight is indeed a wonderful point from which to predict the future, ¿no? But only if you could be in both places at once, the past and the future.

Por ejemplo, how many mistakes would you have made on last week's quiz on the whereabouts of Batista between 1944 and 1948 had you the benefit of the notes—if you will be so kind as to notice, albeit late in the game, that I have had the generosity not to make notes in red ink all these years to ease some of your anxieties, to allow for the luxury of a lie for those of you who needed it after class when asked what grade did you get—by notes I mean, agreed-upon dates, señores. Sí señor . . . or as in the words of señor Alvárez, had you had 'em there next to you, would any of you have written the same essay?

Entonces, señores Chávez or Ostrovski might have; after all, an A is an A, ¿no? And there is a certain school of logic that would suggest that if you did no preparation for the quiz, some reading—if nothing, on the bus ride to school that morning—might have made the task less arduous, less boring. But this in itself might be asking too much. And—I don't mean this facetiously—it's possible that even the most prepared of you could have come in to find that the rules could have changed, the world had suddenly shifted, and you could have come in to find that I had written the essay question on the board in Mandarin, and still have had the same expectations of all of you.

Por ejemplo—for those of you who had no idea last Friday, Batista had two presidencies; señores Chávez or Ostrovski can tell you what he was doing in between them—what material difference did it make or would it have made for a person like my mother at the time, a maid from the provinces just happy to have a job that didn't involve a farm implement; or someone like doña Liliana who was white, at least while she was still in Cuba, and wealthy to the point she could be without regulating the light switches in her house unless she chose it as a hobby? Not unlike many cubanos whose lives were hinged to the rhythmic underpinnings to a passacaglia—sí, sí sí, yo sé, señor Ostrovski, I will bring an example of a passacaglia for you all to listen to so that you'll understand what I am talking about—no matter, igual, what it's like is the pendulum swing or the consistent rhythm of time. Yet time itself belongs to others, was set by others, so long ago that we all were all born into it without recognizing its pulse. It seems it's only when life slaps the shit out of us in some good or bad way that we . . .

Well, no matter.

Think of it like a shift in this country from Democratic to Republican parties or vice versa, and the effect that it has on your lives; does the number of CDs that you can or cannot buy greatly differ from administration to administration; the movement is first quick, and then quick to remind us of its contiguousness by rocking rocking rocking back to an evenness. What one read in the morning or evening paper or heard over the radio that spoke of difference or a skip in the pulse of the familiar, by the time that it was retold in a downtown La Habana barbershop or in the dentist's waiting room seemed to have already separated fact from rumor and by the time it was repeated it ran as thin as wet tissue paper, not even chisme worth repeating. So that when she heard that there were boys in the mountains, it sounded to doña Liliana like yet another watery lie.

Which is why when I tell you that as she emerged from the pangola at that summer retreat in Santiago of one of her father's business associates the summer following Batista's Time magazine cover, and she could hear Helen Ellen calling her name, you'll understand when I tell you that instead of hiding or heading toward the house, she simply walked to where she could be seen by all of the friends and friends of friends having drinks out on the lawn and put her foot, shoe and all, into a steaming color pot.

She says they called to each other to come watch as she plunged her toes in deeper and could feel the earth begin to warm, and it was as if the mercurial swirled—blue and green; white and baby vomit; ocher and blood—ink of the hole sucked and churned, filling her pink silk pump, soaking her stocking.

Oh my God, Liliana, what the hell are you doing? Ellen Helen yelled it seemed not being able to help her English.

Though she stood on the bluff above doña Liliana calling for her to come up, calling for her to stop being so silly—What have you finally gone loca, loca?—neither Helen Ellen or any of the others made a move to get doña Liliana out.

They called, poised as if watching a street juggler, like sacks of linen sausages in their light-colored clothing balancing cocktails and cigarettes and cigars and plates of canapés and a sombrilla or two and several pairs of sunglasses, concerned that someone they very seldom called by name—most just said querida when they telephoned her looking for a shopping companion, company at a benefit, a fourth or a sixth at a dinner party, a suitable date for a cousin visiting from Spain; the type of girl that went with you when you went to pick out a new car, someone whose father had just a little bit of pull with the government to get minor charges dropped and court records expunged, the girl they wanted to remain a virgin forever, young forever, so that she could be fucked open in their heads night after night before going to sleep only to dream of fucking her open again; the girl they counted on later becoming fat, losing her hair, or better her front teeth, she was either to marry a homosexual or a man who would beat her ugly, married and to bear a child for each year that her husband was still alive to only—within a year of the birth of her last child while just beginning her fifties—have to watch her husband die a long agonizing death that between his medical bills and his gambling debts would leave her penniless and destitute. And even though they had all somehow pinned their speculations of their own futures onto hers, depended upon her as a balm between themselves and aging and decay, not one of them came down to help her, came down to see if she had fallen into the color pot or chosen it.

At her calf the ring of mud that turned her stocking a mossy-green and fecal-brown felt icy compared to her toes that felt like the hots on the ends of cooking pieces of coal.

She was no longer interesting to half the crowd on the bluff, who turned away and to each other. The rest wondered out loud why, and what was she thinking as midthigh, nearly to her hip—I hope it's worth the ruin of a perfectly good stocking, darling Ellen Helen laughed—sweat broke over her brow and shoulders, and her neck knotted as if on a tension wire or her spine was being pulled taut by a spool at her tailbone. She says that at that point she knew that she couldn't bear it much longer, she would soon have to free her leg and head back up the bluff as a topic of inquiry and curiosity. However, she had already planned—before she had decided to test, find out what the earth did inside—not to tell any of them what she had found out.

Don't fall in m'dear, Helen Ellen called down spilling her drink as she stumbled over her own shoes and then the brown-and-white wing tips of the man beside her. But it would be years before doña Liliana would tell anyone that she couldn't if she had wanted to. The earth pushed back, pressed itself up from itself onto itself; it took all the force that she had to hold her position and not be thrown into the mud beside the color pot. A vector aimed directly upward, split and wrapped in bands around her leg. Tight. Burning. She held one hand out for balance and dug the nails of the other into her palm. She says she winced yet wouldn't cry out, wouldn't entertain those on the bluff any further; her eyes began to water as she threw her head back and her hat—something Ellen Helen had picked for her—fell into the mud, and she says that she could hear the ooze seep into the stiffened damask silk; lichen from the sea, microbes from the air, hungry and swift, began devouring the ribbon band, unthreading the weave of the fabric and swallowing it whole, propagating and feeding on it, sloughing skins and extruding wastes that ripened and fermented. And as she raised her head and brought her chin to her chest in response to a bright flash of finely sharpened concertina wire that tore through her, she says that it was the earth that let her see, the earth squeezing her eyes clear of enough tears to reveal them on top of the bluff dotting it like the little crosses marking the dead strays as Ellen Helen roamed between them, thin and rat-like, molted as if suffering from mange, before the color pot forced her out.

A lovely weekend; a lovely afternoon; a lovely evening spent; so nice, the dresses and the flowers, the music and the dancing; the light off the ocean; the mist in the air; you'd be reminded of, doña Liliana wrote back when her father wrote to ask about her trips away from the city: off of the island; an excursion with Helen Ellen to Paris, another that she went on with other friends to Cairo; to England; and when people asked about the unrest in her country, she'd smile and they would back away from the question as if they had invaded her privacy, but she says in reality she had nothing to say at the time.

She went to Miami to find that she had missed her father by just a few hours, and when she returned home she was told that he had just left. If it was true, we can't tell anymore, not one of us thought to ask Amá—it had never seemed important—before memory began to come at such high premiums.

Doña Liliana began to note sometime afterward that her father's closet—a walk-in dressing room, really, she explains—marked the seasons for her: summer clothes were exchanged for winter ones; and then warmer ones for lighter ones. Occasionally she would come home from a routine shopping trip before there had been time for one of the maids to remove a recently tapped cigar from an ashtray, and the room would still be fragrant, nearly radiate, with the grassy aftershave that she says that was nearly always somewhere underneath the smells of tobacco and body of the crushing hugs that he would lock her in even when they had only been separated for the day.

Querida—as if he had been there yesterday, doña Liliana says—he'd write that the larches in Panama were no substitute for the palmas reales that dot our island; the sky went lavender as he sat on the deck of a boat docked—so close yet so far away—near the Bay of Biscayne, longing, aching to be home; pero querida, negocios keep me from what I love, he wrote, what I long for, as if he had no control or contract over his feelings or his business, as if somehow the island so dear to him had ceased to exist as a living vibrancy except for in the flickers of memory.

There was no mention of possibilities for his daughter's future, nor did it seem to her that he hoped for or dreamed about the future of his only child, the child he wrote was light, the beacon he saw at the end of the day when he wrote he was tired and irritable and it was all that he could do to find his bed; he never asked if she had aged or become fatter, had she seen the first wrinkle in the mirror. She imagined it an island, without radio or newspapers; negocios with no connection to anything close; like the sensations of warm experienced waist-deep as the tide comes in, she imagined it a helplessness and thrill of giving yourself over to change without having control.

Se armó la catástrofe, las viejas cubanas say, or a shithouse built. A secret place, a quiet quiet sanctuary where headlines reading Moncada—so close to the place where she had put her foot into the color pot a few months before—or the twenty-fifth of July that year had come and gone as another change of shirt and tie.

She says that she still wonders if he ever imagined her—the girl he wrote remembering as looking wide-eyed and fascinated by a tray of pastries in Rome—needing her convent school prayer—Dios, por favor, ayúdame; Quítame este dolor, por favor; Llena mi soledá con tu amor; Llena mi soledá con tu amor—as she came home late at night, as at every turn, places she was used to and knew, had been comfortable in and familiar with the ways in which they welcomed her back, were suddenly queer with men in uniforms. Men who in the past would have never spoken to her, carried guns, and occasionally asked her dates where they were headed so that a walk in the park, an evening stroll had elements of the criminal, made her suspect. Her father wrote to her of Gypsy dancers in Granada, gelato had at the house of a business partner and his wife—a sunny italiana with the most agreeable disposition who supervises each step of the making of ice cream—that reminded him of a café in Palermo. He wrote and wrote, though no matter how recent the event, he always told it from the long view of hills: nothing predicted anything that would happen, nothing was said of that that will happen, everything had happened in what he told her, she says; it was as if he was living his own memoir.

The hem of a woman's dress at a dinner in Washington, D.C., reminded him of her mother's laugh, a deflated beach ball tangled with seaweed let loose an entire summer when he was seven and he and all his cousins ran naked through the cane fields, scaring the cutters, floating on their backs in a murky pond for hours thinking of nothing, nothing at all.

Once, she says she said—on a sleepless night that doña Liliana roamed her father's well-appointed house in La Habana's El Vedado, she first noticed a world gone sepia; Helen Ellen had yet to make it back from a recent trip to the States or who knows where, she says, and the house was calm, cool and still with just the servants, and her only duty was to clear the fragments of half-eaten cat off of the patio the few mornings; horse-drawn carriages creaked stone streets, boulevards wide enough to accommodate street traffic and cars and the perambulators of the well-to-do vanished; she says she even ran the poet Plácido, whose picture if you did not do the reading for last night you missed as we unfortunately had to sacrifice it to bring Roosevelt and Martí together, no matter, she says that she ran the poor poet backwards between houses; she could send the marauders that chased him, wanting him dead, back to their dinners, their children, their wives with full fat tetas that made them burst with pride; she says she could collect the poet's blood off of the sand, scoop it up in her palms out of the street; she says she talked with indios and babes that lay centuries in typhus, influenza and smallpox crypts before they vanished before her; she says, if you can believe it, she believed that all that was left was the rare and blue-green glittering dazzle that she had read about in history books—and once, she says she said was all she said before she let her father's ashes loose in the wind.

The box had been surprisingly light in her hand. All the weeks that it sat on the table in the great hallway of her father's house next to piles of condolences that she never got around to writing thank-yous for, she had imagined it much heavier; imagined something that might remind her of the heft of his belly, or his broad shoulders, the groaning sound that he made when he was getting out of chairs.

El cortejo headed toward La Plaza del Cathedral had been a long black uncoiling of chauffeur-driven cars and propriety in the late-morning sun that passed through her with a handclasp, a word, a teary yet cool embrace and then it was gone. The list of associates, business partners, their wives, their children that claimed to have understood her loss, her sorrow, in a way that each individual mourner in an effort to convey the personal replicated the person in front of him. The telegram that she received from Batista was identical to the letter from Earl T. Smith, the then U.S. ambassador who incidentally señores is not mentioned in any of the pages of your text just in case you were wondering if we had already cut him out; each spoke of his contributions, each expressed regret that something so tragic should happen at this time of unrest; each equated her sorrow, her loss, her unhappiness in a way that when doña Liliana says that she attempted to try them on to see if they fit, they became tangled, seemed inside out; ill-fitting as ermine on a woman of twenty-four, she says, the bereavement they were talking about was an older woman's or a young widow's, however, she says that at the time she felt like an infant although her mourning was like the wear of a ring on the finger of a woman older than she had ever known.

Ellen Helen hadn't been at the funeral, which had been a week of pageantry and show that included a procession to her family crypt complete with prayer and consecration yet without interment. Doña Liliana says all she had was the box and a gaggle of sentiments; no one had told her how, and she used the time between the last of his letters and the arrival of the box at her door—delivered by a soldier and a man who identified himself as a member of Batista's cabinet—to approximate when. And then nearly three months later, Helen Ellen arrived very tanned and relaxed—hairless nearly everywhere, darling, doña Liliana says, Ellen Helen claimed to be fresh from retreat in Lucerne where the waters were salubrious, the masseurs suave y fuerte, varonil; well worth the trip, she said, Helen Ellen couldn't possibly think of money better spent. At the airport, doña Liliana says she noticed something reptilian—a lack of eyebrows—like dry fish scales her back felt when she hugged me, doña Liliana says.

Ellen Helen came with a bodyguard, which at the time, doña Liliana says, was simultaneously thinkable and unthinkable. A curious young man: strong, tall, but with stark white hair, and nearly colorless blue eyes that gave the impression that despite the brute force he projected, and the bulge his shoulder holster made, under the black suits he wore in spite of the heat, he held fast to a great shock, a singularly definitive moment in which time—calibrated towards the emphatic—shook him both backwards and forwards, leaving him somewhere in between. Silent when he accompanied

Ellen Helen to parties or nightclubs in the evenings—he even stood outside of the changing rooms of the finest dressmakers of the day that La Habana had to offer—doña Liliana doesn't recall ever being introduced or his shaking hands with any of the men they knew. He was just there. He ate in the kitchen, shared a room with the driver; and even the times that they thought that no one was looking, that they thought that they were concealed by the dark, he simply grabbed Ellen Helen by the hair and lifted her skirt and took her quickly, silently from behind; afterward, while she adjusted her clothing and smoothed her temples, he'd let go a great loud spattering piss, the puddles of which the dog avoided when leaving its victims. But by then, there was very little to bury, she says, she imagined the dog growing fatter and fatter as she began only finding bits of bone and fur when she went out in the mornings.

With little to do to occupy her time, the following fall doña Liliana took a lover. Her first. At twenty-four, an orphan, the girl who had been well known, documented in the slyest of language in gossip columns as a tease, an heiress, a catch, they read, the extraordinarily well outfitted daughter of a well-appointed house in El Vedado found herself between an acne-scarred man—who called her chiflada, she says in the most affectionate of ways—three years her junior and the greasy, shit-smeared sheets in his student apartment.

It was a relationship, she says, in which they never stopped making each other. Over and over, daydreams, fantasies from a past of long wonderings of what this moment would be like had materialized. She had shirts made for him by her father's shirtmaker in London; he bought her used books that he wanted her to read, and lost patience with the rate at which she read and insisted that he read them aloud to her. If you loved me, one would say to the other before one of them would request a pot of coffee brewed, or the other would desire love in the form of a trinket stolen from a sundries store; would he run naked around the block in the dead of night; would she tell her high society perra americana friend to go fuck herself; did she mind too much that he flashed the crack of his ass to the entire mezzanine at the ballet; could she forgive him for dropping grapes into her décolletage during dinner at the home of one of her father's former business partners?

Fuentes, Horacio Fuentes, she says his name was, though Fuentes was all she ever called him. Fuentes was all she heard anyone call him. And even though his friends and their girlfriends wanted very little to do with doña Liliana until the bill came around in a restaurant, not one of them let the opportunity go by—when Fuentes was in the bathroom or deep in conversation with someone else at the table—to let her know that she wasn't good enough for him. He was a genius, she was told by one well-meaning friend; soon to be one of the island's most revered philosophers, by another; he would become a politician like this country has never known, doña Liliana says a woman, an artist who never showed her canvases—I mean nobody saw them, not even the three people she lived with—told her as she helped herself to the entire pack of cigarettes doña Liliana kept in her purse, not because she smoked, but because the more Fuentes talked, the more he smoked, and there had been a bitter evening followed by an equally bitter argument in which he asked her how, how, how, how could she, how could she?

If you loved me, she says she said, and in the middle of the afternoon, fully dressed, he stood in the fountain of El Palacio de los Capitanes, singing a bolero in which the air was dusted by the black and violet wings of mariposas and a woman scorched his heart, left him stupid and awestruck y solamente, wanting.

He only agreed to escort her to an evening at the opera

once she had strung the pearls she was wearing around his neck. He needed to tell her she was day, she was night, she was his reason for living, and she needed to blush when she heard it. If he loved her, he would take off her shoes, reach under her skirt, remove her stockings and rub her legs and feet; if she loved him, she would take something to his tía Sofia who was a santera, he said, just a few herbs and things that she can't grow herself. She says that when she cocked her head and raised her brow towards him he said, No need to worry, querida, just business, he said, he and his friends would load the car at her house; sus hermanos y sus tíos would unload it; she would—if she loved him—just need to drive. Alone; she shouldn't take the driver; no, he couldn't go himself, or he would; he had plans; just business. Don't worry, querida, she says he said as he kissed her forehead, I'll be here when you come back.

There is something to being thought both pretty and feckless, doña Liliana has always said, no one expects any more of you than to have a fresh face on and to be appropriately dressed for any occasion; like a disguise the world offers you from itself. Had he thought more of her—thought she might stop the car outside the city lights and look, make sure for herself—he never would have asked.

She says she felt the length of the barrels of the bundle of rifles, the handles, could smell machine oil through the heavy canvas bag, and knew immediately what Fuentes thought of her, and she was pleased. Relieved that each time—moments in bed, on a drive, walking in the park—when they said if, they both meant if.

A light rain scattered across the tops of palms above her, the diesel engine of the black-finned Caddy chugged and there was no need for a flashlight. If he asked, she'd kiss Fuentes' shoulders, his back. His arms, she allowed him to push her head around his body, think she was his to move about and play with at will. And she knew at that moment that she would continue to let him, she says, because without him, she—one gossip columnist had called the girl who can go everywhere when she returned from Egypt—wouldn't have been standing in the mud nor would she have been headed toward the Sierra Maestra. At home she would have been watching Ellen Ellen powder something or another as she prepared to go out for the evening; Horacio Fuentes—if he loved her—whoever he was, hardly mattered; he thought her silly, frivolous; thought he was making her to his advantage. In exchange—the second and third times he asked for her love in the form of a trip to the mountains—she, while his friends loaded her car in the carriage house, tried to remember how Ava Gardner made up her eyes, or what she might wear that made her both alluring and secretive; she says, she wished that she had paid attention when Helen Helen giggled over the bottle of perfume that they said the actress wore, so that to Fuentes she was mysterious and luminous as any projected image that held his fascination in the dark of a movie house. Doña Liliana says she had no idea where he was headed, or why exactly she wanted it, she says, she simply knew it was what she wanted.

. . . IT WOULD BE nearly dawn when she would come home on the nights that Fuentes would send her, and doña Liliana says that her skin was hot, and she called, Mireya, Mireya come quick. Doña Liliana says Amá appeared in her nightgown with her hair tied up, apologizing that—Amá says because she understood that this, according to Marta, to be seen by the mistress of the house in one's nightclothes, was something that was to never happen—she was not already dressed and ready. Doña Liliana shushed her, grabbed Amá by the arm and took her into her bedroom. Amá says that she had never sat on the bed that she made sometimes twice daily before, never seen doña Liliana's room from that perspective; the dresser and vanity that she dusted; the bottles she put back in their places. Mireya, doña Liliana says she said, I have something to tell you, I have something I need to tell somebody, y Mireya, she says she began for the first time in her life to open up to somebody.

And it was doña Liliana yelling Amá's name—¡Mireya! ¡Mireya!—as she negotiated the grass and mud of the uneven terrain in high-heeled shoes and pink suit, the skirt of which for a while has been too tight for her now-broad hips—¡Mireya! ¡Mireya!—that caused Amá to stop dancing, and I watched as Wicker Park began to materialize for her.

The people from the Jesus bus tried to encourage her with cries of Praise be and Light everlasting, but they soon became disoriented by Amá's confusion. Distracted by her whirling around to find the source of where her name was coming from; the drum stopped and those who had been dancing around her followed to the clink of the tambourine against a hip as they headed with her across the field. ¡Mireya! ¡Mireya! where my calls of Amá hadn't worked, my implorations for her to come with me, and each time I had been able to grab her arm either she or one of the people from the Jesus bus would wrench me away and take her back with them in the dance. It was either the pounding of the drum or wild fear I could feel in ears and nostrils, but no word as neat as home that described exactly where I wanted her to come would come to me in Spanish.

Mireya, doña Liliana called and she and Amá held each other for a moment until we heard the sound of Naty Valdez McIntosh's bracelets as she waved—Hola; Hola; Hola—from the opposite end of the field.

She was walking on tiptoe so that the heels of her shoes didn't sink into the mud while she balanced herself with one hand on Román's shoulder. Ay, Señora, Naty said when they were finally close enough, I have no idea you could dance so good, I seen you, you keep so many secretos. Amá slumped on doña Liliana's shoulder trying to locate the girl who was talking to her.

Cállate la boca, chiflada, doña Liliana snapped. Which set the two women into an argument—a rush of shivering bracelets and pointed, sharpened and lacquered fingers—in Spanish about Naty's stupidity and doña Liliana's bitchiness. And when Román and I joined in to stop them, I watched the same look come over the faces of the people from the Jesus bus that were in front of us the day on the commons that doña Cristina says started his English. Faces just like ours, Román's, Amá's and mine. I know that look, seen it before: black faces wondering how Spanish came out of our mouths. What are you? the boys taunted after I stopped Román before he could repeat what they had told him that he had to say as fast as he could—the red ants run up the black ants pole, the red ants run up the black ants pole—if he wanted to get by; whatareyouwhatareyouwhatareyou, a question that I wouldn't hear until I asked it of myself years later when, after weeks of following Aureliano into his bedroom, I woke to an arm dead with sleep underneath him, and to wake him I whispered, This, this what we're doing, what does it make me? and he pulled me closer around him and said, Mine, inextricably mine; what are you, and I told them in English to fuck off, and said vamos to Román, but he stood there wanting to please them in some way—the red ants run up the black ants pole, the red ants run up the black ants pole—wanting to fit in; his eyes were focused on the lips of the biggest one, and I watched as he mouthed the words—the red ants run up the black ants pole, the red ants run up the black ants pole—practiced before he said them; I don't remember what I said, but it was in Spanish, and as immediate as the need to vomit, the first punch was thrown.

Naty began to cry and doña Liliana was yelling, pointing at her face when Amá straightened up and took Naty in her arms. No, no mija, eso es, eso es, eso, eso, eso es, she said rocking her in her arms. She looked over Naty's shoulder and saw me. Mijo, she said, take us home.

Doña Liliana says that Fuentes sent her two more times, and each time she came home she told Amá what she had seen, what had happened. Of the gruff brother and uncles, and how the vieja who had first pretended to be the santera in need of herbs no longer showed up. She also told Amá about her evening with Fuentes, the things he talked about with his friends, and how she couldn't help it, even if anyone thought her una malita, she nearly always let him slide his fingers up her leg and under her skirt; it felt just that good.

A month had gone by since he last asked her to go to the mountains, and she says that each time that she read more about what was going on there, the more anxious she became to get closer, see. She couldn't bring herself to ask him if his tía needed more herbs; like in bed, her enthusiasm would betray a clearing in the miasma he looked through when he looked at her. She had to wait. All the experience that she had planning menus, arranging parties—a distant cousin was getting married and needed a trousseau that Liliana was happy to provide—there was the house, and the cars, and the signing of things that kept her busy. Until she realized that it had been weeks since she heard from him.

His apartment didn't seem in any more disarray than usual. And for as long as she knew him the lock never worked. Another week went by and she happened to run into the woman—the artist who didn't show her canvases—who told her, after collecting lunch and all of the change and the pack of cigarettes that doña Liliana kept for Fuentes in her purse, that he had been taken away in the night several weeks before. Which night? Doña Liliana says that she asked, but the girl didn't know.

What she did say was that Fuentes had whimpered, whimpered like a little bitch, she added, you think after all that talk, everything he was saying all the time, he'd have at least been man enough to be taken away like a man.

But doña Liliana knew better. No, she says she immediately thought how every second with him had been like wishing someone would write you a love letter, wishing someone would fly into a jealous rage, wishing someone couldn't be without you, wishing someone needed you, wishing, whether it was true or not it fills your life in the most extraordinary way. No, she says she told the girl.

Amá says doña Liliana had been gone more than a week before Ellen Ellen noticed. In fact, it had been at a party that Helen Helen was throwing for her own birthday—she had complained bitterly, Amá says, that doña Liliana had not been around to plan a party; she forged Liliana's signature on the invitations, ordered the staff around and charged all of the food and wine to doña Liliana's account—guests were arriving, Amá was taking their coats and Ellen Helen asked ¿Dónde está nuestra anfitriona? And Amá said that she went to the mountains the week before.

Now it depends on who you ask, señores, doña Liliana wasn't there and Amá has always claimed to not remember the incident other than the slap. However, doña Liliana says that she heard that both Amá's admission of doña Liliana's whereabouts and the slap had taken place in front of a room full of Helen Ellen's guests, the curse that Amá threw on Ellen Helen has always remained in doubt.

Amá denies it, pero noticed shortly afterward that Helen Ellen's hair began to fall out in large patches that she would find on the side of the bed, in the toilet and wastepaper basket of her bathroom, at the vanity. Ellen Helen took to staying in her room that was kept dark when food was brought up to her and she hid in the bathroom when it was being cleaned. The front door was opened to at least three or four doctors, a wig maker and a funny little person who, she could not tell, was either a man or a woman who wore a lot of dramatically drawn eye makeup and the most cleverly folded silk scarves on her or his head. And it is only because one of the doctors had suggested that she go into hospital that anyone of the household had seen that in a short period of time she had gained a considerable amount of weight. One hundred and fifty, maybe two hundred pounds, and her skin must have been splitting and she was walking with a cane and wearing one of those wonderful head scarves the small person had worn. And it is only because Amá made the suggestion that the cook increase the butter and cream as well as the portions that went on the trays that it was thought by most of the household staff that was left—because many took what they wanted from the house when no one was looking and left during those months doña Liliana was in the mountains—that Amá had put a curse on la americana, which Amá says at the time she neither refuted nor claimed because of the power it gave her. She was only aware that combined with the fact that she was the only one who knew where doña Liliana had gone, had helped her pack, it gained her a certain amount of respect among the other household workers in that they began to believe that she knew things that she didn't necessarily know.

Amá was suddenly promoted to the person to ask about the type of flowers doña Liliana would prefer on the piano; which rooms needed airing and cleaning. Was she well doña Liliana? Amá was asked, and she would cross herself and pray after she answered, Of course she is. The other staff directed friends of doña Liliana and her father's former business partners to Amá when they asked if anyone had any idea when the lady of the house would be returning. And it was a question she avoided for the longest time by saying, In due time, and in due course; when asked if she knew if doña Liliana had become, you know . . . and then they couldn't have finished their sentences, Amá says she said, Well, you know la señorita, and left it at that. And invariably the asker would indulge in a long contemplative nod from which they would recover refreshed and reassured. It was only when Amá heard herself slip and say, Any day now—can you imagine, Any day now, she says, after months of putting people off—that she sweated herself sick wondering if she may have somehow put doña Liliana in peril by saying something that she had no idea if it was true.

She says she never thought herself wishing Ellen Ellen bald and fat, although she found that once la americana was hiding herself in one of the guest rooms, she was completely content to think that she got what she wanted without having any idea what it was that she wanted. But by the same logic it seemed that things could go awry.

For the first time since she arrived in La Habana she needed her mother—mi abuela that Amá had called to her face a foolish old woman as she left, who never learned to read or write, who would take the letters Amá wrote her to the letter writer who would read them to her and transcribe Abuelita's responses in the most florid of scripts that Amá imagined must have looked like vines to her mother; pero, however, at that moment, her mother's clear vision, her way of knowing how and what and where, astounded her, took her breath away, and all she says she said was, Ay mamá, and within the hour doña Liliana, hugely pregnant, had fainted in the front hallway.

When hearing this story Aureliano Franciso García Carrera speculated that she had come and gone through Holguín, driven herself from La Habana, and there someone had to have shown her the way in, it's the only way she would have found it; if what she says is true, he said. Entonces, he, like all of the Ostrovskis I have had, wanted dates to match and time to click by as neatly as serpentines of upended dominoes. We were at the blue house that he rented each year for the three before the first one that we were there together, directly across Lake Michigan; on the Michigan side, past—somewhere between Stevensville and I don't know what the next city is, it's so small, he said early on when I met him—New Buffalo.

The house is on a dune, just a getaway from the city; at one time I thought that I'd like to own something like this, now I know that it's just enough to be able to say that I've been there one more season each time I have to close it up in October, he said, isolated, looks over the lake, at night there are so many stars it'll make you crazy, mad loco in love with me; like an island, he said, y dije, sí; a walk on the beach, no one will see, don't worry, hold my hand, ven, ven para acá, come here, come here; y dije, sí.

Sí, it hardly mattered, nothing really seemed to matter so far away where everything seemed to matter; that first week—of what would be many, many weeks over the next four years—there, spent in nothing but pairs of beat-down chancletos, y sí, the water was blue when, sí, the sun on our shoulders began to be too much, y sí, his vaca frita tasted just like Amá's, crusty bread, garlic and butter that ran down the corners of my mouth, y sí, sí, sí, no I would never doubt his cooking again, y sí, the fires were warm, y sí, I too loved the smell of burning cherry, so rich the smoke, sí, there was nothing in the world like it, y sí, sí, I'd swim in the moonlight, y sí sí sí, no it really didn't matter if you could distinguish what was in front of you as long as you knew someone was there, y sí, put out a hand and find another, y sí, hear the sound of someone else's splashing, y sí, I saw the gooseflesh run up his arms, stand the fine black hairs on end; sand everywhere, ven para acá, comeherecomehere, he said, y sí, dije yo.

Sí, through Holguín, he said, buttering a piece of toast—carefully, from corner to corner, a very exacting man he was, Aureliano Francisco García Carrera, except he had a carelessness about him that only men who are completely unaware of how good-looking they are can afford—she must have gone through Holguín. He knew it well and told of a winter two years before that he had been sitting at his drafting table in his office at work designing the entryway to an office building his firm would one day, long after he was dead, call one of their finest efforts. He said there were feet and feet of snow shoveled to the sides of the streets—sooty snow, hauled up into parking lots—when the dart he threw at the map of the island across from him landed in Holguín.

He said it is twelve maybe thirteen hours of solid driving from Chicago to Montreal in bad weather, and you needed to lie when you get to the border between Detroit and Windsor; he said he was waved right through, and all he said to the man was something about skiing, but he never looked at the car at all to see if he had skis, he said the only warm clothing that he had was what was on his back, he had read the temperature for the ten days that he had planned to go was predicted to be in the nineties. Cheap, chartered flights direct from Mirabel to the tarmac at Frank País Airport.

He had no idea, really, all he knew is his sister Pilar had hundreds of letters their mother had written on blue stationery to La Sierra Maestra, to sliced guayaba lying on a pink plate turning brown in the afternoon heat; years and years of the watery tether of fountain pen ink that stretched over miles and miles to a cove on a shoreline she was certain nobody but she and a prima who was always a young girl whose braids kept coming undone no matter how old Ana got; his whole life when people saw him, heard his name, met him, heard his Spanish, they'd ask that question that so many of us ask without thinking—Where are you from?—knowing Miami or Chicago does not answer the question that was asked; more than once his father slapped him cubano, slapped him exilio, slapped him manly and silent into the straight upright position of disposed royalty; until he slapped him hard and fast away. It was Pilar who called about their father's stroke—¿Poncho? she asked for on the phone when she called—and Pilar's husband who managed the particulars of their father's managed care.

Silenced by his own blood and placed out of the way, his father knew nothing more about his son than when they all returned to the island, when the island was gotten back by its rightful owners, there were fincas of coffee, coffee, coffee. And there was some part of him, Aureliano Francisco García Carrera—not that he said, but spend enough time alone with one person and you know what they don't or won't say, they invite you to, y sí, sí, sí, dije, sí—that I know that dying before his father simply wouldn't be enough; he had been as part of a group trip in college, fourteen days, all of the high points, and another time part of a conference of architects, his firm sent him because he was the only one who had been Institute certified that spoke Spanish, for the days that were to be spent in hotel meeting rooms, but sitting in his office that snowy February in Chicago, he needed to not only see that what his father saw no longer existed, but that fidelismo had become a windmill his father battled and all it really had done as far as the island was concerned was cut a brutal fissure that opened it to quick ripening, and turned it into a country that neither his father nor any of the revolutionaries whom he fled in nightmares would be able to name.

Amá says that Julio and Román came quickly, six weeks later, an easy birth, she says the doctor says, one right after the other, no problems, no complications. But from the time that doña Liliana fainted in the hallway of her father's well-appointed house in El Vedado, through the birth, and for a while afterward, she was never completely conscious of what she said and what she did. The same doctor who first pronounced the differences in color between Román and Julio was the result of Román's being smaller, the second to come out—give it time, Amá says he said, soon there will be no one on the island that can tell either of them apart—was the same doctor who claimed there was nothing wrong with doña Liliana—nothing at all—he had known many women, hundreds, who had fever, who had problems right before and shortly after multiple births, but they go away; Amá said that he said that multiple births took a lot out of a woman; and they really had no idea what her life was like, what kind of nutrition she had had.

But that was the last that they saw of him. Amá says that was when she began to notice that, little by little, El

Vedado began to crumble. Not all at once, but something like paint peeling and sooty windows, little things. Por ejemplo, from the street she could see urns that had once held some of the most proudly yellow, vibrant overflowings had become overgrown with green moss and the plants inside withered. Gravel from a drive had begun to wear thin in places, and previously well tended lawns began spouting long grasses and wild pineapples. What she says was most disturbing, what she missed most, was the hum of refined traffic that she had become accustomed to in the years since she came to doña Liliana's house in El Vedado: carriages on their way to, people coming home from, something that reminded girls who had come in from the country, men who delivered in trucks, someone who had wandered in or wanted to see what it was like, that there were those who traversed the world in a much more stately manner.

The black-finned Caddy was gone, as were her shoes, doña Liliana had been wearing a dress that scarcely accommodated her belly that we all knew that she would have never have chosen for herself, the soles of her feet were very swollen and cracked open in so many places, Amá says, pero Aureliano approximated eight hundred to eight hundred and fifteen miles from Holguín to El Vedado; she surely didn't walk; and he recalled being hit by a wave of heat at País after so many months of being so cold, so unbelievably cold, and he found that nothing else seemed to matter. All he had needed was the sun.

Amá says that the cook was the only one who had been there in doña Liliana's father's fine, well-appointed house when doña Liliana's mother lay there dying, and pleaded and begged them not to carry her there, but it was the only room in the house that could be completely secured from noise and traffic from the street, and the doctor had said that she needed quiet, the only room in the house where there was morning and afternoon sun, and the doctor said that she needed light. Amá says that when she called at the doctor's office the phone rang and rang. When she called at his house on a hot hot night that doña Liliana had sweated through all the sheets, burned with fever, teeth chattering as she called out ¡Dios! when Amá called the doctor she was told he was not in.

And it was only until she went to his house at the opposite end of El Vedado that she found that his house was empty except for a tiny little maid, Martina she was called, Amá says, who told her that they had left the week before, just left, she says she said.

There are boys in the mountains, Amá says doña Liliana woke as if in midsentence, boys scratching themselves, all with the same beard, like monkeys, all with the same name, boys. You think, you think, you think, but it's just the same, boys.

The cook stood in the room holding ice at doña Liliana's temples and then at her feet every now and then she would call out to Changó to save this girl, or if she had to go, let her go as quickly and as quietly as her mother did: you must take her, let her go as peacefully as her mother.

Saving and damning, saving and damning, Amá said doña Liliana called out until she was hoarse and was only whispering, the word scratching, whispering, scratching, scratching, boys.

Julio helped me set the table once we got Amá home from Wicker Park. It's hard to act as if nothing is happening when for everyone in the room something is happening, or everyone except for the one person for whom everyone is pretending nothing is happening.

Amá seemed to perk up at the smell of garlic and onions, and just their sizzle made my apartment seem hotter, the air thicker. None of the curtains around the open windows moved. In the kitchen, Román, still in his dress shirt with the sleeves rolled up and tie, sat in front of the piles of quimbobó, green pepper and plátanos that he was cutting with the edgy sort of grin that he gets when he feels that he's doing something well; sitting across from the dining room table in Amá's little little casa blanca just off of Ashland Avenue, I can tell you, señores, there was many a time I wanted to rip his tongue out of his mouth as he curled it around his lip when he finished his geometry before I did.

The hiss of the pollo hitting the hot skillet sat Amá upright in a chair in the living room as the smell of something that we had all come to depend on her making us began to happen around her. Her eyes skittered back and forth between then and now as I watched as she watched doña Cristina come up behind doña Liliana to help her off with her jacket, wipe her brow and tie an apron around doña Liliana's waist as she stood in her stocking feet—spatula poised—uncharacteristically, in front of the spattering pan.

When Amá has told it in the past because doña Liliana won't, she claims not to have any memory of it at all—doña Liliana, she remembers being in the mountains and the way the air smelled fresh and clean, thinner, clearer than in La Habana when she tells it to Julio, Román and me; doña Cristina says once doña Liliana told her that she remembers the air being fetid with their smells, their jokes, the stench of machine oil and farting, brutish though at times very kind, muy dulce, suave, serio, concienzudo, high-minded and well-meaning, and you never had any idea which combination would come up on the surface of them at any point in time; she told the escribano who had been summoned to the house to record the birth of the gemelos, their father's name was Fidel, they all called themselves Fidel, they all believe it, their own fidelidad, and sometimes I do, sometimes it's true, you never know, Amá says she said, and the escribano grabbed her hand and said, Pobrecita, pobrecita—Amá remembers the cook asking Changó for the kind of peace that he had granted doña Liliana's mother; preserve this child from suffering, allow her rest, and doña Liliana suddenly sat up in bed and yelled ¡No!

Naty sat between Julio and Román jabbering about what she heard that Señora Figueroa had been saying about the shop, and what would happen to it and how she nearly went off and went to the woman's house and told what it was she thought of her but then how she thought otherwise because she might end up kicking her where there ain't never been any sun and then she thought of what Señora would say about it not being at all the sort of thing a lady of refinement might do no matter how loudly she thought about it, while we waited for Amá to take her first bite of pollo con quimbobó y plátanos. Amá placed her fork back onto her plate, and just began to chew when Naty with a complete mouthful and her free hand poised in the air around her face shook her bracelets down and said, You know Señora, what would set them all right is if you were to let me go ahead and open the shop at least until you get better and could come back, then it would be like you never went or nothing, you know, I know it all, you know, what you taught me and I can keep all them silly perras what work for you in line too, you know that and that way everybody keeps they job and nobody is the wiser that you had a hard time or nothing.

Naty kept talking and eating without noticing that doña Cristina gasped and pulled most of her napkin into her mouth and that Amá had gotten up from the table.

¡Perra estúpida! doña Liliana hissed and in soft yet harsh tones—I suppose that Amá couldn't hear—she began to enumerate from the tops of Naty's dyed hairs to absolutely deplorable taste in shoes why she thought that Naty was the simplest woman that she had ever met in her entire life.

Naty had begun to talk about a woman who had been coming in for years—for years regular she's been coming, even though she's not old, still young, but with two or three kids, Naty added—Lila, La Señora will know her, she said, and will remember her as being a small B cup if she had tetas at all, y entonces, I seed her the other day and damn if she ain't bought herself a D, no.

And Naty was swearing to God, the woman, Lila, had had it done as sure as she was sitting there when doña Liliana—who never allowed us boys to use the word tetas, once washed Julio's mouth out with soap when we were just teenagers for looking too hard down the front of a woman's dress because she was sure he was thinking the word tetas so loudly that she could hear it—interrupted her to ask about her güero in the chocolate-covered Porche.

Naty squealed with jingling delight, Ay, didn't I no tell you, he was married, goddamnit.

How did you ever find that news? Doña Liliana sneered.

Well, I had to ask his wife, flatly stated, who else was going to tell me? He wouldn't give me his number except for his cell, and we never went back to his place after that first time; and I began to think that it looked too clean and nice for just a bachelor's; so one night after we had went to a motel out by O'Hare, I followed him back, and damn if a woman didn't open the door when she seen him coming up the walk.

You are kidding me, doña Liliana perked up in her chair. You, you didn't go to this woman, his wife, you didn't make a scene.

No, of course not, Naty assured her before she told us, I went straight home; got a good night's sleep, so I looked good; got up early; dressed all nice and did my face real perfect; and went back right after he had called me from his office to thank me for such a nice time like he do; and then all ladylike and all—I was no raunchy or nothing—I knockeded on the door and said, Excuse me.

And as Naty began to tell us what the wife of the man with the chocolate-colored Porsche said, and then what she said, and then what the woman said, and then what she answered, and the fact that maybe there had been a little bit of yelling. But really if she were the woman, Naty said, she would have been grateful that someone like her had come to her door rather than some puta or another. Which was when doña Liliana returned to her hissing low voice as she started in on Naty's sexual promiscuity and the slutty way that she carried herself, and Amá came back into the room and handed Naty the keys to the shop.

If you ask doña Liliana all she remembers is really the shock of the strength at which the gemelos pulled when they nursed; it's not what you expect, she says, that she was sitting in her father's well-appointed garden in the patio that had become completely sprouted with wild pineapple and she had Román to her breast, marveling at how something so small could pull so hard as she heard the commotion in the streets. She says that she covered his head and her breast with her shawl to see what was going on, and she was told the world had changed, the boys were coming down from the mountains, and she yelled after the women who had been the maids of the women who occupied the house next to her father's finely outfitted house in El Vedado, I had babies, told them, I had babies as they rushed by her and passed her on the street as if she weren't there.

Not bad, needs salt, Amá said with her second mouthful.

Tears filled Naty's eyes. Ay Señora, are you sure?

Sí, Mireya, are you sure? Doña Liliana asked, looking at the keys in Naty Valdez McIntosh's hand.

Ay, Liliana, make it sleep, Amá sighed; the girl, she started, but then she turned to Naty and said, Nenita, you have a yellow baby inside you that you need to catch.

Doña Liliana was about to say something when Román interrupted by saying to Amá, doña Mireya, there is flan for dessert; store bought, he said, of course, none of us has learned how to make it con guayaba.

Sí, no, of course, store bought, Amá said as she continued eating.

Which I think is why when doña Cristina tells the story of Román's English to the chismosas in the shop that she has a way of making everything, even bad news, sound so peaceful, nice, con garbo, elegancia.

. . . MEMORIA, SOMEWHERE BETWEEN hope and nostalgia, a famous fado to which I can remember all of the words but have oddly enough forgotten the melody. And who we used to have a record of singing it, I can't remember either, señores.

Amá now says that it was Pirata when I ask.

Someday I'll take you home; someday I'll take you back, the refrain goes, but no matter.

Yesterday afternoon, doña Cristina and I sat in the dark as Doctor Canales showed Amá slides on the wall.

Un caballo.

Un barrilete.

Un paragüero becomes a basura. No, she said, a wastepaper clothes, no, a hamper para basura, no she says. And Doctor Canales goes on to the next slide.

Cinco, Amá called out when the number five appeared, but a picture of a plum seemed to shock her, frighten her. Flustered, she asked for a minute to think, said that she thought that the number seis was coming next, but this thing in front of her made her want to say siete, which she knew wasn't what we called siete en inglés, pero, how can you call this? When Doctor Canales said plum, ciruela, Amá nodded as if she were seeing one for the first time. Nodding at something she didn't know, but had to believe because someone said it. Nodding like she nodded, listening into the receiver as Marta told her, Vas a Chicago, nena, there's a place for you here, I train you, you see, you'll love, it's happy. Though, señores, it's a voice that, I now know through letters—cryptic notes, really, scribbled on scraps I found in a box marked Cosas that Julio and I had stored in the basement after the fire that I found while looking for Amá's health insurance policy—someone from the past already familiar to Amá. Doña Liliana says that Marta had been the maid that trained Amá to be a maid when she first came to La Habana; always seemed to be the same age, one of those women who after puberty looks middle-aged for the rest of their lives; warm, dark-skinned, always called everyone mija, so you never knew how old she was. And it seems it was to Marta Amá went when things didn't make sense in doña Liliana's father's house: the laundress; the butcher; how to fold the corners on a sheet so they looked like the flaps of an envelope. There's a note—Mija, América, Sitting, Calm, In Own House—that appears to have been handled, folded over so many times it is smudged and splits at the middle.

Dieciocho.

Diecisiete.

Dieciseis.

A man in a hat turned into Facundo Machado. Pero, no it couldn't be Facundo Machado, Amá said, so many wives, three, pues . . . such an empty house. Three, she said before she stopped abruptly and asked Doctor Canales ¿Está enfadada, verdad, Doctor? And the doctor replied, no, she wasn't angry; she simply wanted Amá to do the best she could. Pero, what can I do, Doctor, Amá said, Facundo Machado is his own man, follows his own heart. He only wanted the womens what spoke her own minds, and cursed God when they runned through his fingers.

Doña Cristina must have felt me looking at her. Her eyes were darting from the screen to Doctor Canales, and back to Amá when she shrugged her response to my inquisitive glance about this Facundo Machado that I had never heard anything about. We watched—doña Cristina sitting on the edge of her chair, as if she were attempting to coax the answer that matched the picture, little sighs of relief came out of her—as a pen was a pen; a chair, una silla. A pint of blueberries—something none of us, not even doña Liliana, had seen before coming north; blueberries that we had no idea were eaten in yogurt, with cream, sprinkled over things and embedded in pancakes; each of us—me, Amá, las doñas Liliana y Cristina, Román y Julio had had that wonderful moment of discovery of just one of them crunching between the teeth to fall sweet, sour, both sugar and dirt on the tongue into something for which none of us had any Spanish; talking about them we started sentences out with como and then we would fill in the blank that followed with something that we all knew; in a sentence completely composed in Spanish, like the flip of a yellow penalty flag, blueberries was the only word that we could think to use—when all of a sudden, Amá smiled brightly, as if someone new had walked into the room and said, Los arándanos.

Doña Cristina closed her hand tightly around mine, and sucked in deeply as if in realization of her own mistake, as if driving away from the house, overcome by the sudden recollection of leaving a window open and the cat walking away. And just as quickly all of the tension in her hand seemed to give way when Doctor Canales responded, Sí, and went to the next slide.

Setenta; bolígrafo; una taza de té; a Oldsmobile, una casa, a apple, thirty-nine. And I wondered about where in this jumble of familiar and strange, and the familiar gone foreign, and how the foreign gets placed with the familiar. Los arándanos, she had said, as if she had always known it.

When a rose appears on the screen, Facundo Machado reappears with his lonely hollowness, babies snuck away in the middle of the night, the mark and whisper of the cornudo branded on his back—the first one left him for some yanqui, she said they said, the second lives with a woman they had seen her kissing, touching her breasts, who they called Cuca; the third was lame; you'd think he could hold on to a woman who could scarcely walk, she said they said—as he sat watching the ocean. And she said that she used to dream herself walking from the road and going down to the shore to sit beside him—long after we had left, after she had no idea what had become of him, nor had she heard from anyone who would know to speak of him—that she was feeding him los arándanos. One by one, whispering, Don't hold, let it happen, enjoy it and let it go.

The three of us sat and waited as several times the word for stone would come to Amá but would never make its way past her lips.

Doctor Canales, finally confident enough to give what's going on inside Amá's head a name, recommends melatonin and vitamin E; she switches Amá off of the donepezil that I set out for her and she sometimes takes or sometimes I find wadded up in a paper napkin beside her breakfast plate, to rivastigmine, an anti-inflammation drug, much more aggressive, she said, long walks and tasks that might challenge her abilities to think, but when I asked what that would be, or to be more accurate what wouldn't that be, she neglected to name any specifically. She sighed and said it was just a matter of time, but there's no way to tell how much. We should begin to think about what next, which hospice, what plan. When Amá returned into the room after having her blood drawn, Doctor Canales told her that she had given doña Cristina and me a whole new list of vitamins that she should take and suggestions of some exercises that might help brighten some of the dark corners that seem to close in on her quick, that Amá has described to her to be like sudden turns into blind alleys of the familiar and the impossible. Amá smiled, nodded, and then she reached out and touched the doctor's hair. Stop doing this yourself, I'm begging you, nenita, she said, Naty's running the shop now, she'll take care of you, I'll tell her.

Call it what you want, it's all the same, señores. Amá stops on a street corner, in the grocery store, underneath the archway between the living and dining rooms in my apartment, unable to recall if she is headed toward the bathroom or dizzy on the ground in front of the table where mi abuelita was throwing the corie. It will all eventually collide and mix until the same mechanism that recalls and forgets and then recalls again that she once knew how to close a button will be attached to the one that reminds the body to breathe. It's so much like knowing that the place that you think of as home, the place that held every dream you had before you got to it, ancestral dreams completely made up of then and will be, is the same place that you'll pack and leave or simply flee into the night, it's just that horrible.

Después de tanta ira y desamparo, y el amor se convierte en otra cosa. What it turns into, I couldn't tell you. Sometimes it's nothing. Other times it can send you out to smash a pool cue over the head of someone who had not even looked at you in the wrong way. It's a foaming bowl of piss—helplessness—that you hold to defend yourself against the path of a shark. And the odd thing is that just because you know something in advance, are completely aware of its inevitability—like the headlights of the truck coming towards you—doesn't mean that you accept the inevitable or that its blow is somehow softened.

Withhold and endure. Withhold and endure. A box of matches; ninety-nine, which she seemed to like to say for its n's and its t, resolved itself as quinientos, which she seemed to know was wrong but didn't care; un lápiz de color; a hairbrush, probably a G. B. Kent & Sons, they come from England, Real Bristles, it'll say on the handle, Amá said; and I sent her over and over in my mind through witchgrass and sand to sit by Facundo Machado's side. If I strained could I hear her say something tender, something enduring, something he'd keep forever? Aureliano Francisco García Carrera, por ejemplo, was dying the day that I met him. Sick, he told me so when I met him. But then sick is all anyone said back then. Then saying anything else was the same as telling what you were, and waiting for a narrative of what you thought was your life to be rewritten and retold to you: who he is was how many partners he had had; where he went and what he did when he was there would be examined and compared to all the lives around him. The year before we met he had awakened to feel his lungs filling and knew—had read in the paper, had heard it rumored, had had a friend of a friend—what was happening was happening to him, but he still lay there, shivering in the cold morning light knowing that the moment that he went to the phone to call for help his entire life—invisible cities in shapes that he had yet to imagine that had roamed his head for years faded on the ceiling above his bed—was now measurable, real.

Ven, ven acá, come here, come here, he'd say to me when he wanted to hear a story of long-ago-and-far-away. Ven, ven acá, come here, come here, he'd say when he wanted to hear about people arriving to a place, landing on a new shore where the past was behind and what was going to happen had yet to happen; a place of make-believe, or what was believed or wanted to have no past. Like husking time: save the pretty—no wars, no famine, no, no—like paradise stilled right before shit begins to happen, he said, ven, ven acá, come here, come here.

And easy as knowing that you are about to begin a

marathon completely composed of backflips, señores, even if you never do it, have never done it in your daily life, you pray, and then you start.

Father Rodriguez was having his hair cut in my kitchen this anoche when I came home from work. Naty was doing the cutting, while Amá lectured the priest on the benefits of daily scalp massages; even at your age, Amá told him, there's really no time like the present to start; it would be nice to have hair the rest of your life, she said, even if you are a priest, ¿no? I mean you need to be attractive to somebody if only to yourself or to other priests, so better you should hold on to as much hairs as you can in case you find yourself needing a new job later in life, she said, Amá.

Naty nearly cut Father Rodríguez with her scissors as he jerked his head around to watch Amá leaving the room. ¡Ay Padre! Naty cried out, be careful, you know I have no idea what I'm doing. You will, Amá called out from the dining room. Father Rodríguez, she said, you'll stay for dinner, ¿no? There's leftover pollo from last night and you know is always more better the next day.

In between getting dinner ready and setting the table in the other room, Amá came in and rewet Father Rodríguez's hair and recut it, all the while telling Naty that there was no need for tears, she'd learn eventually; she really wouldn't need to know how to give a good haircut in the beginning, Amá said, she would just need to know how to hire people who did, which seemed to cheer Naty considerably enough to pull her into a flurry of sweeping up hair and getting dinner ready.

Between the in and out of their bustling, Father Rodríguez whispered that he had come over because he was concerned about Amá, Señora Figueroa had said that she had closed the shop, and he hadn't seen Amá in the church lately.

And I said, Sí.

He wanted to know if there was anything that he could

do, anything at all, after all we had been members of the parish for many years and this was very difficult for him to see, a member of his parish . . . and then he stopped.

And I said, Sí, sí debe ser dificil para usted, Father Rodríguez.

He drinks whiskey, Father Rodríguez, you know, señores, pero will have rum, with a little ice, a little lime, and a little soda if you haven't any. In even lower tones, closer to him—like when his breath is coming from the other side of the sheer curtains all the ladies in the parish keep so clean, very white, dust free in the confessional—he asked if I had sought guidance.

¿De quién, Father? I asked.

De Dios, of course, he told me, before he suggested that I make his next drink short; then again it's always just the two, no more, I don't know anyone who has seen him drink any more than what will allow him to talk clearly, speak, give advice thoughtfully; a blessed man, an anointed man, if you notice, señores, he's always very clean; I don't want to spoil your mother's dinner, he said. And then he let me know that across the back garage where the priests park their cars someone—in letters that he has approximated as being nearly six or eight feet tall—has implored himself delivered from that crazy fuck Delossantos.

God, he said, but I couldn't pay attention because I was so incredibly thrilled by this vandal's soul that one of you or so many of you possess; it took me completely out of there for a moment and made me wonder about the man the artist would become. Imaginen, señores, the stealth and the agility; and what Father Rodríguez said was true, for those of you who haven't seen it, señores, go quickly, I went this morning, and Father Rodríguez is planning on having it painted over as soon as possible, he said to save me any more embarrassment. Pero, the letters are fat red-and-yellow balloons that run the length of the fifteen-car garage—¡Madre de Dios, porfa, Deliver Me from This Crazy Fuck Delossantos!—and what better use of the space do you think there could be, señores?

There aren't even fifteen cars in there—maybe at one time—but now there are scarcely enough of them living in the rectory to seat two to a vehicle; and I couldn't help but wonder where does it come from—the urge is in all of us to violate something in such a grand fashion, yet the ability to execute always falls short, seems to dissipate before we head to the store; and an industrious motherfucker, he—¿no?—given that he would have needed to go to the suburbs to get spray paint because it is illegal for any of the stores to sell it here in the city; and it makes you wonder—¿no?—did he or they take the train or drive out in a car during the day, with fake identification to prove he was eighteen when he went to make the purchase, or was it a father supporting his son, providing him with the tools that would allow for self-expression—Father Rodríguez says that it must have happened in the still of the night, at least that's what he told Ms. Jonas in the teachers' lounge this morning, however, things can happen right in front of his face without his notice, my God, I was there when Joaquín-Ernesto, the Santiago Boy, slipped right through his hands like so much water cold and icy—though I would like to think that as beautifully rendered and artfully placed on its canvas as it is, that it was late afternoon and many of you were filing out of the building onto the commons and the green, and that some of you had the opportunity to see the fixed and concentrated look on the artist's face right before he spewed what in my mind is one of the most splendidly articulated fuck you's I have ever seen.

God, Father Rodríguez said again, and of course the boy and his family; there is a divinity, mijo.

¿Mijo? I stopped him mostly because I had no idea if he

was calling me mijo, or if he was speaking on the behalf of God. Well, you never know, ¿no?

Sí, mijo, he said to me, you have always been my son, you all have been my sons over the years, and even though you have had transgressions, forgiveness, there is bounty to the love that I have had for all of you.

We've all needed to be forgiven from time to time, I said.

From time to time, he said, holding an ice cube between his teeth and then taking it out of his mouth and rubbing it in his open collar before he exhaled that he thought that there is a very clear message for me here. He asked if maybe we didn't have a fan. I shook my head, no, and he took the handkerchief from his pocket and began to wave it in front of his face.

Thirteen.

Fourteen?

Naranja for a bicycle. And I began to wonder what orange bicycle, on what bicycle was she eating an orange, was she riding a bicycle, ringing its orange-colored, orange-shaped bell into an orange grove, an orange-colored sky?

I asked Father Rodríguez what he thought that that might be, and he asked me what, and I asked him what he thought the message to which he had referred earlier might be, and he asked me what, and I asked him the message he felt that God was trying to send me, and he asked me what I thought that that might be.

The mean eyes of a school of remora for the number eleven.

Un patín de cuchilla.

Straightening himself in his chair, Father Rodríguez told me that we all are sent messages from time to time. And I asked him, what was God telling him now? And he told me of how he had spent the afternoon going to the homes of the older parishioners, making sure they had water in all this heat, did they know that there were places for them to go to if they simply couldn't take it anymore? The lonely, mijo, he said, people who maybe wouldn't eat unless someone came to make sure that they had food and a little company. He said that his heart was nearly broken in two when he went to the tiny apartment of this little dominicana that had hardly been to mass in the past couple of years—long and frail like one of those long-legged spiders, he said—sweating to nothing with only Telemundo to keep her company, just lots of shit all around her; pictures of the farm she grew up on in La República Dominicana, her daughter who died of an overdose nearly twenty years ago, pictures of a shih tzu that she had; and she crochets—my God, he said—there was a doll whose crocheted skirt covered the extra toilet paper roll in the bathroom, and another whose crocheted skirt spread out on the small couch that she had, and another one who guarded the remote control, and yet another whose skirt was being assembled while we talked, and he said that all he could think was, Oh my God, I know that you're trying to tell me something to tell her, but I don't know what it is.

He declined a third drink like I knew he would. But I asked anyway, it only seemed polite.

And then I asked him what he thought that might be, and he asked me what, and I asked him what message he might give to the dominicana, and he asked me what, and I asked him what message he felt that God was trying to tell him about la dominicana with the crocheted doll skirts, and he asked me what I thought that that might be.

She hadn't known a slice of pie, Amá.

A blonde boy with blue eyes and a bully T had been a niño.

Father Rodríguez asked me if I played cards.

And I said, No.

I asked him if he watched baseball; was he a Cubs or a White Sox fan?

And he said, No.

Jesucristo had been a golden ring or a yellow O, I couldn't tell, and Doctor Canales hadn't answered, she just went on to the next slide.

Amá called dinner, and we walked into the room, where all of the candles had been lit on the table and on the sideboard. While we were still standing, Amá asked Father Rodríguez to give the blessing, and in his generosity and wisdom, he had us clasp hands around the table, and asked that not only that the bounty given us be touched, but that it healed and soothed our wounds, made us whole, one again.

He was seated next to Naty Valdez McIntosh on one side of the table and Amá indicated that she wanted me to sit at the end opposite from her. Across from Father Rodríguez and Naty, Amá had set a place—wineglass, water glass, plate, cutlery and small glass of rum that caught the light from the candles and threw it into the dark corners of the room—with a photograph of Aureliano Francisco García Carrera that was taken at the blue house across the Lake, one of the last that he would allow, right before all the wasting began and he hardly looked like himself; it was the photograph—the first thing his sister, Pilar, saw after he was gone and she came to our house with some sense of entitlement to see where her brother lived; Poncho, she called him; no one called him Aureliano at home; Francisco or Poncho he was called in another life, like someone I had never known at all; she wanted things, Pilar; paintings off of the walls; a table that she said had been in their family for years; the microwave; his life insurance policy; his journals; letters; pictures; she felt it a right to go through the drawers in which we had both kept our underwear and socks. How did you know him? she asked; I was his friend, I told her in the same way that I told her that I was a history teacher, lived in the neighborhood adjacent to this one nearly all my life, born on the island but that was another story that seemed so long ago, was all I said, and because all it says on his death certificate was heart attack, she believed what she heard. To have found it Amá would have had to have gone through years of pictures taken by the remote timer of the two of us happy on the beach, in the sand, in the sun; pictures taken in bed and in the shower, on the toilet, giving each other the finger, laughing. She had put it into a frame with a singed corner that had been in the little little little casa blanca off of Ashland Avenue, though too big, the frame, for the photo and doña Liliana's father's well-appointed garden in El Vedado, although somewhat faded, spilled out on either side of him.

What's all this? Father Rodríguez said.

Dinner con familia, Padre, Amá said, eat before it all gets cold.

I know Señor Father Rodríguez, he's tan cute, ¿no? I don't even know who he is or why La Señora invited him, but I'm glad she did, he reminds me of this tipo I know once, good-looking, liked to dance and everything, had a good job, pero one night we was getting ready to go out and everything and he's lying on the bed and he telled me that he thought my nalgas was falling, can you imagine that, he said this to me, to me, so I told him that he always had the bad breaths, and sometimes it was all I could do to kiss him; and that was it, it was on then, we was throwing shit—ay, perdóneme, Padre, sometimes I embarrass myself, I can be so nasty—we was throwing stuff, and they had to call the cops that time, and we swore before God—but not in a bad way, really, she said grabbing his hand—to kill each other if we was to ever see the other one again; but you know how love is, Padre—or maybe you don't—so I will tell you, it was like something that couldn't keep us away from each other later that night, if you know what I mean, I couldn't help myself, but kiss the bruises what I give him. I don't know what happened to him but he was muy guapo, like that guy, she said, pointing with her fork, and when she noticed that Father Rodríguez was still staring at the picture, she told him to eat; is not good cold, she said.

I watched Amá's eyes as they followed something that seemed to flutter and light around the top of the room, move from perch to perch, banyón to flamboyant, around the top of the room, before she became very still. So still that she would forget it was dinnertime.

But I had to ask you one question, Padre, Naty asked, have you noticed if my nalgas they are falling? I worry, she said.

. . . Y ENTONCES, SEÑORES, Jesucristo, powerful and mighty, maker of all things good on heaven and earth, gave doña Cristina her second birth at the feet of Las Madres Escolapias. She says she was told that had they not found her begging and dirty in the street, right there in front of the school on calle Real, eating out of a garbage pail, she would have easily perished. Told her that she had no language, no voice, just a squeak, so at that moment she became two even though doña Cristina is certain she must have been older, must have been shown by someone else how to fend for herself, make a life on the streets, but she can't remember it as a life through language. There were always people around that picked her up and smiled at her, gave her food and sat close to her. But it was the nuns who called her Cristina María Teresa de las Madres Escolapias, and said she was to say—when she could, if anyone was to ask—that she was delivered to them by a winged messenger.

And it's funny, señores, how your textbook lists there was a Revolution, something they call the Cuban missile crisis—as though it was a crisis for everyone—and then on to Panama. Think of it as an entire country on a thirty-seven-page tour, give or take the few pages that we ripped out.

No matter.

Cárdenas, doña Cristina says, is one of the most beautiful places on the island, but then she stops and says, no, she isn't sure if that's true, she says, or if that's what the nuns told her. When she thinks hard about it, when other people's stories don't get in the way of memory that she actually lived rather than one that she is holding for someone else, Cárdenas and La Habana were the only places on the island that she had seen in her entire life.

What do I know? she says. When you talk to her, Cuba opens as a complete surprise, full of excitement, something delightful and exotic. And the chismosas at the shop ask her, How can you not know, didn't you get out before all the atrocities happened with the rest of them? She says she says, Sí, sí, sí, because she is certain that's what they want to hear; none of them are cubana anyway, they'll listen to what they want to listen to; and for the very few cubanas that come into the shop—atrocities, brutality and longing—that was what they wanted to hear about too; they liked to hear about longing.

She remembers standing on the grounds of the convent school that sloped wide with sumptuous gardens and was speckled with fruit trees, and being told by a nun she was now to think of herself as a fortunate girl. To live in a house with lots and lots to eat, she says she was taught to say made her privileged and she should pray thanks for her bounty, it made her blessed.

They made her work, they taught her to read, and prided her on her silences, praised her reserve, and her willingness to give over her will to God. And she says she remembers thinking at the time, even though she scarcely used her voice then, It's only land.

Live outside long enough, she'll tell you because she remembers nothing of her first birth or of the mother that she assumes abandoned or lost her somewhere along the way, and you'll know there's so little difference between yourself and what's around you.

Tree.

Uva.

Vine.

Watch a drop of water long enough as it runs down the side of a wall and you'll have no idea when it has let you inside of it. What she says she remembers clearly is that she was following a beetle into an aceituna that had fallen and had begun to have that sweet ripening smell they get right before they rot away when one of the sisters plucked her by the collar. And after that, inside, things were named, called things, and as much as she pressed her hands against the glass or wrought iron of the windows of the rooms they would put her in, she already knew that the opportunity for her to crawl into an aceituna would never come again. She believes it to be the price she paid for allowing herself to be brought inside. Says, in fact, that she didn't know enough at the time the nun's hand came down on her neck to be afraid. It was only until she was brought in, scrubbed down and dressed in the same uniform as all the other girls that she knew fear.

Aureliano—a building man, a man who had towering spires in his eyes—would have agreed. Agreed wholeheartedly, nodding so his hair flopped about, nodding unable to wait until he had finished the mouthful he was chewing to say as he often did, houses, huts, castles, cathedrals, the sheds people put their dogs in, took on the fears and ambitions of their owners; hold it in secret places, dust pockets and empty corners, filling up to bursting; there was nothing anyone could do, not even the best could keep it from seeping into the everything from foundation to weep hole.

How often, he said, that he had watched his mother run her fingertips along the upstairs balustrade so many times, that he knew too well the palpable shriek that always threatened to blast that house apart, a howl that set him and Pilar running from it the moment they were old enough, that he knew that hurricane season she opened her house, Ana would have gathered the sides of a summer robe around her. Doubled the cinch in the belt so it would not fall open from the weight of her stomach and breasts.

She turned on all of the lights in the room and rounded Alberto's side of the bed and went into his bathroom. His collection of balms and salves, shaving creams and colognes, shattered glass shelf upon glass shelf like a parade of dominoes with just the weight of her shoulder. She turned on his hair dryer and his exercise bike and his radio and his electric razor. A cloud of talc came up from the floor and clouded the air as the windows were opened easily with the phenomenal strength she found that she had in her wrists. It swirled through the dressing room passage that connected her bathroom to his, creating a bay-rum-scented funnel that escaped as she opened the windows at the other end.

The chandelier swung in the cove of the catwalk that surrounded the main stairs to their rooms. The lights dimmed and flickered; its crystals sounded cries against each other. She listened as one by one a few would give way every second or so and smash against the tiles in the front hallway.

The door slammed closed behind her in Pilar's room. Ana could feel the plush pile of the pink carpet between her toes. Everything was exactly the way the girl had left it as though Graciela somehow knew this day would come. All the riding and swimming medals were dusted and placed back; the dolls and stuffed animals, exactly where they had always been. Even clothing that Ana had not seen her wear since she had been in high school was folded and pressed and hung neatly in her closet.

Across the room, through the windows, Ana could see Alberto's sunfish bang and bang against the dock, however she could not hear it. The wind screeched, it howled, its pitch was so high, so violent she could not tell if it surrounded the house or haunted her head.

She motioned to thrust all of the things off the girl's desk—scholastic awards, pictures of friends, a miniature volley ball—with the back of her arm when Ana recognized the woman in a picture behind a stuffed hippopotamus. A small silver frame tooled long ago, she wondered how the girl knew to hide it away all of these years. Ana had cut the woman out of almost all of the pictures long before either of the children was born. All the newspaper clippings of La Flaca assisted by her driver in front of her father's city home in El Vedado; La Flaca at the Hilton in La Habana with her high-ranking government companions; La Flaca sunning herself on a private beach near Santiago de Cuba.

Where? Had she and Pilar been clearing out closets of things to go to charity? From underneath Christmas decorations and yards of fabric that looked like mattress ticking.

She stared at the incredibly supple thin S of her figure that had set her apart from women who were—even in their teen years and early twenties—beginning to round in curves that suggested matrons. Like a princess, the girl said. Sí mija, Ana responded, like a princess who lived in a castle that was surrounded by the sea.

The window gave way to her push. She used the desk chair and the screens collapsed on themselves and flew out toward the gardens. The blotter and the rest of the things on the desk went with them. She banged the frame against the edge of the desk several times before the glass broke and the frame could be bent in half, freeing the picture.

Qué bonita. How strange, how foreign, that hand folded underneath her chin, warm, fragile though moist. Her head tilted in that way. What in the distance could she have been listening to—that scratchy Dulce María Mora record her tía listened to over and over again with sherry stolen from the kitchen, or just the leathery fronds of the palmas reales like the slapping of thighs through trouser material around a domino table—Ana could not tell. She, she thought, her there, dancing in the wind, surrounded by the sea, jeweled wildly in exuberant flamboyants, fragrant with orange blossoms. From the dark spreading in wide root, springing into hard stalk, her there, she was born of azúcar. Azúcar planted in a draft of a letter written late in the August of 1881 to her great-grandfather back in Barcelona that started: Cuba is a place deep in its own filth; Savages and flies that swelter in an insufferable heat and outnumber the whites a thousandfold. The script was cultivated and precise; the paper was very fine. It was written from a place—here on just a lump of dirt, it read—that would become one of the most famous and prosperous of the estates that surrounded Camagüey. Although, she knew, before he could make any of his dreams come true, however, he would have to marry a woman from unforgiving blood. Island blood. Either criollo or negro, they said they said; nobody was sure; what they did know was that her dowry outweighed her a thousand times over—acres and acres of cane that abutted her abuelo's land—and made her appear paler, more Spanish than she actually was. The word azúcar was underlined with a flourish, and he wrote of the chopping that he would one day hear and the grunting and the sight of wagons filled to their maximums, and the creak and jangle of reins around the necks of burros as they headed toward Santiago and sale. She had no idea if another version of the letter draft was sent. By the time that she was old enough to play in her grandfather's desk in what had been his office in the by then decaying finca, he was merely an oil painting above the great fireplace floor; the cool breeze that caused them to shutter it even on the hottest of nights.

Doña Cristina says there's so little difference between hot and cold if outside is all you know. The shade of a tree, the warmth between two buildings or a cove or just a piece of board to block the wind. La niña doesn't even have sense enough to bring herself out of the rain, she says that she overheard one of the nuns saying, though she says now she knows she could have told them it was not the rain that should be feared, but the extremes, lives lived exclusively in or out of the weather. She had no idea how to say it then, but even as a little girl she had discovered something intrinsically evil about knowing better. How hot can it be if you've no idea that people ride around in air-conditioned limousines, she'll ask you, or you're never as hungry as you are once you've had that first opportunity to turn away food, she tells you. The other girls imitated the nuns and called her ratita when in a cloudburst her instincts sent her scurrying under a bush to watch the puddles she'd splash in afterward instead of pushing her inside the warm dry confines of the school, and cucarachita when they discovered that she saved and hid the crusts and scraps they left on their plates.

She says doña Liliana was only at the school a year, but it was a year that disturbed the balance of the ordinary for the nuns. Routine and daily life were nearly set aside for this girl—too rich, too spoiled for her own good, too wild, she says they said, that all the girls were not to indulge her and to pray for her—who had come to their arms as needy as doña Cristina. Only with a different need, she says they said.

There was crying and fits of wailing at bedtime. The entire dormitory had been awakened by doña Liliana's demands for water, demands to go home, and to the delight of most of the girls, doña Liliana is said to have cursed like an estibador, however, doña Cristina says, because she had no idea what any of the words that made the other girls giggle or the nuns blush and rush at Liliana meant, she found anyone who could get that much of a reaction from anyone fascinating and exquisite, although doña Liliana claims to remember none of it.

She does remember wetting the bed every night, and the severity of its consequences those first months until the girl who worked in the laundry with the same eyes that looked at her through the gate at her father's house in El Vedado years later helped change her sheets and turn the mattress before morning bed check.

Amá says that in the past she had always been frightened by nuns even though she had seen them her whole life. She never could put her finger on it, but it had something to do with the severity, the white wimpled habit of them made them look as if they were about to perish; in a breeze, a group of them together made Amá think of women in the stranglehold of a wave. But here was this very innocent, scared-looking child that she and doña Liliana were trying to find clothes for.

The two red streaks ran from the inside pocket—stained red as blood, Amá says—and doña Liliana insisted that it be burned at once on the patio; pero, doña Cristina told them to wait. And they watched as she scraped fresas—there must have been fistfuls of them, they say—from her pockets.

Julio, Román and I were one and two, and she immediately set herself to the helping of our care, and the care of Ellen Helen, who under doña Cristina's watchful eye returned to her normal weight, but only went into La Habana once before she was frightened into not going outside until she had to. And las fresas, they would dry to dust and seed on a towel doña Cristina kept in the room she was given and there would be two seasons of them, ripening wild and prolific in any space they could find between the cracks and around the pineapples that sprouted in doña Liliana's father's well-appointed patio before they knew anything at all about why she had left Cárdenas.

Doña Cristina says that children don't know to call it hungry, they just cry out when something hurts. For her, she says, it's been a life of instinct rather than words. She says we wouldn't have known—and when she says we, she includes herself along with me, Román y Julio; we were three and four together that year—when we began to see men in the bushes around the house that no one else saw.

She says that she has had a life of that since her second birth, would have always felt hungry—that hole in the center of her stomach—had she had some history to retrace over and over again, some story that meant something to someone when now upon meeting her they say, So you're from Cuba. Hungry in a life of someone else's reason, someone else's logic, someone else's why did you come here.

Por ejemplo, señores, Ana García Carrera née Pérez, Aureliano's mother, used every muscle of her will to keep herself from leaving the framework of the window. She was completely soaked through and hard gusts of air tempted her to straddle them. She was certain she wasn't losing her mind; even Graciela had said that she could see her sometimes on a clear night floating; only forty-five kilometers away, señora.

She, her there, Ana thought, thin as a slipper, radiant y moreno floating within arm's reach, knows nothing about where she's from. They said they said her beauty was her mother's: slow emerging; a fine dancer; a graceful hostess, una mujer de la fortuna from one of the best families in Santiago. So thin when she was born her mamá hardly cried out in pain; so pale you could have forgotten she was the granddaughter of a woman of unforgiving blood; if she squinted, she might remember them taking her to her mamá's side as she lay in the last of childbed fever.

A cut across the palm of Ana's hand left a smear of blood as she cleared away the rest of the things off the desk. And without even releasing her thumb and forefinger, the photograph—she, her there—was snatched from her. It spun, it whirled, it split into ribbons, then slivers, then vanished. She, her there, sailed out toward Alberto's sunfish. Over the yard and the garden and gazebo where hundreds of

Alberto's friends and his business associates, people they knew from the yacht club, sweated under blue-and-white striped canopies that June afternoon Pilar was married. Over a thousand glazed iced prawns and five hundred baby lamb chops with paper flourish panties. Thirty cases of Veuve Clicquot were set out into tubs waiting to be placed into hired ice buckets, and eight cases of rum were brought up through Mexico for the waiters to pass on trays.

Ana warmed her hands in her fleshy armpits. How often they had ached from being lifted; by nursemaids and housekeepers, a nanny and even a governess before the woman became the mistress of one of the sons of the mayor. By her father—a man whom she knew only by the smell of his cologne that permeated the air and the clip of his heels against the polished wood floors—as he lifted her and set her on the edge of the piano and told her she would like being away at school; she would have new friends her own age. At any time she could close her eyes and watch herself being passed like a souvenir at a cocktail party or a prima ballerina.

When she had returned home on holidays, she had listened as her father y tíos y primos returned on horseback from the end of what they said was an infinity of azúcar: acre after acre, more than anyone could ever want; it would keep her warm and fed the rest of her life; it would make her desirable to marry; every man worth a salt from Santiago to La Habana would fall over himself getting to her; she would be the most beautiful woman in all of the island. Her father's sister brushed Ana's hair each night—a hundred and one strokes—as she told her how she wished that she were as lucky as Ana; to have tobacco like she had nearly coming out of her ears up in Manicaragua; there would be a life ahead of her that she couldn't possibly imagine. Though for her, it was only imagined. All of her acres, the abundance that spilled toward her, was nothing that Ana had been allowed to actually see. She was too delicate, they told her; there was no place for her. Wild animals or savages could attack her, they said, but she knew they just wanted to be able to swagger around, free to piss into the ground and call it theirs.

Doña Cristina says there are no resources in that kind of hungry. Nothing to satisfy you, nothing to fall back on, you become the bird that flies to eat and eats to fly until you're consumed either by exhaustion or old age or the exhaustion of old age, which when she said it most recently, I suppose it reminded her—without her ever saying so—of Amá, and she immediately gestured her hand towards me as if to take it back. Quickly, she remembered the sun over Cárdenas being unlike it was anywhere else that she had ever been, close like if you was walking up a hill, she said, you could simply reach out and touch it like it was the road in front of you. Not like the sun here so far overhead; she complained about the rains and the heat of the past weeks, and thinking that she had distracted me away from Amá and the distance that she had begun traveling from all of us, doña Cristina told me that after doña Liliana had left the convent on the arm of her very proud father to never return. Said that God claimed her again in the form of yet another benefactor.

Father Juan Rodolfo Nietes stayed handsome and youthful-looking her entire life, from the day she met him, when she says they said that she was a voiceless orphan, when he handed her a half dozen or so fresas that she unashamedly caught in her skirt when the other girls naturally took them in their hands, until he pointed across the lawn in Cárdenas fifteen years later; and she says that another one of the girls overheard the sisters question him, the silent one, and all that he said was, Sí, the silent one.

Insensato y estúpido, she's always thought it was to think silence was innocence, to equate quiet with peace, calm with contentment. ¡No! she said smashing her fist down on my kitchen table sending the folded pile of Amá's unmentionables that she will not let me launder—it's just not right for a boy, her son—onto the floor. Doña Cristina says that in all the years that Padre Nietes had come to their convent school out in the middle of nowhere he brought fresas. Big ripe juicy fresas, that brought the girls to him more easily for his council, his blessing and his benediction. Las fresas, he said, that couldn't possibly be grown in Cárdenas because of the heat and the nitrates in the soil. She says that she only needed him to kiss her on the forehead twice as he dropped the fresas into her skirt. The next time he drove up to the convent with the backseat of the car that he was driven in full of fresas, they grew wild along the lawn, around trees and bushes, they threatened their way into the convent and the school so that it became a rotating weekly chore for the girls who were born a second time and didn't pay to attend to keep the fresas out.

She says, doña Cristina, maybe it was her fresas. She was just told he would sponsor her as a bride of Christ; she was such an honored child—she said they said—to live within such a merciful world. And though she knew nothing of the world and its mercies, she knew were she to become anyone's bride . . .

And then she stopped and crossed herself, and said she'd sooner marry the beetle that had been kind enough to invite her inside a rotting aceituna.

THROUGH THE HALL and around to the end of the catwalk, Ana García Carrera née Pérez let the door slam. Aureliano's room rattled around her. He had been gone for more than ten years though held an odor that none of Graciela's cleaning could shake it free from. Late nights wandering around the house long after Alberto had passed out Ana would come into the boy's room. Only after hours of searching would she abandon hope of finding the soiled sweat sock or T-shirt or old pair of tennis shoes. It was different from the soured odor Alberto grunted into bed each night. New, fresh and eager as the boys who pressed into her and told her she was the sea, the wind, the rain, everything that made living on the island worthwhile, at parties. Whispered in her ear, her hair, along the slim arch of her neck, like candy, they said, azúcar.

The windows in Aureliano's room faced away from the water. Ana could not see it, but she could hear it slam Alberto's sunfish into the dock over and over. Light from one of the outside floods flickered between torrents of rain. The room was pounded like a tin box juggled in the air. Ana pulled a chair to where, for the past couple of years, she had noticed a tiny corner of wallpaper had begun to pull away from the wall. The first strip gave new start to the next; each that followed started another. Chunks of plaster came with them. Dust clung to her hair, mouth and eyelashes.

She fell against the bed to catch her breath. And she, her there, in the mirror, panted back. Flesh heavy and slack around her frame, her hair dusted and wild around her broad face, it was hard for Ana to remember swallowing fireflies for boys to chase their light to her belly. The papers said they waited for her for hours outside while she purchased hosiery, lunched with girlfriends; they followed her in their cars while she walked her dog.

If you follow the clippings that Aureliano left in a box in the basement here, there were reports of engagements to American actors, diplomats; a diamond bracelet was delivered anonymously. They said they said a man once jumped from the deck of his boat in full evening dress just to swim in the water she had just emerged from. On heat-slick patios, lined with colored lights, they pressed her close and whispered that she was night, she was day, she was the wind, the shore, the sea.

Earlier in the evening, Ana had sat around a canasta table with women who called life el exilio. En el exilio they only spoke of home, where the fish were fresher, the servants nicer, the nights were darker; they slept more soundly and dreamt less. The shopping was better; the restaurants were cleaner; the air was healthier for you. There you didn't have the crime; or the worry; or the thinking about who was behind your back. Each had left one or more fincas—tabaco, azúcar—more jewels than you imagine; was swimming in dresses from France; and had had hundreds of admirers in tow. They all had pictures of themselves getting off of planes at Miami International in crisp silk dresses, sunglasses, gloves and fresh lipstick. They had only packed what they would need for the season, they had Batista's promise; in the newspapers they had all seen the same kinds of pictures of him taken on the very same airstrip. Since, hundreds of letters had been written. Since, thousands of appeals, cries of anguish, had been sent up to La Virgen del Cobre for the rings that were hidden in the vault behind family portraits; for the coffee plantation in the mountains; for an aching heart last seen surreptitiously on the corner of calle Veintiuno. Until one night, after hours of canasta and too many cocktails, any one of them would ask Ana if she would not mind staying behind the others. And over cafecito cubano, any one of them would pull Ana's hand across the table and say, I need to tell you the pain of mi historia; Ana, soy . . . soy La Flaca . . . you know, the one you would read about in all the newspapers back home, I am she. Ana would never say anything as she looked in their eyes with understanding. Ana listened as they told the story as it had been in the newspapers of how she had been at the coming-out party of a friend: You know at the Hilton Habana. They added details of the dress they had been wearing: some were blue others were green: As you know this was my favorite color. They all made excuses for why Ana may not recognize them now: their lives were a series of living hells en el exilio; no one knew who they were; no one treated her the way she was intended to, meant to, born to be treated. They told Ana, each night she longed for her stolen identity and every morning she woke to who she knew she wasn't. They all told her that they were not looking for her pity, they just needed someone to tell, and they knew that their secret was safe with her.

Ana had watched their waiter go to each canasta table in the game room at the yacht club to tell them of the approaching storm. By the time he reached their tables they all knew the message. Ana could see he was sweating. He bowed at the waist over his cocktail tray and began, Perdónenme señoras, when one of the other women at the table interrupted to imitate his same provincial accent and say, I'm afraid that it is only kind to warn you the news report talks of a very bad storm coming up from the south. The other women laughed while the woman who had done the imitation ordered more drinks for all of them and waved him away by saying, One more drink, one more hand and we're all out of here. The man had bowed again and backed away from the table. Ana had turned the first card she was dealt over to find she was holding the queen of spades. She had placed the second card on top of it in the palm. By the time the hand was completely dealt she had managed to get the queen of spades into her lap. By the time the waiter had returned with her drink, she had folded the card in her lap over twice. She had feigned counting her cards, and then made a joke, telling the woman who dealt that she need not bother to finish her last drink. The card had been replaced with the two of diamonds and they had begun to play. Ana could not think of why she was cheating. The missing card had no clear consequence to the outcome of the game. She only knew that the blood rushed in her ears like the deafening sound of waves as the game went on and as she—with her hand hidden under the table—folded it over and over and over on top of itself until, finally, it was so small it could disappear under her heel into the carpet.

A spiteful demon, lethal venom in the form of drying quinceañera wreaths, dance cards and fans, sea-worn stones and casino chips, flattened hats and a brocade vest, a riding crop for who knows what, he said, Aureliano, mixed with the smell of mothballs to keep the rats out the moment that you walked into that house. An invisible something, he called it, houses hold it, and at the time I said that I had no idea for sure what he was talking about, it is only now that I know exactly what it is.

Julio, Román, doña Cristina and I would see the men nobody else saw come into the house and go through doña Liliana's father's splendid desk, his important papers, his magnificent bureau, throw files about the room; I don't remember, but she says that I pointed at a wall shouting, He did, he did, and although no one believed me, she says that later she took me aside and told me that she did.

There was something about Ellen Helen—about the way that she insisted that Román, Julio and I made up imaginary men to cover our misbehavior, and that doña Cristina was soft with the boys, loved us up too much when we really should be beaten, and that she was covering our tracks—that reminded doña Cristina of being told that she was blessed when she had thought that she was blessed to have found garbage that seemed fresh and delicious when Las Madres Escolapias found her with their love.

Nena, I know all about love, doña Cristina says Helen Ellen told her, I know boys, she says she said, and they will test you at each turn, don't start them out letting them get away with it so young or they'll never turn out to be decent men, as if there were such a thing.

Pero, doña Cristina says that she knew all about tests of love. She had had a lifetime in which she had to prove herself deserving of it, worthy of it, so much so, she said, that whenever the word was said to her it made her think of tentacles first pulling from one direction to the other. How worthy was she of the benevolence of the sisters and their charges, she says she asked God every night as instructed, how worthy of the light they had bestowed on her, the life opened to her, the misery she'd left behind, the joy she could anticipate in the everlasting? What hand had touched her on the shoulder that brought about Father Nietes' attentions? more than one nun suggested that she pray as she counted her blessings in her counsel with La Virgen del Cobre.

And she did, each day, one by one, until she had affixed a number to them all, was certain of their tally and wanted to cash them in during the confession prior to taking her vows.

Nietes had come to tell the sisters that the school was to be closed down; Castro, he announced in his speech to the nuns. It seems as if God has left the island, he moaned. Doña Cristina says that she watched a bead of sweat break on Nietes' brow, heard it thunk in the spine between the pages as he read the benediction of the Host. And another, fatter one slithered from under his carefully combed mantle of bangs, and rang against the chalice as it joined the blood of Christ. He began to rain down on the altar cloth as he raised the monstrance in the air and soaked the front of his surplice.

She and the other sisters made him lunch and talked about where they might go, and how the church would support them now that they had no place anymore. Though as they ate, doña Cristina said that she remembers his wet thumb and forefinger against her lips, a sheen of light in between the upstanding hairs on the back of his hand, as he announced she was about to receive the body of Christ. Christ in His new and everlasting light; she said Amen to His body divine in its covenant with His people so that sins would be forgiven.

Rather than in a confessional, she says she sat directly across from Nietes later as she asked him to bless her for she had sinned. He called her his child and asked how long it had been since her last confession and instead of answering, she dropped three very ripe fresas into the lap of his cassock. The reddest ones she could find. Sweet sweet, she says, the grittiest with seeds she had grown that would break open against your teeth with a crunch that sent shivers through you, stopped you from thinking of anything else. Though when he didn't seem to understand, Bendígame, Padre, she kissed him on the forehead, Bendígame, as she reached under his cassock and undid his belt.

So much can be traded in for language just by watching the movement in nature, doña Cristina will tell you as she cures a bad stomach virus with a root she finds down on Milwaukee Avenue. There's no need for anyone to tell you, no need to know how to tell anyone else. It's all monkey, she says, it's what you get to know from watching monkeys, sometimes all you need to do is find the monkey in you and you'll know exactly what to do next.

Ana García Carrera née Pérez pushed herself up from her son's bed and walked through the scraps of wallpaper that surrounded her. At the window, she looked past the basketball net and lawn where she had taught the children how to play croquet and Alberto had rolled around on the ground with them when they were little when he came home from work. Just past it, rain and hail battered at the wrought iron table and chairs. She knew they would not give way to the wind. They were bolted to a cement slab poured into the ground and had then been covered with sod and flagstones to make them look as if they had pushed up from the earth.

Ana looked past the wrought iron table to a slope in the road where she could see a truck struggling in the mud against the wind. It slid a few feet up the incline and then would be blown back again. The grinding of its gears was taken up by the high-pitched howl in the air. The boy's room shook and whistled from gaps in the molding. The gutters overhead clattered loosely against the terra-cotta. A rose trellis from the back of the house flew by; the entire root system, cleaned of all traces of dirt, flapped like the tail of a kite behind it.

She turned into the room, and with just the tips of her fingers flipped over a table of magazines and baseball cards. She used the back of her hand to clear away glass animal figures and soccer trophies. She pulled the empty drawers from the dresser onto the floor with a single tug of her hand. Bottles of ink, flung from the desk drawers, bled into the carpet.

The windows came open easily, almost by themselves.

She could not think of how many times Graciela had suggested that the señor have a look at them. The suck of air that followed forced the door open and gave the strips of wallpaper life out the window. Ana grabbed fistfuls of pens and notebooks to follow them. His catcher's mask and glove. Socks, clean from the drawers at the back of his closet. T-shirts and underpants. Tennis shoes and an old pair of Alberto's wing tips. Baseball caps and boldly colored ties. Out. He would no longer need anything that bound him to this place.

Much in the same way that after it was over, doña Cristina says, Padre Nietes first fell down on his knees and then became prostrate on the floor in front of the crucifix in the little chapel weeping over himself, over his weakness, over his unforgivable sullying of a young child. And she says that she asked, what made him think that God had not forgiven him long before he thought of touching her, and why was it that he had sullied her? She says that he wouldn't look at her through the rest of his visit, and in exchange for love he came to her cell that night he was leaving and told her that he would take her anywhere on the island that she wanted, but she couldn't stay there.

Doña Cristina says she had no idea where to go, but it seemed that in El Vedado was a place that she could ask for something before it was given to her. She had no idea what to say at the gate, no voice, no language all over again. She stood there mute until doña Liliana recognized her. Though once again, she was completely voiceless, nothing in her life had prepared her to enter doña Liliana's father's house. In fact, her entire life prior to that moment had been to deny her worthiness of it, to clean up and move silently out of the way of girls who had come from it, and to acknowledge and accept that a kingdom was hers were she to repent—repent that very minute—and step away from the door. And even as she allowed herself to be ushered into the vestibule, she felt her throat beginning to close, her tongue stilled, as spiders from when she still slept on the ground, under palmas, out in the open, when she was a little girl who couldn't distinguish herself from the landscape around her, returned to sew her mouth shut. A crystalline thread of wait and see, look and learn, until she was confident of how it was she was to say what it was she was to say, until she learned the names of things.

It had been in a moment following the invasion of La Playa Girón—one of the many titles assigned to a date in your textbooks, señores, that I've asked you to change; you'll find a big black line through its English cognate if you've done what I've asked—that she decorated him, endowed Aureliano with everything of her in spite of Alberto's historia of greed. Everything he would need. Solamente sangre cubana, an unforgiving blood, thick with savages and flies, without heiresses to court, without deals to make, without fincas to collect, without political parties to join or governments to overthrow. Solamente sangre cubana, sin azúcar.

The chandelier swung on its mooring as Ana García Carrera née Pérez rounded the catwalk and headed down the stairs. She tightened the belt of her robe knowing that around canasta tables all over Coral Gables las chismosas would have claimed to have seen her shopping at Versace; would disagree and say she was in Paris, or Barcelona. Though Ana must have known all she did was open the door and walk outside where she was night, she was day, she was the wind, the shore, the sea.

One night, while we were all asleep in doña Liliana's father's well-appointed house, doña Cristina says that she performed her second test of love by pouring all the powder, and all of the flour, the sugar, the spices left in the cupboards, onto the shiny shiny floors. But then again, doña Cristina will tell you that it was at that moment she could see herself becoming something that up until that point she had been told her whole life, by the sisters and the other girls, that she either never would become or never should become, but which she wasn't sure. Prayers began, Lord I'm not worthy, though she had no idea whether that meant that she should strive to earn merit or was each breast-beating mea culpa a cry to retain valuelessness. Their whispers, the sisters in their cells, the girls as they dreamt—to live a most humble life unto the Lord; asked, is this the most humble life unto the Lord; gave, with this penance, in my humility—choked her, caused her to rip at her nightgown, slip out of a window and roll on the grass until she was cool, disinterested and no different from the churning of dark above her. A useful life, she says that she could hear them dreaming for as she lay there wondering whose was useful; who had more value and who got to choose. Útil; Provechosa; she says she rolled the words around in her mouth like marbles as she tried to think what else to say. And it wasn't until she found herself squatting in front of one of us—either me or Julio or Román—on doña Liliana's father's luxuriously fragrant patio uncoiling the braid that ended at the middle of her calf—that the nuns told her was only a sign of her vanity, her weakness, her unquenched desire for secular life, a life of the flesh, her flirtation with pecado, peccadillo at its worst and most treacherous—uncoiling her braid to dab at a sloppy mouth or a bucket of crocodile tears that with relief she realized she was neither anyone's nursemaid, nor servant, nor bride, nor handmaiden. No. If Julio or Román or I shoved, she shoved back; we all splashed with our clothes on in the fountains at the far end and center of the garden; she ate as many of her fresas—that took over vases and window pots, vined and spread out onto trellises—until she was just as sick as we were, but with us, ate as many the next day, until we all rolled around on the ground holding our bellies; she helped us bring the peahen and her nest in the house when the wind threatened to take it from its roost, and wept along with us when Amá threatened to throw them all out, particularly when she was stopped in the hallway by the cock who spread his tail and hissed at her. Each day during our time together in El Vedado is marked by a lost tooth, a broken vase, a sprained wrist and a mild concussion as though they were her own and woven into, inseparable and just as real as the flying carpets and chests of gold that Amá and doña Liliana read to us about before bed. It was just a glance passed between the four of us—doña Cristina, Julio, Román and I—that confirmed the footsteps that passed along the corridors at night, a look of knowing the same as the wordless secret we passed between each other watching a caterpillar spin a cocoon; there's a moment, when the sea is at its calmest, between waves as they break against the shore, that you're so certain that's it, no more, or at least we thought so. And I suppose to them—the men who came and went through drawers and closets, opened hatboxes, listened as they rapped their knuckles on walls—we appeared to have no mouths, no eyes, just as they were invisible to Amá and doña Liliana. Amá had punished Román, Julio and me by sending us to bed without reading to us; doña Cristina remembers overhearing her tell doña Liliana that maybe Ellen Helen was right, those boys might do with more discipline, might could want for a good smack every now and then. And doña Cristina says all she could think of were the times a hand had been brought hard across her mouth for saying that she saw God outside, she saw God in the holy water font, a turtle was once carrying God on its back headed toward the convent, and she stole doña Liliana's compact, and the face powder off of her bureau, and containers of sulfa dustings and bromide elixirs that so many had brought to heal Helen Helen's many maladies. And by morning everyone but Helen Ellen knew that the house was no longer safe.

When confronted with moments of uncertainty, hang

out long enough and something's bound to happen, Aureliano would say when we had been given the wrong directions while diving in an area we didn't know, fishing with an unbaited hook, when there was a lull in conversation long enough to make others uncomfortable—hang out long enough and something is bound to happen—and everyone seemed to be happy and smile after that. Something, he'd say, not expecting anything at all, just something.

Doña Cristina says that the morning after Amá and I left the island, she drew Ellen Helen's bath at noon as she had every morning since the day she arrived. And while she bathed she and doña Liliana burned all of Helen Ellen's clothing in the yard and laid doña Cristina's habit on the bed. When Ellen Helen appeared from the bath on the patio in a towel and a turban holding the habit asking what was the meaning of this, it was doña Cristina who told her that it was time for her to go.

No one could say what it was that persuaded Ellen Helen to leave the house; they only knew that after she did they would find traces of footprints for a long while afterward. Up until a day a year later that they would board one of the last of the Freedom Flights.

Helen Ellen's nameless dog however turned up dead—long dead, months or maybe years dead, it was so decomposed and stiff when she found it on the patio of doña Liliana's father's well-appointed house in El Vedado—with a gold bug in its mouth.

Of all the things gathered up to head to the airport the day they left for good, doña Cristina says that she has no idea why she went into the garden for a pocketful of fresas. She was certain at some point in time, between juggling luggage and the boys between them, the fresas would get crushed and spoil the first suit she ever owned, one that had been one of doña Liliana's favorites.

The airport was jammed with people. The counter, the

last counter to get to America that anyone knew about was crushed. Doña Cristina says that they knew someone wanted something in doña Liliana's father's well-outfitted house, but they really never knew who it was that wanted it, or what it was they wanted. They had ransacked the backs and false bottoms of drawers for American dollars that seemed to appear like doves out of a silk top hat, and she and doña Liliana had cautioned each other about anything that would garner them attention at Martí.

So she was shocked as she saw doña Liliana pull all of it out and put it on the counter. Doña Cristina said she heard the man say, Señora it is the same for everyone, you only buy two. Never in my life have I heard Liliana sigh so deeply, doña Cristina says it was the kind of silent hysterical scream that she had become so accustomed to, living with the sisters, a hysteria that can't articulate itself but remains muffled to everyone unless it's someone who has done it herself, she says.

And she reached into her pocket and she pulled out a fresa and gestured to Román, and as he came she says she said to the man at the counter, No, señor, this one is mine.

. . . PERO, SEÑORES, puso un circo y le crecieron los enanos, las viejas cubanas will tell you. It all costs. A señor Martínez from four years ago—or maybe it was when I was a student here, I don't remember—snuck food all the last week before he was to take the state middleweight championship title; two, three Milky Way bars in a single period, two on the green; never made weight, didn't wrestle. And even if he doesn't think about it, he left an entire graduating class poised with what if's that lead to nowhere; and then what it was that we all thought that he was, he wasn't, and we could no longer take that away with us.

Before, I had been skeptical when people said things happened or time just passed, but they did and they do. A morning can just as easily spend itself in an office behind a desk as it can on a couch in aimless thought; all the books can be taken down off of the shelves and saved from dust, or they can gather grit and become gummy with the summer's humidity. Bulbs should be uprooted, dipped in bonemeal, tubers thinned. The carpets cleaned along with the slipcovers. Dune grass needs to be planted for erosion control. Check books out of the library only to return them unread a week and a half overdue, to check them out again a week later. Three boulders can be moved to the far end of a property line only to be moved again to another location that won't harm the birch. There is a fencing class to be researched, shopped for, and not taken as well as classes in German and figure drawing. Party and dinner invitations were accepted and then canceled. Fourteen irreverent essays on city government were written but not submitted. The orchids in the living room perished in the winter and the violets along the kitchen sink flourished between periods of lavish attention and lavish neglect.

Rent a blue house on the other side of Lake Michigan for years and years until you eventually buy it, señores, and you still won't own it as much as it owns you. And even though you spend the entire week in the city in a classroom waiting for a return of the same feeling, it isn't the same.

Por ejemplo, cafecito after cafecito, Aureliano Francisco García Carrera said he watched his father, pero there simply wasn't enough Cuban rum in all of Dade County to make it 1958 again and put him in the arms of a woman who danced the merengue in a dress so thin so red so tight, Tan sexy, he said he said, he thought he had died and gone to heaven.

Say, No, just to swim, when friends ask what do you go there for with their faces set in expectation to hear of something great, something like you've come to read or write or paint, or that you thought it a good investment. Draw a map on your hand, point and say that there is the shore; the other side unseen, a tidy place to keep wishes, and watch how their faces drop, listen how quickly they change the subject when you tell them that you can be anywhere, before going to bed take two Halcion with a glass of scotch, shed whatever you're wearing on a rock or a log and simply walk in without testing the water with your toe.

The properties of water propel and envelop at the same time. In a dog paddle just a half mile from shore, a wave can send you high enough to see the desolate glow of the house as an enormity set to swallow you. A quick suck from an undertow can turn it all to miniature; the light from the living room will spill out onto the deck, the dead brush poking up from arid tufts of snow at the onset or end of winter can seem as if they can fit into the palm of your hand. An ice floe is either a terror or an invitation, the moon either a guide or a hindrance.

Perspective is the thing. Flotsam is jetsam if you're dead center in the middle of something. No, señor Ostrovski, no, none of the years of Ostrovskis can have this one, not this one. This one I know, I was there! Know what it is like not to know anything, know what it is like to not even be sure of your own name, or where you are exactly.

Amá and I spent a week in the dark the year we lost the Santiago Boy, Joaquín-Ernesto. And I would say that darkness has its own light. Separate from air and water, it's the space between the horizon and anywhere you might sit on the shore. The gulls neither travel through it nor on it the way that you might think, but negotiate the tissue-thin membranes despite their razor-like talons and beaks as if they know corners where there aren't any, can find things where you only see the water-colored, the sun-dried, the rubbed-down of sand and bone and disembodied fish heads.

Amá spent the next week looking for a job that she could go to after she was done at Marta's. It would only be for a short time, she assured. The landlady let her use her phone and allowed her to run a series of extension cords from her apartment to our kitchen. I sat in the corner on the floor as Amá made dinners of borrowed rice, fríjoles negros and salt pork on a borrowed hot plate by candlelight. After we had eaten and we cleaned up, I did my homework at the kitchen table until it was time to go to bed. It was my job to put the leftovers on the back porch so that it would be fresh for my lunch the next day. Each night, in the new dusting of snow, moonlight blasted the porch and exposed a trail of large bare footprints that ran from the alley up the stairs to our kitchen window—where they paced back and forth for a better look around the gaps in the curtains—and back down again. Though each time I would go to tell Amá, I would find she was already asleep on the couch. Her brow was so smooth and her mouth nearly smiling like the day we got the mangoes, I didn't tell her.

By the beginning of the next week Amá was hired at Walgreens to work between ten o'clock and three o'clock. In the mornings, she walked me to school and then made her way to Marta's. At three o'clock, she picked me up from school and walked me back home. Marta paid her extra to come back after hours and do the cleaning up. Amá could sleep for an hour in one of the operators' chairs before taking the bus downtown. Our landlady would be home to look in on me, or if I needed her in an emergency. And I was to never ever open the door for anyone. Amá asked me to show her how I could light a candle and put it out several times. I was to clean up my dishes and study until nine, make sure I brushed all of my teeth before going to bed; I needed my rest; I needed to study, I would need to be good at long division when I became a diplomat.

If you were to go to the blue house across the lake in the dead of winter, señores, it's hard to imagine it as the same place with all its dizzying white light that blasts so the annuals burn up within an hour if they are not kept soaked through July and August. Typically at the start of winter there is a leaf storm rising from the forest preserve that engulfs the dune; it takes the entire sky, washing it a dark that won't go clean until late April. The lake swells to meet it. It is just at that time of year that Aureliano Francisco García Carrera would cut the clematis close to the ground. He would cover the rock garden with a tarp and mulch the roses; and by then he would have hipped them so that they could be dried and crushed into sauces for rabbit and venison, or have them wait in glass jars, labeled, ready in the dark to mellow the sharpness from bark tea. At that time of year there is no beach, no real daylight. It is a murkish haze that meets the water swells as they throw up floes of ice that become miniature and comic through the window like fat on top of gravy. During the day, dry and barren, it has the look of withering skin. There's no sand. No sun.

Here—with the exception of this year with its horrid heat and torrid rains that seemed to come out of nowhere—here, usually, you can hardly smell the earth until late April—almost May—and it's only then that you realize you've nearly forgotten it. It starts with your being able to smell mud, then dog shit. Then you suddenly realize the tulips have come and the lilacs are in bud. Amá predicted if it could stay cool enough for the next couple of weeks to keep an opened jar of mayonnaise from spoiling, she would have enough money saved to have the electricity turned back on. In the mornings, increasingly longer shadows of light would draw against the walls of our apartment, and the chatter of high-pitched birds woke us earlier and earlier. The wind no longer burns your nose, and sky gives way to great festoons of blue light.

And it was on a morning just like that that Joaquín-Ernesto—the Santiago Boy—appeared to a fisherman in the eddies at the basin of the Fox River. Bloated and discolored—pale as fish bellies, they said—his body was first thought to be a buoy lost the summer before.

Though by then, there was nobody to claim him. They called his father's house to find the number had been disconnected. A committee headed by Mr. Sáenz and Father Rodríguez went with the police to the house. They found a month's worth of wet and disintegrating newspapers on the front steps. All the windows had been left open and the doors unlocked. Breakfast dishes for three were left on the kitchen table; drawers in the girl's room had been pulled open and emptied; the contents of Joaquín-Ernesto's mother's jewelry box had been poured out onto the carefully made bed; his father's truck was still in the garage and the keys were in the top pocket of his winter coat that had been neatly arranged—in tight armless folds like in a department store—and placed on the back of the living room couch. Eventually, Father Rodríguez and Mr. Sáenz called the gas station Joaquín-Ernesto's father owned and his tíos came to claim the body. Confused and unable to understand exactly what to do at the moment, the tíos gave Joaquín-Ernesto's body over to the community and it became ours to bury and mourn.

I've spent every Monday morning for the past thirteen years here in front of this classroom trying to pretend that the weekend before I try not to fight the want to sleep whenever I get to the point that I'm a mile offshore. If I've forgotten to turn off the lights in the house, it will float up like a tiny vista, a panorama on the dune. Like Christmas, it's both real and fake enough that I never ask where I am or where I'm going or where I was. It's neither the warmth of scotch in your belly nor the cool steel buzz of the Halcion in your head. Plaintive like hissing, it directs you toward it.

By squinting, I can bring the little blue house on the other side of the lake into focus with all its disorder and peeling paint, the deck that will need resurfacing by summer, and the under hum of Aureliano's lingering like his smell in drawers and closets and corners that now seemed to be completely other than anything that I know. I can point—this house; this place; this time—as if they were part of a story of something that never happened, yet it still feels like someone is standing on my throat every time that I tell it to myself as history.

Relaxing into the crest of a wave, however, the light blurs and spills over me, portentous in its invitation to come, ven, ven, ven aquí, come here, come here, he'd whisper even though there was no getting closer; chico, he'd say, through Spain, the year before we met, then Jamaica two hundred dollars got him a plane, a hotel room with bad plumbing and crawling mildew in a place his mother said was the most elegant of its day, and a walk until he thought his legs would drop off down El Malecón that he said looked nothing like the memory played over and over to him; and I offered a beach I could scarcely remember being at only because the last time that I was there—Amá, Román, Julio y las doñas Liliana y Cristina—I had no idea that I would need it one day when he couldn't walk, or eat, or weighed so little he needed help sitting up. We'll like it there, he said, in a way that seemed at the time like dying twice; though play something like that over in your head over and over for years, señores, like anything learned by rote, even swallowing glass, can feel natural.

Father Rodríguez and Mr. Sáenz organized the second funeral. School was canceled that day, and Marta closed her shop for the rest of the afternoon. We crowded in cars, work and delivery trucks; cab drivers from the neighborhood or who lived in nearby Latin neighborhoods refused fares and waited while we stood underneath umbrellas out of the steady shower of cold rain.

Amá and I came home to our slowly darkening apartment. She did not make dinner nor did she pack her bag with her comfortable shoes to go to Walgreens that night. Instead, she sat looking out at the daylight as it moved over the buildings across the street. Pobrecito, I heard her whisper, pobrecito, pobrecito, and I knew she was crying.

She was still crying by the time the room had gone dark and still crying when she connected the line of extension cords from the landlady's apartment. In the dark, the sound was isolated to the run of water into the pot; the shuffle of her feet across the room. The glow from the borrowed hot plate sizzled with her tears. And as the coil grew redder, it seemed to reach up to drink them in through a story she was telling herself that was bathed in the wet warm that comes after a hot Habana day, when her neck and shoulders smelled like lemon and jasmine water. Y qué bonita, they all whistled, eyeing her from the gardenia behind her ear, down the tight sea-green dress she had made herself, to her slim ankles. Dance with me negra, she said they said, as she was bringing our plates to the table, they said, Dance with me. Dance with me luna negra, she said they said, and then began to give thanks for our dinner, Dance with me, cariño. As the moon slid up to the kitchen window, I could see Amá sitting there, turning the rice and beans over with her fork. Luna negra, dulce luna negra, she said they said, as she cleared our plates and washed, dried and put them away.

She brought my books to the table along with the candle. Estudia, she said, as she hunted in her pocket for the matches, when suddenly the lights came back on.

Because she was nearly late getting to Walgreens, Amá had to wait and call the electric company the next morning. We took the food off the back porch and put it back into the refrigerator. I overheard Amá tell the landlady that they said that the bill had been paid for at least two years. When the landlady asked by who, Amá said they didn't know. When she opened the shop for Marta that morning there was an envelope addressed to la negrita who makes flan con guayaba like home, but there was no note inside. When Amá suggested that maybe she should call the police, Marta asked her what would she tell them. Tell them what, arrest the man that paid your light bill? Amá called again and started to tell the woman on the phone that there had been some mistake, when Marta pressed the button down and asked Amá, What was she, una loca? But Amá insisted she would take charity from no one. The first client of the day—an old woman who often spoke of the talking burro that predicted the weather in the mountains on her father's coffee finca—called Amá an ungrateful bitch, una tonta who couldn't tell the difference from un milagro and a lamppost.

For days afterward, Amá tried to find out who paid our light bill. At Marta's, in the laundería, at the grocery, women would look at her blankly, as if she had done something wrong to have come by it. Others looked at her puzzled, looked at her as if she were doing something wrong by questioning it. Each would cause Amá to bite her lip and curse under her breath, and continue to work at Walgreens for a little longer every time she had decided to quit, as if she was certain something would come along to take our milagro away.

As school wound toward end, Father Rodríguez added veiled cautions to our morning prayers. We were to think the thoughts of exemplary young men and if we didn't know what that meant, a summer project could be to look up and record the definition of each new word we came across. We were to keep open eyes and ears toward improvement. We were told our lives should begin to take on new meaning; but there is no way of telling if any of us heard it. Even when Mr. Sáenz came in one day to tell us that fine young men took part in things like the 227—young men interested in the outdoors, marksmanship and the community—nobody listened, nobody joined. The most gloriously fat warm breezes would take us—one at a time—out the window and over the park toward a green vista near water.

Those of us who were already part of the 227 spent the beginning of the summer vacation painting our wall against the carnicería white. The butcher had donated an outside wall of his shop next to where a building had been torn down so long ago no one had been there long enough to remember what had been there before. The mural had been Mr. Sáenz's idea. A mural that expresses all of the great aspects of rising Latin values of manhood, Mr. Sáenz said cheering us on, though it only caused laughs and groans. Older boys were trusted on ladders; the rest of us took their lewd jokes and planned accidents in our hair. Even though I didn't want a part of it—swore that I would sit and read at the shop or the library or even the apartment—Amá said it would be good for me, besides, what will you do all day and all night while I'm working?

Within four days, the wall was white with three coats of

paint. That evening, Mr. Sáenz took each of us home in his van. Every time one of us got out, he said, Think quickly hombre; we want to get our mark up there before the graffiti guys take it over. He waited and watched until each of us got walked through our front doors and an adult came out to wave that we were in safely.

Our landlady let me in our apartment. She said that she would be out for an hour or so to make sure that her husband was really working late like he said, then she would come back and heat up my dinner.

I opened all of the windows and the back door. I sat at the kitchen table and rolled my sketch paper out. Someone said that he was doing a superhero; a gladiator had been taken; a couple of cowboys would fight off a pack of wild Apaches; already, a forest ranger was going to be on the lookout for out-of-control fires. Without an idea, the pencil poised itself over the sheet of paper as if it were in no way attached to my arm. As the light started to fade, I held the tip toward the breeze that was coming through the back door and waited for a conquistador to ride out with sharpened point or an astronaut's heavy lunar float to make the air a liquid, when Joaquín-Ernesto's father stepped forward and pressed both his hands against the screen.

¡Shh! he said putting a finger between the gap in the screen door to flip the hasp.

His hair was long and matted in places. He was barefoot, his pants were dirty and his shirt had no buttons. It was hard to tell the difference between dirt and hair, each ran so thick. As if he had been asleep under the leaves, under the snow, under the winter, he smelled hot like earth, like dog shit, like rum, like the trail of smoke from a hundred thousand cigars, like a night with stars I could almost remember near Santiago when Amá and I chased each other around and around until we fell tired with laughing and were surrounded by a field of new casabas.

His arm was curled around a brown paper bag. For a while he stood there and stared at me. I couldn't say anything, my heart was in my throat as he slowly came toward the table and looked at the blank piece of paper in front of me. He made a clicking sound with his tongue and stroked the back of my head, and then one by one he began taking guayabas out of the bag. Fresh and verdant, they filled the page and then spilled over onto the table; some rolled off onto the floor. Maybe only thirty or forty but it seemed like hundreds.

He was sweating heavily when he finished, and he went over to the sink and put his mouth on the spigot. Watching his back heave up and down like a wounded animal, I felt less afraid and was able to move. I was going to the cupboard to get a glass for him when I realized out loud that it was he who had the light turned back on. He pushed past me making a groaning sound, opened the freezer door and put his head in for what seemed a very long time. Gracias señor, I whispered, though he continued to groan. I cleared my throat, gaining courage, and said, Señor gracias, again, when he pulled out the ice trays, crackling them, sending cubes in a scatter across the floor.

He scooped up three and forced them into my hand. Holding on, he pressed his forehead into the ice causing it to melt black down my arm. He moved my hand down his face and chest and into his pants. I felt the back of my head slam into the refrigerator door; the beard on his cheek cut against the side of my face. And as he rocked back and forth against my belly, I could hear him sing sweetly, low and deep, from an unforgotten place in his chest.

I stood fixed until his feet hit the bottom of the landing and then slapped against the bricks and echoed at the end of the alley. Forever after that—after I had wrapped the guayabas in the drawing paper and hid them in the bottom of the garbage—the only thing ever talked about when anyone mentioned Joaquín-Ernesto, his family or the milagros that followed that winter he seemed to disappear through the ice. Anyone who could have seen into our apartment after I had changed my shirt, after I had wiped up the floor, after I had turned all of the lights on and sat at the table to wait for the landlady to come to heat my dinner, might have said, How good that boy is—that one there across the alley—the one whose mamá makes flan con guayaba like home.

Buy a lottery ticket, mix an orisha, throw the corie pero luck has nothing to do with it, Father Rodríguez called out in his clearest voice to the thirty or so of us who stood in the field with him as he blessed our mural. He and Mr. Sáenz decided that the commemorative service should take place on the fifth of July rather than the fourth because it should be independent from the yanquis' Independence Day and everyone will have the day off work anyway. The two of them stood in front of a carefully rendered painting of Spider-Man because someone had sprayed the word fuck across his chest plate in the night. After the prayer, Mr. Sáenz proclaimed the mural a work of creative force that needed to be cultivated and respected. Not to be upstaged, Father Rodríguez said it came from the kind of faith that comes from the ability to dream. Behind them, a gladiator plunged a sword into the heart of a dragon as it emerged from a cracked fissure near the Great Barrier Reef; two wrestlers, caught in the Sea of Cassiopeia, were in a clench and appeared enormous next to a spaceship carrying a Martian who waved at a muscleman balancing a thousand-pound dumbbell in each hand. One of the wings of the figure I painted crested above them all, the other—at an angle—dipped between Spider-Man and the Martian; the feathers along the wingspan were translucent to flurries of sky and light and color underneath them; his face could have belonged to any one of us brown-faced boys who needed help getting just that high on the scaffolding.

After Father Rodríguez and Mr. Sáenz finally stopped their speeches, a boom box let out a trumpet squeal that fell into rhythmic drumbeats that caused the hips of a grandmother in a flowered housedress to remember a rumba she danced with a man whose name she could no longer remember; It had to have been more than thirty years ago, she said. Those of us in the 227 ran wild in the weedy field in between card tables and families and converted industrial drums—cut open and turned on their sides—which had been wheeled out for the occasion. The air was flavored with the smoke of lighter fluid y charcoal y carne y plátanos y bacalao y pollo. Someone's mother cranked mango ice cream in one of those old machines that needs rock salt, and there were kegs of beer and brown paper bags of rum. Even the puertorriqueños stood on the sidewalk with their bikes, slowed their cars on the street to find out what those pinche cubanos were doing.

There was an argument that nearly turned into a fight over how much anyone should be expected to pay for a used car that was only going to die twenty minutes after its new owner drove it; and in whispers around the backs of hands, the questionable length and shocking neckline of a certain red dress that had managed to find its way into more laps than really could be considered respectable was discussed thoroughly with anyone who would cross her arms, roll her eyes or click her tongue in agreement. No one spoke of snow or wind or sleet or rain or ice. O milagros. For a long time that day, the sun was hot and bright and directly overhead, and we all stayed together in the field until it slipped behind our mural, and the dark came, and complaints of tired feet and too-full stomachs and sunburned eyes and work in the morning, and little ones sprawled worn out across their papis' shoulders, and teenage girls tested the stickiness of their boyfriends' T-shirts before allowing them close, and the last of the coals had gone out and food had been packed away for lunches. It's just what we do here, aquí, so far north.

But I suppose it's how we live our lives, señores, some

of us calling ourselves exiliados, others of us asking each other where are you from, bringing entire countries with us while leaving the same country behind, all the while pretending it doesn't hurt. Even if you're comfortable now—the Babcocks I've had over the years and the Tylers, all too good to be taught by me, by immigrants, yet too poor to get the fuck out of here—in jobs, at college, somewhere out in the world, even if you were born here, even if you are like everyone else or you think you're like everyone else, you are like everyone else in that you'll find that wanting what is going to happen in your life next while standing still so that even saying that you came from this place—Chicago, this neighborhood, this school—is both the same agony and the same pleasure as being sucked into a back funnel or a whirlpool.

What resilient creatures we are, señores, when I think of how many times when I least expect it—in line in the supermarket, while planning lessons, when my apartment was still my own and I'd often sit at the kitchen table having cafecito while I read at the end of the day—that he comes flying, señor Santiago, Joaquín-Ernesto's father, dirty and ugly, back from wherever it is he went so lonely and sad, and I take him in my arms again, and again, again the same way as before, each time—eso, es, eso, es, eso, eso, eso, es—before I let go, forgive because I know, I know. The same way that I know that this will be the year that I can let go of the blue house across the lake. I no longer need it. Perhaps in the same way that I no longer need señor Santiago, Joaquín-Ernesto's father, to turn our lights back on, as much as I need him to need me, as much as I need Amá to believe we were saved by milagros that first year, as much as I need to know—in what I now know is simply dead center in the middle of my life—that it is just that, dead center from the time that Amá first felt me ticking.

Ay, señores, but to get there you pray, pray, pray like anything, like nothing you've prayed for before; so hard and long that it feels like cursing, like forgetting: each novena, each rosario, rippling a squall. Even if you're buoyed eight or nine feet in the air there is no chance of bringing the blue house on the other side of the lake into focus. Mouse fur and droppings float on a layer of dust in the backs of cupboards, missing window cranks, the smell of stilled damp, everywhere, everywhere. Far from. Far distance. Away. Move into the current, and let go of the window broken in the second bedroom, the drip that prevents the pipes from bursting in the cold. Swim in and that fucking fucking fucking salsa he played on the stereo, the party with friends on the deck, toadstools and mold that creep up the side of the kitchen sink quick as the start of a fistfight; the need for a home-cooked meal; or to imagine your abuela sitting by herself in her chair every time weather fronts from the south and the north meet in a storm overhead so that you can watch her index finger stroke down the list of names of each family member left behind.

Bring your knees to your chest and breathe in. Go past where you've been before, you will begin to tell yourself that it is all in your head. Breathe in, 'mano, it's mango, you like it, cabrón, waiting for you on a pink plate sprinkled with just a little bit of lime. Come here, come here, ven acá, ven, ven, ven aquí, he says, mira, in my eye a woman spins in the warm air just because she likes her new yellow and blue dress, mira, he'll say, until you're completely surrounded by melons. Aliento, amor, breathe, comeherecomehere, until you feel as if you can get no closer. Shh—sí, he'll say before pushing you up, pushing you back, letting you go by saying, I know this moment it is so far away it might never have happened, so much like something that you think happened that you think you know, pero it's not here, not now, no. Further.

SHH, AMÁ WOKE me anoche or early yesterday morning from a dream about nothing at all—not even floating or silences, nothing—to say that she had something that she wanted to show me. Something I want to give you, mijo, she said.

Descansa, Amá, mira el tiempo, Amá, I said as the dark of the room blurred into focus. I reached for my glasses and felt Amá's hand stop me. No, no, mijo, she said. I rolled to the other side of the bed and reached for the light, and again Amá's hand stopped me, no, no.

We'll look in the morning, when it gets light, I told her, Amá porfa, I'm tired, you're tired, descansa, I told her.

No, mijo, now, she said as she has said each time since she moved to my apartment that Pirata has delivered a cool shiver from someone or brought a friend who moved from Santiago to a farm near Bayamón, or once it had a ruby in its beak that it had plucked from one of the scuttled Spanish and American battleships that she says you can see off the coast of Caimanera at low tide, though in the living room all we found was a red bead from a dress that had fallen out of one of the sooty boxes from Amá's house that doña Liliana says that she wore and wore until she had shaken most of the beads off.

I turned away from the sound of Amá's voice. It's just

this thing, this one thing I want to give to you, and then I live you alone, I live you to sleep, she said.

Amá, porfa, I pleaded, descansa, it will wait until morning, I'm sure.

Amá was quiet, still like she often is now. I imagined her eyes darting, lost, her body forgetting that it was part of, parked on an object in motion in space.

In the dark, there was such a great nothingness around us that it was hard for me to know if I was awake or had slipped back into the same dream when Amá said something I'm sure that she was certain would hurl us backwards to doña Liliana's father's well-appointed patio in El Vedado—¿Quién es mi capitán? ¿Usted es mi capitán, señor?—and it had already begun to become overgrown with everything that made it prized as well as everything else that in the past had been manicured out. ¿Quién es mi capitán? ¿Usted es mi capitán, señor? she says she chased me through the thick lawns that had grown to the middle of her thigh, but just covered the top of my head as she watched me weave a path, she says, cut like the bow of a ship towards the back of the garden as if it were headed to places that she had never heard of or only seen in pictures; a head full, she says, of the most beautiful pelo fino; pelo castellano, that felt so fine and silky in your hand, against your lips and cheek, mi hermoso, hermoso niñito, she tells las chismosas at the shop.

¿Quién es mi capitán? ¿Usted es mi capitán, señor? she said and I sat up awake, ready to follow.

Amá stopped my hand at the light again; no, she whispered, Román's asleeping on the couch, I let him in; no to disturb him, this I want you to know about first, she said as she arranged my slippers at my feet, handed me my glasses and helped me into my bathrobe, guiding me to the door. We go out the back, she whispered in the hallway, and it was not until we were through the kitchen, on the back porch, and she was pulling the door slowly closed—so as no to creak it, shh, she said—that I realized that in all this heat she had put on her mink coat—the coat she bought only once the deed on the house was settled, and after she waited and waited until there was enough to bring las doñas Liliana y Cristina, Julio y Román up from Miami, and then only used would be too good, she said—over her nightgown.

Amá, where are we going? I asked and in the light that came off of the streetlamp across the alley she first looked at me as if she had no idea who I was, and then I realized that she had no idea what I was saying.

¿A dónde estamos yendo, Amá?

And she asked, ¿Quién es mi capitán? ¿Usted es mi capitán, señor? the same way that she would admonish me for a lie, or stealing the candies, the little mints she would place into the dishes that went on the side tables in the room doña Liliana is talking about when she says the salón in that way that lets you know that—somewhere in the locura she will quickly slip in and out of when someone brings up something that she had long thought forgotten—she will go back and briefly check for dust on the bookshelves, run a finger along the marble top of a gilded empire table.

Vamos, mi capitán, Amá said and she had me help her carry her wire grocery cart down the back steps into the alley.

What's in this? I asked and she either didn't understand me or hadn't heard because she grabbed my hand and raced me down the alley; I asked if she didn't want to go wherever it was that we were going by car—Amá, we can go around front and I'll take you anywhere you want; we'll follow Pirata all night—and she said, Shh.

Shh—¿Quién es mi capitán? ¿Usted es mi capitán? Amá woke me from a dream about climbing; I had envisioned mountains as very simple triangles—brown on the bottom with a crust of white on top; purple or green on the bottom with the same crust of white on top—and I was traversing them one at a time with a pickax—Shh, she said.

No, as I reached for the light, and she sat me up in bed, turned me around towards her in bed.

¿Quién es mi capitán? ¿Usted es mi capitán?

Sí, Amá, I answered, I am your captain, in the same way that had won her smiles before, in the same way that caused her to throw her arms around me and kiss my neck, I am your captain, I am your captain, I am your captain.

And will you go round the world with me?

Sí, Amá, I'd say.

Twice, three times around the whole globe for me?

Sí, Amá.

Would you put out your arms for me, she asked, and I said, Sí, Amá.

No, she said, not over your head, no, not in back of you. One at each side.

Y dije, No, Amá, it's too hot, I don't want my coat.

And she said, Shh—¿Quién es mi capitán?—vamos. And I said, No it's too hot, and she said, Shh—you don't want to wake the whole house, do you?

And I remember shaking my head no, thinking that she could see me in the dark. Julio and Román are sleeping, so is doña Liliana, you don't want to wake them, do you? she asked, and again I shook my head, and was still shaking my head until she hooked my glasses around my ears—the second pair, the pair that I wasn't supposed to touch after I had broken the first pair trying them on Román—and then she stopped my face in front of hers; in the dark, I could feel her breath against my forehead. This is our secret, she said, no one else will know about it.

¿A dónde estamos yendo, Amá? I asked as we reached the end of the alley and she shushed me as if her wire shopping cart full of things weren't rattling behind us.

Don't worry, mijo, she said, is no far, you'll like it when we get there.

We walked the three blocks hurriedly on to the night-bright of Ashland Avenue. Few cars pass at that time of night, the traffic lights change and wait in anticipation. The few cars that did pass us either thought nothing of two people in their pajamas, Amá in her fur coat, pulling a shopping cart behind them, because they either sped along—flew through red lights—or crept down the street weaving between the yellow lines. It's only at night, señores, that you notice, really notice, the debris, the dirt that blows about, what people throw away. Only then when you're watchful of everything that you see it.

Amá, I called.

Shh—she said as we tiptoed through the highly polished floors spilled with moonlight that came through the windows of doña Liliana's father's well-appointed house. Doña Cristina met us at the iron gate out front, she was standing with two men and a woman that I didn't know. There was a car there not running. I pulled close to Amá, and then tried to pull away. The fear like a trapped feral made me rigid at her side, made me vomit down the strange man's back as he carried me while she and the lady that I didn't know pushed the car and doña Cristina steered away from the house and out of El Vedado before they started it.

¿A dónde estamos yendo, Amá?

¿Quién es mi capitán? ¿Usted es mi capitán? And when I didn't answer, Amá whispered, You are my captain, as she pulled me close to her in the back of the car, there is so much of the world that we'll have to see together, ¿no? she asked and when I didn't answer, she said, Sí, you'll show me everything that I have ever dreamed of seeing and places that I never dreamed of seeing; will you take me to India? she asked, and then replied, Yes. Will you show me the blue masque we saw in a book and the Taj Majal? and she said, Yes. Two more men that I didn't know were waiting for us at the shore, and I was juggled between arms and good-byes until I realized that I was watching doña Cristina and the car get smaller and smaller; for two days, I now know, ¿Quién es mi capitán? ¿Usted es mi capitán, señor? as we rocked back and forth—I believe that I even slept with my arms around Amá's neck; the three strange men and the woman said little to us or to each other; I remember one of the strange men handing me the water bottle and another laughing, Careful, he spews, but I also remember not taking it, not drinking anything unless it came from Amá's hand. Can we go to the Louvre? she asked when the boat would pitch from side to side and even the most stoic of the men on board clenched his fists whiter and whiter; the opera and the ballet. Mi hermoso, hermoso niñito, she said, ¿Quién es mi capitán? ¿Usted es mi capitán, señor? Spread every map out in the world from end to end till we're there, she said.

We spent nearly a year in Miami waiting for Marta to call to say that arrangements had been made. ¿Quién es mi capitán? ¿Usted es mi capitán, señor? she said when I complained about having to stay with other women and their children when Amá went out and cleaned motels, or when I complained that she took care of other women's children. Will you be my captain? she asked.

So little has changed at Amá's little casa blanca—everything she hoped for, prayed for, long before she knew she wanted it—since we were all there for her birthday. Neither Román nor Julio nor I have been to cut the grass in the past couple of weeks, and Amá and I struggled to drag the wheels of her shopping cart. The day—you remember yesterday—was already coming up hot and angry, there was a heavy scent to the air, a mixture of night, a too-early summer, and the starting up of the chocolate factory floating up from Pilsen, as around us lights flicked on in windows and a car engine choked a couple of times before starting in the next block.

Just something to show you, something for you, she said, something I want to gave to you dropping the handle of the cart and running ahead, waving me on, like a child towards a game or finding a puddle full of minnows, to follow her.

She parted the elephant ears forming a circle at the center of the garden that now stand nearly seven feet in the air, and went into the little room they formed with their enclosure. The stalks and leaves of the elephant ears rustled while I waited, the burnt smell from fire had gone sour and old and something so disconnected that it seemed to have nothing at all to do with any of our lives anymore. More lights went on in the houses around me and there were more starts of engines, no one seemed to notice me standing there as they went on their way with the exception of señora Figueroa who passed by her living room window several times thinking I hadn't noticed, though, with a head full of pink rollers, I was confident not even she would come out to find out what I was doing there in my bathrobe and slippers.

Amá appeared from an opening between the stalks and looked at me as if I had been making an unexpected visit. Ay mijo, she said, how nice for you to come. Come in, she gestured, come in, I got a present to gift to you, very nice, you'll like it.

The space inside the elephant ears held the heat and the humidity of the day before. It was stifling and thick, Amá sweated in the heavy coat. And all I could do was think of ways that I could get her out of here, safe back home.

Mira, she said, as she pointed at a small green shoot coming from the ground.

Sí, I said.

No, mira, she insisted, grabbing my neck and turning my head to look more closely at the plant.

Is nice, ¿no? she said.

Sí, Amá, pero what is it? I asked.

Ay, mijo, sometimes you make me wonder. Es un banano, of course, is that time of year, ¿no?

Sí, I said, verdad, pero Amá, they can't grow here, they don't grow here. I think it might be something else, I said, looking at the circle of pebbles that had been carefully arranged around it, seeing how neatly the soil had been raked away and flattened. No, Amá, I told her, I think it's something else.

And then she looked at me for a very long time before I realized that she was watching me grow up into a man nearly middle age before her eyes, and it frightened her.

Sí, could be something else, she said, and then she say, No matter, is for you. OK, she kissed me, I had to go now.

Go where, Amá? I asked.

Go while you can still say I say, say is banano, then is banano, she said.

The problem inherent with saying it's un banano, señores, is that if it isn't, it isn't. And you have called something that it isn't something else, therefore renaming each of the things that they once were, and then the question still remains do either still exist. Pero, however, if it is un banano, the question always comes up—at least with my mother—how did she do it, which of course, you never ask. She'll only tell you that you do what has to be done, and then you do some more.

Besides, the last time I saw her, she was halfway down the street.

It had been Amá's turn to talk when Marta died quite suddenly and peacefully in her sleep—really quite unexpectedly; she had given three perms that day, a comb-out for a woman, she said, hardly didn't have no hair to comb out at all; she went home and made dinner, had an argument with one of the three boyfriends who attended her services; watched some television, ate half a bag of Oreos; set her hair and went to bed, never to wake up again—and when it was discovered that the shop and all of her savings had been signed over to that little negrita that was too rough with the comb and rinsed too cold on purpose—they knew—the chismosas decided that was the least Amá could do.

A year after Joaquín-Ernesto, the Santiago Boy, came up in the eddies, six months before las doñas y Román y Julio came to live with us, what could Amá say of the woman who had given her a second and third life; shown her how to sprinkle lavender water into the sheets as she made beds, or to think of surfaces in the room as clocks when she dusted so that things went back into the same place; money to bring us from Miami had come from Marta, as well as money to have my teeth fixed when we first got to Chicago, it was Marta who paid for Amá's training.

Amá stood in front of the church with one knee threatening to shake the grip she had so tightly fixed on the podium that I thought her knuckles would break as the short speech—just a few lines really—she had rehearsed in the tiny apartment we shared off of Ashland became a barely audible scratch against the air. When she got to the part in her speech that has always reminded me of the note that Marta left—for Mireya and her yellow boy—she stopped at the word give, and made it gived, and then looked at me panic stricken, and waited for me to nod—nod vigorously as if I was sending her off, giving her wings—as she changed gived to gaved.

Y ayer en la mañana, this morning, I cleaned my glasses, knotted my tie, and after toast and coffee and a cigarette, and very brilliant reports I thought from señor Ostrovski about what you get if you call it the Bay of Pigs and señor Chávez's rather scattered version of what he called El Conflicto en Playa Girón—complete with a rather odd diagram that, I must agree with señor Martínez, looked like a dick—I taught my third- and sixth-period classes, attended a staff meeting in which we celebrated Señorita Jonas' early departure to tend to her pregnancy.

After she had unwrapped the gifts she was given and

we were all eating cake, señorita Jonas walked around giving everyone, even Mr. Sáenz, a chance to put a hand on her belly. When she insisted despite my protests—Feel him kick, fuerte, like a footballer, she said—she was right, I did feel better, like so little in the world mattered for that second. It was something like a jolt or a shock that zigzagged a wire up my arm and threatened to pull me inside out there in front of señorita Jonas, Father Rodríguez, Father McMillan and all of the rest of them for whom I am a questionable story, something that they tell other people about; sí, that señor Delossantos. I was already running inside as I excused myself and said good-bye to my colleagues.

Strange that. Knowing your body is doing something before you're actually doing it.

Inside, I had begun that rhythmic panting, the way that you do when you hit stride, and heat and pace and the thwacking of the ground underneath you means nothing, all before I'd reached the hallways that I was told never to run down for years before I was telling you to never run down them; out across the green, I left my car in the parking lot, and headed out onto North Avenue; my tie, my shirt and then my T-shirt either landed in the garbage cans I pitched them at along the way or became finds or trash—no sé—I had become this efficient machine detecting neither hot nor cold, unable to think of anything else but running, running, running, running, running, the five miles that on the snowiest of nights on the way back has seemed like leagues of mud; passed what changes so much—changes at nearly a weekly or daily rate—that day to day I can never be assured I could recognize it; running until I was covered slick straight through to my undershorts when I reached into my pocket for change as I stopped at a pay phone and called doña Liliana to tell her that Amá had given me un banano.

SHE EITHER HUNG the phone up or dropped it, it hardly mattered, because by the time that I had gotten home she and doña Cristina were already there and it seemed that she had been yelling at me for some time already. When Román arrived he suggested the police, and it was he who took the phone away from doña Liliana who kept repeating the word how over and over, even after Román informed us that the police were coming to take a description and get information from us.

Like hiccups they were, doña Liliana's how's, one after the other. Neither the water doña Cristina brought her nor the level-headed words of comfort Román offered—She's OK, mamá, he said, don't worry, we'll get her back—seemed to comfort her. Not the tea we made, or the pillows she said she needed immediately that we brought for her feet and her back and her head stopped the how's from coming. Though she was able to contain them a bit when doña Cristina offered her a pastelito that she found in the kitchen; though when doña Liliana found that it had gone stale, her how's immediately turned into why's that came in more rapid succession than the how's and brought on a torrent of tears. Because, señores, as Amá says, sometimes you stand too close to a thing to see it. And they only stopped when Julio arrived with Naty Valdez McIntosh.

We all sat there for a while.

Each passing car sent one of them to the window. Every time someone else came or went from the building, around the room, we all sat up in our chairs, or turned an ear.

Someone said something about dinner, but nobody responded.

Doña Cristina peeled at her cuticle.

Julio slowly paced in front of his mother, who was only left with an occasional low sigh.

Román didn't move.

And I watched.

Naty's eyes, as she sat in her chair, moved from Julio and then to Román, and then she looked at Julio and then back at Román, and then to doña Liliana, then to Román, then Julio—Naty Valdez McIntosh—thoughtfully rubbing her belly while her bracelets jiggled a sound very much like the lady's hand door knocker tapping, tapping, tapping.

ESCUCHEN PERFECTOS—hombres jóvenes; all of you who have sat in these seats over the past several years; mensajeros del futuro.

Mis iluminadores.

Mis casas.

Mis escuelas.

Mis corazones.

Mis playas.

Mi sentido común; mis yucas locos—I forget all the names that I have had for you all of these years—Shiny Distant Shores. Too far away, a fever's dream.

Entonces, señores, next we will go, then, you and I—when the evening is spread out against the sky like a patient etherized upon a table, like the poet says—on to Panama as your textbook demands. Because so much time was spent in Cuba, we will all probably be working on the canal when the semester ends. And this time we go as friends, you can be my guide. It's time you start thinking about yourselves that way.

Not to tell you what you don't want to know, won't believe if I were to tell you now, pero as much as you rail against it, most time gets passed floating—sí, floating—in something so buoyant and mostly pleasing that little else will matter. The clicking in your ear—ven, ven, as one anniversary simply ticks off the onset of the approaching next—when will suddenly becomes was, and you'll realize here was once there.

You'll graduate and go before you realize that you're in the movement that you thought was around you, that you thought you were watching. Sí, sí, sí, no need to laugh, it's a moment of self-reflection that can be predicted for even a Chávez. There's a great world out there inventing itself every day that he knows nothing about, that none of us know anything about—possibly because it has very little to do with the seemingly inexhaustible song and variation that he produces from his nether regions, no sé—pero, this too could be thought of as great.

Yo me voy too, pero, señores, not back into history. No. As a brilliant man once said, it is the nightmare from which I'm trying to wake. I don't remember who, but I'm sure señor Ostrovski will be able to tell us all one day who. I recall it as a man waking from a thousand years' journey and really only wanted to get some rest.

You'll get back to us, señor Ostrovski, ¿no?

No, señores, history is not the demon that I want to carry for a while. My ability to live in the what if and when seems to be acrimonious towards my desires for a happy and rather simple life.

For me, right now, dreaming about the past in relationship to the future . . . well, I've done it so well for so long that I thought it was true: I could nearly taste a lifetime of dinners spent, plan ad infinitum vacation destinations; I've nearly placed a carefully chosen sofa in front of thousands of different fireplaces in any number of countries.

Whether this has been true or not, at times it has been so glorious that I want to leave before that fantasy is destroyed for me, and I can still learn new things.

Señores, let me introduce myself.

Soy Óscar Delossantos—porfa, call me Óscar—y finalemente—I exist in time, and am set towards something that is like a stoked fire, a warm embrace, the most tender kiss that is for me and me alone. And I'm blindly, stupidly, ignorantly, unabashedly running towards the hands that will hold mine in the movies, rub my feet when my work goes bad, share the last tea bag, pour the whiskey when we decide it would be fun to get drunk together. There are books, and movies, and politics to be argued over in a bed somewhere so far away that I can't tell you where it might be; there's an argument to be had over whether or not there regularly should be half-and-half or two percent in the refrigerator, and one over whether or not Oswald acted alone, and another over something that really matters. There are cashews to be roasted, Christmas ornaments to be packed in tissue paper and lists of mutual friends whose conversation and company we simply could not live without if trapped on a deserted island.

There's a football hurtling towards me in a snowstorm on one of the coldest days of a future winter where there is someplace warm to cuddle afterward, and I'm afraid of what I might become—of what I may be becoming—if I do not make some gesture to catch it. Were I dreaming a cure for an uncurable illness or a way to stop time, I could just as easily turn over and go back to sleep. But to more than occasionally spoon and kiss the sleeping back that wants and is in demand for nothing more on a Sunday morning sounds oddly reasonable, sounds like something worth getting up early for. And, true, none of this may ever come to fruition, but I can't help think that I need to move toward a clearing where it is, at the very least, a possibility.

Entonces, señores, we'll go on together to Panama, to the end of the semester, through the lesson plans I made the summer before, through convocation, into the next summer, in and out of thousands and thousands of collective loves, to battle good, be good, be good at battle, battle evil, or battle the evil that's good.

Señores, like a letter recently forwarded from my prima Carolina still in Cuba, whom I never met, sent to Amá but really meant for all of us, says, It's not here, it's not here anymore, tía; I don't know whether it is there or is it further—like me, caught somewhere between one place and another, caught in the net of might never leave, there's something between the time when things get painted over and when things fall apart that makes me want to whisper to each of you, Cuidense, señores and those who care for you—you may take them when you go, pero still go—get them together and throw a party, serve wonderful food and incredible wine, wear a garland of peony, dance.

With or without music, señores, when what you feel feels less like wanting to stand or walk—so tired and wrung out—much less move yourself through this thick thick air. Much easier to simply sit there than follow some inner rhythm, some dislocated hum, a buzz that haunts you awake as a memory just under the skin, an imprint. As if windows and doors were simply for letting air in and out, they might say, you said he said. Or ways in and out of rooms, rather than ways of keeping you exactly the way that you are, preserving you, framing you, marking your position, and therefore allowing someone else to chart your territory, set your course, give you country and mouth to tell it, tell it as if it invents it. Wretched or sick, hungry or poor, as the lady says, but I'd have to add bold and wealthy and house-proud, and as awkward as it feels, no matter how much you want to glance over your shoulder, blush to the quick, until your cheeks feel as if they would burst, eager to jump at the chance at something so imperfectable that imperfectability, discrete as a prime number, becomes the perfect that you were looking for. Somewhere in each of you allow it to come over you, if only for just once, wash you through as if it wrings and slips your spine, ay señores, into something that bites and yowls so much like hunger you'll know it's there, will be familiar with it as infants know to search open-mouthed as it calls out—Come here, come here, ven, ven, ven aquí—sin tu rumba yo me muerto.

¿Como?

Ay carajo, cariños.

Sí, sí, sí. No laughing. Or, OK, go ahead, laugh if you want to, and then remember it. Remember it always, señores, you'll need it someday, you'll least expect that you will, pero you'll need it. Sí, sí, sí, this too is love.

I dance myself, señores.

I mambo—loose-limbed and free-hipped, dizzying myself and my partners, real or imaginary; I mambo, dug in deep down through the center of the congas, in that place that sets the lights wet bleeding into you and you think you'll never come out—sí, I mambo, pero only when it pleases me.

AGRADECIMIENTOS

Escúchenme. If you are lucky—and only if you're *very* lucky—no one will tell you that a novel is a whole lot of writing. And believe them, if you will, the alchemy of so many lonely nights fretted by cigarettes y cafecitos, entonces usted está más loco de lo que yo estoy.

This book wouldn't exist without MY MOTHER'S INSISTENCE that shelter and dinner were equally as important as time to write. In addition to putting off a trip to Switzerland for nearly half a century, she raised mis hermanos—SUSANA, MARÍA, CRISTÓBAL, DANIEL y ÁNGELA—and their babies—JESSICA (LA MINOUCHE), DANIELCITO, JILIANA y MISS SYDNEY—so that I was sure that I knew that I was loved with or without the book.

SHANE R. CONNER, pragmatist, logician, lawyer—when I met him ten years ago—told me that he didn't believe in fiction, but he believed in me, and has unflaggingly propped me up, set me on my way, made sure I was standing, and still reminds me of who I am and where I'm headed.

ANNE CALCAGNO—brilliant writer, extraordinary teacher and loving friend—who somehow knew about this book long before I did, and marshaled to protect it by creating a cadre of people—TODD C. PARKER, MICHAEL MENZEY, JUANA QUIÑONES GOERGAN and JACKIE TAYLOR—in the DePaul University community who nursed and guided it long before I was ready for literary parenthood.

If you think about approaching the page, setting pen to paper even for the most idly rendered haiku, make sure that you have a first reader and first editor like DEE DOLAN GEORGE, someone who can make sense of, spin gold from, any "Mongolian Pig Fuck" you throw in front of her.

Books take time. Expect to lose some of those dearest to you along the way. PATRICK (EDWAR) WERTHMANN, a photographer who taught me all I know about "seeing," DENNIS O'DEA, the master of the "go-and-do," the originator of the "life as art project," who showed me the meanings of "largesse" and "abbondanza" in one glorious extended dance, and JULIO JUAN CARLOS CARRILLO MONTENEGRO, mi hermano and, no doubt, my first real friend, all breathed life into these pages but couldn't wait to see them finished.

When you're about twelve, put in your life a painter like JULIO MARIO DE LA PEÑA, and hold fast to him like you've never held on to anything before; he'll remember thirty years of lost domino games, drunken pees had in alleys, first kisses and heartbreaks on canvas for you.

In addition to the vatos you play pool with, you'll need a 'mano like MARSHALL BOSWELL, who helped me believe what he saw with just a few words as we were both leaving Vermont early one morning.

Borrow patience of those like that of my committee members at Cornell University—SUNN SHELLEY WONG, PAUL SAWYER and MARY PAT BRADY—they seem to have it to spare. Secure funds and community: DEPAUL UNIVERSITY, THE NEWBERRY LIBRARY, *GLIMMER TRAIN* MAGAZINE, THE CONSTANCE SALTONSTALL FOUNDATION, THE BREAD LOAF WRITERS' CONFERENCE and THE CORNELL UNIVERSITY ENGLISH DEPARTMENT have been very good to me, and have kept this project afloat long after I could have ever anticipated.

You may need a scientist; choose one like DENNIS VAN ENGELSDORP GASTELAARS, the biologist who proved to me that in this day and age people can go invisible only to leave something so much like a throb or an ache that you eventually get used to.

Allow a champion like SUSAN BERGHOLZ to be your champion, and throw the doors and windows open to the wisdom of an editor like ERROLL McDONALD, who—without nearly saying a word—can tell you what you're thinking, or what you should be thinking, before you think it. And get someone like ROBIN REARDON—an Atlas in disguise—to hold it all together for you.

What you call a "project," as if saying the word "novel" would cause it to disappear, is a lonely place to hang out in by yourself. You'll need someone like my agent and compadre in imaginary things, STUART BERNSTEIN, who believed without seeing, and for so long said the word for me.

Days, months and years will pass without gateau and tickles unless you bring in the constant, warm glow thrown off by someone as dear as ANDRÉS LEMA-HINCAPIÉ, who will keep you from "loosing" too much.

At the very last moments, right when you think that you can see the end in sight, find a seafaring man like JOSEPH T. PAGILLO, who, without a boat, can sail you to the middle of something and show you real peligro.

Keep a poet about. Not just anyone. You'll need one in whose work you hear your own music. If you live your life without the love and generosity of genius of una mujer like GINA FRANCO, I beg you not to start yet. Who else will fight you word for word; who else would pan through the crumples in your wastepaper basket for what you can't possibly see?

And when you think you're ready, when you're really ready, grab hold of the hem of the coat of a writer like HELENA MARÍA VIRAMONTES; in this writing life you will need a guide, a scold, a harbor, a mentor and a friend who can set an unparalleled example of pursuit in flight.

Then, and only then, are you *very* lucky.

Ustedes tienen una fortuna.

Vayan. Escriban.